Thanks so much to Jean Forside for loving my books—thank you for your service in the army!—and sharing them with her mother, Darlene Zimmerman, who is in a nursing home. They couldn't see each other because of COVID-19 for a long time. But she loves the sexy wolves just as much! Who would have thought Donna Fournier, my friend and beta reader, would discover that her cousin Jean and her aunt Darlene read my books too. So thanks to Jean for making this a wolf family affair.

THE BEST OF BOTH WOLVES

TERRY SPEAR

Cover design by Stephanie Gafron/Sourcebooks
Cover illustration by Craig White/Lott Reps

Published by Sourcebooks Casablanca, an imprint of Sourcebooks
P.O. Box 4410, Naperville, Illinois 60567-4410
(630) 961-3900
sourcebooks.com

Printed and bound in Canada.
MBP 10 9 8 7 6 5 4 3 2 1

CHAPTER 1

Everything had been looking up for Sierra Redding, a retired army finance officer, since she'd moved to the Portland, Oregon, area before Christmas. At least she thought that. After a day working in a mixed-media-collage intensive workshop for teachers, she was excited and looking forward to setting up "official" art assignments for wolf kids of all ages in the red wolf pack, starting on Monday. The job was just a part-time one, but she had her army retirement pay, and that was all she really needed.

She wasn't sure if she could do this since she'd never taught kids before, but she'd had so much fun at the workshops that she knew this was just what she wanted to do. Initially, she hadn't really thought of what she wanted to do once she retired, but her pack leaders, Leidolf and Cassie Wildhaven, had hired her immediately to teach art classes to the pack-schooled kids. Cassie was eager to find someone trained in art already and who had a talent for it since a couple of the students showed real promise and needed someone who could teach them more skills.

After the long day of art-teacher-training workshops, Sierra entered her Portland hotel room, ready to order some seafood from room service and chill while watching a movie on TV. As soon as she shut the door, she got a call from Cassie. She hurried to answer it while dumping her bag of notes and art supplies on the extra queen-size bed. "Hi, Cassie."

"Hey, how's it going?" Cassie was a wolf biologist, the perfect occupation for a wolf who already knew all about wolf biology on a personal basis. She was often on tours educating people about wolves, when she wasn't home helping her mate lead the pack.

"It's going great. I'm having a blast. I'll be all set for starting classes on Monday, and I already have some adults lined up for art classes at night." Sierra appreciated that Cassie had called to see how she was doing. She hadn't expected to hear from anyone.

"I'm so glad to hear it. I'm thrilled you're all settled in. We couldn't be more pleased that you've joined the pack."

Sierra knew part of the reason was that there were fewer females than males in the pack, and they were always on the lookout to entice new females to join them. It helped when the wolf had a skill the pack needed. They'd even paid for her workshops and her hotel, which was really nice of them.

"I am too." Though Sierra wasn't really settled in—yet. She wouldn't be until she began working and felt she had a mission and purpose in life. She'd loved creating sketches and paintings when she was a kid, and through the years while she was in the army, she'd won a few contests with her wolf portraits. She loved that she'd had such cooperative wolf models. She was always learning new things, and her next great adventure was creating digital paintings from photographs and sharing how to do that with the kids.

"I'm so glad that you haven't changed your mind."

Sierra laughed. She was sure Cassie and Leidolf worried she might still return to Texas to be with her boyfriend. "Yeah, we're good." For now. She had to see how teaching went, how she got along with the pack members, and decide about Lieutenant Colonel Richard Wentworth, the army officer she was still dating back at Fort Hood, Texas.

"Okay, well, I'll let you go now. Leidolf is fixing dinner, and I need to help him with the kids."

"Thanks for calling. I'll talk to you later." Afterward, Sierra called in an order for shrimp scampi at the hotel restaurant and was watching an espionage thriller on TV when her twin brother called. She paused her movie.

"Hey, how are you doing at your workshop?" Brad asked.

Loving her brother, she smiled. He had retired as a Navy SEAL and had mated one of the Portland pack members, which was one of the big reasons she had come here. When they had kids—and often wolves had more than one at a time—she wanted to be here to help out. While she and her brother had both been in the military, they hadn't had a lot of time to see each other, though they'd always been close, so it was time to bond again.

"Great. I love it. Why aren't you busy making little Redding wolves?"

He chuckled.

She teased him about that all the time, though she knew he wasn't waiting to have kids with Janice. She also knew he had called because he wanted her to love what she was doing and stay in the area. Her parents were waiting for her to say if she was going to remain in Portland before they made any move from Texas to join them.

"Okay, well, I just wanted to check on you, and I'm glad you're enjoying it. See you soon."

"Thanks, Brad. Sounds good." They ended the call.

She started the movie and then her phone jingled again. *Now* who was calling?

She paused the movie and grabbed her phone. Her boyfriend. She sighed and answered the phone.

"Hey, Sierra. I hope you're getting tired of the rain there."

Not "Hey, honey, I missed you"? Something was seriously wrong with their relationship.

She was starting to get used to the rain as she listened to it softly hitting the window. "I'm glad to be here." She'd met so many wolves in the pack who were friendly and welcoming, something she had certainly been hoping for.

"I miss you."

"I miss you too. I'll be seeing you." She'd told herself she had to give herself time to learn how much she liked it here before she made any decision to return to Texas. Sure, she felt somewhat conflicted about leaving him, but he was doing what he wanted to do, and this was what she wanted to do. Not only that, but she hadn't missed him as much as she'd thought she would.

"All right. I hope that means you're coming back for good."

"We'll see." She was beginning to think that for him, absence made the heart grow fonder. Though she also suspected he was afraid she might find a new wolf to interest her and Richard would be history. He was doing a lot more checking up on her than when she lived in Killeen, Texas. She was really trying to be objective about this and not let any bachelor wolves sway her from her mission: settle in, work with the kids, and see if this was what she really wanted to do.

But she had to admit there were some real bachelor male hotties in the Portland-area wolf pack that she was interested in seeing more of if things were going to work out for her here. Police Detective Adam Holmes with the Portland Police Bureau was on top of the list. He had been all smiles, welcoming her to the pack as if she were staying for good, and had made her feel really great about being here. She supposed another reason he was on her good list was he'd been the first one to sign up for her adult art class for Monday night, though—according to him—he couldn't even draw a stick figure.

Someone knocked at the door, and she figured her shrimp scampi dinner had arrived. "I have to go. My meal is here."

"Home delivery?"

"I'm in Portland at the art workshops this weekend, staying at a hotel. I've got to go. 'Night, Richard." She'd told him last week and reminded him again a few days ago where she was going to be for the weekend. He especially worried about where she was and what she was doing during the weekends, but he never remembered after she told him.

"Later," he said.

He could be controlling, used to being in charge in his position as a commander. And she was tired of him never having time for her when she was actually living in Killeen. Now, he continued to call, email, and text her, hoping she would get her "visit" to Oregon out of her system and would move back to Texas.

Yet she just couldn't give up their relationship. As much as she hated to admit it, she loathed the idea of getting to know someone new as a potential mate.

They ended the call and she answered the door to get her meal delivery. "Thanks," she told the delivery guy, then shut her door.

She knew Richard was miffed at her for not staying in Killeen. No matter how much she had told him she wanted to be with a pack, he just didn't get it. He was more career-minded, wanted to make more rank, and joining a pack was definitely low on his list of priorities.

She settled down to eat a meal that was the best shrimp scampi she'd ever had while finally finishing the movie. Then it was time to shower. She pulled off her clothes and laid them on the bed, then went into the bathroom and brushed her teeth.

The problem was that Richard lived for promotions, which was fine and good—for him. But she was done with the military and wanted more. Once she'd retired, she knew she needed to do something important with her life again. Sure, she enjoyed being with him, when he made the time. But there wasn't a wolf pack in Killeen, and now that she didn't have to transfer to a new location all the time, she wanted and needed the socialization that went along with a pack. Once she had children of her own, she would really need that. Plus, she wanted her kids to live close to Brad's so they could get to know their cousins.

Richard wasn't about to change his mind about moving anywhere else, and certainly he wouldn't leave the military.

She'd had to make so many changes in her life while in the army, and he had been her one constant. One boyfriend for three years.

Of course there had been no other wolves available for either of them to date at Fort Hood either. So naturally, from the first time they'd met, the attraction was there between them. But now that she didn't have a full-time job to keep her busy, she wanted more. She wanted…something different. Her parents were happy with each other, and though her dad had made general in the army, he had always had time for her mother, who had been in the air force, both retired now. Richard wasn't like that with Sierra.

She removed her makeup, then started the water for her shower. Soon she was in the bathtub soaping her hair when she thought she heard her hotel-room door shut. She listened. She didn't hear any sounds other than the shower water pelting her and running down the drain. She must have heard a door close for another room close by. That was the trouble with her enhanced wolf hearing. Everything could sound much closer than it was.

She was in the middle of washing her hair and face, soap all over her body, the hot water sluicing down her back, and she was feeling dreamy when she heard a drawer in the chest of drawers squeak open. Her heart began to race and her skin chilled despite the hot water. The bathroom door was wide open because she wasn't sharing a room with anyone else, or she would have at least closed it and could have jumped out of the shower and locked it.

No one should have been in her room, and now she suspected the key-card noise she'd heard just minutes earlier had been the real deal. Who the hell had a key to her room? Whoever it was didn't say a word. The scary part was that even though he had to hear her showering, he ignored it, like he knew he was safe, that she couldn't harm him. And that made her angry. And even more worried.

Another drawer opened in the bureau, and then another. She hadn't unpacked her bags, except for hanging her rain jacket, a shirt, and a pair of pants in the closet. The rest of her things were still in her bags. Her purse and her laptop were also in the closet, where she always put them when she wasn't using them. She knew she should be careful, not worry about her personal possessions and only think about living through this, if it came to that, but she was instinctively a territorial wolf. Allowing him to steal from her without a fight wasn't in her blood.

She quickly washed the soap out of her hair and off her face and body and left the water running. Her phone was sitting on the bedside table, so she couldn't reach it to call the police. She didn't have a weapon… Well, maybe not a gun or knife, but she did have a different kind of weapon. One she was born with. It would have to do.

She called on her wolf, heat rushing through every bone and through every muscle. Confronting a human like this wasn't something wolves would normally do when they were taught to hide their identity at all costs from humans. But the intruder couldn't see her shift and she was afraid—since he was bold enough to remain there when she was taking a shower—she could be in a world of hurt if she didn't do something to protect herself.

As soon as she had turned into a big red wolf with big ears, big teeth, and big wolf paws, she pushed the shower curtain aside with her nose, leaped out of the tub, slid on the bath mat, and tore out of the bathroom and into the room. As soon as the man saw movement, turned, and noticed her coming at him, the would-be thief jumped straight into the air. He cried out with a strangled sound and made a dash for the door.

That was what she liked to see. Him scared to pieces and running for his life. Though her own heart was beating triple time, the adrenaline surging through her blood preparing her to flee or fight. Fighting was more what she had in mind.

But his leaving the room pronto wasn't good enough for her. She had to get a better look at his face so she could identify him in a sketch and the police would have something to go on to catch him. Not to mention she wanted to scare the crap out of him so he wouldn't pull this again with some other unsuspecting guest. No telling how many robberies he'd already committed and gotten away with.

Imagine him thinking he was robbing a defenseless human but suddenly was faced with a snarling wolf!

He had to assume the only occupant was a woman, since her bra, panties, jeans, and sweater were piled on the bed and a pair of size seven women's boots were sitting on the floor next to the bed. There were no men's clothes anywhere in the room.

His back was to her while he was in fleeing mode, and she lunged and tackled him, her large paws slamming into his back and knocking him flat on his chest on the carpeted floor. She wanted to bite him! But she couldn't or chance turning him into one of their kind. They couldn't have that happen no matter what. It was bad enough if they did it to someone accidentally, but doing it on purpose to someone who exhibited criminal behavior? No way.

She was growling, snapping her teeth next to his neck, letting him know just how dangerous she could be. And how stupid he'd been for breaking into her room with the intent of stealing from her.

She smelled urine and growled again. She would have to switch rooms or smell his pee in her room for the rest of the time she was staying here.

On his belly, he struggled to get free of her, terrified, crying out, his body pressed against the floor, trying to unsettle her. She had her front paws firmly on his back, pinning him down, her hind feet on the floor, giving her traction as she spread her large wolf paws out. He was trying to twist away, and then she realized he was reaching with his right hand for something in his pocket or at his waistband under his hoodie. A gun? A knife?

Don't bite him, she warned herself. She desperately wanted to. To show him he wasn't in charge here. In the beginning, she should have let him go, she figured in retrospect, just scared him and forced him to run out of the room, shifted, then locked and bolted the door and called the police. And hurried to get dressed. Now, she assumed he was armed and could be more dangerous than her—only because she couldn't take a bite out of him.

She wasn't sure what to do. Keep him pinned to the floor so he couldn't hurt her and howl to get help? Uh, yeah, that would go over well.

He smelled of beer and pot and pee, and she would remember his scent anywhere now. If she didn't have to turn back into her human form, she could have tracked him down once he left the room. He finally managed to roll over so that she lost her grip on him, and then she studied him, growling.

His face was filled with fear as he sat up and scooted away from her like someone doing a fast crab scuttle. She was glad she could get a good look at his long chin, the bristly dark hair covering it, pale thin lips, and wide hazel eyes. His hair was cut short, and he had a rattlesnake tattoo around his neck.

He quickly scrambled to his feet and continued to back away toward the door and, at the same time, pulled a gun out of his pocket. She remained in her spot, ready to dodge if he fired a shot, but she suspected he didn't want to use the gun if he didn't have to and alert everyone within hearing distance that someone was firing a gun in a hotel room.

Still, her heart was hammering triple time. What if he shot her accidentally, if not on purpose? She wanted to sit down, to show him she was letting him go, but she was afraid to make any kind of move at this point.

He backed up all the way to the door, probably having heard that you never want to turn your back on an angry dog. And she was an angry *wolf*.

He bumped against the door and fumbled behind with his free hand to reach for the handle. She should have locked the safety bar across it after the man delivered her meal. And especially before she stripped out of her clothes and took her shower. *Damn it.*

Then the would-be robber pulled the door open and maneuvered around it, his eyes on her the whole time. Yeah, she had a real good idea of what he looked like and *smelled* like.

As soon as he made his way out of the room, he pulled the door shut as fast as he could. She raced to the door, shifted, and shoved the security latch in place. Then she ran and got her phone and called Police Detective Adam Holmes, a red wolf like her. If she couldn't get him, she would call Josh Wilding, also a red wolf with the pack and Adam's former police detective partner, recently retired. She knew they would take this threat seriously.

Thankfully, she got ahold of Adam right away. "I've had a break-in at my hotel room." She gave the name of the hotel and found an address on a notepad. "Hurry. You might catch him! I'm in room 308."

"Are you all right?" Adam asked, his voice deeply concerned.

She heard Adam's Hummer door slam shut and his engine roar to life. "Yes. He ran out of the room, but I've got to get dressed." Still naked, she hurried into the bathroom and turned off the shower, but she was glad Adam was coming to aid her and that it wasn't someone she didn't know.

"You were showering?"

Astute wolf's hearing.

"Yes, but I'll be dressed before you get here." She put the phone on speaker and grabbed a towel to dry herself off. Then she seized her phone, returned to the bedroom, and dug in her suitcase to find a pair of panties and pulled them on.

"Hell, Sierra. I'm on my way. What did he look like?"

She slid her bra straps over her arms and fastened it. "I'll draw you a sketch, but if you see him race out of the hotel or anywhere in the vicinity when you get here, he's wearing a black hoodie, blue jeans, tears in several places on the thighs and knees, black sneakers, white male, approximately mid- to late twenties. He was scrawny, had short, brown hair and bristly chin whiskers, and a rattlesnake tattoo around his neck. He smells of pee and pot and beers, oh, and he has a diamond or fake diamond earring in both ears."

"And he has *your* description," Adam said, sounding worried that she was an eyewitness and the guy could retaliate against her.

"As a red wolf. Yep." She fumbled through her suitcase for a flannel shirt to wear.

Adam didn't say anything for a moment. "You shifted?"

"That's the only way he would have my description as a red wolf. Got to go, Adam. I need to get dressed." She could envision the police at her door while she was still trying to dress!

"Be there soon. Calling it in now."

She finished dressing and then started drawing the sketch of the man on her sketch pad at the little table for two in the room before she forgot anything.

It wasn't but about ten minutes later that Adam was knocking at Sierra's door. "It's me, Adam Holmes."

She hurried to let him in. He looked so spiffy in his suit, like an FBI agent, his green eyes narrowed as he considered her appearance, and she knew he was making sure she was okay. She was surprised that no one else was with him.

"I have men downstairs talking to the clerks and trying to learn how he got a key to your room. I wanted to talk to you privately first. Are you okay?"

She folded her arms. "Yes. And I know I should have secured the safety bar on the door." She figured he would lecture her about that and about shifting.

"Correct. Did he see you shift?" He was still frowning at her.

"Of course not! I was in the shower, and he was rummaging through the empty bureau drawers." As if she would do something so foolish. If he'd come into the bathroom, well, she would have shifted, but behind the shower curtain, not in front of him.

"But he heard the shower going and that didn't deter him from staying in your room?"

"No, which was why I was really worried. The bathroom door was wide open, and I couldn't jump out and lock it without him catching me at it. Oh, and he had a 9mm gun."

"Sierra." Adam sounded totally exasperated with her.

"What? I had to chase him off the only way I knew how. I didn't bite him, but I would have if I'd known it wouldn't turn him. I didn't know he had a gun."

Adam let out his breath. "We're certain this guy is part of a team of thieves who have hit numerous hotels. We still don't know how they're breaking into the rooms using the hotel keys, but you're the first one who has actually witnessed a break-in." He looked over the sketch and glanced at her. "Hell, this is really good."

"Thank you."

"You're hired."

"What?"

"We need an additional sketch artist at the Portland Police Bureau. It would be part-time so you can still teach your art classes. I'll talk to the boss when I get back, if it's something you would consider doing for us."

She opened her mouth to speak, and Adam said, "The kids need you for your art expertise, but we need you to help us catch criminals. You're hired."

She smiled. Adam had such a way with words. And the more she got to know him, the more she really liked him.

CHAPTER 2

Seven months later

Adam was glad Sierra had come to work for the Portland Police Bureau seven months ago as their part-time sketch artist and still had time to teach art lessons to the kids a couple of days a week and adults in the pack at night, mainly because she was so good at her job and she seemed to love doing both. He'd had a ball when he had gone to her first adult art class where she'd showed them how to create photoshopped artwork and was teaching them about perspective, lighting, and shadows. Most of her class had been made up of bachelor males vying to win her attention, even though she was still seeing an out-of-state wolf who used to work with her in the army.

Adam had been trying to learn about art from her, but he was truly smitten with her—the way she smiled at her students and the way she tirelessly showed them over and over again how to create a simple picture using clip art and different layering techniques, laughing at some of their sillier comments and questions. She appeared to enjoy teaching them as much as they enjoyed getting to know her better.

But now it was back to the grind for him. Since he had to investigate the case of a stolen rental car from the airport and Sierra had to catch a flight, he was on his way to her house to give her a lift, which worked out well for both of them. Though the reason she was flying out of Portland bothered him. She was still seeing her boyfriend in Texas, and he sure wished he could convince her that she didn't want to leave the pack. To be honest, Adam didn't want the boyfriend to join them here either.

On the way over to her place, Adam got a call on Bluetooth from Sierra's brother, Brad. He suspected Brad hoped Adam could convince Sierra she didn't want to leave for Texas today or any other day. Not that Adam had told Brad he was taking her to the airport. "What's up, Brad?"

"You should tell Sierra you're taking the boat out the weekend she gets back. We'll go with you. Ask Josh and Brooke and my sister-in-law, Dorinda, to come too, and maybe Sierra won't think it's anything more than a family and friends get-together."

Adam chuckled. "I've asked her before, and she said no."

"Yeah, but right after she has seen her boyfriend, she's more willing to go out. I think she feels everyone understands she's 'with' him so none of the bachelors make a move on her."

"I'll ask." Adam was certain she would decline the invitation again.

"Okay, I'll keep working on her at this end."

Adam laughed.

"It's hard for Sierra to deal with change all at once. Retiring from the army, then moving here, she's having a hard time letting go of the last tie she has there. But he's not good for her."

Adam didn't know if that was really true or if Brad just wanted his sister to live close by.

"Okay, I'll ask."

"All right, good. And be sure and take another art class of hers. The more we can convince her that everyone needs her to stay here, the better."

Adam smiled. "I am. She put them on hold to take a trip back to Texas, but I'm on the list for her next one coming up." He didn't think he'd ever really be able to do anything art-related that was newsworthy, but he was having fun taking the classes because she was teaching them. "Talk to you later."

Adam dropped by the coffee shop and picked up a chocolate-caramel-hazelnut coffee for Sierra—her favorite. He'd gotten into the habit of getting it for her at work once she'd teased him about drinking boring coffee and he had learned that was her favorite. Of course his former partner, Josh Wilding, had told him it was obvious Adam was making a play for her.

After Sierra had drawn the police sketch of the man who had tried to rob from her hotel room, the police had also rounded up three staff members at three other hotels who had given the robbers access to the rooms. Sierra identified Dover Manning in a police lineup, though the robber denied he'd ever seen her before. Because he'd been armed with a gun and threatened her with it, even though she was a wolf at the time, he was charged with first-degree robbery. During the trial and his testimony, he had stated that he'd been protecting himself from a vicious guard dog. Of course no one—hotel staff, cleaning crew, or police officers—had seen any sign of a "guard dog" so Dover Manning was looking at twenty years in prison.

Adam arrived at Sierra's one-story brick home with flowers filling its flower beds and planters. He hadn't realized she was quite the little gardener, never having been to her place before. While he was getting out of the Hummer, she came out of the house carrying two bags and he loaded them in the back of the vehicle.

"Thanks, Adam." Sierra pushed a loose red curl behind her ear—the rest of her curly hair held in a chignon, a few wisps of tendrils framing her face—and climbed into the passenger seat.

He sure wished he could change her mind about going back to Texas so *he* could date her. He couldn't imagine successfully being in a long-distance relationship like that. And the fact that she'd left the boyfriend behind had to say something about their relationship.

"No problem. I had to be at the airport anyway," he said. Her eyes were a clear blue like her brother's and were spellbinding. She was petite but when she tussled with her brother as wolves, she was more than aggressive, and Adam would love to play with her like that. "Did you get everything you needed?"

She checked her purse. "Yeah, I've got my ID. We're good. Last year, I was behind a woman at the check-in counter at the airport who had forgotten her ID. She said she would never get back to the airport on time if she went home to get it. She was in tears when she left. I always remember that whenever I have a flight scheduled and check to make sure I have my ID on me."

"I don't blame you. I bet the woman was upset."

Sierra took a deep breath of the aroma of the coffee and eyed the cup sitting in the console for her. "Ohmigod, I can't believe you got my favorite coffee before I go on my trip." Sierra smiled at him. "You are my hero." She sipped some of the coffee and sighed. "You sure know how to help me unstress in a big way."

He smiled at her and drove in the direction of the airport. In a subtle way, he kept hoping he could convince her she didn't need to return to Texas to see the boyfriend ever again.

He was glad he had convinced Sierra to work with them at the police bureau. He loved watching her work on witness sketches. She always had such good rapport with everyone at the bureau and with witnesses she worked with. And with the pack members too. She was fun to be around at pack functions, but she avoided going out with any male wolf alone that could signal she was dating someone other than the out-of-state-wolf.

He didn't think she would say yes to a boat outing, but since Brad had spoken to him about it, he had to ask. Again. "Hey, I was going to take the boat out the weekend after you return from your vacation and—"

She gave him a look that said he was pushing his luck.

He smiled. "It would be with your brother, his mate, and his sister-in-law. And Josh and Brooke will come too."

"I'll see how I feel when I get back."

He figured that was a no.

Ever since she'd moved in with the pack, Adam had been interested in her but disappointed she was still seeing another wolf. He'd hoped once she began working for the bureau as a sketch artist and teaching art to the kids in the pack, who adored her, she would realize her home was truly here with the pack, her brother, and his mate. Even though Adam was an alpha wolf and would love to try to change her mind about dating the other guy, he just didn't feel right about it. He considered himself one of the good guys.

Stealing another wolf's potential mate wasn't something he was interested in doing. He supposed it had to do with that happening to him when he was a younger wolf in love with a she-wolf. A wolf passing through had convinced her to leave the pack and go away with him. Adam figured the woman he'd been dating wasn't as interested in him as he'd been in her, but he wouldn't do that to another wolf.

"I'll see if my brother can pick me up at the airport when I return." Sierra was wringing her hands and appeared to be uncomfortable about something. Flying? Seeing the boyfriend?

He hoped she was having second thoughts about returning to see the guy.

"Sure." Adam didn't offer to pick her up. He could be in the middle of an important criminal case when she returned for all he knew and wouldn't be able to spare the time. He didn't want to dig deeper into the feelings he had about her. The fact that she was seeing someone as a possible mate—that she wasn't free for him to pursue. If he had been seeing her, he would have damn well made sure he could pick her up from the airport. Criminal case or no.

He wasn't the only one who didn't want her flying out to see the boyfriend in Texas. Even her brother had told her several times she needed to give the guy up. Adam suspected Brad knew who he was, but he wouldn't tell anyone his name. Neither would she.

If she was *that* interested in him, wouldn't she have mentioned him by name at some time or another and let on how much she cared for him? Maybe she wouldn't share her feelings with the guys, but why not with the she-wolves in the pack?

He got a call from his dad and answered on Bluetooth.

"Hey, are we still on for fishing this weekend?" his dad asked.

Adam and his dad were close, and whenever he had a chance, Adam tried to run down to fish with him at the pack leaders' ranch or they would go out on the boat. Since his dad was a retired police officer, he was working security for the pack leaders' ranch now. So was Adam's mother, who had met Adam's father on the police force. His mother would undoubtedly be going on a shopping trip in town with some of her lady friends when he and his dad went fishing.

"I sure am, Dad."

"Hey, about Sierra..."

"I'm taking her to the airport." Adam had to warn his dad she was in the Hummer before his dad said something that would get Adam into trouble. "She's off to see her boyfriend." Why did she always have to go to see the boyfriend? Adam wanted to tell the boyfriend it was *his* turn to make the effort and come see her. He should have checked out the pack to see that Sierra was fine living here with them. Did he at least pay for her airfare?

"Oh, hey, Sierra, have a great time. I've got to run," his dad said.

"Thanks." Sierra frowned at Adam.

"See you and Mom Saturday, Dad." Then Adam ended the call. *Hell.* He shouldn't have mentioned on their last fishing date how he wished Sierra would call it quits with the boyfriend. His dad had instantly believed Adam had the hots for her and had started in on how Adam should change Sierra's mind about leaving town to see the guy. No matter how many times Adam told him there wasn't a lick of truth to it—because he didn't want his dad slipping up like this in front of Sierra—his dad knew him too well and didn't believe him.

In reality, a bunch of hungry bachelor male wolves would jump at the chance to date her if she wasn't still seeing the guy.

She looked over at Adam. "What about me? What was your dad going to say before you cut him off?"

Great. He would have to tell his dad not to mention anything more about this. "I have no idea, but I wanted him to know you were with me."

She stared daggers at Adam.

He shrugged. "Who knows?"

"You do. You know just what he was going to say." She let out her breath in a huff. "You're going to be in the doghouse, you know."

"With you?"

"Well, until you tell me what your dad was going to say about me that you were so eager to stop, yes. But no, I wasn't thinking of that."

"Then what?" Adam couldn't think of one reason why he would be in the doghouse over anything except for the other matter.

"Did you tell anyone beside your dad that you were taking me to the airport?"

"My boss. Well, not him either. I just let him know that I was going there about the stolen rental car." What had that to do with anything?

"Okay, good. For your own sake, keep it that way. Unless your dad tells everyone. No one else would take me to the airport. Brad and many of the bachelor males made sure of it."

Raising his brows, Adam glanced at her. "Seriously? Why?" He was surprised because whoever had an in with her might end up with a mate if she dumped the boyfriend.

"Yeah, seriously. I'm surprised you didn't get the word. They don't want me returning to see my boyfriend."

"What about your brother's mate, Janice? Or her sister, Dorinda, who is rather a rebel? Wouldn't they have offered to take you to the airport?"

"Nope. Maybe Cassie would have if she hadn't been on a wolf lecture tour back East. Then again, maybe not."

"Because they don't want you to see the boyfriend?"

"Because they don't want me to mate Richard and leave Portland for good."

Richard. Now if only Adam had a last name. Yet even if he did, what good would it do him or anyone in the pack?

"I could have driven my own car to the airport, but I didn't want to pay the parking cost, or I could have taken an Uber, but I figured someone in the pack wouldn't mind taking me. That was before I began asking pack members for a ride and everyone said they had obligations and couldn't do it at that time."

"Which could be true. In any case, I don't have any heartburn over it." Though he did, for the same reason other pack members did, but he was going to the airport anyway.

Since Adam was a detective and worked with Sierra, several of the bachelors in the pack had asked him to investigate this out-of-state boyfriend of hers. He told them he couldn't do it. It would be unethical. So why was he trying to learn who her boyfriend was on his off-duty time as if he didn't have anything better to do with his life? If she had a boyfriend and didn't want to date anyone in her new pack, so be it. She would eventually mate Richard, and she would leave the area to join him. Or he would join her here. It really wasn't anyone's business, though the males still wanted to know just who he was and how serious the relationship was.

For all Adam knew, she corresponded with him all the time, called him, texted, emailed, sent him letters in the mail. Despite telling himself he didn't care and that it wasn't his business, he did have a wolf's curiosity.

"Okay, so tell me why Richard"—Adam tried not to say the guy's name with animosity, but it was a struggle because he didn't believe Sierra deserved that kind of treatment—"doesn't come out to see you. Is he afraid of meeting the pack members?"

"He wouldn't be afraid of the pack members, if we even saw anyone else when he visited. But he's got a very important job."

"Like you don't?" Crime was up across the board in Portland. They needed all the help they could get, and she was great at the job.

She folded her arms, tilted her head to the side, and didn't answer Adam.

"You deserve better."

"It's my choice to see him." She looked out the window.

"So he has offered to come out here, but you preferred to see him out there?" Maybe Adam had it all figured wrong. What if Sierra was afraid the pack wouldn't like what they saw and would try to discourage her from seeing this Richard, so she thought she was protecting him.

"No, and it's really none—" she began to say.

"Of my business. I know. Sorry." But Adam wasn't. He knew he'd irked her over it. He also knew her brother did too.

"I hear enough from Brad about it so I don't need to from you too."

"What do your parents think of the situation?"

Sierra gave him a look that told him to back off. Her parents had met when her mother was in the air force and her father in the army while stationed in San Antonio. They retired there so they might want her to return to Texas. First, Brad came out to Portland. Now Sierra. Brad said their parents were considering moving to Portland if Sierra stayed and mated someone though.

Sierra looked back out the window and didn't answer Adam, so he wondered even more what they thought of the situation. He suspected they didn't like Richard, or she would have said they thought he was great or something. That was why she was mad.

Adam let out his breath. He supposed she had something really special going on with Richard since she kept returning to see him. Yet she wasn't mating him, and that made Adam suspicious that things weren't all right in paradise.

Sierra couldn't help being annoyed with Adam, though she understood he was concerned about her. She still appreciated he'd gotten her favorite coffee for her and was taking her to the airport.

But she also knew he was like the other bachelor males of the pack who didn't want to give her up to an out-of-state wolf. Her parents and Brad had given her enough grief over continuing to see Richard. But damn it, it was her decision to make, no one else's. She didn't mean to be so grouchy with Adam over it, but she guessed she was feeling some of the same things that others were telling her—that Richard should have paid her airfare, that she needed to move on with her life.

So what had Adam's father been about to say concerning her? She suspected Adam had been talking to him about her. If it had been about work, she was certain Adam's father would have just said what he had to say, not shut up over it.

She sighed and rested her hand on her purse, felt the postcard in the outside pocket that she'd received in the mail this morning, reminding her that she needed to hand it over to Adam. Not when he was driving though. He'd want to examine it right away and she didn't want him to pull over the SUV when he might make her late and miss her flight.

She glanced at Adam as he drove them to the airport. He was tall like her dad, his hair a lighter shade of brown, and he had dimples when he smiled. He smiled a lot whenever he saw her, as if she always brightened his day. His workload had doubled, and the chief hadn't found a replacement for Josh yet, though Adam always had a smile for her.

Butterflies were flopping around in her stomach. She wasn't sure she was doing the right thing by seeing Richard any longer.

The last time she saw Richard, she ended up sitting in his apartment for hours on end while he worked. Even though he was *supposed* to be taking off from work to be with her. That was the whole point of going to his house. Seeing *him*.

He had his sights set on making full bird colonel, which was a nice goal…for him. And she totally understood where he was coming from. When she was in, she'd worked hard to make rank too. She liked that he was goal-oriented and doing what he wanted to do most.

On the other hand, she'd been happy to retire from the army to pursue her first love—art. She loved reconnecting with her twin brother, Brad. Of course, her parents wanted her to move to San Antonio, but she didn't want to be part of the pack down there. She'd met a few of her parents' friends and they were fine, but she really liked the Portland pack. And she loved her part-time job as a sketch artist at the Portland Police Bureau and teaching art classes in the evenings or during the week when she could. That was the nice thing about teaching kids in the pack. They had her come in whenever she could. Her hours weren't set in stone. She didn't want to move to wherever Richard would be reassigned next when he was finally transferred. She wanted to be with a pack, and she wanted stability. And someday, she wanted kids.

So why was she still going back to see him? Trying to come to grips with ending the relationship? She wasn't a quitter, which was why she had stayed with the service until retirement, and she suspected that was why she was having such a hard time breaking it off between them. Richard hadn't seemed to want to end their relationship either.

As soon as they reached the airport, Sierra pulled out the postcard she'd slipped into a baggie as if it was evidence of a crime. Just in case it might end up being so. If anyone needed to give her advice concerning the postcard, it was Adam.

"Here we are." He pulled into the airport lane for dropping off departing passengers. He got out of the Hummer to help her with her bags. "Can you manage okay? I guess I should have already asked you that. I'll be parking in the tower anyway to investigate the stolen rental car and I can park, then help you with your bags."

"No, I'm fine. And good luck on the case."

"Thanks. I look forward to seeing you when you return." He pulled her bags out of the SUV and set them on the sidewalk.

She handed him the postcard with a German shepherd pictured on the front and a hand-drawn X on top of the dog. On the back, the card said: *I don't know how you got away with hiding your dog at the hotel, or maybe all the police were conspiring with you so I'd get more time for threatening a woman instead of a dog, but I've got your number. DM*

Adam read the back of the card and frowned. "DM. Dover Manning?"

"But the postcard wasn't sent from the jail where he's being held without bond for previous weapons charges and breaking probation."

"It's from Portland. Hell. And he's got your home address. Someone else had to have mailed it for him."

"Someone who would kill my dog, if I had one."

Adam looked up at her. She knew that dark look. He was thinking she could be the target. She agreed, but she didn't want to consider it right now, not when she needed to catch a flight. "I've got to run."

"You need to move back in with the pack. Stay with your brother and sister-in-law. Or with Leidolf and Cassie. The whole pack will offer you the best protection."

"I'll think on it." She didn't want Dover Manning to intimidate her from jail. If someone broke into her house, she might consider the situation differently. For now, she was going on a two-week vacation to be with her boyfriend, and that was all she had time to contemplate. "Thanks again! See you when I get back to the job."

She grabbed the bags and hurried into the airport to check in. Then she checked her bags. She didn't want to think about the situation with Richard and that he wouldn't ever visit her here. She was beginning to believe she didn't want to waste her time and money to see him if he wasn't willing to do the same for her.

CHAPTER 3

Adam figured he should have handled that better as far as confronting Sierra about her boyfriend not taking the time to visit her out here. He knew he shouldn't have brought it up. Hell, if he'd been dating her, he would have taken off to be with her, moved here even, or attempted to convince her to rejoin him. He couldn't imagine being apart from her if she really meant something to him, like this guy should feel.

His dad called him back. "Hey." This time he didn't say anything more as if he was afraid Sierra was still with Adam.

"Yeah, Dad, she's not here. What were you going to say about Sierra before? She was not happy with either of us."

"Sorry about that. I was going to tell you not to drive her to the airport if she asked you to. The word had gone out—via her brother—that no one was to drive her there."

"I didn't get the word."

"Obviously."

"I had a job to do at the airport. I would have taken her with me anyway, even if I'd had word from Brad not to take her."

"You have a soft spot for her. Your mom and I are trying to come up with ways for you to change her mind about seeing the boyfriend any further. Oh, but maybe this worked for the best anyway."

"How's that?"

"You taking her to the airport when everyone else refused to. If things don't work out with her boyfriend, she'll see you as the good guy."

"I was just doing a job."

"Sure you were. So you're working on the case of the stolen rental car at the airport?"

"Yeah, how did you know?"

"It's been all over the news. Do you need any help with the case?"

"Not right now, but you know when we go fishing, I'll bounce some ideas off you." Adam's dad had retired from the police force two years ago, but he couldn't let go of solving crimes. "You know they have an opening in the cold cases department."

"Nah, your mother would kill me."

Adam smiled. "She could join you there."

"She likes being retired from the police force."

Adam glanced at the postcard in the plastic bag sitting on the passenger's seat that DM had sent to Sierra. There was no return address, and Adam was afraid this could mean trouble for her.

"Got to go, Dad."

"Okay, call if you need any help. Talk to you later."

They had never discovered who Dover's cohorts were in the hotel thefts. His workers were either lying low or hitting up other businesses. Or had they gone clean? Adam doubted it. There were enough robberies in the city that his partners in crime could have been involved in any number of them.

Adam parked his Hummer in the short-term parking lot and went inside to speak to the woman at the rental car counter. "Hi, I'm Detective Holmes from the Portland Police Bureau." He showed her his badge.

"Yes, oh, I'm so glad you're here. We had a second rental car stolen minutes ago."

Forty-five minutes later, Sierra felt a slice of apprehension slide through her as she boarded her flight to the Killeen-Fort Hood Regional Airport. When she finally arrived in Killeen, she texted Richard to let him know she had arrived. She had hoped he would be there waiting for her, all smiles, with a big hug and kiss and a promise of more when she arrived.

She didn't get an answer as she waited for her bags on the carousel. The last time she had come to see him, he was still at work, couldn't get away, and she swore they were having an office party the way it sounded with all the laughter and talking in the background. He better not do that to her this time too.

She texted him three more times, gave him a call that went to voicemail, and gave in and hailed a cab. She wasn't waiting forever at the airport on his return call. And she knew just where this fiasco was headed. She was glad she had made one last effort though, and she would call it quits in person, face-to-face, unless he made this right between them.

When she arrived at the apartment, she saw lights on in his windows. She frowned. So he wasn't at maneuvers in the field with his division or at work in the office? With a spare key to his apartment in hand, she paid the taxi driver and pulled her bags up the sidewalk to the apartment door, glad Richard lived on the first floor at least.

She didn't bother knocking. She was too angry that he hadn't bothered to answer her call or texts. Unlocking the door, she let herself in, leaving the suitcases in the foyer, shut the door, and heard the sound of a man and woman in the throes of making love in the master bedroom in the back. *What the hell?*

Unless he was making unconsummated love to a wolf or had mated her, the woman was probably human. *Lupus garous* could have sex with humans if they weren't mating, but if they were courting a wolf, they didn't screw around with anyone else.

She stormed down the hallway, smelling his wolf's scent and no she-wolf's scent, so it was a human woman. She smelled his brother's scent too. He must have visited recently.

When she reached the bedroom and saw a blond-haired woman riding astride a man, though she couldn't see his face, she said sharply, "Richard!"

The woman squeaked and rolled off the guy. The guy looking back at her was not Richard. It was his twin brother, Jethro. She would have been embarrassed under different circumstances for walking in on them, but not now. Not when she was too angry with Richard. And not when Jethro was in Richard's bed.

"Ohmigod, Sierra, what are you doing here?" Jethro's eyes were round with surprise.

"I could ask you the same question. Where is Richard?" And what was Jethro doing in Richard's master bedroom having sex with a woman in Richard's bed? Sierra bet he wouldn't have allowed it.

"He's on field maneuvers. Didn't he tell you to cancel your trip here?" Jethro covered himself with the sheet and sat up in bed, while the blond frowned at her, the sheet pulled up to cover her breasts.

Don't bother on my account, Sierra wanted to say. The damage was already done.

"Obviously he didn't. It must have slipped his mind." And that said a whole lot about their relationship. "Fine." She whipped around and headed down the hall. She wasn't about to tell Jethro she was done with his brother. Jethro would surely tell him what had happened when Richard returned home. That could be a couple of weeks from now, depending on how long he'd already been in the field. She didn't care. She was too pissed off.

"Sierra!" Jethro said, chasing after her, wearing the sheet around his waist. "Wait!"

She grabbed the front door and jerked it open, then seized her bags and headed to the sidewalk, leaving the door wide open. Now what the hell was she going to do? No way was she returning to Portland and having to explain to anyone why she needed to cancel her vacation to see her boyfriend. Not that she had to explain it, but she'd feel compelled to give some reason and she wasn't lying about Richard, that was for damned sure.

Besides, she'd paid for the trip out here and she had the time blocked out on the schedule. She was here now, though there wasn't anything she wanted to do in Killeen. She could see her parents in San Antonio, but she'd seen them before she left for Portland, and she knew her mother and father would both give her grief about Richard. That would make a great vacation. *Not.*

She googled a map of Texas and decided South Padre Island could be fun. She got on her phone and looked for a flight today to Brownsville, the closest airport to South Padre Island, and found one leaving in two hours. Perfect. She made the reservation.

Still wearing a sheet, Jethro called out, "Sierra!"

She didn't answer Jethro and the door shut. She called for an Uber. While she was waiting for the car to show up, she made a reservation at a rental unit right on the white sandy beach on the island. Terrific. She would enjoy getting out of the Oregon rain, get a nice tan before she returned home, and she wouldn't let on she had broken up with Richard until she had a chance to do so with him—over the phone. So much for this face-to-face business.

A few minutes later, Jethro opened the door wearing a pair of jeans shorts and hurried down the walk toward her just as her Uber ride showed up. "Don't say a word," she said to him and got into the car, and the driver took her to the airport. Even though none of this was really Richard's brother's fault, she didn't want to talk to him about this situation.

This was between her and Richard.

Later that afternoon, Adam was at the scene of an armed robbery at a jewelry store, just wrapping things up. Thankfully, the owner of the store recognized the voice of one of the two masked men, one of whom was his nephew. Adam headed to his SUV when he got a call from Brad Redding, Sierra's brother, surprising him since he usually didn't get calls from him when he was working. "Yeah, what's up, Brad?"

"I got a call from Jethro Wentworth, Richard's brother."

"Richard, the guy Sierra's seeing?" Already Adam was worried about Sierra. He got into his SUV and drove off toward the bureau.

"Yeah, how did you know?"

"She finally told me his name was Richard. What's happened?" Normally, Adam kept his cool under pressure, but this time he couldn't shake loose of his concern that something bad had happened to Sierra.

"Richard's in the field on maneuvers with his division, his brother said. She left the apartment angry, and he thought I should know because he can't get ahold of his brother *or* Sierra to try and iron things out."

"I take it she hasn't contacted you." Adam figured that had to be a given.

"No. I'm sure she thinks I'll tell her I told her so. I had hoped, since you work with her, she might have texted you in case she was returning to work earlier than scheduled."

"No, she hasn't. Did you check return flights to Portland?" Adam assumed Brad would have, but he had to ask.

"Yeah. She would have gotten into Portland forty-five minutes ago if she was on the flight coming home. She wasn't. I thought since you're a police detective and have sources at the airport, you might be able to check the airlines and see where she went."

"You think she went someplace else?" *To lick her wounds?*

"Yeah. She already had the vacation time scheduled and I know her. She wouldn't have wanted to return straight here after what had happened. Everybody would have sympathized with her, but I imagine she doesn't want to deal with it right now. And she had already paid the money to go out there. I just need to know she's going to be okay and that she knows we're here for her if she wants to talk. Now I feel kind of bad because I instigated the situation with no one driving her to the airport. Thanks for taking her."

"I had a case to work on there, so yeah, I took her. Okay, do you know which airline she took where she flew to initially? Do you know where this guy lives?"

Brad gave him the details of her flight times and the airline and destination. "He's an army officer stationed at Fort Hood, so that means Killeen, but she wouldn't have hung around the area. There's nothing much to see there. She was stationed there before she retired, and I visited her a few times. I called Mom and Dad and she didn't go see them in San Antonio, probably figuring they would give her grief over it. They've been telling her since she retired, like I have, that she needs to settle down in Portland and find a mate—one who is there for her."

"Um, yeah, I agree. So that means Richard didn't tell her that he was going on field duty and had no plans to see her?" Adam couldn't believe the wolf.

"Nope. And she pays her way out there every time. If it wasn't that it's her business to handle this the way she sees fit, I'd punch the guy out."

Adam felt the same way and knew her brother would actually do it too, for upsetting his sister. "Okay. Let me look into it. One other thing..." Adam hadn't told anyone about the postcard yet, except for his boss. Normally he wouldn't tell family members or others about a case he was looking into unless the person it pertained to wanted him to, but they were wolves and handled things a little differently. "When I was dropping off Sierra at the airport, she handed me a postcard from a person that used the initials of DM." He explained to Brad what the card had said.

"DM? Dover Manning, had to be, damn his hide."

"Yeah, so I turned it in to check for fingerprints. It came from Portland, not the jail, so someone mailed it for him or sent the message on his behalf. I just wanted to let you know in case she needs to move back to the pack's ranch temporarily until we catch this guy."

"Or guys. You thought there were more than the one you caught, in addition to the hotel staff."

"Right. I'll get back with you as soon as I learn anything about where she's gone to and what's going on with this veiled threat."

"Thanks, Adam. Are you going to tell Leidolf?"

"Yeah, that's next on the agenda." Not about Sierra going somewhere else for the rest of the vacation but about the threat to her life, if that was what this was. The pack was always there for each other.

"Okay, then I won't have to."

Adam was swamped with cases because of losing his partner to retirement, but when it came to one of their red wolves, that situation shot straight to the top of his list of important missions.

"And thanks for trying to locate Sierra. I owe you," Brad said.

"Think nothing of it." Adam arrived back at the bureau, but before he went inside, he called Leidolf to explain to him what was going on in case Sierra needed a security detail.

"Hell," Leidolf said. "I think she should move back to the ranch. No one who plans any mischief would get to her here."

"I agree, but I still think it should be her call as long as nothing is going on. It may be just a veiled threat, and nothing will come of it."

"Okay, just keep me informed."

"I will." They ended the call and Adam gathered the paperwork on the jewelry store robbery and headed inside the bureau.

He'd just set his paperwork on his desk when a woman wearing a light-gray suit with a skirt walked into the suite of offices. She had long legs, high heels, her dark hair in a bob, and a smile that was at once disarming and put him on alert at the same time.

Some of the guys smiled at her, a couple were gaping at her, but luckily none of them gave a wolf-whistle. No sexual harassment was allowed here.

Adam's boss called out from his office, "Looks like your new partner, Tori Rose, is here."

Adam looked back at her. If she'd been a wolf, he might have been interested in getting to know her better—as in courtship. But Sierra dominated his thoughts and now maybe he would even have a chance with her if she and Richard were on the outs with each other.

"Adam Holmes," he said, stretching his hand out to Tori.

She joined him, her dark brows instantly rising, and her ruby lips parted. "You certainly are one of us." Her words were soft, for his ears only, as she shook his hand.

He instantly cataloged her scent and smelled she was a red wolf too. How could he have gotten so lucky? "Hell. All right! Have you talked to Leidolf and Cassie?" He wanted to introduce her to their pack leaders as soon as he could.

"Leidolf. He's the one who convinced me to come here and apply for your former partner's position. He said it would be best for both of us to work together as partners. Cassie is still on a trip. I wanted to meet you right away, but you've been busy all day."

"Yeah, Josh Wilding retiring has put me in a bind. I don't blame him though. He wanted more time with his new, uh, mate."

Tori smiled. "I don't blame him either and now I'm here. I'm eager to get started. I spent all morning doing the paperwork to start the new job. What do you want me to do first?"

"That was Josh's desk over there. It's yours now. If you don't mind, go through these cases stacked up on my desk that I've been working on. See if you can come up with anything to nail these guys with. Armed robberies have priority, but if we can't solve those right away, just take your pick."

"What are you going to do in the meantime?"

"I'm trying to track down our part-time sketch artist."

"Sierra Redding? Leidolf said she was one of us."

"Right. She is."

"So she has gone missing?" Frowning, Tori sounded concerned.

"Her brother called me and said he's worried about her. I'll fill you in on the details later." Not about Sierra's private life though. That was for Sierra to share if she was so inclined.

"Sure. If you need my help with it, let me know."

Glad that Tori was fitting in right away, he nodded, pulled his phone out, and pointed to the stack of folders on his desk. He would tell Tori about the postcard Sierra had received once he located Sierra and made sure she was safe.

"Right on it!"

Man, was he glad to have a partner again. He hoped she was as good at the job as Josh had been. There would be some getting used to a new partner. He swore Josh and he were like twins, able to anticipate the other's moves in a crisis without any trouble. If Adam wasn't so concerned about Sierra's whereabouts, he would have taken a picture of Tori and sent it to Josh to show him his replacement.

"Hello, Fred. This is Detective Adam Holmes with the Portland Police Bureau."

"Hey, Adam, glad to hear from you. What do you need?"

"I'm trying to locate a woman by the name of Sierra Redding, one of our"—Adam didn't see anyone within hearing distance—"pack members. She took a flight out earlier this morning from Portland, Oregon, to Killeen, Texas. Then booked another flight somewhere else. Thanks."

"Yeah, I know her. I'm on it."

It helped to have a red wolf working security at the airport!

CHAPTER 4

On South Padre Island, Sierra finally settled into her condo on the Gulf, the fresh air blowing in her face as she sat on the patio on the second floor. She smiled as she looked out on the blue water, a light smattering of white clouds drifting across the blue sky, then took in a deep breath and sighed. She'd been upset with Richard the whole flight here, not knowing what to expect, but now that she was here, she was glad. Someone was sailing farther out in the Gulf, and a couple were walking along the white sandy beach, hand in hand. Four kids—anywhere from toddler size to maybe about eight—were building sandcastles, their parents sitting nearby watching them. Seagulls screeched to each other high above, eyeing Sierra speculatively, hoping for food. But she'd read the signs on the second-story balcony. *No feeding the birds.* She could imagine the mess they would leave behind as they congregated on the patios looking for handouts.

Heck, if Richard had been at home and she'd stayed with him, she wouldn't have half as nice a time. They would be sitting in his condo eating what she had cooked and watching TV. He didn't take her anywhere. They just enjoyed each other's company. It was all right when she actually lived in Killeen, but not now, when she had to spend a lot of money and time to visit him.

But if she'd been *here* with him, that could have made the experience perfectly fine.

She had even had the notion that while she was staying with Richard, she didn't have to worry about the message from the cryptic DM. So much for that thought, because she was on her own—not that DM's cohorts would come all the way out here to make trouble for her. The thing of it was that if Richard hadn't encouraged her so much to come to Killeen, saying that he missed her all the time, she probably would have ended the relationship already.

Sierra went back inside her condo to put her bathing suit on and glanced at her cell phone, sitting on the chest of drawers in the room. She had turned it off when Jethro had called her number several times. She didn't need to hear his explanation of what was going on with him and the human woman. She only needed to talk to Richard, and she knew that wouldn't happen. When he was in the field, he was focused on that and only that.

She grabbed her suitcase and pulled out the blue swimsuit she'd thought she would be using to swim at the clubhouse pool with Richard. This place had a swimming pool with a view of the Gulf and the sugar-white beaches. Even better.

She glanced at her phone. *Nope.* She was on vacation. She didn't have a care in the world. After she swam in the pool and went out someplace to eat a seafood dinner, she would take a wolf run on the beach when it got dark. Then? Maybe she would curl up in bed to watch something she wanted to see. She was *not* going to let Richard ruin her two-week vacation.

And that was just what she did. It was a moonless night, the beach free of people, and she left her condo as a wolf. They did allow pets; she made sure of it. She raced onto the beach and ran for a couple of miles, enjoying the Gulf breeze in her face, the sound of the waves gently washing ashore, the feel of the sand between her wolf toes, and the smell of the salty sea in the air.

Later that night, she was enjoying a historical adventure on TV when the hotel phone rang. She answered it, thinking there was something wrong with her credit card or someone had seen her let her dog run out on the beach off leash or something. "Hello?"

"Hey, Adam here."

She sat up straight in bed. "Adam? What… How…" If he'd tracked her down, something had to be terribly wrong.

"Jethro called your brother who called me to use my expert detective talent to locate you. Your cell phone must be turned off."

She muted the TV and relaxed in bed again. "Can't a woman take a vacation without interruption?"

"Not when her brother is worried sick about her because things fell through with her vacation and she has disappeared off the face of the earth."

She was glad Adam didn't mention the reason things fell through with her vacation. Despite not wanting to feel that way after what Richard had put her through, she was glad to hear Adam's voice. It was deep and warmly reassuring and she couldn't help but think about the difference in the two men's voices. Adam's was soothing, comforting, when he wasn't being in charge of a crime scene. Richard's voice was just as deep, but it didn't have the warmth that Adam's voice had. Why in the world was she even thinking of that at a time like this?

"Hey, not that you would want me to come join you or anything, but if I wasn't swamped with work and didn't have to teach my new partner the ropes before I can even *think* of taking a vacation, I would do it in a heartbeat. South Padre Island? I had to look it up, and I have to say it really looks like a nice place to visit."

"It is. So you have a new partner?" She was surprised to hear it because he hadn't said anything about that before. She guessed he had just learned of it. She hoped the new partner worked out as well as Josh had. The two of them had made a great team. And being wolves in the same pack had made it even better.

"Yeah, and the best thing is that she's a red wolf too."

Sierra couldn't believe it. She was thrilled that he had another wolf partner, but she was really shocked to learn he did. And that the detective was a she-wolf on top of that? Sierra was almost disappointed. And she didn't know where that feeling was coming from either. "You're kidding."

"Nope. I couldn't have hoped for better."

"Because she's a she-wolf."

"Hell, she may be married or engaged to a wolf. I don't have any idea. I just stuck her with a bunch of my cases and have been trying to locate you ever since."

"Oh, I'm sorry." She truly was because she knew how hard Adam had been working on his caseload and she wished her brother hadn't burdened him with her problems. She was glad Adam had a partner to lend a hand now, but she was surprised he hadn't made the time to learn more about his new partner, though Sierra appreciated that he'd looked into her disappearance for her brother.

She hadn't thought anyone would know she wasn't at Richard's. She just planned to return home after her vacation and take an Uber to her place, and she hadn't intended to tell anyone what had happened. Jethro had totally screwed that up for her.

"No problem. I know how you feel. I went through the same thing with a woman a while back. I just couldn't let go and she couldn't either. Then I got shot and she dumped my butt. No doting girlfriend there. She wasn't the caregiver type."

"Probably not me either." Sierra didn't know why she even said it. He wasn't looking for a girlfriend. And if his new partner was available, he could have a built-in partner/girlfriend. "But that is horrible." She guessed she should have said that first! "Did you tell Josh about your new partner?" She could just imagine him laughing. If the woman was the right age and available.

"No. I was concentrating on finding you."

She smiled. "Richard wouldn't have bothered, even if he knew I had come and gone."

"He's an ass."

She let out her breath, glad Adam agreed with her, though she hadn't planned to waste her breath talking about Richard when Adam was so nice to have tracked her down and called to check on her. "Yeah, he is. And thanks. Tell my brother I'm fine. I'll turn on my phone. I'm sorry for wasting your time."

"Are you kidding? You're a valuable member of our pack and with our police bureau and my favorite art teacher. Enjoy your vacation. Oh, I sent the postcard from DM to fingerprint analysis. I'll let you know if I get anything back on it. If you need anyone to talk to, you can cry on my shoulder, and I'll tell you all about my ex-girlfriend."

She laughed, feeling much better. "Thanks. You never know. I might take you up on it."

"Good. No sense in feeling bad alone when we can swap stories and commiserate. I'll let you go now and get back to your vacation."

She was thinking about his offer to go boating with him and her family and how much fun she'd always had with her parents and brother when she'd still lived at home and they'd had a boat. "Um, hey, uh, do you *still* have room on your boat for one more person?"

"Yeah. I've been saving the spot just for you."

She smiled. "Okay, good. 'Night, Adam. See you when my vacation is done."

"'Night, Sierra."

As soon as they ended the call, she retrieved her phone and turned it on. When she did, the ringtone jingled a tune. The caller ID revealed it was her brother. She sighed and answered it.

"Do you want me to come there and punch him out?" her brother asked before she could say anything to him about wasting Adam's time searching for her when he was so busy with real criminal cases.

She smiled. Brother to the rescue. "No. I don't want you locked up."

"Did Adam tell you he would beat me to it?"

She couldn't believe Adam had told her brother that and hadn't even let on he had! "No, he didn't say anything about that."

"Well, he would. I hope you're not going to see the louse anymore."

"That's a given. And sorry, Brad, for worrying you. I only turned off my phone because Jethro kept calling me. I didn't ever think he would end up calling you."

"I gave him hell to pass along to his brother. Are you all right?"

"Yeah. Thanks. It's just beautiful here. I'm going to enjoy the sunny days."

"Okay, I'll let you go then. I'll pick you up from the airport when you return."

"I can take an Uber."

"No way. We need to talk. Enjoy yourself."

She sighed. She should have figured he would want to know everything that was going on between her and Richard. "Good night." She was taking an Uber when she returned.

"'Night, Sis."

She ended the call and stared at the TV, no longer interested in watching the movie. As much as she thought she would enjoy her time here, she suspected she would be bored if she stayed longer than a week by herself. With a friend, she would have had a blast staying for the two weeks.

She turned off the TV and her bedside lamp and settled down to sleep. She wondered what Adam's new partner looked like and if she was mated or courting someone already, like Sierra had been.

Sierra hadn't a clue why she wanted to know those particulars about the new woman, who undoubtedly would soon be a member of their pack, if she wasn't already. Sierra wasn't dating again until she was ready. And if the wolf's job always took a priority over her, she… Well, she couldn't fault the person if he was someone like Adam who was always on call when he had cases he was investigating. Richard should have told her to cancel her flight, but she suspected that was an oversight on his part. Which meant he hadn't really been looking forward to her visit, or he wouldn't have forgotten she was coming!

Adam closed his eyes that night, and all he could think of was the pretty redhead and her brilliant blue eyes, envisioning her lounging on a sunny Texas beach. Man, did he wish he could be there with her, making her forget all about the ass she'd been dating. Being in paradise for two whole weeks by herself might be what she needed, but as he heard the rain hitting the bedroom windows, he wished he could be there to enjoy the time with her. Not as a boyfriend but as a friend, a fellow pack member. He could use the break too.

It seemed as though he had only closed his eyes when he got the call the next morning that there was another home invasion and now a homicide.

He hurried out of bed, again wishing he was far away from the wet Portland weather, on a beach enjoying the sunshine with Sierra.

When he arrived at the crime scene, the rain was finally letting up and Tori was already there taking notes. He was glad to see her there, making him reminisce about how dedicated he and Josh had been to the job—at the office early, usually having cups of coffee and working over cases, trying to shed new light on them with each other.

"Did you get ahold of Sierra?" Tori asked.

"I did. She's enjoying herself on South Padre Island, Texas. Safe and sound." He crouched down to see the muddy footprints on the tile kitchen floor.

"I'm glad she's fine. I bet you wish you could join her."

Wondering if Tori had the wrong impression about his checking on Sierra, Adam glanced up at her to see her expression.

Tori smiled and began taking more notes. "Oh sure, you were checking on her because her brother called you and asked you to and because you're a police detective and can get the work done. But"—she pointed her pen at him—"there's more to it than that."

She's a wolf, he wanted to say, a pack member. And wolves looked out for their own and other wolves in need. He wasn't about to admit he had been thinking the very same thing about being with Sierra.

"I asked her brother what's going on because I want to be her friend when she returns home. Especially since she works with us too. Her brother said she's having boyfriend trouble and it might be over for them. At least Brad hopes so." And so did Adam. Sierra needed to be here with them in the Portland area, forgetting about returning to Texas unless it was to see her parents or go on a vacation. "I think we all feel the same way."

"You should date her." Tori shrugged.

"She might not want to date for some time, if she's even given up the guy for good."

"Well, I would sure convince her to drop the bum."

He hoped Sierra didn't need any further encouragement.

"I wouldn't wait too long on the sidelines when she gets back. I'm sure a lot of bachelor males are waiting to see how this all unfolds."

He wondered if Tori was mated or already seeing someone out of state. He hadn't even asked where she was from or anything else about her. He'd been too busy trying to track down Sierra and then working on cases again. Yet even now, he didn't want to ask Tori if she was seeing someone...or mated. It might sound like he was interested in dating her. Maybe after he had worked with her a while, he would feel something different for her. For now, he was more concerned about how Sierra was feeling.

They maneuvered around to the back door where the glass window was broken. "A paver was used to break the window," Tori said.

"But no one was home at the time, correct?"

"Right. Their neighbor called in the break-in. Then the renter walked in on the would-be thief, now wanted for murder."

Dr. Patrick Silverson, the coroner, arrived. He was a gray wolf who had moved into the area a couple of years ago and was glad to be with a pack, even though it was a red wolf pack. "Another Ryson."

"Yeah, the last of three brothers," Adam said. "Probably same thing as before. Selling illegal drugs in another drug lord's territory. These guys never learn."

"Too much money to be made," Patrick said. He glanced at Tori and smiled. "Do you work with this guy?"

She smiled back at him. "Yeah." She offered her hand and he shook it. "I'm Adam's partner now. Tori Rose."

"Adam sure lucked out. I'm Patrick Silverson. Uh, you're not with anyone, are you?" Patrick asked.

"Nope, not yet. Are you?"

He smiled. "Not me."

"Good, then why don't we go to an Italian restaurant—tonight, if you're free," she said.

"Hell, yeah. Would seven be all right? I'll pick you up at your place."

"Sounds like a deal."

They exchanged cell numbers, and she texted her address to the doc.

Adam couldn't believe the doc was hitting on his partner over a dead body and making a date. But he *was* a coroner. And they were wolves.

Then they finished their business there, and Adam and Tori headed for their cars.

"What do you think of the coroner?" Tori asked Adam.

"He's a good guy, cares about his job, enjoys seeing people, fun to be around at a party. As to dating, I haven't a clue."

Tori laughed. "I might have waited for you to ask, but I think that's a lost cause."

"Oh?" He figured Tori was referring to him being interested in dating Sierra.

Tori just smiled and shrugged and wouldn't say. "So why did Doc wait to ask me to go out?"

"You would have to ask him."

"I think he was waiting to see how you responded, worried he might be stepping on someone's toes. That's why I asked him to go out first. To let him know I was free and available. You know why I know you have some draw to Sierra? You didn't once ask me if I was free to pursue." Tori smiled.

"Maybe I was giving you time to get acclimated to your surroundings and your job."

"Nope, you were too busy being worried about Sierra." She patted his shoulder and headed off to her car.

"Don't tell Sierra that when you meet her."

Tori only smiled.

Hell, he needed to make sure Tori didn't let on that he really did have a thing for Sierra. He could see that getting him in hot water immediately.

CHAPTER 5

A WEEK LATER, THE POSTCARD SENT TO SIERRA WAS STILL nagging at Adam on his drive home from work. He was traveling through the flooded streets in Portland when the summer storm turned vicious and the case took second billing. At least the Ryson case had been solved. A rival drug gang had ordered the hit and was searching for his drugs. One of the gang members was in jail awaiting trial for the murder.

Winds suddenly picked up and shook Adam's car, making it feel like an earthquake was breaking up the road. Thunderstorms were roaring through the area, but he hadn't thought it would get this bad.

Rain poured down in a deluge, making the roads slick and slippery, his wheels sending floodwater shooting through the air. His wipers struggled to clear the persistent falling rain, covering his windshield in an avalanche of water. Lightning struck all over the place and thunder followed with tremendous booms. His heart racing, Adam saw a dark-gray funnel headed a little south of him. Tree branches were torn from trees and flew across the road in front of him. A blue-and-white patio chair flew off a front porch and bounced off the black roof of his Hummer. If that was all the damage his Hummer suffered, he'd count himself lucky.

He wondered if he should have stayed at work until the worst of this was over. Then the funnel headed farther south. He could still see it dipping down from the dark sky, the swirling motion of the clouds, and what looked like black birds flying through the air—but were really shingles or other debris torn up and tossed and swirling in the high winds.

It was rare to have a tornado strike in Portland, Oregon, but it had occurred the year before too. Some said that everyone nationwide could experience "weirder" weather. He believed it.

He worried about the wolves in his pack and whether they were safe right now. He worried about his fellow coworkers with the Portland Police Bureau and hoped everyone was okay.

A red cedar tree suddenly uprooted in the yard next to the sidewalk, making the most horrendous noise, and crashed across the road in front of his vehicle. Adam slammed on his brakes and avoided hitting the tree branches extending out several feet.

Another red cedar was ripped out by its roots in the eighty-mile-an-hour winds and landed some feet away on the other side of the one blocking his path. The second tree hit a house with an awful bang and crunch. Despite the driving rain and wind, Adam had to take the chance and see that those inside the house were safe.

Before he could do that, a pin oak cracked in half and landed on electrical wires, bringing several down onto the fallen tree in front of his vehicle. All the porchlights, streetlamps, and lights on inside the houses in the neighborhood went dark in one fell swoop. It was early evening on a summer day, so the sun had a long way to go before it set, but the storm was making the sky appear as dark as if the sun was already setting.

Adam saw a man video-recording the wild storm from an upstairs awning window. He suddenly reached out to close the window against the growing wind. Struggling, he couldn't make any headway, and the wind tore the window out of his grasp, and it flew off its hinges. The window sailed through the air for several feet, disappearing behind a fence.

Adam yanked off his seat belt and hurried to remove his suit jacket. Then he got out of his vehicle in the deluge and raced to the two-story brick home where the tree had crashed onto one side of the roof. His shoes filled with water as he ran through the deepening puddles on the road, and he was quickly soaked from the heavy rain.

He pounded on the door. "Police detective with the Portland Police Bureau! Is everyone all right?"

A gray-haired man answered the door, his gray eyes widening to see Adam soaking wet, standing on his porch, the rain coming at a slant and still soaking him, the roar of the wind deafening. "Thanks for checking on me and my wife." He shook Adam's hand. "We're okay, Detective, but we'll have to leave the house. It's not safe staying here. My son's trying to make his way here to pick us up." He motioned to the garage. "No way to get the car out now."

"Okay, I'm calling in some assistance to help clear the roads and take care of the downed power lines and trees." Once Adam was assured the couple were okay and on their way to safety with their son, he returned to his Hummer and called the electric company servicing the area and the city about the tree removal.

Then Adam's phone rang, and he saw the call was from Leidolf. "Hey, Adam, I got an emergency call from Sierra."

Adam immediately worried she was in trouble. "She's still in South Padre Island, isn't she? Or did she return home early?" He wished she'd told him, and he would have picked her up from the airport. Then again, her brother had told Adam he planned to take her home whenever she arrived at the airport. Adam suspected Brad wanted to talk to her about not seeing the boyfriend any further.

"She arrived at the airport and took an Uber, but after she left the airport, the storm got bad. A tree fell on the roof of a woman's car that was driving in front of them. Sierra wanted the Uber driver to stop so she could assist the woman in her car. The Uber driver let Sierra out and set her suitcases on the pavement, and then tore off and left her stranded. She's attempting to get the woman out of her wrecked car. Sierra tried getting help, but everyone's tied up. I thought of you, since I suspected you were headed home, unless you're still stuck working on a case or got caught up in this weather too."

"I was on my way home after work. Trees, power lines, and branches are down all over, but I'll get to her. Where are they?"

Leidolf gave him the directions.

"They're only three blocks over from where I am. I'm on my way. I'll let you know the outcome later." Adam began to back his vehicle up, but there were so many tree branches down that he couldn't drive out that way without moving a bunch of debris. He called Sierra's number. "Hold on. I'm on my way to help you out."

"Adam?"

"Yeah, I'm only three blocks away from your location, but I need to move some branches out of the street first. Be there in a bit."

"Thanks! Be careful!"

"You too." He hated that she was stuck out in this weather with no shelter. If he could have, he would have arrested the Uber driver for abandoning the women like that.

Sierra had sounded as harried as he felt as he got out of his Hummer and hurried to clear the street behind him, and then he backed up and pulled into a driveway. Then he reversed and was on the street again. The wind was dying down but still slamming into the car. He was a block away when he saw live wires on the street and couldn't drive any closer. He parked his vehicle and ran down the block to reach Sierra and the woman she was trying to help. The wind pushed him faster than he'd ever run. The rain continued to soak him as debris was flying all over the place—patio furniture, parts of roofs, some fence slats. He was dodging and ducking, again wishing he could be wearing his wolf coat.

Tree branches whipped by him, one striking his shoulder, another scraping across his cheek as he ducked and missed the full brunt of it.

When Adam finally reached the area where Sierra was supposed to be, he saw just as many trees and power lines down over there, the wind still tearing things apart, roof shingles flying, leaves and twigs whipping through the air. The funnel had passed by, but the winds were still wreaking havoc over the area, the rain still pouring down, and lightning striking all over the place.

And then he saw the tree on the roof of a red Suburban and Sierra trying desperately to get the passenger door open behind the driver's side.

He rushed to join her and noted right away that she had been hit by flying debris, her forehead and her left arm bloodied.

"I can't get the driver's door open. The woman is eight and a half months pregnant. And she has a toddler in the back in a car seat," Sierra shouted over the wind. "I called an ambulance but they're having trouble getting here really fast. They are on their way though."

"Good." Adam tried the driver's door and Sierra rolled her eyes. He allowed himself a small smile. What if he was just stronger than Sierra and could get the door open? "Is she okay?"

"She said she is. Upset, anxious, naturally. She's called her husband, but he's a firefighter and was dealing with a fire. He's on his way. She's calling her brother now. The toddler is crying but appears to be all right."

Adam just hoped the pregnant woman and the toddler really were all right. He tugged and pulled at the driver's door while the pretty, dark-haired woman was calling someone on the phone. Sierra held on to the car to maneuver to the other side in the strong winds and tried the rear passenger door.

"You're going to be all right, honey," Sierra said, talking in a mommy way to reassure the little one.

If Adam wasn't fighting so hard to get the driver's door opened, he would have smiled at Sierra's motherly instincts.

With another hard yank, the door opened on Adam's side, and he kept his back against it to keep it from slamming shut.

Sierra got the door open to the back seat and unbuckled the baby.

"Are you okay, ma'am?" He could just envision the woman going into labor before they got her out of here.

"Yeah." The woman was holding her belly, and he was afraid she might have been injured. "What about Sarah?"

Adam hurried to unfasten the woman's seat belt.

"She's fine. I'm afraid to take her out of her car seat just yet and move her into the wind and rain," Sierra said, "but she's smiling at me."

Just then, an ambulance came down the street.

"Here!" Sierra shouted, waving her arm to indicate the driver of the vehicle was the one who needed their help.

Since the ambulance was there already, Adam didn't help the driver out of the car, concerned she might have sustained injuries and would need prompt medical care. There wasn't any threat of the car catching fire. Before the ambulance arrived, his main concern had been getting her to a hospital.

The EMTs were running a gurney around the debris on the street to reach the car, one of the men tossing branches back onto the sidewalk or yards to clear a path.

As soon as the EMTs helped the woman out of her car, they lifted her onto the gurney and began checking her vital signs. Each of the men acknowledged Adam and Sierra, and then one of them checked the toddler over.

A bright-red pickup truck showed up while Adam was fetching the woman's purse and handing it to her.

"Rosie!" the driver said, getting out of his truck. "I'm her husband and Sarah's father."

"We're taking them both to the ER to check them out," one of the EMTs said.

"Thanks. I'll meet you over there."

Then the ambulance and the fireman took off for the hospital.

Adam took hold of Sierra's arm and began helping her back through the wind and rain to his vehicle. He hoped the pregnant woman and her daughter were going to be all right. And he was proud of Sierra for helping her and the toddler in their time of crisis.

"Are *you* okay?" He worried about Sierra's head wound. Her forehead was still bleeding, the blood dribbling down her skin and mixing with the rain.

"Yeah, sure. What about you?" she asked, glancing at his cheek.

"Scratch. But you have a wound on your head."

She reached up and touched it. "I don't feel anything." But then she looked at the blood on her fingertips. "Yet."

"I'll take care of it, if you need me to."

"I have a medical kit at home. I can handle it." Another lightning strike and subsequent thunder struck close by, making her jump.

He grabbed her suitcases and began hauling them to his Hummer, then put them in the trunk. "I'm going to move branches out of the street that came down after I parked the Hummer. You back the vehicle up for me, okay?"

"Yeah, sure."

He opened the driver's door for her. Once Sierra was secure in the vehicle, he went behind it and began pulling tree branches off the street so she could back up. Then he hurried to take over the driving and she slid over the console. Another lightning strike lit up the dark sky, thunder booming all around them.

They were soaked to the skin, and Sierra was only wearing a swirly skirt and tank top, both glued to her feminine curves. She pulled off her wet pumps and set them on the floor.

She pulled a tissue out of the package in her purse and wiped the rainwater off her face. Then she handed him the package of tissues. "Help yourself."

"Thanks." Adam took a tissue and wiped his face. "I guess we're going to have to do some navigating to find a street that will take you back to your house."

"What about your place?" she asked.

"I don't know. I never made it home before Leidolf called me that you needed assistance."

"Thanks so much for coming to my aid. I sure didn't expect to run into a tornado when I returned home."

"Hell, me either."

She looked up reports on the phone. "Looks like no one was killed by the severe weather yet anyway. Just trees and power lines downed, some mobile homes overturned, and a few roofs damaged, as far as they know. All kinds of videos and pictures are coming in, showing the devastation."

"That's bad on the damage, but I'm glad no one has died in the storm." Adam started to turn down the street to take them to her place but saw it was blocked. Then he turned and went another way.

"It looks like none of the homes in this area have any electricity. I don't know if mine is on or not, but if we can get to my place and we have electricity, you're welcome to stay and have dinner."

"Yeah, sure." Adam wanted to ask her about her vacation, but he was afraid to bring it up because of the reason for her changing her destination. Not to mention he was really concentrating on the road conditions and having to zigzag because there was so much debris in the streets.

"Okay, after we eat, you can check with your electric company and see when your electricity will be restored if it's out," Sierra said. "I'm not sure what we can eat, but I think I have a couple of steaks in the freezer."

He had to stop the Hummer so he could get out and move a couple of tree branches out of the street, but he checked with his electric company to see if he had power. "Anything would be fine with me. Yeah, my electricity is out." Even though they could see in the dark, he thought she might need to talk to someone who would understand what she'd been through, and he would enjoy the company. Since they both worked at the police bureau, they could at least catch up on cases, if nothing else.

When they reached her home, Adam had to move more debris out of her driveway. Her house looked good, no damage on the one-story brick home, and he was glad about that.

"No lights," she said.

A lot of branches were down on the streets and in the yards. Streetlights were all out. No lights were on in any of the homes and no porch lights either, which meant her electricity was out too.

She raised her brows at Adam. "Any other ideas?"

Sheet lightning flashed across the stormy sky.

He sighed. "We could go out to the reindeer ranch and eat dinner with my former partner's brother, or we could drop in on our pack leaders' ranch farther south, since neither of those areas got hit bad. They might still have electricity. But the weather's so bad, it probably would be better just to eat at home. Do you have a grill under a patio cover?"

"I do. I'm sure I can find something in the freezer if I don't have a couple of frozen steaks. Uh, I also have hamburger."

"Either would be fine. It won't take long to grill steaks or hamburgers, depending on how thick they are." And he really liked the idea of spending some quality time with her. Not to mention that if the weather got worse, he wanted to be here for her.

CHAPTER 6

Finally, having arrived home safely, Sierra sighed with relief. She opened the passenger's door, grabbing her purse, and got out of the Hummer. Before she could hurry through the rain to the house in her bare feet, Adam was at her side, swooping her up in his arms to navigate over the twigs and other debris littering her driveway and walkway to the front door. She hadn't expected that, but she sure appreciated it.

He set her down on the porch and she entered the numbers on the keypad, then opened the door. As soon as she walked into the house, she flipped up the light switch, forgetting that there was no electricity. "Old habits die hard."

He laughed. "I do the same thing. I guess your keypad had battery backup."

"It does." At least with their wolf vision, they could see in the dark.

"I'll get your bags." Within minutes, he was carrying them into the house.

"Thanks!"

"You're welcome."

She'd forgotten all about the ton of drawings and paintings cluttering her dining room table. She'd been working on some portraits of wolves—some of pack members in their human form and some of members of the police force—before she took off on her vacation.

"Sorry for the mess."

"Don't be. Everything looks fine, and don't bother to move anything. We can sit at the kitchen bar if you want."

"Okay." Sierra opened the freezer and frowned. "Oh, I, um, cut my steaks in half and repackage them to freeze because I can't eat a whole one at a sitting." She sighed. "Is that okay?"

He chuckled. "Yeah, sure. Two halves are as good as a whole."

She pulled three halves of steaks out of the freezer and handed them to him.

He set the steaks on the counter. "Let's take care of your head injury first."

She realized then it was throbbing. "Okay, sure. And your cheek is cut too. I need to get out of these wet clothes and so do you."

Adam opened his mouth to speak, and she said, "Don't tell me you are fine. You're soaking wet like I am."

She led him to her master bedroom where she had left another couple sketch pads on the side of the bed she didn't sleep on and smiled. Her artwork had taken over the house. She pulled some black sweatpants out of her chest of drawers, an old antique piece she had hand painted with a country setting of flowers and rabbits and a little pond. "I think the sweatshirt will be too small for your broad shoulders." She liked clothes that fit. If she'd had something larger, it probably would have been fine.

"That'll work. Let's take care of your forehead first." They went into the bathroom then.

She brought out the medical kit from the cabinet down below, and he washed her forehead with a gentle touch. She winced when he wiped it with antiseptic. He covered the injury with a bandage. "Head wounds bleed a lot, but it doesn't look like you'll have any trouble with it. No need for stitches."

"That's good." Then she did the same with the cut on his cheek, taking care to be gentle. "Did you want me to cover it with a bandage?" She suspected he wouldn't.

He glanced at the mirror. "No thanks, it's good. Let me see your arm."

Even though it wasn't as bad as her head or his cheek, he was sweet to take care of it, but he had to bandage it too. "Thanks, Adam. Are you ready for dinner?"

"I sure am." He moved into the bedroom and unbuttoned his wet shirt.

She left the bathroom to get her clothes and suddenly felt like they were getting ready to have sex in her bedroom. Where that notion was coming from, she had no idea.

She grabbed some clothes from her closet and chest of drawers, went into the master bathroom, and shut the door. Even though *lupus garous* stripped out of their clothes and were naked before they shifted into their wolves, this felt way too intimate with a bachelor male wolf when she wasn't dating him.

She quickly removed her clothes and dried herself, suddenly remembering she should have gotten him a towel too. "Towels are in the linen closet down the hall!"

"Thanks!" He left the bedroom and she envisioned him totally naked when she left her bathroom. There was no sign of his wet clothes or him, but she heard him in the hallway, opening the linen closet door.

She pulled on a pair of panties, shorts, her bra, and a T-shirt.

A big bang sounded, and the light came on in the living room, went off, came on again, and she heard him say, "Hallelujah!"

She smiled.

With her own wet clothes and her small amount of dirty clothes in the laundry bag in hand, she walked through the bedroom and out to the hall where she caught an eyeful of one sexy man. He was butt naked, his skin still wet, his wet clothes on the floor, and he was drying off one of his legs. Hot buns, hot legs, back, and arms, and when he turned to see her gaping at him, the rest of him was just as hot.

"Uh, I'll throw your clothes in the wash with mine and then dry them, now that the electricity is on." Her face was flaming—speaking of hot—as she scooped his clothes off the floor, all but his shoes. She didn't wait for an answer as she flipped on the hall light, then hurried to the laundry room on the other side of her kitchen. She turned on the light in there and tossed the wet clothes and her dirty clothes into the washing machine, added soap, and started to wash them.

Before she reached the kitchen, the lights on the house flickered. She paused, and the lights went out. "Well, it looks like I'll have to wash the clothes when the electricity comes back on."

"No problem," he said, easygoing about the whole affair.

Sierra was glad because she still couldn't get the incident with the pregnant woman and toddler out of her thoughts and she needed only positive vibes right now.

She fetched a lantern out of her pantry and set it on the patio table while Adam joined her wearing her sweatpants and nothing else, still towel drying his short light-brown hair. She smiled at the length of the pants on him, the hemline reaching about mid-shin. His bare chest was buff and lightly haired with dark, damp strands, his nipples pebbled from the chilly air. She rarely saw him get naked, certainly never in her house. So eating with him when he was wearing so little that way was definitely a first. And thoroughly titillating.

"The pants are good enough," he said, catching her smile. He got the grill ready. "Thanks for washing my clothes—when the electricity comes back on."

"You're so welcome. I'm glad I at least had *something* for you to wear."

She was relieved the winds had died down, but it was still raining hard. Thankfully, she had a nice-sized patio that kept everything dry. She went back inside to set up a lantern in the kitchen too. After that, she grabbed a couple of baking potatoes out of the bin and washed and wrapped them in foil, then took them outside to set on the table. He started the potatoes first on the grill.

With the storm creating such a mess, she was glad she had

Adam's company tonight. It was more fun riding out the storm with a fellow wolf. She brought the corn on the cob out of the freezer. She covered the cobs in butter and lemon and pepper spice and wrapped them in foil.

"Hey, thanks for everything," he said.

"I need to thank you for coming to my aid with the pregnant lady tonight. I thought she might deliver her baby if the ambulance didn't get there in time. Not to mention I wouldn't have had a ride after she and her toddler were picked up."

"The Uber driver should never have abandoned you like that."

"He was afraid his car would be damaged in the storm, and it's his only income." Sierra felt she had to see the driver's point of view. Not all people were born to be heroes. She was glad Adam was.

"He still shouldn't have left you and the woman and her child to fend for yourselves." Adam took a deep settling breath. "Why did you call Leidolf first and not me?"

She was surprised that he thought she should call him first. She would have, if she had thought he was close by. "I didn't know where you were. I thought you might still be in the middle of a case like you can be. I called Leidolf, since the ambulance couldn't get there right away, hoping one of our wolves would be close by. He said you had headed home and thought you were nearest to my location. As to another matter... About the driver's door?" She had struggled and struggled with that door, and she figured there was no getting the woman out that way.

He smiled. "Yeah, it just needed a little more muscle."

"Ha! I loosened it for you."

He laughed, then he started the steaks.

She went inside and set up several candles on the bar and lit them. Once she'd put the silverware and place mats out, she was thinking this looked more like a date than just something nice to do during an electrical outage and bad weather. She brought out a tub of butter and set it on the bar. "Do you want some red wine?"

"Sure, that would be good."

She opened a bottle of burgundy and poured each of them a glass of wine. Then she fixed them each a glass of water.

He gave a quick call to the hospital to check on the pregnant lady and the toddler. "Thanks," he said, then ended the call. "Both the pregnant mom and little girl are fine."

"Oh, good. I would have worried about that tonight if you hadn't checked on them."

"Yeah, me too."

When they were finally ready to eat, they sat down on the leather barstools. This was really nice, she thought, looking at Adam's bare chest as he began to eat. *Really* nice.

She sure hadn't expected this to happen! "So how is your new partner?"

Adam wasn't entirely surprised Sierra would ask him about Tori. The guys all wanted to know about her, naturally, but so did some of the women, curious if he was interested in dating her.

"She's good. She's prompt. Hell, she often gets to work before I do. She has a good head on her shoulders when it comes to investigating a case. She's former FBI, but she wanted to work with me because I'm a—"

"Wolf, naturally. So she knew you before? How did *that* come about?" Sierra sounded surprised because he'd never mentioned her before.

But he didn't know her. "Leidolf knew her, apparently. I had never met her before. He convinced her to come here to join the pack." He buttered his potato.

"That's what a good leader does. Looks for valuable assets to add to the pack. So is it a matchmaking effort on our leaders' part?"

Adam smiled at Sierra. He swore she was fishing to see if he was actually dating Tori or even interested in dating her. "Maybe. But several bachelor males in the pack are interested in dating her. I'm sure that was another consideration for convincing her to join us." He carved up some more of his steak. He guessed if Sierra was going to get personal with his life, he might as well ask about hers. "Did you have fun on South Padre Island?"

"Yeah, I did. It was relaxing. I swam in the pool, walked on the beach, swam in the Gulf, ran as a wolf at night on the beach. I even sketched some drawings of people at restaurants and at the beach. I had a great time."

"That sounds like the kind of vacation I would have enjoyed, only I would have been building sandcastles and taking pictures instead of drawing. My drawing is in the vein of stick figures."

She laughed. "You did great on the first photoshopped photo art that you created. Sandcastles, eh? That would have been fun." She took a sip of her wine.

"But you came home early."

"It would have been more fun to have stayed two whole weeks if I'd had a friend along . I would have too. I certainly hadn't expected to come home to a tornado."

"I so agree. I thought about you on the beach while we were socked in with rain. I would have been there in a heartbeat if I could have been. It sounds like the perfect place to take a vacation."

"It is, but knowing you, you would never have the time."

Adam suspected that he was in the same boat as her boyfriend as far as the notion of dating her went. "Especially after Josh retired, though with Tori to help, we'll get caught up eventually. So what happened with the boyfriend?" He wanted to know if Sierra was still dating the ass or if she had finally given up on him and ended the relationship.

She sighed and picked up her corn on the cob. "He's going to bite the dust once I'm able to tell him so."

That was good to hear. Adam didn't like that anyone would treat her with so little regard. "You still haven't talked to him?"

"Jethro, his brother, finally got through to me once you asked me to turn on my phone. I told him I was fine and having fun, not to worry. He was anxious about me telling Richard that he had been having sex with a human woman in Richard's bed. I thought he was also concerned that I was upset that I had come all that way to see Richard and he wasn't even there."

"So are you going to tell on his brother?"

She chuckled. "That's all you guys would worry about."

"Not me. If I had a brother, I would never have abused his trust like that. So are you?"

She ate the rest of her corn. "I doubt it will come up in the conversation whenever, *if* ever Richard calls me."

"Do you think Jethro will have told him you were there and angry about Richard not being there?"

"Yeah. And Richard will undoubtedly smell that I've been there. If he ever checks all the messages I left him, he'll know."

"And you still aren't sure Richard's going to call you back?"

She took a deep breath and let it out. "Let me put it this way. His work always comes first. When he's back at the office, he'll be busy playing catch-up."

"And when he's home at night?"

"Maybe then he'll think to call me."

"You're not going to just call him and get it over with?" That was what Adam would have done. Ended the relationship right then and there.

"Ha! I texted him three times. I don't know when he's getting out of the field. It could be another week if he had just gone out before I arrived. I'm not going to keep calling and texting him. It would sound like I'm desperate to get in touch with him."

"Did you call it off between you and him in your texts?"

"No. I wanted to talk to him in person. I feel I owe him that much. Though I guess I really shouldn't feel that way. And if he doesn't respond in a couple of days, I'll just email him a Dear Richard letter." She took another bite of her steak. "Not to change the subject, but did you ever get any response on the sketch I did on the suspect with a shaved head?"

"Not yet. It's a great sketch, but either no one wants to come forward with any information, or he's not from around here. Next time he hits up a liquor store, we'll get him." At least Adam hoped they would.

"Well, darn. There's nothing that matches him in the database, I suppose."

"No. He might never have been caught before so he wouldn't be in the database. Or he just started his life of crime. Oh, and by the way, the redheaded guy you sketched the day before you left on vacation? We got several leads on him. Hopefully, we'll get him soon."

"I sure hope so. Anyone who commits armed robbery shouldn't be running free. Oh, what about the rental car theft?"

Adam smiled. "Now that worked out great. A second rental car had been stolen just before I arrived, and I took off after it. With a couple of police cars also in pursuit, we nabbed the car thief and learned about the chop shop where they were dismantling the cars and selling the parts."

"That's great!"

"Yeah, it was. We've missed you. Everyone has," Adam quickly said. He hadn't realized until she wasn't there how much so, just seeing her smiling face when she was coming into the office to do a witness sketch or frowning in concentration as she was drawing the eyewitness's account. Or thrilled when he brought her the special coffee. "I think Willy Blanchard's getting tired of being our only other sketch artist. He's crabby, short-tempered half the time."

"As long as he doesn't retire."

"Right, like Josh did." But Adam was thinking that was where this was headed with Willy, and he hoped Sierra would consider taking his place and working full-time.

"But at least you have a great partner to replace Josh."

"I do."

"Maybe Willy just needs a vacation. Mine wasn't what I had planned for, but it turned out great. It recharged my batteries." She took another sip of her wine.

"You could always go full-time and take over Willy's position if he decides to really retire." There, he mentioned it, hoping she would consider the idea favorably.

"Thanks, but no thanks. Willy and I have a great arrangement. He does all the dead body sketches; I do the witness sketches. Now that I'm back early, I can relieve him of some of the load I'm sure he has been feeling. Maybe that will help."

Adam didn't have the heart to tell her that Willy had been telling him over and over again that he was going to retire. Adam suspected it was going to be sooner rather than later. After Willy had snapped at a witness for making him change a sketch several times, Adam knew it was past time for him to retire. He was a great guy, but this work could take a toll on anyone.

Suddenly there was a noise like a transformer had been fixed and the lights came on, shut off, came on again, and stayed on. He'd forgotten Sierra had turned the living room light on. He was glad the electricity was back on. The washer turned back on too. And her food wouldn't spoil.

"Great. Maybe my electricity is back on too." Adam checked with his electric company on his phone. "No, it's still out."

"Well, you can just stay here. You have to anyway, until I can wash and dry your clothes."

"Thanks."

Adam glanced at the picture of a family of red wolves and one of two young wolves sitting together on the mantel of her fireplace. "Your family? Is the other of your brother and you when you were little?"

He had never met her parents. When they had visited Brad from San Antonio, Adam had been busy working. He wondered if they would move here, now that both Sierra and her brother lived here.

"Yeah. I need to get a photo of Brad and his mate now too."

Adam looked around at the oil paintings on the wall of landscapes, birds, boats, seascapes, wolves, and flowers. "All yours?"

"Yeah, as you can see, I ran out of room. My parents' home is filled with them. And I'm working on Brad's new home. He wouldn't take any until he retired and settled down, not wanting any of my paintings to be ruined in shipment. I want to do one of Mount Hood when I have time, since I live here now, and it's just part of being in Portland. I've started selling some of my floral oils in Brooke's shop, which has been really cool."

"That's great and they're beautiful."

The rain was still pouring outside, but the lightning was moving off and the thunder rumbled farther in the distance, not as loud. Adam was glad the storm was dying down so when he left, he would get home easier after all the damage was done. Though he was enjoying the time with Sierra and wasn't eager to leave just yet. About half an hour had passed and the wash was still going, though he figured it wouldn't be long now before it was done. He'd still have to wait for his clothes to dry. Maybe he and Sierra could watch a movie or something after they finished eating while they waited for his clothes to be finished.

Suddenly, there was a knock at the door. His first thought was that someone needed help because of the storm. Hopefully Sierra wasn't a target for Dover Manning's continued harassment.

"Expecting someone?" Adam asked, ready to protect her. He was off his barstool in a hurry.

"No, I'm not expecting anyone." She went to the door and looked out the peephole. "Ohmigod, it's Richard." And she didn't say it in a good way.

"Oh," Adam said and returned to his seat.

She sounded shocked and not happy about it in the least. What in the world was Richard doing here? But would she finally break it off with him?

CHAPTER 7

Sierra couldn't believe her boyfriend, Lieutenant Colonel Richard Wentworth, or the ex—because that was just what he was about to be—had shown up unexpectedly on her front porch all the way from Fort Hood, Texas, without letting her know. Was he crazy? What if she'd been out of town or not home? And she wouldn't have been here if she hadn't gotten bored being by herself on South Padre Island.

Or—she glanced back at a very underdressed Adam—had been entertaining a bachelor male wolf, no matter how innocent the situation was.

"The boyfriend," she whispered to Adam, not having opened the door yet to let Richard in. "Uh, ex, as soon as I tell him the news."

"Good." Adam continued to eat his steak as if the news that her boyfriend was standing on her front porch didn't alarm him. Wolves could be territorial and confrontational over something like that. And she suspected if she had any trouble with Richard, Adam would take him to task, if *she* didn't.

Sierra sighed. She wasn't sure how Richard was going to take this, not that she should care how he felt after what he'd put her through. She was calling it quits with him. No backing down on it.

She opened the door and gave Richard an annoyed look. She couldn't muster a smile for him for anything. His blond hair was cut military short, his blue eyes all-assessing as he smelled the air and she knew he smelled Adam's scent in the house. Richard was wearing jeans, a T-shirt, a rain jacket, and loafers. He looked relaxed as if he had nothing to worry about as far as their relationship went.

"Why in the world are you here? You never even answered my texts or called back after all the phone messages I left." She just couldn't believe it. Unless he thought the only way he could salvage their relationship was to come here. He sure didn't look like he was glad to see her or even itching to kiss her or do anything with her that would show he really, really wanted to prove she shouldn't want to dump his butt.

Richard looked over her shoulder and saw Adam raise a glass of wine to him, his chest and lower legs and feet bare, candles lighting the bar, setting the stage for a perfectly intimate evening.

"It looks like I'm a little late to the party." Richard didn't sound like he had anything to be concerned about.

Maybe he figured she wouldn't do that to him unless she'd called it quits first, and she hadn't, not in any emails or texts or phone messages.

He came inside and dropped his black bag on the floor like he planned on staying a while, despite it looking like she already had a new boyfriend and Richard was on the outs. Richard took off his rain jacket and handed it to her, then closed the door behind him.

Okay, so they needed to talk before she sent him packing anyway. No matter what, he wasn't staying the night with her, and he would have to get his own transportation to a hotel and then to the airport whenever he could get a flight out. She wasn't going to do anything for him, just like he hadn't taken the time to pick her up from the airport when she'd visited either.

She'd told herself his actions had been a passive-aggressive reaction on his part, annoyed that she'd retired from the military and had moved out of state and wasn't still available to date just any old time he wanted to get together with her.

She hung his wet jacket on a coatrack. "Richard, this is Police Detective Adam Holmes with the Portland Police Bureau. Adam, this is Lieutenant Colonel Richard Wentworth, infantry officer at Fort Hood, Texas."

"Her boyfriend," Richard added, in case Adam needed to know that.

So her *ex*-boyfriend *was* annoyed at seeing Adam sitting there with barely any clothes on, eating a steak dinner and having wine with her after all, not to mention the candles all lit on the counter, making it look like more than just a dinner together. Richard didn't even kiss her like he normally would have when they met up with each other. Of course she would have kissed and hugged him, if she wasn't planning to call it quits with him.

"We had storm trouble, if you didn't notice as you were on your way here to Sierra's home. We had a tornado touch down in Portland, if you didn't hear," Adam said. "And the electricity was out."

"Yeah, I heard about the tornado on the airplane. I noticed the lights suddenly came on in the houses and the streetlamps as I was riding in the taxi through the dark residential areas."

"I'm going to check on the wash for you, Adam," Sierra said, then walked quickly down the hall, trying not to appear to be in a rush. How long did the darn wash have to go? Not that she wanted Adam to leave right away. Richard was the one she planned to get rid of quickly.

She didn't want to leave the two men alone together for too long. She should have just told Richard it was over between them and goodbye, but she was more tenderhearted than he was. She was feeling guilty that he had flown all the way out here to see her, maybe thinking he needed to resurrect their relationship, but as far as she was concerned, it was too late for that. And why should she feel guilty about it?

She reached the laundry room and saw that the timer on the washer said it had just a minute to go. Yes! She folded her arms and tapped her foot on the floor, waiting for it to be done. And then it buzzed, indicating it was finished. She started pulling damp clothes out of the wash and throwing them in the dryer as quickly as she could.

"So you say you're here because of the trouble with the storm?" Richard asked Adam. He sounded like he was trying to keep his cool, but she could hear the undercurrent of annoyance in his tone of voice.

"Yeah. We had to give a pregnant woman and her toddler assistance, and both Sierra and I were soaked to the skin in the pouring rain."

Sierra started the dryer and hurried back down the hall to the kitchen, where she turned on the light.

"You couldn't go to your own place to take care of your own laundry?" Richard raised a brow at Adam, as if he knew there was more going on between Adam and her.

She was glad Adam didn't tear into Richard about how he'd acted toward her. She needed to deal with it. Not her friend.

"Did you lose your phone?" she asked Richard.

Richard gave her a conceited smile. "I was in the field."

"You're not today. Did you not get my text messages? Phone messages? Emails?" She had figured something would have gotten his attention.

"Why do you think I'm here?"

A phone call would have sufficed!

"You couldn't give me a call or text before you came?" That was one of the things that annoyed her the most about all this. The silent treatment. As if she didn't matter enough for him to bother talking to her before he came. To even say he was sorry. Oh, yeah, not once had he even said that! At least that would have been a beginning. Thinking back on it, he always thought he was right. Maybe that was due to being in charge of men and women in the military and believing he would look like less of a commander if he had to say he was sorry for making a mistake. She kept feeling like it was her fault! Lack of communication between partners could really kill a relationship. "Did it slip your mind that I was flying out there to see you?"

"I had a lot on my mind."

"I reminded you I was coming a week before I left for Killeen. And you said you couldn't wait! You *do* have prior notice about your field duty." Richard could pretend he didn't, but she knew better. "Which means you forgot about me coming. And that's the issue right there. Nothing is more important to you than your next promotion. Certainly not me. You know it wouldn't hurt if you said you were sorry for not telling me you were going into the field."

"You should have paid for her airfare," Adam said.

Yeah, he should have, if he really wanted to apologize for his actions.

"I wasn't talking to you," Richard said, sounding really pissed off at Adam.

"No, you weren't, but you could make amends for what you pulled by at least paying for Sierra's airfare and Uber ride."

Sierra shook her head at Richard. "Go back to your job. Make your promotions. It's over between us. Go." Sierra really hadn't wanted to say all that in front of Adam, but she had to end this now. "We're through."

She stalked over to the coat tree and grabbed his wet rain jacket. "Here. Go. I'm sorry you had to travel all that way to learn I'd planned to call it quits. We have gone in totally different directions. You didn't even have the decency to call or text me not to come. You know how upsetting that is when no one is there to greet me at the airport when I've flown all those hours and paid all that money to get there? You don't need me."

She handed Richard his rain jacket. "We had fun when we could while we were assigned to the same army post, but that was it." She knew if he'd been the right wolf for her, she would have stayed with him and worked wherever she could, or she might not have retired.

Someone rang the doorbell, and she wondered who else would be here on such a stormy night.

Richard pulled on his coat and was texting someone, probably trying to get a ride out of here.

When she looked out the peephole, she was surprised to see it was DEA Special Agent Ethan Masterson, also a red wolf with the pack and also a bachelor. What in the world was *he* doing here?

"What brings you here tonight?" she asked, letting the agent inside. She figured Richard *really* wouldn't like seeing another bachelor male arrive at her place.

"Hell, you have a revolving door around here for red male wolves?" Richard grabbed his bag and brushed brusquely against Ethan on his way out. "I should have known that's why you left the service. All your talk of not seeing anyone. What a damn waste of money and time."

Man, was she glad that was over between them.

Ethan raised his brows as he considered Richard's scowl.

She'd never had anyone but a couple of female wolves over before. She couldn't believe Richard would show up unexpectedly and she would have two other bachelor males at her place the same night.

"That was the *ex*-boyfriend," Sierra said to Ethan, remembering he didn't know who the other wolf was as she closed the door on Richard's departure. He would have to wait on her porch to try to stay dry until his ride got there. Then she smiled. It might take a while because of the bad weather and downed power lines and trees. She realized Adam had gone out back to clean the grill. "Adam's on the back porch, half-nude, but before you get any ideas about the two of us, don't."

Ethan smiled.

Adam opened the back door and saluted him. "You got here just in the nick of time."

Ethan eyed his attire.

"Don't tell me you called Ethan to come to your rescue," Sierra said.

Ethan smiled at Adam's clothes. Or lack thereof. "I like your outfit, Adam. It suits you."

"Wiseass," Adam said.

Ethan glanced at Adam's plate with its remnant of the steak and the wineglasses. "Looks like I missed out on all of the fun."

"We just finished dinner. Adam's leaving just as soon as his clothes have dried. Unless he wants me to just bring them to work tomorrow and he can go home like he's dressed."

Ethan removed his raincoat, and Sierra took it and hung it up on the coatrack. She really was feeling like she had a revolving door tonight. "Would you like a glass of wine? I can make you a grilled cheese sandwich, if you haven't eaten anything."

"Sure, on both accounts. Thanks." Ethan pulled up a barstool and sat down.

"Would you be fine with wheat bread?"

Ethan smiled. "Just the way I like it."

She loved it when people were so agreeable. "Okay, so why are you here exactly?" she asked Ethan again as she finished making the sandwich. She added some potato chips, while Adam poured him a glass of wine like he was her wine steward. She gave the plate to Ethan.

"Thanks, Sierra, Adam."

"You're welcome." She cleaned off her and Adam's plates and put them in the dishwasher.

"The truth is Adam did call me. Not for his rescue, exactly. More like for yours, if you had needed it, but if you were going to patch things up between you and the boyfriend, then I was still here for moral support." Ethan took a bite of the grilled cheese sandwich.

"Okay, all is forgiven then."

Ethan smiled. "Good, and this is a great sandwich. I hadn't expected to get dinner when I came here."

"The cheese is extra sharp, making it the best."

"I'll need to get that when I go to the grocery store. Steaks on the grill would have been nice too," Ethan said.

"I'm sure the ex-boyfriend was miffed he didn't get one of those, but I did instead." Adam looked like he was enjoying this just a little too much.

"So now you're available," Ethan said, smiling, saluting her with his glass of wine before he took a sip.

"I'm just getting over ending a relationship with my boyfriend. You know what they say about rebound." She poured herself and Adam some more wine.

The guys exchanged glances, and she suspected they didn't believe she was having that problem. How did she know how she'd feel a few days from now? Tonight even?

Relieved. That was how she felt right this minute, and she loved that Ethan and Adam were here for her if she had needed some moral support. Tonight after they left, maybe she would feel differently about ending things between her and Richard. But she really didn't believe so.

"So how are things going in the DEA business?" she asked Ethan.

"Too busy." Ethan bit into a potato chip. "How about the rest of the crime business?"

"Same," Adam said. "If I didn't love the area so much and the pack, and hell, now we even have yet another eligible she-wolf, I might have considered moving to someplace quieter, less crime-ridden."

"You would be bored." Sierra was sure of it. Adam would be so intensely involved in a case that no way would he want to work somewhere that didn't have any real crime to speak of. "Can you imagine getting calls about treed cats and such if you went to a town where nothing ever happened?"

He smiled. "True."

"It would waste all of your detective talent." She heard the dryer quit finally. "Sounds like your clothes are probably ready. I'll get them and set them out for you in the guest bedroom next to my room so you can change."

"Thanks so much for doing that," Adam said.

"Thanks for coming to my rescue! I could have still been wandering around in the storm without a way to get home." She headed down the hall to the laundry room.

As soon as she was pulling clothes out of the dryer into her laundry basket, she heard Ethan ask Adam, "So are you going to ask her out first, or should I?"

She smiled. Yeah, dumping Richard was a good idea all right.

CHAPTER 8

Adam and Ethan left Sierra's house at the same time, both men believing she was feeling fine and not upset over the breakup with Richard. But Ethan didn't have to ask Adam who should ask her out first. Of course, she'd heard. She was a wolf!

And she needed time to get over this, Adam thought.

Ethan drove off to his home and Adam to his, and he was almost home when his boss called him. "Hey, Adam, I heard Sierra has returned home from her vacation early."

"Yeah, she came in tonight." Adam wondered why his boss would be calling him about that.

"Willy turned in his papers tonight."

"Ah, hell."

"Yeah. First Josh, now Willy. Don't *you* get any ideas."

Adam smiled. "No, I'm good."

"Anyway, I need Sierra to come in tomorrow and start working full-time temporarily if she doesn't want the full-time job permanently. Otherwise it's hers. You probably know her better than anybody at the bureau. What do you think she'll say?"

"Uh, well, she really liked the previous arrangement."

"I know. She did most of the eyewitness sketches and Willy handled the dead bodies. Sierra's a known quantity as far as her witness sketches go. She does an outstanding job with handling distraught eyewitnesses. We don't want to lose her, so if you can convince her that we need her and no one else will do, I'm going to tell her tomorrow she's got the job. I've got to go. My wife is calling me to change out a light bulb for her."

Adam smiled. Every time his boss called him after Adam had left work, he ended the call saying his wife needed him to do something for her. Adam often wondered if she really did or if that was his convenient excuse to end the call.

"Okay, I'll talk to Sierra. See you tomorrow, sir." Adam wasn't about to call Sierra with the news tonight. Not after she'd just broken up with her boyfriend. Since she'd already told him she preferred the way things were, Adam didn't want to hit her with the news that Willy had retired and the boss wanted her to take his place.

In fact, Adam had every intention of letting the boss tell her what was up tomorrow morning. Then if Adam still had to convince her she was the only one for the job, he would certainly attempt to do so. He really liked to work with his wolf kind because they could talk about their wolf halves while on an assignment when humans weren't about. That was one thing that he enjoyed while working with Josh. He didn't see Sierra as often, but if she worked full-time? He would see more of her, and he would enjoy that.

He hoped she would really like Tori. He knew Tori would try to convince Sierra to work full-time too. Or at least he hoped she would.

Early the next morning, Sierra felt good about calling it quits with Richard. While she was having a cup of orange tea and just chilling, Sierra got a call from her boss. "Adam needs you to do a witness sketch this morning. He said you had arrived home from your vacation last night."

"Uh, yeah, okay. I'll be right in." Her boss was always all business. She hadn't expected him to appreciate that she was home early or ask her how her vacation had gone. He never took a vacation, and he didn't really think anyone else should either. Not when there was work to be done. And truly, there was always work to be done when it came to trying to solve crimes in the area. She wondered how his wife went along with it.

Sierra hurried to finish getting dressed. Even though she was only part-time and was more on an on-call schedule, she was always ready in case she did get called in. She hadn't expected to get a call this early though. Willy usually handled the cases until nine. She guessed he was busy on another case.

When she arrived at the bureau, she expected to see Adam there and maybe his new partner. Adam would want Sierra to speak to a witness right away. Instead, he wasn't there. Neither was anyone who looked new who could be Tori.

"Redding! I need to see you. Now!" Police Chief Arnold Covington hollered.

She entered his office, and he motioned to a chair. She took a seat, wondering what was up now. He usually only had someone sit down when he wanted to scold them about something.

"You're it. You're taking over Willy Blanchard's full-time job."

"You want me to do what?" she asked her boss. She really hadn't expected that. He'd called her in because Adam needed her to do a witness sketch!

The chief had round, pudgy cheeks that were always a little flushed, a bulbous nose, and a rounded belly that made him look like he ate too many of the chocolate-crème-filled cookies he had tucked inside his upper desk drawer. She knew because she'd seen him grab a couple to eat with his morning coffee, and he would down a few more when he returned from lunch.

He wore a butch haircut, the sides of his hair sporting gray, the top black. He reminded her of a sergeant she had worked with in the army, except that the sergeant had been in a lot better shape and beer had been his vice, not chocolate cookies.

"Okay, look, yeah, we still need a police sketch artist when someone hasn't caught the perp's face on a cell phone or a security video hasn't captured it. So then witnesses can help you create the person's image on a sketch pad. And you do a damn good job at it. But when you don't have a witness sketch to do, we really need you to do a different kind of sketch, one to identify the victim instead."

"As a forensic sketch artist working from deceased facial photos from the crime scene or the morgue, sure. What happened to Willy Blanchard? He always worked those cases." She would much rather do sketches of criminals based on witness accounts. She hoped Willy hadn't been fired.

"He retired. No notice, just said he had grandchildren on the way and he needed to leave. Usually we get two weeks, but he's taken leave for the last two weeks. We need you to fill the vacuum that he left behind. Now, I know you can do it because you're a damn good artist. So you've got your first case. Willy always went out to the crime scene and took his own photos and measurements. Detective Holmes will take you out there. He's waiting on you now."

"What about the witness I was supposed to sketch for?" That was what her boss had called her in for. Sometimes she had a one-track mind.

"The witness's mother called and said she would bring her in later today."

"Okay." Sierra had no idea if she could create a face from a dead body if it had deteriorated a lot. She hated that she might draw something that was so unlike the person who had died that someone might think it was their beloved missing family member or friend when it wasn't. Or if she couldn't draw it well enough, that no one would be able to recognize the body.

She had never been involved in gruesome work with dead bodies. Her real love was creating art. Not like this kind of art. She shuddered.

She was so glad Willy hadn't been fired though.

"All right, I'll do the best I can. I love working part-time on the witness sketches so I just want to do the full-time job until you can find a replacement for Willy's position." She didn't want to give up the part-time job because it gave her real purpose.

"We can do that. But if you decide you like the expanded benefits and money working full-time before I find someone else to replace Willy, the job is yours."

"Okay, thanks."

She figured after she did one sketch of a cadaver, she would be history as far as forensics sketches went. She had enough money from her army retirement so she wouldn't be hurting for a paycheck. Maybe she could work for a different police department if the bureau hired someone else full-time and they didn't need her here any longer.

"I appreciate that you're helping out since Willy left." The chief sat back in his chair and folded his arms across his chest, his mouth a grim line. "You're good at what you do, and once you start a thing, you have to finish it. You know the families and friends, not to mention the police and the victims, need all the help we can give to identify the bodies we find."

"There are more than one?" She envisioned a mass grave of thousands of bodies.

He cast her a small smile. "Only one in the field. For now. Get your feet wet. See how it goes. But I'm telling you right now, I have every faith that you can give us a good idea of what the man looked like, a hell of a lot better than what we have now, or I wouldn't have asked you to do this. I want to see what you come up with after you have a chance to do it," her boss said by way of dismissal.

"All right. I'll give it my best shot."

She left her boss's office and saw Adam coming into the bureau. He solved cases involving anything from robberies to kidnappings to carjackings, and he was always needing her to do a witness sketch for him. "I hear you need me to see a dead body."

"Yeah, sorry about this, Sierra. I know how you feel about it." Adam was dressed in a dark suit and was already wearing a raincoat.

"It's not your fault that Willy decided to retire." On the way out, she grabbed her raincoat and the camera bag containing the bureau's camera Willy had used. "What is this case about?"

"This one involved a carjacking. The driver crashed into a tree and flew out the front windshield, and his face was shredded badly. Sorry, Sierra. Truly. I wish Willy had handled this one before he left. We don't have any video on the carjacker and no way to identify him, so we really need your help with this."

"Okay, I'll do my best. The boss said you told him last night that I returned home from my vacation early."

Adam smiled down at Sierra. "He did, did he? He told me last night that he heard you had returned. You know him. He seems to know everything about everyone on the force before we even do."

"True."

Adam glanced down at her high heels and raised his brows. "You might want to wear some more sensible shoes from now on if you're going to be doing this kind of work."

"I *was* wearing sensible shoes when I came into work this morning. How was I to know my job description was going to change so drastically? The boss called me in to do a sketch for a witness of yours. Besides, not all sketch artists go to the crime scene. I *could* do this from photos."

He shook his head. "I know you. You're too particular. I'm sure you would want to see the body after you saw the photos because they didn't capture the remains the way you wanted them to. Thanks for helping us with this. We're doing DNA testing and checking into dental records, but all that takes time. He might not have either on file anywhere. If you can make a sketch of his facial features, maybe we can find someone out there who recognizes him, and we'll catch a break." He unlocked his SUV's doors and Sierra climbed into the passenger seat.

"I might not be able to do this. I've never done a real, live postmortem sketch before."

"You'll be able to do it. I know you will. You've taken the training. You can do it." He glanced at her as he pulled out of the parking lot. "By the way, have you ever seen a dead body?"

"Only on TV."

He cleared his throat. "Okay. If you get sick, move away from the crime scene."

"Thank you. Good to know."

He pointed to the glove box. She opened it and found a baggie.

"Use that to barf in if you need to."

Oh, just great. She *really* didn't want to do this now. But if she didn't actually see the person and get the pictures that she thought she needed, she might not be able to capture the actual person's features well enough to make the sketch recognizable to family, coworkers, and friends.

She pulled the baggie out and set it on the console, then closed the glove box.

"Are you free this weekend?"

She glanced at him. "I am. We're boating on Sunday, right?" Was he interested in a date? She wasn't really planning on dating anyone for a while. Sure, dating someone new could be an ego booster and make her feel that someone really cared for her after what she'd gone through. It could be fun. But she wasn't sure she was ready for that emotionally. "I'm just staying home and chilling otherwise."

"Yeah, we are boating on Sunday. The rest of the time, we could have more work for you then."

She frowned at Adam. "The boss said there was only *one* body."

"Today. At the crime scene. That's not including the three in the morgue already."

She'd had an idea this day wasn't going to go well as soon as the chief called her into the office so early this morning.

Instinctively, she knew to bring some humor to the table when she was helping a witness recall everything she or he could about an assailant. A little levity could go a long way in helping the witness relax and recount details of his experience—or vent, whatever was necessary to help in the cognitive process. Often a witness would blank out the assailant's face in their mind, terrified of the ordeal they'd gone through. They often wouldn't remember seeing anything that would help. She'd just ask things like *Was he smiling?* And suddenly the witness had a description of his mouth. *Was he frowning, eyes narrowed?* Then she had the color of the eyes, the size of the eyes, the expression.

Sierra wasn't sure she could manage when the victim was dead.

Adam knew Sierra was a terrific artist, but he wasn't sure she would have the stomach to view dead bodies to do her work. Maybe she could work just from photos if being at the scene didn't work out for her.

Sketches didn't always mean a victim was identified or that a criminal was either. It could be hit or miss. That didn't mean the sketch didn't look like the person. Other factors came into account, like no one who knew the person seeing the bulletins or news or the person not being local. Or someone knew and wasn't saying.

Sierra had a higher success rate than Willy at getting a better picture of the assailant while doing witness sketches, and Adam thought it was because she was so good at putting the witness at ease. He'd really enjoyed watching her work while he took notes about the description the witness gave.

She was easy to get along with and he liked working with her, so he didn't want to see her fail and quit the job. He didn't want to see anyone else take her place either.

Today, Sierra was wearing a black raincoat over a navy-blue jacket and skirt meant more for office work. He glanced at her shapely legs, her high heels way too spiked for the kind of terrain she would have to manage. He agreed it didn't matter what she wore when she was doing witness sketches. She was often sitting down at a desk, drawing the sketch. Most of the time, they brought in the witness or had the witness come to see her. Sometimes she would go to the scene of the crime to speak to the witness, but it normally wasn't in a muddy setting.

With all the traipsing through the grass in the rain where the body of the carjacker had landed when he went through the windshield, the area would be muddy. Adam hoped she didn't slip and fall, but he would be right beside her every step of the way to catch her if she did.

He drove her out to the site, and she glanced down at her sandals in his Hummer that she'd left there when he'd picked her up during the storm last night. "Sorry about leaving my sandals in your car."

He smiled. "Tori gave me a hard time about them when we went to a crime scene earlier this morning. She said here she'd considered asking me out, but if she was going to find a she-wolf's clothes in my car, that was the end of that."

Sierra laughed. "She didn't."

"Yeah, she has a great sense of humor."

"What if she wasn't kidding?"

"I told her why they were in the SUV. She said she suspected as much."

"Oh, I bet. Hmm, as long as she doesn't think there's something going on between the two of us."

"Only police business."

"So is she dating anyone in the pack yet?"

"She went out with the coroner. Just once though. She told Leidolf to spread the word to the bachelor males that she wants to get settled first and meet everyone. It's a lot to get used to—working with me, working a new job, working with a new boss.

She took the job and started right away, but she has to move her household goods into her house this weekend."

"Does she need some help with any of it?" Sierra asked.

"She has professional movers helping."

Sierra let out her breath. "Right, but does she need some help? When I moved to Portland, even with professional movers, I had so many boxes to unpack it would have taken me forever. The movers just set the boxes and furniture in the rooms where I wanted things. After that, it was up to me to do what I needed to with the contents. It was really nice when my brother and others of the pack helped me to empty boxes and sort through things and break down boxes, then haul them away."

"Uh, yeah, Josh and I were busy on a case that weekend. I remember that." He'd regretted he hadn't been able to help her back then and get to know her a little better. Then about a week later, he learned she had an out-of-state boyfriend, so that had put her off-limits with him and the other bachelor males of the pack.

"I can help her if we don't have bodies to sketch all weekend. Oh shoot, if I'm going to be full-time, I won't have as much free time to do things I like to do. I won't be able to teach art to the kids in the pack on Tuesday and Thursday starting next week either. I was still supposed to be gone all this week, so I wasn't scheduled."

"You could do some classes on the weekend though, if you don't have to work." He'd forgotten that she was teaching art to the kids in the pack. Though next Monday, he was looking forward to her adult art class he was taking. "As to Tori, we can ask her when we get back to the office if she would like our help, if she's there."

"Sure. We could do it on Saturday. It would be a nice way to visit with her and get to know her while helping her out."

Adam agreed.

When they arrived at the scene of the crash site, several police vehicles were there and some of the police officers glanced in their direction and waved. They looked a little surprised to see Sierra out there. Especially when she got out of the vehicle in her high heels.

She hadn't grabbed the barf bag, so Adam did, just in case.

Being the wolf that he was, Adam wanted to carry Sierra through the muddy grass to where the man's body rested. But he figured Sierra would want to sock him if he did that to her in front of all the police officers there. Instead, he stayed close to her in the event she fell. He hadn't expected her to get stuck in the mud after they had barely left the roadway.

She grabbed his arm to steady herself and pull her heel out of the mud. The rain was coming down hard, but she had her hood up over her head and didn't seem fazed by it at all. Four more steps and her heel was stuck in the mud again. This time, she grabbed his arm and yanked off one heel, then the other.

He smiled down at her. She released him, handed her heels to him, and squished through the mud in her bare feet. The police officers were all smiling at him and at her. This was a side of her none of them had seen before.

The rain let up and was now just a light sprinkle.

When she reached the man's body, Sierra turned suddenly, and he knew from the way her eyes were round and she was trying to keep it together that she was about to vomit. He quickly pulled the barf bag out of his raincoat pocket, handed it to her, and then seized her arm and moved her away from the site.

"Sorry, Sierra. I probably should have given you pictures of him instead. You could have tried to reconstruct his features that way for the first time."

Sierra threw up in the bag, then handed him the used barf bag, pulled a tissue out of her pocket, and wiped her eyes and mouth. "No, no, I need to do this. You know me. I'm thorough, if nothing else."

He glanced down at her muddy heels clutched in one of his hands and the barf bag in the other.

She held out the used tissue, and he offered the bag so she

could stuff it in. Then she took hold of his arm and made her way back through the mud to the man's body.

"Who found him?" she asked, releasing Adam and pulling out the camera from the camera bag.

He hadn't expected to bring her to the site and end up carrying her muddy high heels and barfed-in barf bag. He cleared his throat. "The police were following him in a high-speed chase, and then he lost control of the stolen car."

"So it was an accident."

"Right."

"And he did it alone." She took several pictures from different angles, her feet squishing in the mud. Her toenails had been painted a pretty red, but now every time she lifted her small feet, her toes were coated in the slick mud.

"He did."

"Was the owner of the vehicle hurt?" She snapped another couple of shots.

"Yeah, the carjacker pistol-whipped the owner, who is in the hospital now with a concussion. He'll survive but he was injured badly."

"Then he'll be glad to know this guy won't be hurting anyone else like that."

"I know we are."

"Did you or anyone else know Willy planned to retire?" Sierra eyed Adam, watching his reaction.

That was the thing about wolves. They were good at recognizing if another was telling the truth, but he was surprised she would question him about that now.

Adam didn't say anything for a moment, thinking about the conversation he'd had with their boss last night. "Willy had talked to me about it a number of times. But no one thought he would really do it. I mean, he has been saying this for a couple of years. I think it was the combination of working the last case—"

Her brows rose.

"He was tired of it. And his new grandson was just born in New Jersey and he wanted to be there. Another daughter is having a child in two months, and he wanted to help out and get to know his grandchildren. That's all."

"The last case?" She finished taking the pictures she wanted, then tucked the camera away in the bag, slung the strap over her shoulder, and seized his arm to make her way back to his vehicle.

"It wasn't a bad case, but he was ready to do something else with his life. He's sixty-five. He's been doing this for nearly forty years. He was past wanting to retire. And then here you are, all bright-eyed and bushy-tailed and doing a great job."

She rolled her eyes. "And throwing up my breakfast after seeing the remains."

"Everyone does it the first time they see a dead body. That isn't just on TV."

She smiled and looked up at him. "Did you do that the first time you saw one?"

"Uh, no. Maybe not *everyone*. But a lot do." He handed the barf bag to a police officer.

"Evidence, sir?" the officer asked, frowning.

"No. Just dispose of it when you have a chance, will you?" Adam didn't want to take it with them in the SUV, not with their heightened sense of smell. "About Willy, I didn't know he was going to leave like that. But the boss did call me last night and told me to tell you, to convince you that you should take his place in the full-time position."

She narrowed her eyes at Adam. "You knew and you didn't tell me?"

Adam let out his breath. "You'd just broken up with Richard. I was afraid you would be worrying about taking the job on top of that last night, and you didn't need the extra concern. I told the boss how you felt comfortable with the prior arrangement you'd had with Willy. After the night you'd had, I didn't feel calling you with this was appropriate."

"You were worried I wouldn't be able to sleep last night?"

"Something like that." He unlocked his vehicle's doors and glanced at her.

She was still eyeing him, but he couldn't read her expression. "Thanks, I guess."

He waited for her to climb into the passenger seat, then handed her heels to her. He shut her door for her and climbed into the driver's side.

"What do you think about drawing a sketch of the guy's face?" He started the Hummer.

"I can do it."

"Good."

"I don't know if it will be as accurate as the sketches that I do from eyewitness reports," she warned him.

He glanced down at her muddy heels in her hand. "You'll do your best. That's all we can ever do. Do you want me to drop by your place so you can get cleaned up? And grab a different pair of shoes?"

Her feet were caked with mud, and she had mud splatters all the way up her legs.

She hesitated, then said, "Sure, thanks. I could try and clean up in the ladies' room, but I would make such a mess." She glanced down at his muddy shoes. "You can clean up there too. I'm afraid I've made a mess in your car."

"It's inevitable when we're doing work like this. Think nothing of it." He was just glad to be working with her no matter what the circumstances were.

CHAPTER 9

Twenty minutes later, Sierra and Adam were at her home and she was hoping her place was halfway straightened up after last night's wild adventure. If she'd known she was going to have company again, she would have done more. He would think she never cleaned up the place.

With the sandals she'd left in his SUV overnight in hand, she wiped some of the mud on her bare feet off on the grass before she entered the house. Adam did the same with his shoes on the grass, and then he did it again on her doormat. But then he just pulled off his shoes and walked into her house in his stocking feet.

At least the mud left on her feet was dry. She hung her raincoat on a coat tree, and he pulled off his raincoat and did the same.

Luckily, the place didn't look half-bad—a romance book was lying on her coffee table where she'd left it last night with a bookmark saving her place. A pair of blue fuzzy slippers were sitting beside her recliner, her fuzzy blue robe tossed over the back of the couch, and her aqua hoodie was hanging on the back of her dining room chair, her sneakers sitting beside it from an early morning run she'd taken before she'd gotten the call from the boss. Her gardening gloves were resting on top of a kneeling pad on her kitchen island, with packages of Pacific Northwest wildflower seeds of baby's breath, flax, phlox, cosmos, coreopsis, bluebells, blue lupines, and more sitting next to that. She'd planned to plant them this morning before she got the call from the boss to come in. She hoped to do it this evening now that she was working full-time. At least during the summer, the sun set later.

The kitchen was clean after they'd had dinner and her breakfast plate was in the dishwasher. Adam didn't seem to notice anyway, which made her wonder how his place looked, and why she was even thinking about that, she didn't know.

"I'm going to take a quick shower. Can you be away from work for that long?" She would wash her shoes later and put on more sensible shoes for her new job.

"Uh, yeah, sure. It's all part of the job."

"Good. Because I'm too muddy to just wash off my feet." She headed into her master bath and closed the door, then began stripping off her clothes. She could imagine that everyone who had seen her at the site where the body was found would be joking about her and her heels and making poor Adam carry them for her. Then she had to go and barf into a bag, and he had to carry that too.

She'd never envisioned him in that role before. A real sweetheart who didn't have any issues with his masculinity.

She needed to fill out a bunch of paperwork when she returned to the office to change her status from part-time to full-time, at least until her boss could open the position to other applicants and find someone who was qualified to do the job.

Washing off the mud in the shower took longer than she thought it would. She could imagine trying to get it off her shoes when she returned home after work and how hard that would be once it dried on. Here she thought she would have her afternoon free, unless another body turned up or another witness needed her to do a sketch. She hoped she could manage better at the morgue and wouldn't get sick this time.

What she couldn't believe was that after she had dressed in nice slacks and a blazer and boots, she found Adam in the kitchen using a paper towel to dry off her shoes. He'd actually cleaned them!

"Wow, thanks so much." She leaned over and kissed him on the cheek, since appreciating his thoughtfulness and just saying so didn't seem to be enough.

He smiled. "I figured I would do it after I cleaned the mud off mine. Yours were actually easier to clean. Less surface area and not as many ridges on the soles as the bottom of my shoes have."

"Who would have ever thought fewer ridges on the sole of a shoe would be a good thing."

"Yeah, it's harder to make casts of unique shoe imprints in criminal cases though." He grabbed his raincoat. "It's stopped raining at least. Are you ready to go to the morgue?"

"Do you have more barf bags in your car?"

"A couple. Yes."

"Good. Thanks again for cleaning my shoes and all the rest. Okay, so why did you say I might be needed over the weekend for cases in the morgue if I'm already seeing them today?"

"Willy always covered them."

"Ahh."

"Don't quit on us, please. Your eyewitness sketches were always on the money when we finally caught the perp and compared your sketch with the accused. Willy didn't have your innate ability to coax details out of a traumatized victim."

"Yeah, but these are different."

"You'll do great. I have every faith in you."

When they finally reached the morgue, Sierra was apprehensive about what to expect. She was glad Adam was with her but hoping he didn't have too much work to do and she was keeping him from it.

All three victims were men, all having been fished out of the Willamette River recently, their bodies swollen and degraded. She realized—as she wore a mask that did not help to reduce the smell of decomposing bodies because she was a wolf and the smell was so strong anyway—that Adam was right there with her, barf bag in hand.

She quickly took photographs of each of the men at various angles and then did a rough sketch of each of them as she asked the coroner, Dr. Patrick Silverson, "Ages? Cause of death?"

"Drowning. It could have been accidental. Several things come into account when trying to determine if the cause was accidental or not. Cool water slows down decomposition, but putrefaction accelerates once the bodies are removed from the water. We have to consider the water currents, rocks, branches, and other obstacles they could have come into contact with postmortem, which could make it appear that they sustained injuries due to a struggle with unknown assailants. One of the men was caught submerged under tree roots and other debris, another swept up on a rocky beach. A fisherman spotted him as he was headed through the woods to the beach to fish. He contacted the bureau and a search was conducted. The other man was found a mile downstream from the other two. It looked like they were in their forties to early fifties."

"But no one has reported any missing men between those ages, I take it," Sierra said, finishing up her drawing of the last man.

"No. Which is where your help comes in." He smiled at Sierra. "I hear you're our new full-time sketch artist. And you're available now."

"Word gets around fast."

The coroner smiled again. "Yeah, your boss is super pleased about you working full-time. As to the other matter?" Dr. Silverson glanced at Adam. "Well, we're all glad for that too."

She closed her sketch pad. "I will try not to disappoint everyone. About the sketches."

"You'll do great," the coroner said.

She thanked him, and then she and Adam ditched their masks and left the morgue.

"The smell is the worst the first time you have to deal with this," Adam said.

"I don't think I would ever get used to it. Now using our enhanced sense of smell to locate dead bodies? That would be a plus. Having to do an autopsy or anything else with them for a long period of time?" She shook her head. "Thanks for being there for me, barf bag in hand."

"You did really well, all things considered," Adam said as they climbed into his Hummer.

"Thanks. So what do you think? Foul play?"

"It's hard to say. I would have to go along with what the coroner said as far as the drowning being accidental unless we find evidence that says otherwise. They were fully clothed. I've got the pictures of them after the one man was pulled from the water. The others were already decomposing on the riverbank."

"Okay. So they weren't swimming if they were wearing all their clothes."

"I would say more likely they were boating, maybe fishing when their craft overturned and none of them were wearing life jackets. They were wearing lightweight jackets, sneakers, socks, T-shirts, and jeans."

"Wedding rings?"

"There was no jewelry found on any of them."

"Wallets?"

"No. They might have left them in a cabin or a car, not wanting to get them wet or lose them. We're checking all the area cabins but haven't succeeded in locating where the men might have been staying. No cars in the vicinity that would have belonged to them either. All were accounted for."

"No boat found?"

"No. Which makes it my case. I've been looking into any stolen boats that might be resold in the area. The whole scenario leads me to believe someone found the boat downriver and took it. I can't think of any other explanation."

"But no one has reported the men missing."

"Which leads me to believe they were here on a fishing trip and aren't expected to return for a while. Maybe they didn't tell anyone where they were going to be. Hopefully, once you're able to draw the sketches and we share them with the public, we can get somewhere with the case."

"What about DNA?"

"That'll take a while, and if they're not in any system, it won't lead us anywhere either."

"Okay, then I guess it's up to me to help you learn who they are."

He smiled at her. "Exactly."

As soon as they arrived back at the bureau, a brunette dressed in a brown suit and sensible shoes hurried to catch up to them. She was all smiles.

"You're taking Willy's place, aren't you?" the woman asked, joining them and offering her hand. "You've got to do it."

Sierra shook her hand and smiled. "You must be Tori." Sierra hadn't ever seen her before, but she smelled like a red wolf.

"Yes, and you must be Sierra. I'm so glad to meet you. Adam's told me all about you."

Sierra glanced at Adam. His ears turned a little red. She hoped he hadn't told everyone about her failed relationship.

"Well, not everything. He just mentioned you had retired from the army and your brother's here too. And your parents are still living in San Antonio. Here it is, my first day on the job, and Adam hands me all his casework and tells me to get right on it and solve them."

That didn't sound like Adam.

"Your brother had called him, tasking him with locating you. That was most important, for sure. Adam spent most of the day calling airlines, then hotels." Tori smiled. "If I ever go missing, I hope someone is that dedicated in searching for me."

"With a pack behind you, you can count on it," Sierra said, not wanting Tori to get the wrong impression about Adam. What if he wanted to date Tori? "Adam said your household goods are being delivered on the weekend. If you need some assistance in sorting things out, I would love to help. I just went through that rigmarole a while ago myself."

Tori smiled and looked relieved at the same time. "I'd love that. I absolutely hate moves, and if I had to do this by myself, half the boxes won't be unpacked for over a year."

Sierra laughed. She liked the pretty brunette already.

"I'll help too, if you think I won't be in the way," Adam said.

"Nope, that works for me too. Maybe we can order sandwiches for lunch while we're emptying boxes," Tori said. "My treat."

"Sounds good to me," Sierra said.

Adam agreed.

"I guess I'd better work on these sketches if you could give me the photos of the men when they were first found, Adam," Sierra said.

Adam went over to his desk and found the file on them, then handed them to her.

She glanced at the new arrivals walking into the police bureau.

"It looks like an eyewitness just came in for you to do your magic, Sierra," Adam said.

"Okay, that first then." She took the files and set them on her new desk.

A police officer was escorting a teen and a middle-aged woman who looked like an older version of the girl, both blond, both blue eyed, both anxious-looking as the mother rubbed her hands and the teen looked nervously about.

The officer escorting them said to Sierra, "She witnessed a robbery at a drugstore. Can you draw a sketch of the alleged assailant?"

Now *that*, she could do.

Tori sat down at her desk and got on the phone to check on a case while Adam was drawn to watch the way Sierra put her young witness at ease. She began by asking her about hobbies and what her favorite books were and what she loved to watch on TV.

He was much more cut to the chase. Nothing but the facts, ma'am. So it was interesting to see how she worked a witness. The teen had been nervous, subdued, but now she was smiling, animated, talking about everything...but the robbery.

Tori joined him at his desk and smiled down at him. "She's good at it, isn't she? I don't think I've ever seen a sketch artist who could bring a traumatized witness out of his or her shell that fast."

"Yeah, she's good. That's why she likes to do the sketches of eyewitness accounts."

Sierra talked to the girl for a long time and continued to work on the sketch. Then she showed it to the witness. She pointed at the nose and Sierra erased and worked over it again. Then she showed the girl the picture again.

The girl nodded. Sierra had her sign the picture on the back, behind the area of the face so that no one would see it or reveal the witness's name when the picture was scanned. Since it was considered official police evidence, it had to adhere to the chain of command. Sierra thanked the girl and her mother, and they left the building while Sierra handed the sketch to Adam. He scanned it into the system, and the original would be kept on file in the evidence room.

He'd heard the girl remark that the man had a mole on his chin, but Sierra hadn't added it. "No mole, eh?"

"No. As much as I want to really make these look exactly like the person that is described to me, if someone doesn't recall the mole or some other feature I've added, they might think it's not the right person, when it really is. It makes it less likely for the public as a whole to recognize the alleged assailant. More of a sketch makes it better."

"Okay, so no prettier image."

She smiled. "Nope. That's for my art on the side. Like when

I'm doing portraits of wolves and people. Then I can add more fun details."

"Gotcha. I always wondered about that. Do you need anything? I've got to do some investigating."

"No, I'm good, Adam. Thanks."

"Sierra! You need to get over to the personnel office and take care of that paperwork. They're all over me about that this morning," the chief called out.

She smiled at Adam. "I'll have to take care of these sketches in a little bit. Off to fill out paperwork."

"I'm glad you're working with us," Adam said.

"Just wait until you see what I come up with on the sketches of the bodies in the morgue," she said, then took off for the personnel office.

CHAPTER 10

After Sierra filled out the paperwork and had officially become a full-time staff employee of the bureau, Adam and Tori took off to learn about a stolen boat that someone had purchased illegally. Meanwhile, Sierra studied the picture the police had taken of the man they had removed from the water, right after he had been discovered. She did a new sketch of him, since his face was much more preserved than after he had been out of the water for some time at the morgue. When she compared the new sketch with the one she'd done at the morgue, she was pleased to see that the two were really compatible. Maybe she could do Willy's job after all. At least she was feeling more confident in her abilities.

Her boss left his office and joined her at her desk, a cup of coffee in hand. "How are you coming with the sketches of the guys in the morgue and the one of the carjacker?" her boss asked.

"Adam just sent me the photo of the man caught under the debris in the river. I was redoing the sketch since the picture shows him before his body deteriorated and gives a much better visual."

Her boss looked over her other work. "Looks good. Scan them in and then we'll make sure they get out. I got word that the owner of the stolen vehicle just came to at the hospital. Adam will meet you over there. He needs to get a statement from him too."

"Okay, I'll head over to the hospital." After she signed the sketches of the three men in the morgue and scanned them in, she gave them to an officer who would send them out. She hung on to the carjacking one though, wanting to see if it looked the same as the eyewitness's account after she spoke with him. She hoped he was well enough to talk and could remember accurately what he'd seen.

With her sketch pad sitting on the passenger seat, Sierra drove to the hospital. She hoped she could get a better sketch of the carjacker before his face had been destroyed in the car accident. Then she could compare her original sketch with the witness sketch and see if she had been on target. If so, she would feel even better about her ability to draw postmortem sketches. The real test was putting them out for the world to see and finding someone who could identify them.

When she walked into the hospital lobby, she saw Adam looking serious as he texted someone on his phone, frowning, but as soon as he saw her coming, he smiled as if she had brightened his whole day.

"Where's Tori?" Since they'd left to do an investigation together, Sierra had assumed they would both be here.

"She's still questioning the man about a boat he purchased. I needed to speak with our victim concerning the carjacking. A police officer at the house where the man purchased the boat without a bill of sale had to come to the hospital because his wife is in labor and he dropped me off."

"Oh, okay."

"Mr. Kinney, the carjacking victim, is on the fourth floor. Come on," Adam said.

When they reached the victim's room, they found a woman and two teen girls visiting him, all three of them looking worried. Mr. Kinney had a bandage wrapped around his head and bruises on his face and looked like he'd had a bad beating.

Adam introduced himself and Sierra.

Mr. Kinney introduced them to his wife and daughters, and then his wife said, "I'll take the girls downstairs to the cafeteria. We'll get a bite to eat and then return in a while."

Mr. Kinney sighed and looked vastly relieved that his wife and daughters would leave during the interview. They kissed and gently hugged him, then left the room. Sierra assumed he wouldn't want to go over the details in front of his family.

"Why don't you do the sketch of the assailant first, and then I'll ask my questions," Adam told Sierra.

She was glad he'd offered for her to go first because she thought she might put the man more at ease before Adam had to question him, not to mention that she wanted his recollection of the man's description as soon as possible.

"What do you remember about your assailant?" she asked.

"I don't know," Mr. Kinney said. "It all happened so fast. I was on the road when my car got a flat tire. I pulled over on the shoulder and began changing it when a black car pulled up behind mine. I thought they were just Good Samaritans. A passenger got out of the car and said he would help me change the tire."

"They?" she asked and glanced at Adam, surprised that there had been more people involved in this since the boss hadn't mentioned it.

"How many were involved?" Adam asked.

"Uh..." Mr. Kinney glanced from Sierra to Adam, and she swore he looked a little panicked. Smelled like he was too, which confirmed he was suddenly highly stressed.

"There were two other men in the car," Mr. Kinney finally said. "Uh, one driver, and one front-seat passenger at least. I couldn't tell if there was anyone else in the car. The guy who hit me was in his midtwenties, crooked nose, looked like it had been broken across the bridge once. I'm six foot and he was a couple of inches shorter than me. His hair was a light brown, shaggy, blue eyes, chilling. He had a long chin and it had a cleft in it."

She was visualizing how *she'd* seen the dead man after he wrecked the car. He could have been in his midtwenties; it was hard to tell. Crooked nose? She couldn't make it out because his face had been so badly cut. Five ten? She didn't know. But light-brown, shaggy hair and blue eyes? Mr. Kinney was really wrong about that.

"Are you sure about the hair and eyes?" It seemed like Mr.

Kinney was describing someone entirely different. He probably wasn't remembering it right because of his head injury. She was afraid her sketch of the body would have to do then. In reality, the carjacker had short-cropped hair, nearly black, and dark-brown eyes.

"Uh, well, yeah, but you know, I might have things a little mixed up."

"That's understandable. Go ahead." She was supposed to make the eyewitness comfortable, not make him doubt himself. If his recollection wasn't as good as her visual of the carjacker, she would just go with her own sketch.

"Uh…even so, I really thought the carjacker had left the back seat of the car to come and help me. I shook his sweaty hand and he assisted me in changing the tire, though I could have managed on my own. I thanked him and said I had no cash to pay him, but I really appreciated his help.

"Then he pulled a gun out of the back of his pants. He told me that was okay about the money. All he wanted was the car. He gave me a cold, calculated smile, and I was afraid he was going to kill me. I quickly told him he could have the car and handed him my car keys. It wasn't worth dying over it. But he struck me with the butt of his gun, a 9mm, I think. I fell to the ground and then I saw him get into my car and he drove it off. The car behind mine took off after him. I don't remember anything after that except telling some people who came later to help me that my car had been stolen. Then I guess I passed out before I was brought here in an ambulance. I had no idea the guy would pull out a gun and strike me with it, then leave me for dead and steal my car."

"Okay, you're doing great, Mr. Kinney," Sierra said. "You said his hair was shaggy?"

"Yeah, he looked like a hoodlum. He had tattoos on his neck and arms. I can't say what they were. I just noticed all the ink as he approached. I had felt a little uneasy, but what was I supposed to do? I was already working on changing the tire. I didn't want to run and lock myself in the car. I didn't know he was armed, but he could have shot me through the window anyway."

She hadn't seen any visible tattoos on the carjacker at all. He was wearing a hoodie with long sleeves. She hadn't seen any tattoos on his hands or neck or face, the only skin exposed. Unless he wasn't wearing the hoodie when he confronted Mr. Kinney.

"What was he wearing?"

"Jeans, a T-shirt. I wasn't paying that much attention to his clothes."

"A T-shirt? Was anything written on it?" Sierra asked.

"Oh, uh, yeah, skull and crossbones. I should have remembered that."

"What color was the T-shirt?" Adam asked.

"Black. White skull and crossbones."

"Were there any words on the shirt?" Sierra asked.

"Maybe. I don't recall."

"You could have called roadside assistance," Adam said, sounding like a man with a badge who was thinking of safe tips to offer victims.

Sierra was sure Mr. Kinney had figured that out by now.

"But I didn't need assistance to change out the tire, and I figured it would have taken a lot longer to get back on the road if I had to wait for someone to show up to help."

"I understand," Adam said. "What about the other two men?"

"I couldn't really make them out. They were too far away to give a good description."

"Okay, so did you smell anything about the guy who hit you?" Sierra asked.

"Beer. His face had a couple of days' growth of beard. Thin lips. Bushy eyebrows."

"Good, really good. When the driver got out of the car, was his hair short? Or was there a breeze whipping it about, indicating it was longer?" she asked, even though Mr. Kinney had said he hadn't seen the other men clearly. She found if she just questioned a witness further, often important details they had missed would come back to them.

"A breeze, yeah. His hair was longer, blonder. And he was about the same height as the man who hit me."

She showed him the sketch she was doing based on his version of his assailant.

"His eyes were smaller. Beadier."

She erased the eyes and drew them smaller, then showed it to him. "Like this?"

"Yeah, that's him."

She had him endorse the back of the sketch since it was his recollection, even though it wasn't what she thought carjacker looked like, and then she finished drawing the sketch of the driver, but Mr. Kinney didn't have as many details on him. Once she had him sign that sketch, Adam began questioning Mr. Kinney.

"Did either of the men mention any names?" Adam asked.

"Uh, come to think of it, the other guy, the driver did. When the guy hit me the first time, the driver got out of his car and swore at him and called him Hawk. I thought it was odd, but then I wondered if his name was Hawk. I couldn't remember that before now. Oh, and Hawk told the driver, 'He knows me.' I assumed he said that because he wasn't wearing a mask. And then on top of that, his partner had identified him by name or nickname. So I was certain he was going to kill me."

"You don't remember having seen him from somewhere else at some other time?" Adam asked.

"No. Sorry. I work at a bank as a loan officer, and unless he came into the bank to get a loan, I wouldn't have met him. I have a regular lawn service through a company, and we haven't called anyone for repairs on the house or anything for over a year."

"You haven't had any threats to you or your family's lives, have you?" Adam asked.

"No. I really believe his stealing the car was just a case of opportunity, me on the side of the road trying to change a tire, and it had been late so there wasn't much traffic. You probably won't catch those bastards, will you?"

"I'm afraid we've located your car and the driver had totaled it," Adam said. "The driver of your vehicle, the one who hit you, died in the crash."

Mr. Kinney's jaw dropped, and his skin lost all its color. He touched his head as if it was suddenly hurting.

"Are you in pain?" Sierra asked, getting ready to call the nurse.

"Uh, a mild headache. Thanks, I'm fine." Mr. Kinney frowned at her. "Since the guy who stole the car is dead, why did you need a description of him?" Now Mr. Kinney sounded angry, as if Sierra had tricked him into describing his attacker when they already very well knew what he looked like.

She hadn't mentioned it because she felt it was Adam's job. Adam was frowning at the victim.

"He was badly injured," Sierra explained. "I wanted to make sure I had the best description I could get for your assailant. Hopefully, we can identify him and catch up to the men who were also party to the crime now that we know about them."

Mr. Kinney let out his breath. "Well, at least the one who hit me won't be attempting to kill anyone or doing any more carjacking in the future."

"Yeah, exactly. We just need to catch the other guys who were involved in it. We'll get out of your hair, but you let me know if you think of anything more that can help nail these guys." Adam gave him his business card.

"Thanks for all your help with this," Mr. Kinney said.

"You're so welcome."

Then Adam and Sierra said goodbye to him, and they left his room.

"Do you still have the sketch of the carjacker at the scene?" Adam asked Sierra.

"Yeah, I left it in the car. I was waiting to send it out once I learned Mr. Kinney might be able to give us a better description of the carjacker's face."

"Does Mr. Kinney's version differ much from the one you did at the scene of the accident?"

"Yes. I took pictures of him, so I know he had short-cropped hair, not long. And it was dark, not light brown. He had brown eyes, not blue. Now, it's possible Mr. Kinney doesn't remember, due to the trauma he suffered. I didn't know the carjacker's nose had been broken before the accident, but I'm beginning to wonder if he had that right either. And his chin was so badly cut up, I hadn't noticed the cleft in it, but again, was he only imagining that? His eyes weren't as beady as he said they were."

"Which was why you had made the eyes on the sketch you were doing for Mr. Kinney larger initially."

"Right. I've never seen the accused before I've had to take a witness statement. I had this all worked out in my mind where I would draw his version and validate my sketch of the deceased. It sure didn't work out that way. What do you think?"

"I think you're doing great. I believe either Mr. Kinney has had some impaired memories, which is entirely possible after the head injury he had, or something isn't quite right with his testimony."

She stared at Adam as they walked out the door together. "He couldn't have been in cahoots with these men."

"As a detective, I have to consider every possibility. At first, he seemed like the perfect victim, totally innocent."

She led Adam to where she'd parked her car. "So what are you saying? He wanted his car stolen for the insurance money? That he set it up, only the guy hit him a little too hard and then ended up accidentally killing himself while fleeing the scene?" She couldn't believe it. She guessed she could never be a detective and believe the worst about people.

"Or that Mr. Kinney knew them and didn't want to identify

them, in case that testimony came back to bite him. Hopefully, we'll know one way or another once we get some hits on your sketch. I wouldn't send off the one you did of his recollection." Adam glanced at his phone. "Hey, it's lunchtime. Do you want to have lunch with me?"

She got a call and said, "Hold that thought... Hello, Ethan?" She figured he needed a sketch concerning a DEA job. She just hoped this one was more the usual kind of witness descriptions, unlike the last one—if Mr. Kinney hadn't been totally honest with them.

"Hey, if Adam hasn't asked you out to lunch yet—" Ethan said.

"Uh, he just did." She thought Adam was cute for asking.

"Damn. Okay, I'll have to take a rain check then."

She smiled. "Thanks, Ethan. Talk to you later." She didn't say she would give him a rain check though. She walked out of the hospital with Adam. "You timed having lunch with me just right."

"Don't tell me that was Ethan, trying to get a date with you already."

"Just lunch."

Smiling, Adam shook his head. "Where do you want to go?"

Adam should have figured Ethan would try to get a date with Sierra as soon as she called it quits with Richard. Adam was just glad he had asked her before Ethan did.

Regarding work, now he had a new concern though. He really hadn't thought that the situation with Mr. Kinney was anything but on the up-and-up, but with the way he seemed so nervous—why would he be?—and then was angry with Sierra for having asked him to give a description of his assailant, Adam was seriously reconsidering his "victim's" role in all this. The only reason he could come up with was that Mr. Kinney knew damn well he had lied to them about what the men looked like.

They picked a Chinese restaurant they both enjoyed and had ordered their meals and taken a seat when he got a call from Tori. "Yeah, Tori, Sierra and I are grabbing a bite to eat if you would like to join us."

"No thanks. I already have something to eat. How did things go with Kinney?"

Adam told her what they'd learned. "We can't use his sketch, and I'll tell you the rest later. We'll get the sketch Sierra did of the dead man scanned in and disseminated as soon as we have lunch. What did you learn about the boat?"

"The guy didn't have a bill of sale, the price was way cheaper than what it should have sold for, and the boat had recently been painted. We've confiscated it, but we need Sierra to talk to him about the seller's description. I took notes, but we need her to do a sketch."

"I'll tell her. If we don't have anything more pressing for me to attend to right away, I'll go with her and then return to the office after that." He would have put it on speaker so Sierra could listen in, but he couldn't in the restaurant. "What did you think of the boat buyer? Gut instinct?" He always listened to his partners' gut instincts. As wolves, they could discern a lot more about the humans involved in their cases than humans could. Just as he smelled Mr. Kinney's nervousness when he learned his assailant had died in the car crash. Adam realized he wasn't as upset about the car as he was about not being told the man was dead before he gave his description to Sierra.

"No need for gut feelings in this case. He was sweating up a storm when I asked the man to produce the title for the boat. He smelled of fear and sweat. He made the motion of looking for the title in an old cabinet in the garage, but before he touched it, the cabinet was covered in dust, not a fingerprint on it. When he closed it, the cabinet drawers and doors had fingerprints all over them."

"You think he knows the guys who sold the boat to him?"

"Yep. I don't believe it was a random sale. He was nervous when he gave me the description of the seller. I mean, maybe he knew the price of the boat was too good to be true. And so he figured it was stolen but had been telling himself no one would ever learn the truth."

The food was delivered to the table, and Adam said, "Hey, food's here, Tori. We'll head over there and talk to him after we eat. See you later."

"Talk later."

Adam pocketed his phone.

Sierra eyed his plate. "Hmm, your sweet and sour shrimp looks good."

"Would you like some?"

"Only if you want to have some of my pork and hot pepper sauce."

"Yeah, sure, that would be great. Sorry about the call." He moved some of his sweet and sour shrimp to Sierra's plate, and she gave him some of the pork and hot pepper sauce.

"Don't be. You have an important job to do, and I get to help with it."

"That's for sure." He took a bite of her pork. "Hmm, this is good."

She ate one of his shrimp. "Oh, I love this."

"So the deal is the guy might know the man who sold him the boat. In that case, he can either give them up, which I suspect he won't if he's afraid they will retaliate, or he's just as guilty as them in that he's been working with them for a while. Or he'll give you a false description to use to draw the sketch." Adam took a bite of one of his shrimp.

"Okay, so it could be a waste of time for me to do this. Just like the one for Mr. Kinney was."

"No. If they've lied and we can catch them at it, they can

be charged with aiding and abetting. Sometimes, they'll subconsciously give us features that do match up with the perp. Sometimes the opposite, so he might say the guy is tall when he's short, has red hair when he's really a blond."

"Oh, that reminds me… With Mr. Kinney's description, how tall was the carjacker?"

"Taller than Kinney, six foot one."

"So he was taller by an inch, not two inches shorter. That really doesn't sound like he was telling us the truth."

Adam drank some of his water. "I know. But it's still possible he was just confused after the injury. It's one thing to have a traumatized witness who is trying their hardest to give you the real story. Another to deal with someone who is party to the crime in some way and doesn't want you to find the perp."

"Gotcha." She sipped some of her water. "So why did you go into this business?"

"Both my parents were police officers, and they talked about the cases they'd had to deal with while we were eating our meals. I wanted to be one in the worst way. Once I joined the bureau, my dad and mom retired from the force. I was a policeman for a few years, and then I wanted to do something that I felt would really help in solving some of these crimes. So I became a detective." Adam got another call and he let out his breath and answered it. "Holmes."

"We have a kidnapping in process. We have an Amber Alert out now," the officer told Adam and gave him the location and description of the car.

"That's only a quarter of a mile from where I am. I'm on it."

CHAPTER 11

Adam quickly paid for Sierra's and his meals at the Chinese restaurant and said to her, "A fourteen-year-old girl, Melissa Baeyer, was grabbed at a shopping plaza just down the street from here. The car description was for a blue Ford sedan."

As they headed outside, Sierra's phone buzzed. She looked at the Amber Alert on her phone and frowned. "The license plate and description of the car used in the kidnapping of the girl is of *my* car."

"Hell, your car isn't here." Not believing Sierra's car had been stolen to commit a kidnapping until he verified her car wasn't in the parking lot, Adam quickly called it in to Tori. "The car involved in the kidnapping of the juvenile is—"

"Sierra Redding's car. We just got word."

"Right. Stolen from the parking lot at the Chinese restaurant where we were having lunch." Adam gave her the name of the restaurant and its location.

"I'm already on my way there to pick you up. Be there in a few minutes."

"Tori's coming to pick us up," Adam told Sierra. She looked like she was ready to run down the street and find the car on foot if she had to.

"I can't believe someone would steal my car and kidnap a child!" Sierra sounded as frustrated as he felt.

"I know. At least you were sitting with a police detective when it happened, so no one can accuse you of doing the deed yourself, if that's any consolation."

"It is. But only if we can find Melissa before anything further happens to her."

"Amen to that."

It seemed like it took forever before Tori showed up and stopped so they could jump into her car and take off. They listened to the radio as they headed in the direction where the car had been spotted. Adam began to get an eerie feeling about this when they ended up in Sierra's neighborhood, only a block from her home.

"Go to my house." Sierra gave the directions to Tori.

"Okay, so what am I missing? Your car is stolen, used to kidnap a child, and then what? Deliver her to your house?" Tori asked.

"There is only one person I can think of who would want me to take the rap for kidnapping a child. A guy I put in prison," Sierra said. "Dover Manning."

Adam recalled the postcard Sierra had received before she went on her flight to Texas, and he called it in to the boss. "Sir, we believe the kidnapping could be the work of the man Sierra testified against, Dover Manning. He was angry that no one believed he only saw a dog in her hotel room."

"He's in jail," Adam's boss said.

"Right. I told you about the postcard she got."

"Hell, okay. Keep me informed."

"Will do."

When they reached Sierra's house, Adam really had expected to see her car sitting in the driveway, but it wasn't. He was praying that the kidnappers had pulled the car into the garage and the girl was inside, safe and sound. Tori parked in the driveway.

Sierra was getting out of the car, but Adam told her to stay. She gave him the pass code for her house and he headed to the house, Tori following behind him. As soon as he unlocked the door, he and Tori had their guns out and headed inside.

They found the girl gagged and tied to a chair in the dining room, her brown eyes wild with fear. Adam and Tori quickly showed her their badges, and then Tori began to untie her and pulled the gag off her while Adam searched the house for any sign of the culprits. He found a broken window in the laundry room, glass on the floor inside, and when he returned to the dining room, he saw that the kidnappers had torn up all of Sierra's artwork. He felt sick for her, worried she would be heartbroken about it. Tori was already calling in that they had the girl at Sierra's house, and she was unharmed.

Adam smelled a woman's and a man's scents that hadn't been in the house before, and he was certain they belonged to whoever had kidnapped the girl. He checked the garage, but Sierra's car wasn't there either.

He also called in the situation, saying that the kidnappers were gone, the girl was safe in their custody, and the car was still missing.

"Did they hurt you?" Tori was asking the girl as she untied the rope around her ankles.

"No," she managed between sobs.

"Officers are contacting your parents. You're safe now," Tori said, giving the girl a hug. "Tell us what happened."

"My mother had gone into a dress store and I didn't want to go. She was buying something for my grandmother for her birthday. So I was sitting on a bench waiting for her, texting my friends. A woman grabbed my arm and said my father had been hurt in an accident, that she was a friend of my parents. I told the woman we had to go inside the store to tell my mom. She said my mom would meet us there. It didn't make any sense.

"Of course I was worried about my dad, but I was reluctant to leave without my mom. Then a guy grabbed me and shoved me into the back of the car and said if I screamed, I would be dead. My mom and a couple of people in the store ran out and chased after the car, but the woman was driving too fast. My mom was on the phone right away and someone else was writing something down, so I hoped the police would hurry after us.

"We didn't go very far when they pulled into the driveway of the house. The two of them hurried me inside and then tied me up with the ropes and gagged me. They said they would be sitting outside the house, waiting on someone, and not to make a move or they would kill me. Then I swore I heard the car start up and they drove off. I was trying to get free, but I couldn't. The ropes were too tight, and I couldn't remove the gag."

Adam went outside and waved to Sierra to come in.

"Can I ask the young lady what they looked like so I can draw a sketch of them?" Sierra asked, joining him at the front door.

"Yeah," Adam said. "Don't touch anything."

"How long have I been doing this?" Sierra asked him, her brow raised as she walked into the house.

Tori smiled.

"Right. We just don't want to contaminate the scene further."

"The woman's and man's scents are new," she said. Then she spoke with the girl in the living room. "Hi, I'm Sierra Redding. I work for the police bureau as their sketch artist."

The girl's eyes were huge, and she glanced at Tori, as if silently asking her to protect her from the new threat. Sierra frowned. "I don't have a police badge, but I really do draw pictures of the bad guys so we can share the pictures all over and catch them. The two detectives know me."

"The woman looked just like you...but...she had a tattoo of a snake on her neck. And her hair was fake. A wig."

Dover had a tattoo like that too. Because he and this woman had been lovers? It seemed like too much of a coincidence. "But the same color as my hair?" Sierra asked, sounding worried.

"Yeah."

"Well, after they stole my car from the restaurant where I was having lunch with Detective Holmes"—Sierra motioned to Adam—"they grabbed you, as far as we understand it, and brought you here to my home. So I couldn't have had anything to do with kidnapping you. Where else did they go, besides being in the dining room where they tied you up and—"

Three police officers arrived then. Tori had gone to get her camera out of her car and returned to take pictures of the scene with the chair, bindings, and gag. Adam had two of the officers set up crime-scene tape to secure the area and told the other to make sure no one other than people with official business got beyond the tape.

"They said that the picture of a dog on the fireplace mantel was the dog that threatened to kill Dover."

Sierra glanced at the picture of her family that had been thrown on the floor and stomped on. The one with her brother was gone. "They took the one picture?"

"Yeah. They said it matched the dog that was in the hotel room—the dog that you said didn't exist. Then they went into your other rooms, looking for stuff," the girl said.

"My gun!" Sierra hurried down the hallway and reached her bedroom, Adam right behind her. Drawers were open in her bedroom and her bathroom, cabinet doors open, stuff tossed all over the place.

"Sorry, I should have warned you about that. Where was your gun?" Adam asked.

"In the bedside drawer. And yeah, it's gone." She sounded so dejected that he squeezed her arm consolingly.

"I'll need your serial number on the gun."

"Yeah." Then she headed back to the living room and asked Melissa, "When they left, were they carrying anything with them?"

"I was turned the other way, my back to the kitchen. I couldn't see anything they took in the kitchen, just heard what they were doing."

"Then both of them went to the bedroom?"

"They both went down the hall. The woman said she was checking out the bedroom. He said he would check out the other rooms."

"When they returned, were they carrying anything?" Sierra asked.

"A gun. I couldn't tell if they had anything else. I mean, except the picture. They just hurried really fast out of the house, though before they left, the guy warned me not to move an inch from where I was tied up—as if I could."

"How did they get inside? The house was locked."

"One of them went around back and I heard the glass break."

"The laundry room window is broken," Adam said.

Sierra frowned.

"We'll get it taken care of pronto after we gather any evidence at the crime scene." Adam had already texted the wolf they called on for replacing windows.

"You said the woman looked like me." Sierra sat down to begin sketching the kidnappers.

"With the fake wig, yeah. But she was really dark-haired. Her eyebrows were dark. And she plucked them way too much. They were really skinny."

"What about her mouth? Did she smile at all?"

"No. She acted annoyed with the guy. She kept calling him an idiot. 'Stop being such an idiot. I don't know why you have to be such an idiot. If you were any more of an idiot than you are right now, we would be sitting in jail.'"

"How did he react to that?" Adam asked.

"He said it takes one to know one." The girl shrugged. "He didn't sound mad, just like it rolled right off him. Oh, and she said that if he didn't get some smarts, he would end up just like Dover or Fish."

Sierra glanced at Adam. "So Dover Manning, who is in jail, is in cahoots with some guy who goes by the name of Fish. Maybe Fisher?"

"And they were looking for a dog. A big dog. Part German shepherd, the guy thought. They were supposed to kill it. I was so glad they couldn't find the dog that was in the picture," Melissa said.

"I don't have a dog," Sierra said. "Those are old pictures of dogs we owned a long time ago."

"Oh, they were sure that was the one that had threatened him."

"Did the woman have a long chin like me? Shorter chin?" Sierra asked, getting back to sketching the female kidnapper's features.

"Shorter."

"Wide cheek bones? Oval face? Round?"

"Heart-shaped." The girl smiled when Sierra looked surprised that she would know the different shapes of faces.

"I studied art. I study people's faces. The policewoman has an oval face like you. The policeman has a diamond face shape. Did you know that shape for a man is supposed to be hot?"

Sierra's brows shot up. Tori laughed. Adam smiled. He liked the kid.

"The guy had a widow's peak. His hair was light brown and it was cut short. He had a tattoo of a heart on his"—she looked down at her hands—"left hand. He was as tall as the policeman, but his shoulders weren't as broad. He wore jeans and a gray T-shirt with a crow on it. He had on heavy boots with steel toes."

"You're doing great with the descriptions," Sierra said.

"I kept telling myself if I lived, I had to be able to describe them in detail. Every time I saw them, I would try to memorize another detail. Oh, the woman was wearing a sparkly gold and diamond bracelet and big gold hoop earrings, a gold ankle bracelet and a gold ring, like she was dressed up for something. Um, her shirt had a rounded neck and she was"—she glanced at Adam and her face turned a little red—"like guys like."

"Big-busted?" Sierra offered and smiled at Adam.

He held up his hands in defense. "Not all guys see a woman in that way."

The girl scoffed and tossed her long, dark hair over her shoulders. "Sure, you don't."

She was certainly precocious. And he hoped neither Sierra nor Tori would rib him about it later.

"Was she narrow shouldered like me? Or have broader shoulders?" Sierra asked.

The girl frowned, studying Sierra's shoulders, and said, "About the same as yours. But she was taller. And skinnier. She was wearing pink jeans with a pink short-sleeved top, and she was about your age, I guess."

"Thirty?"

The girl shrugged. "Yeah, I guess." Melissa looked down at the drawing. "Her mouth was thinner. Meaner looking. And she has long, dark hair. When she tied me up, I saw a couple of dark brown hairs clinging to her shirt and they were long. Down to her…chest. They looked like the same color as her skinny eyebrows."

"Okay, good." Sierra sketched some more.

"They didn't have any reason to grab you personally, right?" Adam asked.

"Nope. I was alone, they saw me and grabbed me." Melissa looked at the sketch of the woman again. "That looks just like her. I can draw, but not half as good as you do."

"Here, you sketch whatever your favorite thing is to draw." Sierra handed the sketch pad to her after removing the two pages she had done of the kidnappers.

Adam was impressed that Sierra would give Melissa her sketch pad to draw on, which helped to take the girl's mind off her ordeal.

Sierra said to Adam, "I'll get you the serial number on the gun." Then she headed back to the bedroom.

"Were the man and woman wearing gloves?" Adam figured they would have been, but he had to ask.

"No."

That was good news, if they could locate the car and the kidnappers hadn't wiped it down. "When they grabbed you, did they leave the car running?" Adam asked.

"Yeah. I guess so they could get away fast."

And because they didn't have the keys to the car.

Sierra headed into the kitchen, not touching anything but looking to see if anything appeared to be missing. "I can't tell if they took anything else. Just the gun." She returned to the living room, handed Adam a slip of paper with a serial number on it, and smiled at the picture Melissa had drawn of a horse running. "Now that is truly beautiful. I could never draw a horse like that."

"People are your thing then?"

"I can draw landscapes and other things"—wolves and lots of them—"but horses, not so much."

"I bet you could if you practiced."

"You are so right. I'm so sorry for what they put you through."

"Thanks. You too." Melissa glanced at Sierra's torn-up drawings on the dining room table and scattered on the floor.

"It's nothing that I can't do again. All that's important is that you're safe," Sierra said.

After they finished talking with Melissa, a policewoman took her to join her parents. Melissa had a couple of bruises on her arms where the woman and man had grabbed her, and the police had photographed them, but otherwise, she was fine. She just had to deal with the psychological issue of being threatened and taken hostage. Which was bad enough.

Then Adam got another call.

"They've found Sierra Redding's car ditched about fifteen miles south of Portland, hidden in brush. No sign of anyone in the vicinity," Jefferson, one of the officers working in the office, said.

"Was it in good condition?" Adam asked.

"Yes, sir. It looks like they just ditched it and tried to hide it."

"Okay, great. Impound it and dust for prints," Adam said.

"Will do, Detective."

"Were there any tire tracks anywhere?" Adam asked.

"We've taken casts of the ones we found."

"Okay, good." Then Adam and the officer ended the call. "Your car has been found. And it's in good shape."

"Oh great," Sierra said. "But it's impounded now?"

"Only as long as it takes to get prints off the car and take hair samples. Then it will be returned to you. I can get you back and forth to work until that happens," Adam told Sierra.

"Thanks. What about my house?"

Adam frowned. "You can stay with me for the night. They'll be finished going over the crime scene in a few hours."

"I would take you in, but nothing's unpacked except my clothes and dishes," Tori said.

Sierra smiled at her. "We'll help you get it straightened out. I felt the same way when I arrived, but at least I had a lot of wolf pack help." To Adam, she said, "I just need to get a bag and throw in some clothes and toiletries to stay the night."

"Don't touch anything—"

"I can smell where they've been and what they've touched. I'll be careful, Detective," Sierra said and took off for her bedroom.

"Detective," Tori said, sounding amused. "Better watch out or she'll be staying at someone else's place tonight, and you'd better hope it isn't with another bachelor male like Ethan."

Adam chuckled. He didn't think Sierra was that annoyed with him. At least he hoped not.

They left the house afterward and Sierra said to Adam, "So can you think of anyone named Fish that was involved in anything of this sort before?"

"Yeah, a guy by the name of Jerry Fisher. He's done a lot of robberies. I was surprised he could have done something like kidnapping a girl, but if he works for Dover, no telling what he would do next."

"You think the guy in jail is the one who arranged the kidnapping to set you up then?" Tori asked.

"Yeah, I do," Sierra said.

"We'll nail his cohorts and send them to jail so they can join him," Tori promised.

"Good. I'm all for doing what I can to put the rest of them behind bars," Sierra said.

"You've done it once. I have faith in you doing it again, but I would rather you weren't the actual eyewitness to the event this time," Adam said.

"Well, they're putting me in the crosshairs," Sierra said. "If I could, I would just turn into my wolf and take care of them."

"I can't believe you took the chance to turn into your wolf at your hotel room and show yourself. You have guts," Tori said in a good way.

"I had to protect myself in some way. I just didn't think he would have a gun."

"That could have been a problem," Tori said.

"I figure they tried to set me up over the kidnapping and then kill the dog at the same time for Dover," Sierra said.

"I agree." Adam didn't know what to think, but he sure didn't like Sierra staying at the house alone if Dover was going to have his cohorts or henchmen continue to harass her at her place.

"What are we on schedule to do next?" Tori asked.

"We need to get started on the kidnapping paperwork. Take the sketches Sierra drew and get them out. I'm going to take Sierra to see the man about the stolen boat he purchased so she can do a sketch of the man who sold it to him."

"Do you know of anybody who has been convicted of selling boats or parts of boats that's currently out of jail in the area? Maybe we could take some mug shots and see if he recognizes any. Maybe he can give me the description, I'll draw it, and then you can show the mug shots. With our sense of smell, we can tell if he's lying or not," Sierra said.

"She needs to be a detective." Tori smiled and they got out of the car at the bureau.

"I'm on the team, just doing a different kind of job that I really love to do," Sierra said. "I wonder if Dover knows I'm now working for the police bureau."

"If he was the one who orchestrated the kidnapping from jail,

I would say he knows a lot about you—your car, your house, and probably where you work. I suspect they didn't think you would be having lunch with a police detective and have the perfect alibi though," Adam said.

CHAPTER 12

Sierra and Adam climbed into his SUV, and he drove them out to the home of the man who bought the stolen boat.

"I worry about you being all alone after what happened today," Adam said to Sierra, truly concerned about her and what Dover and his henchmen would pull next. "Anyone who would go to the lengths that they did to attempt to frame you for a federal crime is dangerous. Especially when their leader is in jail but that doesn't seem to be stopping him."

"So catch the rest of the bad guys and put them away. They are not going to keep me from living at my place. I'll only stay with you tonight because it's a crime scene. But once my window is replaced in the laundry room and the police have finished their business there, I'm returning home."

Maybe Sierra just preferred sleeping in her own bed, but he still felt she wasn't safe. "You don't have security cameras or an alarm system set up at your place. I can always camp out at your home if you feel you need some protection. Don't tell me you'll just sleep as a wolf. If they catch you at home in your fur coat, they'll shoot you for sure."

"If I have more trouble, I'll decide then. For now, I'm just staying at your place for the night."

"Tori could stay with you." He wondered if Sierra was afraid pack members would get the wrong impression if they learned he was staying at her house, or vice versa, when they weren't even dating. Since Tori's place was in disarray with her recent move, Sierra probably couldn't stay there.

Sierra gave him a look that said to leave the topic alone.

He shrugged. "Or you could stay with Josh and his mate since he's my former partner and could watch over you. I'm just trying to help."

"I could return to the pack and stay there. Stay with my brother and his mate even. But I'm not going to. I'm closer to work here. And I'm not going to overreact."

"If I stayed at your place, you could serve as bait."

She laughed.

He was glad he could make her laugh, though he still felt the situation was serious.

When they reached the house where they needed to speak to the man about the stolen boat, Mr. Rivers came outside to talk with them. He was frowning, looking annoyed, his blond hair disheveled, his blue eyes narrowed. "What do you want now? I talked to that woman detective when you had to take off for other business."

Adam figured the guy wouldn't like it that he'd returned to question him all over again. But he needed to actually see Mr. Rivers's responses and smell his scent to watch for his reactions to questions. It really helped being a wolf in the police business.

"This is Sierra Redding, the bureau's sketch artist. I mentioned she would be coming here to get your description of the man who sold the boat to you. If you could walk us through meeting up with him and the exchange you had, we would be grateful."

"I gave the other woman the description. Can't you use that?" Mr. Rivers asked.

Why didn't he just give them the description again? Was he afraid he wouldn't remember the same details? Adam didn't trust the man entirely. He always had to consider that if someone was in the possession of stolen goods and hadn't reported it, the person could have been involved in the theft.

"Sometimes I can help a witness provide more details that I need for a sketch," Sierra said in an attempt to get Mr. Rivers to cooperate.

"Fine. What do you want to know exactly?" Mr. Rivers folded his arms in a defensive manner.

"Everything," Sierra said.

"I don't see how this has anything do with the description of the men there."

"It helps if I can see the scene in my mind's eye when I'm drawing the sketches."

Mr. Rivers let out his breath. "All right, so three men were there, and one of the three was in charge. The other two acted like bodyguards or something."

"Had you bought anything from the man before?" Adam asked.

"No."

"How did you learn about the boat being for sale?" Even though Adam knew very well that Tori had asked all these questions of the boat buyer, as thorough as she was when questioning a suspect, it helped to ask the person to describe the events that took place *again* to see if he altered the testimony.

"Craigslist. I told the other detective that. I thought it was legitimate."

"No bill of sale? The price was too good to be true, but the hull number was painted over. Not paying attention to something like that is a big mistake." If Mr. Rivers was innocent of any wrongdoing, Adam had an obligation to tell him what could get him into trouble if he was buying property that might be stolen. "If you ever find a boat where the hull number is missing or has obscured numbers, be wary. Unless it can be proven that it's not a stolen boat, don't buy it. You can see here that the number one was turned into a seven and the five was turned into an eight. The numbers should be clear and distinct." Adam glanced at Sierra who was patiently waiting to sketch the guy. "So what did the guy in charge look like?"

"The guy who sold me the boat—which, like I told the other detective, means I'm out $30,000 when I had to forfeit the boat—had shoulder-length blond hair and pale-blue eyes, a long face, and ears that stuck out. He was wearing torn jeans and a T-shirt and sneakers. He was, I'd say, around forty and had a potbelly."

Adam could smell the man's deception, fear, and sweat and saw his forehead perspiring. "Did it ever cross your mind that the boat was stolen?" The engine number was also what gave the boat away. It hadn't been changed or removed.

"Of course not. If I had, I wouldn't have bought it."

"The blue-book value of the Monterey Bowrider is nearly $64,000. You paid cash for less than half the value of the boat," Adam said.

"Yeah, so? I didn't know it was stolen or worth that much."

Adam didn't believe the man wouldn't have checked on the value of the boat. Most anyone would to make sure they weren't getting a bad deal. Especially when paying that much for a boat.

"Can you give me a description of the other two men?" Sierra asked.

"One was muscular, blond, his hair cropped short. I couldn't tell the color of his eyes. He was too far away. I don't know. Shorter than the seller. Maybe five six. He was wearing blue jeans and a T-shirt, boots, I think. The other guy I gave even less of a glance at. Dark hair, shaggy, he was probably the tallest, leanest of the two."

"Okay, thanks. On the shorter man, spread of eyes? Together, apart? Bushy brows?" Sierra asked.

Adam got a call from Tori. "Yeah, what's up?"

"The three men who drowned in the Willamette River have been identified. One of the men's wives called in to say that one of the sketches Sierra had drawn was of her husband, who owned the boat that we now have in custody, and that the sketches of the other two men were good friends of his. They had reservations at a cabin. We had already checked all the cabins in the area, but she told us they weren't due to arrive there until tomorrow because the cabins had all been rented out for the rest of the time. They were staying at a hotel in the meantime. We found their IDs in their hotel rooms and their truck and boat trailer in the hotel parking lot. A friend in Portland returned the truck and trailer there after dropping them off at the launch site. He was supposed to pick two of the men up tomorrow so they could move their stuff to the cabin. The other one was staying with the boat. The friend hadn't known they'd run into any trouble."

"Okay."

"And we have more of a break."

That was what Adam liked to hear. "What else?"

"The Multnomah County Sheriff's Office River Patrol's *Freedom* stopped this same boat on the Willamette River when they saw three men cruising in it who didn't appear to be carrying any life jackets. Everyone onboard a craft has to have a life jacket. When the patrol questioned the captain of the boat to see if he had a safety education card, required for the operator of a craft with a ten-horsepower engine or greater, he didn't. He was supposed to produce a driver's license, but he didn't have it on him. The officer gave him a citation and loaned them three life jackets that were to be turned in when he went to court."

"Did the description the officers have of the men on the boat match the drowned men?" Adam asked.

"Nope. As soon as I had the IDs for the men from their hotel rooms, I ran the info over to speak to the officers. None of the men pictured in the IDs had been on the boat. So the other men must have grabbed the boat after the men drowned or possibly had something to do with the drowning," Tori said.

"Well, damn, it's too bad that they hadn't had any IDs on them when the river patrol stopped them to question them. But if one of them tried to sell the boat—"

"Yep, we need to have Sierra draw some sketches based off the river patrol's eyewitness accounts. It will be interesting to see just how similar they are to the man or men that the boat buyer described, unless the men weren't the same as the ones who sold him the boat," Tori said.

"Okay, thanks, Tori. We'll head over there next." Adam ended the call. When he saw that Sierra was still drawing but Mr. Rivers wasn't adding anything to the account, Adam said to Mr. Rivers, "Three men died on the Willamette River, and the boat you had purchased belonged to one of the men."

Mr. Rivers's eyes widened. Sierra stopped drawing and glanced at Adam, looking just as surprised.

"It could have been a case of accidental drowning of all three men," Adam continued. "The current is swift and cold, even in the summer. None of the men were wearing life vests. *Or* it could be a case of homicide. We haven't confirmed which yet. Oh, and the good news is that officers with the Multnomah Sheriff's Department have given us descriptions of the seller of the boat. Now we can match the descriptions you offered us with the ones the officers gave."

Sierra quickly hid her smile.

Mr. Rivers closed his gaping mouth. Then he managed to say, "I had no idea."

Adam assumed he hadn't.

It didn't take but a few minutes before Tori called Adam back. "We just found an old case where Mr. Rivers was charged with the possession of a stolen boat in Florida. He got off on a technicality, but the boat was confiscated. Not only that, but the boat he *just* purchased *wasn't* listed on Craigslist."

"Thanks, Tori." Adam ended the call and said to Mr. Rivers, "Sorry, Sierra can get the rest of your descriptions."

"Am I...uh, under arrest?"

"Not at the moment. Detective Rose read you your Miranda rights before I left on another case. Just know that this could be a murder case. That you were in possession of stolen goods. We could conclude that you were involved in a criminal conspiracy." If Mr. Rivers was feeding Sierra a line of bullshit about what the guys looked like, then he might as well know the consequences of his actions. "Oh, and for the purpose of keeping the chain of evidence in a criminal case, you'll be asked to autograph the sketches that Sierra is drawing, per your account."

Mr. Rivers rubbed his chin. "Okay, listen. I'll talk if I can have immunity from prosecution. I didn't have anything to do with stealing the boat, dead bodies, none of it."

"Okay," Adam said.

Mr. Rivers let out his breath. "I met the guy at a bar at a marina. I was wearing my captain's hat, and this guy pulled up a seat at the bar and asked what kind of a boat I had. All right? Well, I didn't have a boat. I'd just sold off one for a damn good price and was looking to get another that wasn't quite so expensive."

"We'll need to see the paperwork on the boat you sold."

"Hell, it was *legitimate*!"

"Then you won't mind showing us the paperwork," Adam said.

"I'll be right back," Mr. Rivers said, sounding exasperated, and went inside the house.

Adam hoped he would return with legitimate paperwork and that he didn't try to sneak out the back of the house if he was involved in everything else.

"I guess it's good I had gotten the descriptions first from him," Sierra said.

"If it's all lies—"

"Then you would have him on false testimony. Do you think he lied about the descriptions that he already gave us?"

"Yeah, I do. That's the reason he wanted immunity." Adam called up the district attorney to let him know what the issue was and if they could go forward with a cooperation agreement. Adam told the DA the situation with the witness and owner of the stolen property. "Mr. Rivers agreed to be a cooperating witness."

"We need to have the agreement signed if he's willing to provide competent and truthful testimony. And that he had nothing to do with stealing the boat in the first place or anything to do with the drowned victims."

"Yes, sir. I don't think he'll tell us what we need to know unless he has immunity from prosecution, and I don't believe he actually had anything to do with stealing the boat or the drowned men. We'll bring him downtown and get the paperwork signed."

When they ended the call, Mr. Rivers came out with the paperwork for the earlier boat he said he'd just sold. He had actually bought it at a boat dealership so everything looked legitimate, but Adam would still verify it with the dealership.

"Okay, the DA says we need to sign the deal so that you can be a cooperating witness. You can follow us downtown and we'll get that done. Then you can finish your story," Adam said. And give the real descriptions of the men involved in selling him the boat. Hell, maybe even their names.

Mr. Rivers agreed to it, got into his car, and followed Sierra and Adam to the courthouse.

"You won't need me now," Sierra said.

"Yeah I do. You still need to finish the sketches of the men he dealt with. Even if he thinks he knows their names, they may be using aliases. After that, I'll run you over to speak with the River Patrol Unit." He smiled at her. "What? Do you think I'm holding you hostage so that I get to keep you safe throughout the day?"

"Are you?" She was wearing a hint of a smile and he knew she was teasing him.

"Nope. You don't have a car."

"I could have leased one."

"I still need you. And when you speak to the River Patrol Unit, I need to learn all I can about what they saw, reactions, et cetera, concerning the men they stopped and gave the citation to."

"Okay, admit it. You want to date me, and this is a way of seeing more of me without officially calling it a date."

He smiled at her. "Hell yeah."

She laughed.

After they finished with Mr. Rivers and got a much-changed account of what the men looked like, the U.S. Marshals arrived to put him in witness protection. In the meantime, Adam arranged to see the officers on the River Patrol Unit.

When he and Sierra arrived, the two officers greeted them.

"Hey, we wish we'd known the boat was stolen," the blond officer said. "We sure would have done something about it."

"Yeah, I wish so too. We didn't find the body of the man that it belonged to and his companions until almost a week later," Adam said.

"Do you suspect foul play?" the officer asked.

"We don't have all the facts yet. The coroner's doing the autopsies now. It's possible the men accidentally drowned, though we're still trying to determine how that could have happened."

"Then the boat was found adrift and these men took advantage of the situation?" the dark-haired officer asked.

"It's either that or they stole it from them. I can't think of any other scenario that would make sense of the situation."

The officers gave the descriptions of the three men on the boat. After Sierra drew the sketches, she showed them to the officers.

"Yeah, these look just like them," the blond officer said.

"Good. It matches the description the man who bought the boat gave us." At least the second description Mr. Rivers gave them. "So we know the same people who sold the boat had taken it off the water," Adam said.

"If you need any more help with this, just let us know," the blond officer said.

"Thanks. This is a lot of help." Adam was glad that the boat buyer had been honest with them once they assured him he wouldn't be prosecuted for the crime.

Adam and Sierra got into his SUV and then drove back to the bureau so she could get busy with other work and he could get the witness sketches out to the public. He hoped they would get something from that soon.

At the bureau, he was surprised to see Ethan. What was the special agent from the DEA doing there?

Tori smiled at Adam. "He needs to borrow Sierra—to do a witness sketch."

Sierra patted Adam's chest and smiled at him, and he realized he was scowling. He managed a small smile. "But she works for us."

"I'll be sure to have her back at a decent hour." Ethan cast him a wolfish grin and escorted Sierra out of the building.

CHAPTER 13

"Adam, you know Sierra's done witness sketches for the DEA before, and they always return her to us safe and sound," the chief said, coming out of his office to check on things. "Has her status changed somehow? You *know* she has an out-of-state boyfriend."

"She ditched the boyfriend," Tori said, smiling. "So all bets are off."

The chief laughed. "Good to know."

Adam thought Tori was enjoying this a little too much. He planned to ask Sierra to have dinner with him and then go with him to Forest Park to run as wolves tonight after the park closed at ten. He hoped Ethan wouldn't ask her out on a date first. But he didn't want to mention any of his plans to Sierra in front of Tori. Hell, he thought he'd have no problem making plans with her tonight since she was staying overnight with him. Then Ethan showed up on the scene.

If Sierra did go running with Adam tonight, she was free to share that bit of news with Tori, but he didn't want Sierra to turn him down in front of Tori, if she had a mind to.

Even though Sierra said she wasn't worried about being Dover's target, he found himself watching for danger, seeing if they were being followed anywhere that he and she went together. He needed to let Ethan know to keep an eye out too, if he wasn't already thinking along those lines.

Sierra knew it was imperative that she speak with witnesses and victims right away because their memories of people's appearances degraded so quickly with the passing hours that they could remember the perps totally wrong by the time she did a sketch. She'd done one sketch of a perp based on two eyewitness descriptions that were so inaccurate, it didn't matter how good Sierra's drawing was. The witnesses had stated the assailant had blond hair instead of dark. Blue eyes instead of brown. Even those details, she figured a witness couldn't have gotten wrong. But because of the time she got there and the trauma they had experienced, they had it all wrong. Luckily, detectives still caught the guy, but not based on her sketch.

Even when Sierra journaled about her experiences, if she tried to recall the more minute details days, weeks, months later, it was amazing how blurry the recollections had become.

On the way to Ethan's SUV, he was reading a text from someone and texted the person back. She figured it was work-related. Then he and Sierra drove to a park to speak to a couple of witnesses about a drug deal that had gone bad. "So has Adam asked you out on a date yet? I mean a real date, not just lunch with him during working hours."

She laughed as they were driving to the city park. "He's working up to asking. We haven't scheduled a date per se."

"He's only working up to it?"

Smiling, she realized she should have known Ethan would be thinking about that and not about his case. Like Adam, he was always really focused on his work, except now that she was available to date. He had always joked with her about the lucky guy who was dating her, so she knew he wanted to date her too, if she ever ditched the other guy.

"Just so you know and don't hear it from someone else and wonder what's up, I'm staying with Adam at his place tonight." She ran her hand over her sketch pad on her lap.

Ethan glanced at her, raised his brows, and smiled. At least he didn't seem annoyed about it. "For your protection."

"No, because my house is the secondary crime scene in the kidnapping case. And I have to have my laundry room window replaced."

"Adam told me you have no security on the house." Ethan glanced at his rearview mirror.

"It's an older home so it didn't come with it, and I haven't had any trouble in the time I've been here. Anyway, I'm staying at Adam's place only overnight."

Ethan frowned at her. "This sounds serious. Though I can understand why, after Adam told me all that had happened. You could stay with Josh and his mate."

"Adam already mentioned that."

"Really? I'm surprised." Ethan smiled at her. "You could stay with me."

Sierra smiled back. "Adam *didn't* mention that."

Ethan laughed. "Of course he didn't. He only offered Josh as protection because he's got a mate."

"Staying at Adam's house is not for protection, and it's only for tonight."

"Those guys mean business regarding you. They wouldn't have gone to those lengths if they didn't mean to cause you more grief. I'm sure of it. None of us want to see you hurt. And you don't want to change into your wolf when you're home alone, with the thought you can scare them off this time." He looked at his rearview mirror again.

"I know. Adam already told me that too. You guys sure think alike."

"We're just worried about you is all."

"Well, I appreciate. Really I do."

When he looked at his rearview mirror again, she asked, "What are you watching for? Is someone following us?"

"It comes with the business I'm in."

"DEA, sure." She frowned at him. "And watching out for me?"

"Yeah, you know it."

"Adam put you up to it. The text message you got and replied to."

Ethan chuckled. "You're good. Truth is, yes, he texted me to watch out for you, but I would have anyway, and I do keep an eye out on suspicious movement because of my work."

"Okay, good. I wouldn't want to think you weren't watching out for me."

Ethan laughed.

They finally arrived at the park where the crime scene was taped off. Two women were sitting together at a picnic bench, and Sierra joined them to start drawing their descriptions of the four men, one of whom had been a shooter. She wasn't sure they would be able to do a good job of it because they had ducked down behind a car to protect themselves when the shooting started, and she sure didn't blame them for that.

The two women began arguing with each other about what the men had looked like.

"That's okay. You're doing great." Sierra coaxed them through the process, helping them to recall further details that she hoped were more accurate than not. "Thanks, ladies. You did really good."

Then she and Ethan were back in his SUV and returning to the bureau.

"Thanks for helping us out as usual," Ethan said.

"You're welcome. I love doing witness sketches, though I'm not sure the women's recollections were good enough this time to assist you in catching the culprits."

"You can only do what you're able to do with what you're given. But in this case, your continued questioning of the ladies worked. When I saw your sketch, I knew who the shooter was."

"You're kidding."

"Nope. He's a known drug dealer who uses a gun when he gets pissed off. He's been in and out of prison for years. We'll get him. I think I know the others who were with him too."

"Wow, that's great." Sierra really did love to do the sketches in the hope that it would help the good guys.

"If you need me to protect you from Adam tonight, you've got my number."

She laughed. "I'll have to let him know that."

"He'll be glad to know that, I'm sure. See you later," Ethan said, dropping her off at the bureau. "The offer still stands if you need a different place to stay."

"Okay. I'll certainly keep that in mind. Thanks." She smiled at him, glad he was sweet enough to offer, and hurried into the bureau. She saw Adam on his phone at his desk, but as soon as she caught his eye, he smiled, then turned serious and waved her over.

Man, working full-time was rough. She was ready to sit down and kick up her feet for a bit.

"Hey, we got five calls about the woman who kidnapped Melissa and left her at your house. It turns out the female kidnapper is Dover's girlfriend."

"Oh, great! Do you have a warrant out for her arrest?"

"We sure do. Her name is Phyllis Kenton." Adam glanced at the clock on the wall. "It's time to quit work. Are you ready to go to my place and have some dinner?"

"Uh, yeah." Boy was she ever. She would sleep well tonight, that was if she didn't have nightmares about the girl being kidnapped. Or about bodies in the morgue. She'd had nightmares about Dover in her hotel room after that had happened.

"'Night, Tori. We'll see you tomorrow." Sierra hoped it would be a lighter workload than today, but if it was always like this, she could understand why Willy retired and why she had been hired to help out part-time prior to that. Not that she didn't like to keep busy, but there was busy and there was exhausting. She realized she needed some downtime during the day.

"Night, Sierra, Adam. See you in the morning. If not sooner," Tori said.

That was the problem with this business. Crime didn't take a break.

"You bought lunch. Do you want me to buy us some takeout dinner we can take home?" Sierra asked Adam as they climbed into his Hummer.

"Yeah, sure. Pizza parlor? Or home delivery?"

"Home delivery. I'm ready to just relax." She got out her phone. "What toppings do you want?"

"Anything but anchovies is good for me."

"Okay." She ordered a large meat-lover's deep pan pizza with extra cheese. "Your address?"

He told her his address and she gave it to the cashier. "Thanks." She leaned back against the seat and closed her eyes.

"It must be tiring for you working full-time again."

"Yeah. But also the business with the young lady being kidnapped, my car being stolen and used in the kidnapping, and my house being the drop-off place for the kidnap victim took a toll on me."

"I'm sorry for all that. You know, this didn't happen until Dover ended up in jail. I'm surprised he's incarcerated and still pulling the strings."

"He's arrogant."

"Yeah, well, he deserves to be right where he is," Adam said.

They soon arrived at Adam's home, a pretty one-story brick house with big, framed windows and a blue bench sitting on a porch out front. He had nice flower beds filled with evergreen plants, but she could envision filling them with flowers too.

They hadn't been home for more than ten minutes when someone knocked on the door and Adam answered it. "Here's our pizza."

"Good. I'm starving."

After she paid for the pizza, Adam set it on the island counter, similar to hers, but his counter and his cabinets were black, while hers were all white.

"Wine with pizza?" he asked.

"Sure, that would be great."

"If you think you could last that long, given that you're so tired, we could go for a run in Forest Park tonight after it closes."

"I would love that. I haven't run in a while as a wolf," she said.

"Good. Then we'll head over there a quarter before the hour."

"To Carver's place, right?" She'd been to the wolf's house before. He and his family had set it up so that anyone who wanted to run in Forest Park could use his place to park their vehicles and shift out of sight since his property was backed up on the park.

"Yeah, it's summer vacation for them. He and his wife and two daughters are away."

After eating their pizza and watching a fantasy movie, it was time to run and they headed over to Carver's place.

It didn't take Sierra and Adam long to remove their clothes and shift in the outer building in the backyard, and then they ran out through the wolf door in the back gate.

This was the perfect way to stretch their legs after a busy day at work and all the rest of the stuff that had gone on. She needed this and Adam seemed to be just as eager to run as a wolf tonight.

They moved off the trails and continued trotting along. The wind ruffled Sierra's fur and she felt exhilarated. She was so glad Adam had recommended going for a run tonight. She knew if she ran, she would feel great, and then hopefully she could sleep really well.

They were having a blast keeping up with each other. With five thousand acres to explore, they had a lot of territory to cover if they wanted to spend hours out here.

About ten minutes later, someone fired a shot at them, and the round hit a tree within a foot of them. They immediately scattered, knowing to put distance between each other so that both of them wouldn't be targets. Her heart was pounding out of bounds. No one was supposed to have weapons in the park, and no one was supposed to be hunting. Well, hell, no one was supposed to be in the park at this time of night!

Another shot was fired, then two more. Another three. The humans who were shooting at them could never catch up to them. But what if whoever was shooting at them had seen them come out through Carver's back gate?

Though Sierra and Adam were still keeping their distance from each other, they were within earshot to ensure they didn't lose each other. They kept running away from Carver's place, and she assumed Adam worried about the same thing. They didn't slow down for several minutes, and finally when they knew they were far enough away that the humans wouldn't be able to catch up to them, they slowed down and then made their way to each other.

Their hearts were racing, and they were panting. She didn't think the humans would ever be able to locate them in the dark now, not without the ability she and Adam had to run as fast as they could. And the shooters wouldn't have the wolves' enhanced sense of smell so they could track them.

But returning to the house was another story, if what she was afraid of turned out to be true—that the shooters had seen them leave Carver's backyard through the gate.

Adam shifted and crouched down in the ferns. "If this has to do with Dover and they tracked us from the house, we can't go there. They could be waiting for us to return there."

She shifted. "Then what do we do? What if we make our way to the front of the house instead, sneak in through the front gate and get dressed out back. I mean, if they saw us naked, they couldn't very well shoot us. Right now, they could say they were shooting at dogs, well, coyotes, not people. I'm sure they figure that at least one of us has to be the 'dog' in my hotel room that day that Dover got caught. And they're determined to kill it. If it has to do with Dover and his people."

"As long as they don't want to kill us even if we're in our human forms too. Carver has a keypad lock to the front door, and he has a security alarm set whenever he's away. We can make our way to the house as wolves and shift in the shrubs before we reach it. You'll remain hidden and I'll race to the house and unlock the door, turn off the security alarm, and wave to you to come inside. Then we can take it from there."

"They have a spare bedroom with clothes for guests who run into trouble. He told me that when I first moved into the area and planned to run in the park."

"Exactly. So I'll grab something to wear in there and let you in. Let's shift and go. There's a break between homes at the cul-de-sac and we can hide there," Adam said.

She sure hoped this worked out and no neighbor saw them running naked through the front yard.

Adam said, "I'll make sure the coast is clear in the backyard, and you come through the front gate. Shrubs hide that area more than they do the entryway and front door."

"Good idea. I worry when I park a vehicle at their house and they're gone, believing neighbors will think I'm breaking in."

"He let his neighbors know he lets his friends use his property whether he's here or not."

"And you know the keypad and security number?"

"I'm a police detective. If they ever have trouble while they're away, they want me to check on it. Or Josh, even though he's retired, or Ethan." Then Adam shifted and so did she.

She prayed they wouldn't run into the shooters on the way back to Carver's house.

CHAPTER 14

Adam and Sierra began moving back in the direction of Carver's house but way around from where they had run initially, just in case the shooters were trying to track them down. She really didn't think they would be successful. Initially, the shooters had a couple of chances to hit Sierra and Adam, but after that, they'd lost that chance. Man, did she want to terminate them. If they had killed either Adam or her while running as a wolf, they would have turned back into their human form. She could just imagine the shooters trying to explain that away and the mess all the wolves would be in, not to mention how awful it would be to lose a pack mate. She suspected whoever survived would have to kill the shooters—not out of revenge, but they couldn't risk the shooters telling what they'd seen.

It took Sierra and Adam a good hour to make it safely back to Carver's house because they were trying to avoid running into the men. They never saw them, though they were watching and listening for any sign of humans tromping through the underbrush in hot pursuit. When they reached the cul-de-sac, she waited in the shrubs as a wolf, figuring she would be well hidden if the men ended up around here somewhere, while Adam, to her surprise, stayed as a wolf too, ran to the front door, and disappeared in the deep recesses of the entryway.

She assumed he'd thought better of running naked through the front yard with the streetlamps giving off a fair amount of light. If anyone saw him as a naked human, they might have called the police, but in his wolf form, they would most likely think he was a dog or possibly a coyote, not a wolf anyway. There weren't any wolves in the Portland area, only coyotes.

She heard the front door open and close. It seemed like it took him forever to turn off the security alarm before he came around through the backyard to the side gate, opened it, and whistled for her to let her know it was him and not anyone else. She raced into the yard and past him into the house.

He was wearing a pair of jeans, and she assumed that was the reason it had taken him longer to come for her.

She shifted. "You can get our clothes out of the shed since you're partially clothed. I'm going to get a glass of water for each of us." She was dying of thirst. She imagined he was too.

He soon returned with their clothes and they dressed and drank the water.

"Well, that was quite a run that I hadn't expected," she said, relieved they were safe for the moment but worried about who the shooters were and why they'd been shooting at them.

"Yeah, and not in a good way either." Adam already had his phone out and was calling the incident into the police. "This is Detective Holmes. My friend and I were sitting out back having a drink and heard gunfire in Forest Park, north of Carver's place." He gave the officer the address. "Yeah, thanks." He ended the call. "They're sending some officers, but I'll need to go with them to help search for the shooters. I know the park as well as the park rangers who work there. Even better than them, actually."

"From running all over the place as a wolf. Besides having the nose of a bloodhound."

"Exactly. I have to get my gun from the Hummer. After the police get here, I want you to drive to my house. I'll most likely be tracking these men down for a couple of hours, and you can get some sleep in the meantime. I'll get one of the officers who is helping with the manhunt drop me off at my house afterward. I have a spare house key, so you can take the one I have with the key to the Hummer." He grabbed his gun, flashlight, gloves, and baggies for evidence from the locked glove box and walked Sierra back inside.

"Are you sure you don't want me to stay with you and help you search for the shooters?" Sierra figured with both of them using their enhanced abilities, surely they would catch up with the bastards in less time than it took for one of them to find the shooters. The police could split up into two teams. She put their empty water glasses in the dishwasher.

"No. It's a police matter for now."

Sierra pulled Adam into her arms and kissed him. "Ever since I met you, I've wanted to do this with you, but then after I broke up with Richard, I was afraid it might seem too soon."

"Hell, no." Adam smiled and kissed her mouth back with feeling that said he was eager to get started on something deeper between them.

She smiled. "Good. Thanks for worrying about me, and you could be right. I'll stay with you at your place if it looks like Dover is behind the shootings tonight. Unless you think I'm too hot to handle."

Adam sighed but wasn't letting her go as he ran his hand over her back. "What if this is just someone else and has nothing to do with Dover? At least this time."

She patted Adam's chest. "Then we're back to me returning home tomorrow. Alone. But we're still dating."

"Hopefully, this has nothing to do with Dover and is just some random nutcases. Though I would still feel better if you stayed with someone. Me, preferably, of course. And don't worry about me. I'm trained to manage too-hot-to-handle cases."

She smiled.

"And yeah, we're definitely dating," he agreed.

It didn't take long after he called it in before they heard three cars pull up in front of the house. Adam said to Sierra, "Go to my place and get some sleep. You're welcome to any bed. I'll see you in the morning." He gave her his keys to the vehicle and house, and they walked outside together so she could leave and he would lead the search party.

She knew why he didn't want her out there. She wasn't a police officer, even though she worked for the bureau. She didn't have a gun if the shooters shot at her. But it was also because she wouldn't have the bureau's backing on her chasing down suspects like this. And it would be hard for her to explain why she could track the shooters and knew the area better than the park rangers—all because she was a wolf and had traveled so much farther and faster than humans could in all kinds of terrain in the time that she'd lived here.

Fine. They could deal with it. She was going to Adam's home to sleep and hoped they would find the shooters without her. She thought he was cute to offer any bed to her. So did he mean he was offering for her to join him in the master bed? She smiled, suspecting so. Was she taking him up on the offer? No way. Not for now, anyway. But she suspected, feeling the way she did about him because he was really the bright spot in her life, they would end up together in the same bed sooner rather than later.

Adam knew Sierra wasn't happy with him saying no to her helping track the men down, but he couldn't justify her being there. Not only that, but he was afraid the police officers wouldn't believe she could track the shooters better than they could. Not to mention he didn't want the shooters to shoot her, and she wouldn't be armed to shoot them back.

He just hoped he could locate the men and have them arrested. And he really hoped they weren't Dover's men. Just some random shooters. If they were Dover's men, that meant they must have followed them to the park, and hell, Sierra shouldn't be home alone. He immediately pulled out his phone and called Tori. "Hey, I know it's late, but—"

"What's wrong? What do you need me to do?"

"Sierra and I were at Carver's place when we heard shots fired."

"Someone was shooting at you while you were in your wolf coats," Tori said, figuring out what he was trying to say without him saying it.

"Yeah, and I'm with a team of police officers, trying to track down the shooters."

"More than one. So you want me to come out and help you track them?" Tori sounded ready and eager, and he felt fortunate that he had her for his new partner.

"No. I need you to get ahold of Sierra and go to my house, if you don't mind. She might need protection."

"I'm on it. And, Adam, we're partners. So if you need help, or any pack members need it, I'm there for you or them. Don't ever feel like it's an imposition."

"Thanks."

"I guess Sierra and I can't both come to look for the culprits, can we?" Tori still sounded like she would rather track down the shooters than babysit.

"Not Sierra. She's not a police officer and she may be their target."

"Dover's men," Tori said darkly.

"Yeah."

"Okay, I'll let you know what happens in a text message when I get to your house. But I'll give her a heads-up too."

"Thanks." Adam gave her his home address, thanked her again, and ended the call. He called Sierra to let her know that Tori was coming to stay with her until he got over there.

"Thanks for letting me know. Hope you find the bastards soon."

"I sure hope so too. They're taking a bite out of my dating time with you."

Then they ended the call and he continued walking on the trail with the other police officers for a good long while, then headed off trail where the shooters had gone—a man and a woman. And damn if the woman hadn't been one of the kidnappers who had been at Sierra's house. He figured this all had to do with Dover.

"Are you sure you know what you're doing?" one of the new officers asked him.

"Yeah, I do." It was understandable that the officer wouldn't have faith in Adam's ability to track the shooters as dark as the park was, though with his wolf's sight, he could see much better than they could armed with flashlights. He was using one too, not wanting to look like he had superpowers. But it was his nose that really clued him in as to where the shooters had gone. The smell from the gunpowder on their hands and that one, damn it, smelled of the woman who had helped to kidnap Melissa told Adam he was right on track. It also meant that Dover most likely was involved in this.

Three of the police officers knew he and Josh were some of the best trackers they had on the force, at least until Josh had retired. One of the two new guys who had questioned Adam hadn't been with the bureau that long. He was a transfer, not a rookie.

The other officers followed obediently along as if knowing Adam knew what he was doing, even the other new guy who followed their lead.

Then Adam kicked a shell casing, though he was sure only he could hear his boot hit the metal. He could smell the propellant from the gun in the vicinity, like dusty smoke, boiled eggs, but hitting the shell casing with his foot was still damn lucky. He shined his flashlight down at the ground and found the casing. "Found a shell casing!"

One of the officers bagged it for him.

The men began searching the area for others then and one said, "Found another!"

They combed through the area and found three more.

Adam was following his nose, searching trees for any more shell casings and hopefully a discharged bullet he could find. He was sniffing the area, smelling the pungent nitroglycerin after the ammo had been fired when he flashed his light on a tree and found a bullet lodged in the bark.

"Found a bullet!" Adam dug it out with a pen knife.

The terrain was rugged in this area, and they would be lucky if no one twisted an ankle as they moved forward, searching for any further evidence. Cell phone service wasn't available in several remote areas, so Adam hoped he would hear from Sierra or Tori before he lost his cell service and that he was still tracking the shooters out here and that they hadn't followed Sierra to his house instead. He couldn't help worrying about both women.

He smelled his and Sierra's wolf scents through this area. The shooters had been tracking them for a while as Adam and Sierra had run off, trying to avoid getting shot, and then the shooters had headed in a different direction. The man and woman must have lost sight of the wolves at that point, which Adam was grateful for. While Adam had been running, he had felt like the shooters could smell him and Sierra and had continued to track them all along and back to the house.

Adam tried his phone to see if he still had service. He didn't. *Damn it.* Tori might have tried to get ahold of him to tell him everything was all right then. At least he hoped so.

One of the officers glanced at him, raising his brows as if he thought Adam should be finding more clues. Adam didn't want to alienate any of the police officers by being arrogant about his abilities. Most of them were glad when he helped track someone down. Usually the skeptics were convinced after he located the culprits or the victims. But a couple of the officers gave him a hard time over it, wanting him to prove over and over again that his ability to locate people wasn't just a fluke. Now, he suspected they did it just to rib him about it. And he had no problem with that either.

Then he got a text and quickly checked it, glad he had cell service again.

Tori had texted: I'm at your house with Sierra. No one seems to have followed her here.

He texted back: Good. I'm still tracking the shooters. They lost our trail, so I'm still searching for where they went next.

Tori: Good luck with that. Sierra's taking a shower. I'm lying down on the couch.

He texted: Good show. I'll let you know when I'm on my way back.

Adam had thought of calling Josh to come and help him search for the shooters, but Josh wasn't with the bureau any longer and the park was closed for the night, though Adam was certain the police officers would welcome Josh's help. Adam thought about Ethan too, though he was DEA. He was also a wolf so he could help track down people.

The shooters had circled back toward Carver's house. They were still heading through the underbrush and not on any main path, then they finally broke through the brush and ended up on a main trail.

"They doubled back," Adam said.

"To…?" the new cop who had questioned Adam before asked.

"Toward the house where Sierra and I were having a drink when we heard the couple shooting. I have no idea what they were shooting at, but hunting isn't allowed in the park," Adam said. "I suspect whatever they were after took off and they chased it all over the place."

"And then back to where you first heard them," the officer said. "Most likely they had a vehicle parked nearby there."

Adam and the officers finally reached Carver's house and the back gate. He didn't smell any sign of the man or woman. For that, he was thankful. Still, he was careful when he entered the backyard but didn't smell either of the man's or woman's scents there either.

He locked the gate after the officers joined him. He let the other officers through the house, and then he set the alarm and locked the door.

He was disappointed they hadn't located the shooters and arrested them, but he was eager to get home to relieve Tori of guard duty so she could return home and get some sleep and he could protect Sierra himself.

"Hey, can one of you guys give me a lift back to my place?" Adam asked the officers.

"I'll take you," the transferred investigative officer quickly said. "Roland Paulson." He shook Adam's hand.

"Thanks, Roland. Adam Holmes. You started just a couple of days ago, didn't you?"

"Yeah. I was working out of New York City and needed a change of pace. I broke up with my girlfriend, and it was time to move on."

"I'm sorry to hear that," Adam said, then waved good night to the other officers, and Roland drove him home. Adam texted Tori to let her know he was headed back to his house.

Tori texted: See you soon.

"I'm sorry we didn't find the shooters. So how do you do it?" Roland asked Adam.

"Track them down?"

"Yeah, Evans was telling me you and Wilding, your former partner, could find the perps like you were a couple of bloodhounds on their trail."

"Just lucky, I guess." That was the problem with having the ability but not being able to share why they could do what they could do with others.

"Nah. I don't believe in luck. You've got something special going on. My aunt always knew when someone was going to call her at home. She just had this really uncanny ability. She would look up at the phone and everyone else would glance in that direction and it would ring. Like clockwork. Of course, that was before cell phones. She wouldn't own one of those. So how do you do it? The guys said you got some of your friends, who live out at a ranch, to help search for a missing six-year-old boy in Forest Park. That he'd gotten away from his parents on a hike and they couldn't find him anywhere. Everyone was looking for him, search parties everywhere, but when you and your friends arrived, you all took off into some really rough terrain and in no time at all you found him."

"Yeah, we were glad to. We had bad storms coming in and it was getting dark."

"Do you sense things out of the ordinary? Like my aunt did with the phone calls?"

"No, nothing like that." Adam appreciated that the officer didn't have any qualms about believing in paranormal abilities, but he knew if he told him the truth that he was a *lupus garou*—which he would never do—that would be a little too much for the officer to handle.

"It was too dark to really see if plants were trampled off trail or branches or twigs were broken, like old-time trackers would use to follow someone. And then pure dumb luck that you saw the first shell casing." The officer cast a glance in Adam's direction, and Adam suspected he believed that he had psychic powers or something like that.

"I just pay more attention to details, listen carefully, watch for movement, breathe in different smells. Like for instance, you ate a hamburger in the car a couple of days ago, you used a pine air freshener, you're wearing cologne, someone spilled milk in the car a few days ago, and a dog has been in the back seat. Oh, and you had ketchup on your french fries that probably came with the fast-food hamburger."

"Hell, you're good. You must have a really great sense of smell."

"I just really pay attention to the smells around me."

"Okay." But Roland didn't sound like he believed Adam.

Adam didn't blame him. If he were Roland, he would think it was unbelievable that Josh and he could find people like that.

"So what do you think they were shooting at?" Roland asked.

"Deer, elk, coyote, maybe." Adam should have mentioned to Tori that the woman who had come after them had been in on the kidnapping. Adam hadn't known that until he'd been chasing the woman's and man's scents, and it would have been difficult to suddenly come up with an explanation that he and Sierra had seen the culprit and she looked just like the sketch Sierra had done. It would have been great to have tied the kidnapper in with the shooter, but he didn't want to get tangled up in a fabrication with the police.

They would have asked him why he hadn't told the officers right away that he and Sierra had seen the men who were shooting off the weapons.

When Roland pulled into Adam's driveway, he thanked him.

"You're welcome. Good working with you." Then Roland drove off and Adam headed into his house, using his spare key.

Tori had her gun readied until she saw it was just Adam, then put it away. "Sierra wanted to wait up for you, but I told her there was no sense in both of us being up while waiting for you to return."

"Thanks, Tori. You're right about that and I'm glad she's getting some sleep. One of the shooters who fired at us was actually the woman involved in the kidnapping earlier today."

"But you didn't tell the police that, did you?"

"No. I told them Sierra and I were having a drink on Carver's back patio when we heard the shots fired. If anyone asks, we went to Carver's house to check on the place while he and his family are away on vacation."

"Okay, gotcha. I'm out of here, but if you have any trouble tonight, just call me. I'll be over in a jiffy."

"Thanks." Adam let Tori out and watched her get into her car and drive off. Then he locked up and walked past the guest bedroom. He wanted in the worst way to check on Sierra, to see that she was fine, but he didn't want to disturb her if she was a really light sleeper like he was. He retired to his bedroom to take a shower in the master bath and was soon in bed, gun sitting on his bedside table. He was worried about Sierra being alone tomorrow when she returned to her own home without anyone to watch out for her. Maybe, once he told her one of the shooters had been Melissa's kidnapper and in Sierra's home, she would change her mind about returning home, if she still had it in mind to do that.

He closed his eyes and was thinking about the day's events when he sensed someone in the room. He opened his eyes, looked over at the doorway, and saw Sierra standing there in a pair of aqua shorty pajamas. "Sierra?"

CHAPTER 15

"Did you catch the shooters?" Sierra had heard Adam's shower run, then quit. She'd drifted off, then woke when everything was quiet and was trying to go back to sleep, but she had to know if Adam and the other police officers had caught the shooters and then she could really sleep. When she peered into Adam's bedroom, she worried he might be sound asleep and she didn't want to wake him unnecessarily, especially if they had some problems tonight and they were both up again.

He opened his eyes and stared at her standing in the dark, woke enough to realize she was watching him, and called out her name in question. He sat up in bed, his chest bare, nicely sculpted as he turned on the bedside table lamp. "No, unfortunately not. But we did find some shell casings and a bullet at the park. Are you okay?"

"I woke and had to know, though I didn't mean to wake you."

"It's no problem." He explained everything to her.

She frowned. "So they must have known we were there."

"I don't know. It seems unlikely that the woman involved in stealing your car and kidnapping Melissa and taking her to your house just ended up in Forest Park when we did. They must have followed us to Carver's place, found a place to park, heard us leaving through the back gate, and then tried to follow us. But instead of discovering us as humans, they saw the two of us as red wolves and figured one of us was the dog that had guarded your hotel room. That's all I can figure."

She frowned. "And they still aimed to kill 'my' dog."

"Right. I don't know what they had in mind to do if they saw us in our human forms instead." He motioned to his bed. "Did...you want to join me?"

She smiled. "Thanks. But no." At least not tonight. "Well, I'm disappointed you weren't able to arrest them, and it's too bad we couldn't add a charge of them shooting at us too."

"Yeah, and if we caught them and ended up convicting them, at least the one for the kidnapping of the girl, can you imagine what would have happened?"

"Yep. Dover's cohort was caught shooting at the same phantom dog in my hotel room." She smiled. "I would have loved for that to happen." Then she frowned. "But only for the first time he shot at us. Not for it to happen again. Thanks for the protection and trying to locate these guys. It's way past time to go to bed. Good night."

"What about tomorrow? Where will you stay?"

Sierra knew he wanted her to stay with him longer because the woman who had been to her house had been shooting at them tonight, and she had said she would stay with Adam if they learned the shooters were Dover's people.

She gave a reluctant sigh. "Okay, I'll stay here. I'll have to pack a couple of bags at my house after work." She really had wanted to stay at her own home and not be a burden to anyone. She did consider how other bachelor males would view this, if things didn't work out between her and Adam, but she didn't want to drive in from the ranch if she stayed out there to have more protection. And she didn't want to impose on Josh and Brooke who were newly mated, though Josh could offer her protection too.

"Okay, that will work. 'Night, Sierra."

She smiled and headed back down the hall to her cozy guest bedroom. But when she settled down to sleep, all she could think about when she closed her eyes and tucked the blue comforter up to her chin was the sound of gunfire, the smell of the pristine woods, and the knowledge that men were chasing them with the intent to kill. She didn't think it would end there either, unless Adam got lucky, arrested the shooters, and sent them to jail.

She felt like she'd barely fallen asleep when she heard Adam on the phone, heading down the hall. He peeked into her room only wearing his boxer briefs and saw her eyeing him. "Hey, I've got to go in to work."

She groaned. She wouldn't have to go in for another two hours normally.

"I can call Josh to come by and watch over you, and then he can drop you off at work. I'm having your car taken out of impound and can have it delivered either here or at work, but it might be a while before someone can get to it."

"You can have my car delivered to the bureau." She really didn't want to have to go in before she had to. "I'll call Josh and see if he and Brooke don't mind me being over there until I need to go to work."

"Okay."

"What's the situation you have to deal with?" She grabbed her phone to call Josh.

"A police officer pulled a man over for speeding, and he looked like the description of one of the men who sold the stolen boat to Rivers. Rivers just picked the guy out of a lineup."

"It's amazing how these criminals can get away with so much, but then their downfall is disobeying traffic regulations."

Adam smiled. "That works well for us. Oh, and other good news—they found wig hair, about the color of your hair, in your car and house and on our kidnapped victim. No fingerprints on the steering wheel or doors."

"That's great news about the wig though. Now we just need to find the wig at Phyllis's residence—"

"Or fibers in her own car. Do you want some coffee?"

"Yeah, sure. One teaspoon of sugar and lots of milk or cream."

"You've got it." He went to the kitchen.

She hurried to get dressed, then called Josh on her cell phone. "Hey, I hate to bother you and Brooke like this, but—"

"Adam said you might need looking after if he couldn't do it. We'll be glad to have you over for as long as you need to be here."

She was glad Josh knew the story, but she wished she didn't have to impose on everyone. "He was called in early to work. I don't have to go in for another couple of hours"—at least that she knew for now—"and I don't have my car back yet. Adam could drop me off at your place and I could help you get ready to open the antique shop, and then, if you don't mind, you could drop me off at the bureau when I have to go in to work."

"Yeah, come on over. You can have breakfast with us. Adam too, if he has time."

"I don't think so, but I'll let him know. And thanks bunches."

"No problem. We'll both be glad to see you. And congratulations on getting the full-time position."

"Thanks." She still preferred the part-time job. Then they ended the call and she joined Adam in the kitchen. "Okay, Josh said for you to drop me off at their place, and he'll take me to work."

"Good show."

She sipped some of the coffee he had made for her and smiled. "Perfect."

"Good. I've got to get dressed."

"Josh invited you to breakfast."

"No time." Adam hurried off toward his bedroom.

"I told him you might not have any."

"Thank him for me for the offer though."

"I will. Oh, and what did he say when you told him he was replaced by a pretty she-wolf?"

"He laughed and didn't believe me at first. He thought I was pulling his leg." Drawers opened and shut in the bedroom.

"I was surprised too. I wondered how Josh would view it."

"Well, if it had just been a female detective, no big deal. But when she was also a wolf?" Adam chuckled. "Tori's been great to work with, and though she's a lot different in her methods than

Josh, she's eager to be a real help in the investigations. She's great at her job."

"I'm so glad for you. I know you were getting really inundated with work."

Adam came out of the bedroom and joined Sierra. "I sure was. Are you ready to go?"

"Yeah, sure." She went back to the guest bedroom and grabbed her purse. On the way to Josh and Brooke's house, she said, "So now one of the men who stole the boat has been arrested?"

"Yeah. He's claiming salvage rights."

"He can't do that." At least she didn't think so.

"No." Adam laughed. "Criminals will come up with anything to get out of a jail sentence. If they had turned the boat over to the police when they found it, that would have been one thing. We would have learned sooner that the man who owned it and his companions had gone missing. Taking possession of the boat and trying to sell it was a criminal act."

"Is there any tie between them and the drowned men?"

"We're asking anyone who saw the boat on the river that day to give us a call. We've had a lot of calls from boaters who saw the men one of the days before they drowned—they'd been fishing and were friendly to other boaters—but not anyone who saw the other men piloting the boat. Except for the officers of the River Patrol Unit. At least not for now. We're still trying to learn if there was any foul play. We didn't find any human blood on the boat at least. Just some traces of fish blood."

"Were there any fish onboard the boat?"

"No. And all the gear the men had onboard was still onboard. That's another way to realize a boat you're buying may be stolen—if personal stuff belonging to the owner is still onboard. Most people who sell a boat would clean it up and only leave items onboard that belong with the boat."

"Okay. If I bought a boat, I'd stick with a showroom boat dealer. Growing up, I loved to go out with Mom and Dad and Brad on boating trips. Dad had motorboats for a long time, and then he got sailboats. They're all fun, though for wolves, sailboats are really nice. Quiet. He always had a motor on one though, just in case we were becalmed. No wind meant we weren't going anywhere."

"That's for sure. I really enjoy my boat, but I get so busy with work, I don't have time for it. I even thought of selling it."

"Oh, no, you can't do that!"

Adam glanced at her and smiled. "Don't tell me that if I didn't have a boat, you wouldn't go out with me."

"Oh, for sure. I love boating. That's just what I need. A wolf boyfriend with a boat."

He smiled. "Does the size matter?"

"Oh, yeah, the bigger the better."

Adam chuckled. "We're still talking about boats, right?"

She laughed. She was glad they would be going out on it in a few days.

They reached Josh and Brooke's house, and both of them came out to greet her. Sierra was planning to do portrait sketches in a few weeks at Brooke's antique store for Brooke's customers for fun. She hadn't realized she would be working full-time now, so she might not be able to do it if she got called in to do a witness or dead-body sketch.

She loved picking up trinkets in Brooke's shop.

"Are you sure you can't grab a bite to eat with us?" Josh asked Adam before he left for work.

"You know how it is. I have to run in. Just keep her safe, will you?" Adam asked.

Josh smiled. "Yeah, you know it."

Sierra shook her head and then went inside with Brooke to help make breakfast. She sure hoped that the bad guys didn't target her friends next because she'd stayed there with them, if they were watching her every move.

Adam knew the look Josh had given him when he told him to keep Sierra safe meant he believed Adam was falling for the lady. Hell, he was. Here he had a she-wolf who could be his partner at work and his mate after hours, but Sierra was the one who kept his attention. He realized he'd wanted to jump in with both feet to date her the moment she had told Richard she was no longer dating him. And yet Adam had been reserved about it because he didn't want to go too fast with her in the event she needed some time before she wanted to seriously date someone again. He sure hadn't wanted to date her and learn later she was just on the rebound and there was nothing more to her interest in him than that.

Then he arrived at the bureau and met up with Tori.

"You look happy about something," Tori said. "Good night last night?"

"Uh, we didn't have any trouble, if that's what you mean."

"No, that's not what I meant, but I'm glad you didn't have any trouble with Dover's crew. Are we ready to talk to the men then?" she asked.

"Yeah. I'm ready. Let's get this done." He sure hoped they could wrap up this case, since they were working on so many others. But he mostly wanted to concentrate on the one involving Sierra.

"So where's Sierra?" Tori asked as if she realized no one was watching Sierra and she hadn't come to the bureau with Adam.

"She's at Josh and Brooke's house having breakfast. You'll have to meet them both. They're really good friends of ours."

"I'd love to meet them."

They walked into the interrogation room to speak with the first of the men—Lonnie Hicks.

"So what's your story?" Adam asked the man.

"Hey, man, I told that cop I was going the speed limit. He's wrong about that."

"Yeah, but I'm here to ask you about the boat you sold off Craigslist to a buyer." Adam knew Rivers hadn't bought it off Craigslist, but if that was the story he and Lonnie had concocted, Adam didn't want him to think he hadn't believed Rivers's story.

The guy's eyes widened.

"The one that didn't belong to you."

"Hey, I told that other cop what the deal was on that. It was just sitting idly in the water and I rescued it. It's the law of the sea. Salvage rights. I claimed it. No one else did."

"And you didn't call the police to let them know about it. Did you even think that someone who owned the boat might have been in trouble?"

Lonnie leaned back in his chair like he wasn't worried about them charging him with anything.

"Did you have anything to do with the owner of the boat drowning in the Willamette?" Adam asked.

The guy's brows shot up. "Hell, no. Is that what this is all about? The boat was just sitting on the water when my friends and I were out fishing. We didn't see nobody on the boat, so we moved in closer. We hollered out, thinking maybe the owner was in the cabin getting some—" The man glanced at Tori. "You know, the good stuff with some pretty blond. But no one answered, so I climbed aboard and there wasn't a soul on the boat."

"And like I said, you didn't bother to call the police or River Patrol to tell them you found a boat with no one on it. It's not like the boat was badly damaged and you had to haul it out of the river."

"How many times I got to tell you people, it's salvage rights, pure and simple. Finders, keepers. If the owner fell off his own damn boat and drowned"—Lonnie shrugged—"he shouldn't be on the water."

"He's dead."

"Well, see there? He's dead."

"And you had nothing to do with it?" Adam asked.

"Hell, no."

"Or the other two dead men who were on the boat with him?" Tori asked, taking notes.

Lonnie's eyes grew bigger again. "Hell, no. You mean you think my friends and I had something to do with the men who died because they couldn't handle a boat that size on the river? No way. We were just fishing."

"And selling a drowned man's boat. Who were your friends on the other boat?"

At that last question, Lonnie wouldn't say.

Sierra wondered what she would have to do today once Josh drove her to work. She hoped she had more witness sketches to do today rather than dead-body sketches. Maybe she would get used to it. She wanted to love going into work like she did before. If her sketches helped identify bodies, she supposed she would feel as useful as when she did witness sketches. She guessed it was because with witnesses, she had immediate feedback from them. They were glad she might be able to help them. She had to remind herself that the drowned men's sketches helped identify them to the boat owner's wife at least.

"Adam's really glad you've taken the full-time position, by the way, if he hasn't already said so," Josh told her on the drive to the bureau.

"He has. Thanks for telling me." Adam had only mentioned it about a hundred times. And she was glad he appreciated her for taking on Willy's caseload.

"It's not just because you're a wolf and a friend," Josh continued as if he wasn't getting his point across.

She glanced at him.

Josh's ears turned a little red. "Uh, he's really glad you're not seeing that guy out of state any longer."

"Richard. Me too."

"Adam's a great friend."

She smiled at Josh. And Josh was a great friend to him for trying to help her see that Adam was interested in her. She already knew that from the way Adam smiled and kidded with her. She didn't need Josh telling her that. She loved teasing the guys. Josh was like her brother and she adored him for it.

"You're going boating with us on Sunday, right? My parents always had a boat when I was growing up, but I haven't been on one in eons," Sierra said.

"I'll have to check with Brooke and make sure she doesn't have other plans. Her shop is closed on Sundays, and she likes to catch up on work at the store."

"Okay." She hoped Josh and Brooke hadn't already told Adam they were going but were now thinking of backing out because they wanted to allow her and Adam time to get to know each other.

Josh pulled into the parking lot at the bureau.

She got out of Josh's vintage Ferrari, a gift from Brooke's inheritance. All the police officers and detectives at the bureau who were either coming or going had to make a detour and check out the car.

"Thanks for the ride, Josh."

"Did you need a ride home tonight?"

"No, thanks. My car should be released to me soon." She saw it in the parking lot. "Oh, there it is. Thanks again for breakfast too."

"You're welcome."

"And don't you say anything to Adam about him having to keep his boat if he doesn't feel he's getting enough use out of it."

Josh smiled and then one of the officers shook his hand. "Good to see you here, showing off your Ferrari again."

Josh laughed and Sierra smiled, then headed for the building just as Adam and Tori were exiting it.

"Come on, Sierra. We've got a job for you," Adam said.

"Dead or alive?"

Tori laughed. Adam sighed.

"Dead. Gotcha," Sierra said. This was going to be a long day.

CHAPTER 16

That night, Adam took Sierra out for a steak dinner, since she'd had her heart set on good red meat—totally a wolf thing—and then to a movie. He wanted to really show her he could take off work and they'd have a great time. He'd even dressed up a bit, no suit since he had to wear one at work, but no jeans on his date. And Sierra was wearing a sundress and looked as pretty as could be.

He had no intention of talking about anything work-related either.

"This is really nice," she said, glancing at the overhead crystal lights bouncing off the rack of wineglasses separating their booth from part of the serving area.

"Yeah, it has the best steaks and great atmosphere, right here in Portland. I thought tomorrow night, if you'd like, we could go to that"—he leaned over and said for her hearing only—"wolf-run restaurant that has live music and dancing."

"Oh, absolutely. You know, I love just doing things with you at your place or mine too. We don't always have to go out, but this is so nice."

"I feel the same way. I love doing either." Adam liked doing both. Despite their busy workdays, he found going out just as relaxing with her as sitting at home and grilling dinner on the grill or ordering pizza delivery.

He wondered if her ex-boyfriend had preferred sitting at home and just chilling with her. There was no way he was bringing up the ex though.

Once their steaks arrived—she got the petite filet mignon, and he went for the T-bone—with glasses of red wine, they settled back and ate their meals, neither of them talking about the cases they were working on. And he was glad about that.

"I have to tell you I'm so glad I came here to live and to join your pack, all at Brad's insistence. He knew I would love it here. And he knew I needed to give my ex-boyfriend up to find someone else."

"I wanted that to happen too. Brad was always showing the guys your picture, whether you were playing with him in the surf on Galveston Island or wearing your uniform and meeting up with him when he came to visit you while he was still in the military. He had all of us interested in you way before you ever arrived here. Then here you are, but you're still dating an out-of-state guy."

"Yeah, I was just having a hard time letting go and getting on with my life. I knew I needed to. And I think the fact that he would never come here to see me should have clued me in that it wasn't going to work out between us. That I wasn't his priority, but I was supposed to continue to see him like he was all that mattered to me." She smiled and took a sip of her wine.

"If you don't mind me saying so, he was a fool to let you go."

"No, I don't mind you saying so at all. Brad, and even my parents, had often said I should have ended things with him before I even left Texas. I guess I just had to finally come to terms with it and let go."

"Well, I'm glad for us that you did."

After they finished dinner, Sierra asked, "So what did you want to see tonight at the movies?" She would have been just as happy to go home and watch something on TV, but she hadn't been to a movie theater on a date in eons.

"Thriller? Mystery? Horror? Animated feature? That's all they have," Adam said, looking up the movies. He showed them to her, and she picked the thriller.

"It seems it goes with our line of work."

He smiled. "You'd think you'd want to watch something else then."

"Nah, maybe we can get a clue, something we've missed, by watching how the other detectives solve their crimes."

"You know, I would have been a skeptic about that theory until it worked for me one time. A man had taken a woman hostage on an airplane so that he could get her bank president dad to open a safety deposit box the kidnapper wanted to get into. After I watched the old movie, I realized the case I'd been working on was eerily similar. So you just never know," Adam said.

"See there? I knew it."

At the theater, they had buttered popcorn and bottles of water and snuggled together. This was sure nice, and unless he objected to her being in bed with him tonight, Sierra was joining him there. The movie was great, an edge-of-the-seat thriller, and she realized he was just as tense as she was through some of the wilder scenes. And the ending was a happily-ever-after, making it the perfect movie for her.

"That's what I like to see. Bad guys lose, good guys win! And the hero got the heroine in the end."

"Yeah, now that's the part I have to really learn how to do."

As they headed out to his SUV, she held onto his hand. "So far, you're doing all the right things to make that happen."

"Good. You let me know if I get offtrack. So about running as wolves tonight—"

"Let's skip it tonight. I don't know about you, but I'm happily tired tonight and I want to return to your house and get ready for bed."

Even though she'd made arrangements today to have video security installed at her home and the window had been replaced, she was staying with Adam tonight. She realized after her home had been broken into, she didn't feel comfortable about staying there on her own. Well, and also because they hadn't apprehended Dover's girlfriend and the other accomplice yet.

"That works for me."

When they arrived home, he had her wait out in the Hummer—just in case someone had broken into *his* home this time. They really needed to catch these people and put them all in jail. She saw a bunch of lights go on inside after that.

Then Adam came out to the vehicle and she hurried to get out. "No problem?"

"No problem." He walked her into the house and locked the door.

"Did you offer me your bed to sleep in tonight?" Sierra asked.

He raised a brow. "With me in it?"

She chuckled. "What? You think I would make you give me your bed and kick you out of it?"

He smiled. "The bed is all yours, with or without me in it, but even better with me in it."

"Okay, I'll take you up on it."

He appeared thrilled!

She smiled, glad for it. "I'm going to take a shower and brush my teeth and join you in a few minutes."

She went to the guest room where her clothes were, grabbed her pajamas, and went into the guest bathroom to take her shower. It didn't take her long to shower, dry off, slip into her shorty pajamas, blow-dry her hair, brush her teeth, and head into Adam's bedroom.

He had already showered and was in bed, under the covers, just like last night, but waiting for her this time.

She sighed, glad she was finally going this far with Adam and not waiting any longer. Even though she hadn't been dating him all these months, she'd worked with him, played with him and the rest of the wolves at various wolf socials, and she knew what she was doing.

As soon as she climbed under the light covers with him, she moved in close so she could snuggle with him. As wolves, it was different for them than dating humans they knew they wouldn't end up mating.

They couldn't consummate the relationship unless they were going to be mated wolves for life. So this was just working up to what might happen in the future. Near future even, if they decided they were ready for a mating. She was ready—as in wanting to settle down, have a mate and some kids. She'd really wanted that for a long time, but with Richard, it wasn't going to happen. She felt completely different about Adam.

She moved closer to kiss him, and he pulled her into his arms and kissed her on the mouth. He appeared to want to get this "game" underway. She was glad that he wasn't holding back.

He was wearing pajama shorts, and she was just working up to this. But once they began kissing, she knew this was what she wanted. Unconsummated, of course. She was open to much more as things progressed.

He slid his hands over her buttocks, the cotton jersey pants sliding over her bottom. Hmm, she was ready to take them off and toss them aside. But she was enjoying slow and easy too. She slid her hand over his backside and felt his firm buttocks through the plaid cotton shorts he was wearing.

They continued to kiss, his masculine lips on her mouth, firm, warm, moving with sensual caresses. And she was kissing him back with the same measured kisses, luxuriating in the feel of him, the intimacy shared between them.

Then he slid his hand over her pajama T-shirt, and she felt her nipple erect and sensitive to the palm of his hand massaging one of her breasts. Oh, man, his touching her made her feel exquisite.

She nuzzled his neck and throat and kissed his mouth again,

her hand caressing his chest, his nipple, feeling the hardened nub against the softness of her palm.

He kissed her again and she reached down to touch his arousal and felt it jump. She slid her hand under his waistband and wrapped her fingers around his full-blown erection and stroked. He slid his hands up her shirt and caressed her breasts. His warm skin against hers felt so good. He began to pull up her shirt and kissed her breasts, then slipped her shirt the rest of the way over her head and tossed it to the floor.

Then she was sliding his shorts down his hips and he kicked them aside. Before he removed her shorts, he cupped her buttocks and pulled her close and kissed her lips again, her breasts pressed against his bare chest, and she felt heavenly. What a lovely way to end the lovely evening she'd spent with him.

He slid his hands beneath the waistband of her shorts and held onto her bare buttocks in a possessive, endearing way, then he removed her shorts and they were both perfectly naked.

He just held her close for a moment, their mouths kissing again, enjoying the nakedness of their bodies pressed together. Then he skimmed his hand down her body to begin stroking her feminine nub and she was caught up in the moment, the way his fingers caressed her, the way he kissed her forehead, her mouth, her chin, her throat. She soaked in the heady feeling as he continued to stroke her. She caressed his arms, the muscles taut as he smiled down at her, his eyes lust-filled, the musky scent of their sex adding to the intimacy. Pheromones were busy at work, telling them to take this all the way, to boldly go where they'd never gone before.

And she was so glad they were doing this now. He gently bit her lip, and she nuzzled his mouth with hers and then tongued him and he tongued her back, the whole time continuing to caress her nubbin. She felt the end coming, but she was certain it would only be the beginning between them.

"Oh, damn, yeah," she cried out as the feeling of ecstasy washed over her, ripples of climax still pulsing through her, making her feel as though the earth had moved for her.

Then she pushed him onto his back and kissed and licked his nipples. She settled onto his thighs and began to stroke his arousal. He caressed her thighs with his hands, drawn under her spell, his face showing the need to finish this, concentration, tension, pleasure. She kept up her strokes, increasing the firmness and speed until he was striving for the end like she had been. And then he exploded, and she smiled. She continued to stroke him until he was blissfully spent. She planned to get off him and let him clean himself up, but he pulled her against him and got her all wet and sticky.

"Now why did you do that?" she asked, smiling at him.

"You know why."

She chuckled. "You are afraid to be alone in the shower tonight."

"You are so right."

He kissed her and she kissed him back. He was fun to be with, even when he was finished making love to her.

She went with him to his bathroom this time, and they showered together, though they didn't wash their hair this time. She helped him dry off while he was drying her off. He made everything intimate and exciting between them, she realized.

Now it was time to snuggle with him before work started all over again.

She cuddled next to Adam, thinking this was truly a new beginning for her in all ways. She was looking forward to going to Tori's house and helping her unpack boxes in three days. She hoped she and Adam could really make a difference for her. And boating on Sunday. But tomorrow night, they would go to the wolf dance club, and they'd have to come up with some plans for Thursday and Friday nights too.

Before she was ready for it, the alarm went off and she and Adam had to go into work. She was glad he hadn't had to go in early this morning, and they had been able to wake up together. They had breakfast and then drove to the bureau in their separate vehicles.

"What time did you want us to drop by on Saturday to help you unload your boxes?" Adam asked Tori as they returned to the bureau after a long, exhausting hump day.

"Let's make it eleven. We can start unpacking, order meals, have lunch, and unpack some more. There's no sense in everyone having to get up so early. Oh, and Ethan, Josh and Brooke, and our coroner said they would drop by to help. Josh's brother, Maverick, said he would too."

Adam shook his head. "Don't tell the whole pack, or you'll have *all* the bachelor males at your place trying to outdo each other."

Tori laughed. "That's the good thing about having more bachelor males in the pack. There are more to choose from."

Sierra joined them outside. "Don't tell me you have more work for me." She looked done in.

"No, we were just talking about what time we need to drop by Tori's place on Saturday." Adam told Sierra who all was coming.

Sierra smiled at Tori. "That sounds like a lot of fun."

"You bet. See you tomorrow at work," Tori said, waved at them, then headed for her car.

"I'll follow you home so you can pack up some more clothes that you might need," Adam said to Sierra.

"I was thinking that maybe I would be all right at home—"

"You're coming home with me." The words slipped out of Adam's mouth before he could stop himself.

Thank God she laughed and wasn't annoyed at his knight-defending-the-damsel declaration. "All right then," she said, still smiling as she got into her car.

At least Tori hadn't heard him say that, or he was sure *she* would have given him a lecture.

He followed Sierra to her house and hoped she hadn't had anyone break in again. He parked behind her car in the driveway, then hurried to get out of his Hummer to go inside her home first and make sure everything was safe.

She unlocked the door, then stepped aside for him while he had his gun in hand and moved quietly into the house. He didn't think anyone would be inside her house right now, but it was better to be safe than run into trouble, especially since Sierra was unarmed.

He checked all the rooms, one by one, recalling when he had been wearing only her sweatpants while they were having a steak dinner when her boyfriend arrived. He smiled, glad the guy was out of the picture. Richard hadn't known when he had a good thing. He sure as hell didn't deserve Sierra.

Adam finished looking through all the rooms and found that Sierra's laundry room window had already been replaced. He didn't smell any new smells. He went out back and no one new had been out there either.

He returned to the front door where Sierra was still standing, arms folded across her chest, looking annoyed. Not at him, he didn't think. But at the situation. He knew how she felt—violated. Her home probably didn't feel safe any longer.

"Everything's clear."

"Okay, thanks." She headed into the bedroom.

"Did you need my help with anything?"

"Why don't you see if there's anything in the fridge or freezer that we could have for dinner tomorrow night."

"Sure. I'll do that." He looked in her fridge and found more corn on the cob and hamburger in the freezer. "Hey, how does corn on the cob and hamburgers on the grill sound to you?"

"Sounds like a winner," she said from her master bedroom. "And in the bread box, I have hamburger buns."

"Okay, got them."

She joined him in the kitchen, hauling a suitcase. She'd changed into khaki shorts, a tank top, and sandals. He smiled. She looked like she was ready to take the boat out for a spin.

"I know we were going to the wolf restaurant tonight, but why don't we skip that and grill the hamburgers tonight."

"Yeah, sure, that works for me."

She glanced at her artwork that was all torn up.

He hated seeing it like that and the upset in her expression. He came over and rubbed her shoulders. "What can I do for you?"

She sighed. "When I have time, I'll redo them. Nothing I can do right now. I packed a lot more than I'll need. I feel more settled now that I have the security installed and I can return home."

He was thinking more like when she had no more trouble—when the guys they were after were in jail, or dead—then she could return home.

"Hey," Sierra said as she wheeled her suitcase out to her car. "I don't want you to think anything of it but if…well, Josh says something about you not selling your boat anytime soon so you could take me out, ignore him."

Adam smiled at her. He loaded the groceries and her bag into her car.

She shrugged. "We were just talking, not about you. But somehow, I mentioned boating, and well, just saying…"

Adam chuckled. "Okay. Thanks for the heads-up. I'll follow you over to the house." He knew Josh was thinking Adam was making a play for Sierra.

When they arrived at the house and parked in the garage, she hesitated to pull in too, but he'd made room for her. He motioned for her to pull her car in. That way, Dover's men wouldn't know it was there unless they had eyes on the place, and they couldn't do anything to it again unless they alerted him and Sierra. Once she parked in the garage, he grabbed her bag for her, and she got the groceries. They went inside, and he locked the door.

"I'll take the hamburgers and corn on the cob out and grill them," he said.

"I'll be out in a minute. I'm going to put my clothes away. You know how it is. Before you're ready for it, you get called to go back into work. I don't want to be trying to figure out where all my stuff is if I have to dress in a hurry."

"I don't blame you. When I have to take trips, I like to unpack first thing too. Feel free to use my closet for your things, and I have a couple of spare drawers you can use." He started cooking the corn first, and after she finished unpacking, she found a bottle of burgundy and poured them each a glass of wine.

"I would have liked to run as a wolf tonight at Forest Park, if we hadn't been shot at there before." She offered him one of the glasses of wine.

He took a sip and put the hamburgers on the grill. "We could drive out to Leidolf's ranch and run there, or to Josh and his brother Maverick's reindeer ranch."

She was watching Adam turn the corn on the cob on the grill and smiled. "Let's run at Leidolf's ranch. We'll still be out at the ranch earlier tonight than if we had to wait until after ten to visit the park."

"Right." He was glad she wanted to run as a wolf tonight. He had really enjoyed running with her the other night, despite the shooting incident. But he was afraid she might be a little spooked about it, just like he thought she was about staying in her home alone. He flipped the burgers on the grill.

She took another sip of wine. "I asked Josh about them going with us boating on Sunday, and he said he had to clear it with Brooke first. I was under the impression they had already both said yes."

"I, um, I'll check with them. I thought they were going too."

"I'm going to call my brother and make sure they're going. I hope everyone isn't canceling."

Adam had thought everyone wanted to go so Sierra wouldn't feel like she was on a date, so he was surprised Josh was waffling about going now. Maybe he hadn't okayed it with Brooke yet. Adam knew Josh loved to boat.

"Hey, Brad. I'm putting this on speakerphone. I'm just checking with you and Janice. You're going boating with Adam and me on Sunday, aren't you?" Sierra asked.

"Yeah, we'll be there."

"What about your sister-in-law?"

"Dorinda made some other plans."

"Okay, we'll see you Sunday then."

"See you both then."

Sierra sighed, sounding relieved.

"Are you afraid of going out with me alone?"

Sierra laughed. "I was afraid everyone would drop out because they thought we should have alone time. But it will be fun having a bunch of our friends and family on the trip."

"I agree." Then someone else could captain the boat and Adam could visit some with Sierra. Otherwise, he was the designated driver the whole time. He served up the hamburgers and corn on the cob, and they began adding condiments to their buns the way they liked them.

She slathered mayonnaise on her bun, and he added a light coating on his. They both dabbed a bit of mustard and ketchup on their buns and a couple of pickle slices on top of their burgers.

"Cheese?" he asked, forgetting that others liked cheese on their burgers.

"No, I'm good, thanks."

They took their plates to the chairs on the patio and sat down to eat.

She smiled and took a bite of her burger. "Hmm, this is really great. I never would have thought I would be having dinner on the grill after work. Except for party functions, of course, I don't get to have grilled fare very often."

"It's been a lot of fun for me too." And a way to show off he could grill meals, especially since she seemed to enjoy them.

"This is going to be fun boating in the summer."

He was thrilled she was thinking of continuing to date him.

"Maybe in the fall we could plan to take the boat out," she said.

"Yeah, anytime we're off and you want to take the boat out, I'm game." Now that was what he liked to hear.

"Good." She took a bite of her corn and smiled. "Hmm, this is so good." She sighed.

"Man, I sure am glad I still have my boat." Adam felt he was winning the competition.

She laughed. "Did you tell Leidolf we're going down there to run as wolves tonight?"

"Uh, no, I'll do that." He texted Leidolf to tell him they were coming for a run in about an hour. They didn't have to give him a heads-up, but they did if they could, just to let him know when anyone was going to the ranch so they would be prepared.

Every once in a while, people would come onto the ranch wanting to photograph it or the surrounding scenery or wildlife. Or hunters wanting to hunt. Once, someone even asked to buy the ranch and all its acreage. No way. Not with all the wolves that called it home. So they had to be watchful that uninvited people didn't show up there and see the pack members running as wolves.

Leidolf texted back: Sounds like you're making progress. Good show.

Adam smiled and texted: I'm working on it.

And then he set his phone on the table.

Sierra took another sip of her wine. "So did you tell him we're dating?"

"That I'm working on it."

She chuckled. "We're *way* beyond working on it."

CHAPTER 17

Sierra thought Adam was sexy and fun to be with, and she was glad she was dating him.

At least their wolf run would be safe tonight. She was looking forward to it and having nothing but fun, instead of trying to escape from shooters as fast as they could run.

After they enjoyed their meal, they drove down to Leidolf and Cassie's ranch. Sierra saw Adam glance at his rearview mirror and side-view mirror on the way there, and she finally asked, "Is anyone following us?"

"Maybe, maybe not. I keep thinking someone is but then they turn off on another road. If someone is tailing us, if they think to follow us onto the ranch, they'll have a welcome committee." Adam gave Leidolf a call on Bluetooth. "Hey, it's Adam. We're on our way to the ranch. We'll be there in about fifteen minutes. If anyone's following us, give them a welcoming that will make them wish they hadn't entered the private ranch."

"I'll be sure to arrange it."

"Oh, and arrest them, because if they are part of Dover's gang, we need to take them in."

Leidolf laughed. "That's supposed to be your job, Detective. See you in a few minutes with men at the ready."

"I'll sketch a picture of the bad guys if I get a good look at them and they get away." Sierra loved the pack. The packmates were always there for each other whenever they needed them to be.

Leidolf said, "That's what I love about the wolves on the police force. Always there to help take down the bad guys."

They ended the call, and it didn't take long for Adam and Sierra to arrive at the ranch. Two pickup trucks were sitting on either side of the gate with two men apiece carrying rifles, waiting for trouble. Two vehicles following Adam's Hummer on the road continued on past the ranch entrance.

Sierra shook her head. "You know, we could have driven onto the ranch, and then if someone was tailing us, they could have tried following us and we could have nabbed them then."

"True, though I suspect they might have looked for another less obvious approach since 'No Trespassing' and 'Private Property' signs are posted all over the place. Leidolf also has security cameras hanging up all over. Though there's so much acreage, they could still slip by unnoticed if they tried to sneak in someplace else. If they see the firepower at the gate, they'll know we're protected at least. I really want to run with you without feeling threatened by Dover and his cohorts tonight."

"I agree."

Adam rolled down his window and waved at the men. "Thanks for helping out."

"You got it!" one of the men said, the others agreeing.

Adam drove up to the main ranch house while the men remained at the gate as guards, probably until Adam and Sierra returned home.

Several homes were also located at the top of the mesa that overlooked the forested and pasture lands as far as the eye could see. The homes up there were for pack-member families that lived and worked on the ranch. A bunkhouse housed bachelor males who worked on the ranch.

Brad and his mate, Janice, came out to greet them, and to Sierra's surprise, her mom and dad, Kirk and Rhonda Redding, were there too. Sierra couldn't believe they had come from San Antonio for a visit and hadn't told her. Brad hadn't either.

Her parents both gave her a hug. And then so did Brad and Janice. Sierra and Brad's parents were just as blond and blue-eyed as Brad was, and she was glad to see them.

"When were you going to tell me you were coming here?" Sierra was thinking maybe she and Adam should have gone to the reindeer ranch where they would have had more privacy for a wolf date. Though they also had a lot more security with all the pack members living here.

But she was really glad to see her parents too.

"We need to celebrate that you're working full-time for the bureau now, Sierra," her mother said, hugging her again.

But her father frowned and folded his arms across his chest. "Brad told us you were having trouble with the man you put behind bars."

Sierra gave her brother a disgruntled look. He wasn't supposed to worry their parents over it. That was why they had come? What were they going to do about it?

Leidolf and Cassie came out too. Cassie gave Sierra a hug. "The two of you go on and run and have a good time. We're going to have some wolves and some men go with you, but not close by where they'll be intrusive."

"I'm going," Brad said.

That was a given.

"We just want to make sure that no one comes onto the property with the intent to hurt you," Leidolf said.

"We'll be so far from the main road, we shouldn't have any issues," Adam said, "but we appreciate the backup. And if anyone sees these men trespassing, have our security take them into custody and turn them over to the police."

Wouldn't that be a great way to wrap this all up? Then Sierra could return home unafraid that anyone would trouble her again, though she had to admit she was enjoying Adam's company—dinners and working with him. The situation had rapidly changed between them now that she was free to date him.

But with her parents here visiting, she needed to spend some time with them too. Her parents were eyeing Adam. She sighed.

Okay, so they wanted to know what was up with him too, she figured.

"We're going to the waterfall," Adam said, which was his way of telling the others that he *was* dating her. That was a romantic spot for courting wolves. For kids to play in too, and families to go to, but when it was a single couple, it was a dating spot.

Sierra enjoyed being around Adam during work and during wolf gatherings—though she was always teasing Josh about one thing or another and not Adam so much. She felt like a sister to Josh and his brother, Maverick, but to Adam?

She hadn't *ever* felt sisterly toward him.

"You can change at our house," Janice said.

"Thanks." Sierra headed for the house and Adam followed her lead.

When they were inside, she went into one of the guest rooms. Adam waited for her to leave the room as a wolf, and then he went into the room and stripped and shifted. Even though everyone was still outside, he must have felt the need to give her some privacy.

She waited for him, and as soon as he left the room, she wagged her tail and licked his face. He nuzzled her face with his, and then they ran out through the wolf door, her first, him following.

"Wait for me," Brad said and headed back inside the house to strip and shift.

Her parents were still talking with Janice and Leidolf and Cassie.

Sierra wouldn't think of running off without her brother and the other men watching their backs. Not that she thought they really needed it this time. But it didn't hurt to be sure.

Before long, a couple of men armed with rifles climbed into a black four-wheel-drive Jeep Gladiator and headed out. Then the wolves spread out and Sierra and Adam took off for the falls.

She was feeling much more carefree again and enjoying the

run. If anyone had followed them from Adam's house to the ranch, they weren't going to be able to see them after sunset at nine tonight unless they were carrying flashlights, and then the wolves could easily see them. At least that was what she hoped. Unless the men had infrared goggles, but she suspected they weren't that well equipped.

Then again, how did they see them in the park last night?

She tried to put the possibility of the shooters following them here out of her mind and just enjoy the time she was spending with Adam. Every once in a while, she caught a glimpse of her brother in the woods running as a wolf, and she saw another wolf farther off on the opposite side of them.

She hadn't been to the waterfall before this. She guessed it was because she didn't think it would be fun coming on her own or with random wolves. But now, running with Adam, she was eager to see what it was like.

They finally reached the pool of water, which was surrounded by a rocky beach on three sides and had large stones in the middle with ferns surrounding the falls. She wanted to come here during the day too. She couldn't believe she hadn't come before this to see the beauty of the falls, despite who she might have gone with or if she had come here on her own. They were just gorgeous. The sound of the water rushing over the cliff and cascading down into the clear water made her feel relaxed and happy. But being here with Adam made it even better.

He was sitting on the bank of the pond and watching her reaction to seeing the waterfall. She closed her gaping mouth and smiled, showing off all her wicked wolf teeth. She woofed at him, telling him she was glad he brought her here. He howled.

She would have laughed but instead bounded into the cold pond, sending water flying everywhere, and headed straight for the waterfall. She didn't hear Adam joining her, and when she reached the waterfall, she looked back at him.

He was still sitting there on the rocky bank, watching her as if he took delight in seeing her explore the pond and waterfall first.

A fish jumped into the water next to her, and she pounced on it—a natural reaction to do so while wearing her wolf coat. She immediately released it when she realized what she'd done, not wanting to take a fish home between her teeth. Glancing at Adam, she smiled to see him still watching her, looking amused in his wolf way.

She suspected if the roles were reversed, he would have done the same thing. As soon as she moved closer to the waterfall, a fine spray cloaked her in mist, and she dashed through the waterfall to the other side of it. When she turned, she saw Adam swimming in the deeper part of the pond to reach her. She woofed, thrilled he was joining her.

He swam into the shallower part and dove through the waterfall to reach her, then shook off the excess water on his fur all over her. He quickly looked at her as if he knew he'd made a mistake after he had already done it. She wanted to laugh. She nipped his ear instead. He licked her face and nuzzled her cheek with his.

Yeah, she was staying with him for now and the foreseeable future. If he was agreeable.

Her brother howled, interrupting the intimate wolf moment, but she knew he must have been alarmed when he didn't see them at the waterfall and thought he'd lost them.

She howled to let him know where they were.

He howled back to tell them he understood and he was glad they were safe.

She nuzzled Adam and thought it would be fun to sit on the shore of the pond and watch the sunset reflect in the pool. Then she dashed back through the waterfall and swam through the deeper section of the pool. She climbed out onto the bank, shook off the water from her outer coat, and turned to watch Adam paddling back to shore to join her.

But then he moved in a different direction and she wondered what he was up to. He got out of the water, shook off, smiled at her, then trotted over to join her. She smiled. Good. He had learned. Yeah, they shook off the water from their coats, a natural reaction, and they might not think about who was within reach of the shower of water, but—as wolves dating—it was a nice thing to think of. Now, if the wolves were mated and had been together for a while? Old instincts were hard to break.

She lay down to watch the sun setting and he lay next to her, their bodies pressed together in a way that said they were more than just on a jaunt to see the waterfall.

This was so nice after a long, hard day. And being with Adam made it so much more special. Shoot. What about all the guys out guarding them? They would surely want the time to be home with their families or doing something fun or productive instead of having to serve on guard duty. She lifted her head to look at the sun. It was going down, but she didn't think she had ever seen it sink below the treetops so slowly. A watched kettle came to mind.

She sat up.

Adam shifted. "What's wrong? I didn't hear anything that could pose trouble, did you?"

She shook her head, sighed, shifted. "I wanted to see the sunset on the pool of water, but it means everyone guarding us can't be home with their friends and family."

"They're watching the sun set too."

Okay, so she would buy that. Relaxing again, she shifted and lay back down and he did the same, snuggling up close to her, keeping her warm in the chilly night air. Now this was nice.

The sun was really beginning to set now, the oranges and pinks and yellows reflecting off the pond and the waterfall—and she wished she could have taken a picture.

And then it was gone, the blue hour upon them when there was still light, the sky not totally black. She and Adam licked each other's mouths, then Adam howled to say they were headed back to the ranch, and of course she had to howl too.

A chorus of howls sounded off—their guards in wolf coats. And then she heard the howls from farther away, at the ranch house and other homes. She smiled at Adam, loving the camaraderie of the pack.

Sierra raced off toward the ranch homes and Adam dove after her. She had planned to run straight back to the ranch and not take any deviations to make the fastest time possible so everyone could enjoy their families, but Adam had other plans. He was chasing her!

And that made her happily nervous—just an instinctual behavior of trying to keep out of the aggressor's path, even though she knew they were just playing. She darted off to her left and then to the right, but he was quick and matched her move for move.

He was so close to nipping at her tail that she thought of turning on him. But she was certain if she did, she wouldn't manage to do it fast enough to get out of his path and he would run right into her broadside. This wasn't working for her, so she turned right, then quickly turned left and rounded on him. He broadsided her. Knocked her down. She knew he would. She wanted to laugh.

He paused for a second, waiting to see her response—be mad at him, ready for retaliation, or amused. She had a brother, and she was used to going on the offensive in a second. She got to her feet and attacked Adam in good fun.

They were biting each other's mouths, front paws hooked over each other's shoulders, standing on their hind legs, having a ball. They nipped and bit and mouthed each other, growling and barking. And then they sat down in the grass and woofed at each other.

She sighed, got up, licked his face, and dashed off. And he was in hot pursuit again.

CHAPTER 18

Adam was having a blast with Sierra. He loved going to the waterfall with her, seeing the sunset, and now playing with her on the way back to the ranch house.

He was still chasing her, not wanting to give up the fun and excitement. He nipped at her tail once, and she turned her head and woofed at him, but she didn't turn to play-fight him again. They needed to get in and let everyone else return home to their own business. He wished they didn't need to have guard support, so they could play longer.

Then they were at the ranch house, and she ran in through Brad and Janice's wolf door. Adam followed right behind her.

She shifted and dressed in the bedroom, and when she came out, Brad came through the wolf door and Adam went into the guest room to shift. Brad woofed at his sister.

"Thanks for being there for us. That was a lot of fun," she told her brother while Adam hurried to dress.

Her brother woofed again, and Adam left the bedroom.

Janice was fixing them all glasses of water. "I think it's just awful what's going on with you and these men."

"We'll get them," Adam reassured her, wanting in the worst way to end Dover's obsession with getting even with Sierra for identifying him.

Before Adam could drink any of his water, Sierra wrapped her arms around him and kissed him. "Adam will get them. All of them." Then she changed the subject. "I really enjoyed tonight."

Adam kissed her back, pressuring for more when her brother walked out of his bedroom and smiled at them.

"Uh, I guess we ought to be getting back," Adam said before her brother threw him out, but Janice was smiling like she approved. "And thanks for the security detail."

Sierra gave her brother a hug. "Thanks for coming with us."

He hugged her back. "What are big brothers for? But I still think you ought to stay with us."

"I'm staying with Adam, closer to work than out here, and I'm—"

"Dating him?"

"Yes," Adam said.

Sierra finished her water. "I am. Where are Mom and Dad?" Sierra asked her brother.

"They're staying with Leidolf and Cassie. When they learned you had dumped Richard and there was no chance you were returning to Texas to live, they decided to check out the pack."

"Ohmigod, they're thinking of moving here?"

"Yep. There's nothing to hold them there now."

Sierra smiled. "Good. How long will they be here?"

"For about a week. We'll all have to have lunch together. Sunday all right?"

"How about dinner? We are going out on the boat earlier, remember?" Sierra said.

"That will work," Brad said.

"Okay, we'll do that. We've got to go." Sierra headed for the door. "Come on, you, before you get the third degree when you're used to being the one who gives them, Adam."

"'Night, Sierra, Adam," Brad and Janice said.

"'Night, Janice, Brad," they both said to them.

They thanked the other men who were coming in from guard duty as they left Brad and Janice's house.

Leidolf joined them and said, "There was no trouble along our borders while you were running as wolves. One of our men followed the two cars that were behind you when you drove onto the ranch. If one of the cars had been tracking you for some dark purpose, they kept going. They could have seen our man leaving the ranch and following them and decided it wasn't a good idea to do anything further tonight."

"Okay, thanks," Adam said.

"Did you want anyone to follow you home and give you protection?"

"No, we'll be fine," Adam said.

"Okay, well, it looks like your parents are planning to join us, Sierra."

"That is such great news. I didn't think they would ever leave San Antonio."

"We're glad to have them. Good night," Leidolf said.

Adam and Sierra got into the Hummer, waved goodbye, and drove back to Adam's house.

"That was a great workout. I haven't enjoyed watching the sun set in forever, and the waterfall was really beautiful," Sierra said.

"It's the perfect place for a picnic too, if you want to have one there."

"I would love that. I just can't believe my parents are moving here. I'm so thrilled."

"I'm really glad too." Adam was thinking more about having kids with her, as far as extended family went, and he knew he was getting way ahead of himself there. But having her brother and sister-in-law there and her parents too would be really important for them.

He focused again on making sure they were not going to have any trouble, looking at his rearview mirror, watching to see if anyone was following them.

She glanced at her side-view mirror. "There's a car back there."

"A couple. But I doubt they are following us with any evil intent."

"Just think, if you didn't feel the need to protect me, you wouldn't have any worries." Sierra sighed.

Adam shook his head. "With the work I do, I've had threats before. At a restaurant that had billiards, one woman nearly hit me with a cue stick when I went to question her husband about a home invasion, and I ended up having to arrest both of them. It turned out that they were both involved in the home invasions."

"It's good that you caught both of them then."

"Yes. And they were both given jail time. After she was released, she followed me in her car several times. I threatened her with more jail time, and that was the last of it. Another time, a mother of two juvenile delinquent sons chased me down in her pickup truck, trying to run me off the road. She was charged with reckless endangerment, and that was the last she bothered me."

Smiling, Sierra said, "Okay, then I guess if I run around with you too much, I may be with you when *you* get yourself into more trouble."

He laughed. "You might be right. I'm sorry I might be dragging you into any trouble I could have at some future date."

"Well, maybe I can help protect *you* then."

"I'm all for having your help." He smiled at her.

They finally arrived home and he parked in the garage. "Did you want anything before we call it a night?" Adam asked.

They entered the house and he turned on the lights.

But then Adam got a call. He let his breath out, hoping it wasn't something he had to go in about, though he wasn't on call tonight. "Yeah, what's up?" he asked the officer, Roland Paulson. "Work," Adam mouthed to Sierra.

She nodded and headed for the bedroom.

Adam hoped she wouldn't be annoyed that he might have to go in at any time for work-related issues. Then again, she also might have to. And hell, there was the issue of him having to leave her alone if he went in.

"We were chasing down a suspect who attempted to burglarize a hotel room. We think he's one of the men involved in the theft ring you broke up when Sierra Redding identified the other man. I.

know you're not on call tonight, but since it was your case before, I thought you might want to come and investigate. You know. Because your sense of smell is so good, maybe you could tell if he was one of the men involved in the other robberies."

The officer was beginning to worry Adam a bit. What did he really know or suspect? "Okay, thanks. I'll be right in."

Sierra came out of the bedroom. Her hair was wet, and she was wearing a pink pajama tank top and pink shorts. She looked huggable and Adam regretted having to go in, yet if the man who had committed the hotel robbery was one of Dover's men, he had to know.

"I've got to go in."

"Okay." She let out her breath and sounded like she was a little frustrated with him. "I thought you weren't on call tonight."

Right, or he wouldn't have gone running as a wolf down at Leidolf's ranch. "I'm not on call. The only thing is I don't want to leave you alone."

"Do you have a spare gun?"

"Yeah, in the safe."

"I'll use that if I need to. Go get it for me and I'll be fine." While he was getting it out of his safe, she asked, "So why are you going in about this instead of the detective on call?"

"It may be related to Dover and one of his men. It was a hotel room break-in, just like when Dover was doing them. Same exact MO."

"I'm going with you." Sierra turned around and headed back down the hall.

Adam smiled, shook his head, and put the gun back in the safe and locked it.

"Are there any witnesses I need to do a sketch for?" she asked.

"There could be. The man escaped, but we can smell his scent and see if we recognize it as the one who had been in your house."

"All right then. Of course I'm going." She came out of the

bedroom wearing a pantsuit, and her damp hair was clipped back in a bun.

"I hate to do this to you," he said, getting into his Hummer while she climbed into the passenger side.

She fastened her seat belt. "It's only eleven."

"True." As long as *she* didn't get called in to do a witness sketch.

Before they arrived at the hotel, Adam explained to Sierra about the officer. For whatever reason, Roland seemed to really like Adam. Maybe because Adam didn't seem to discount his aunt's "paranormal" abilities.

"Well, it's always nice to have a good work relationship with officers on the force," Sierra said to Adam.

"Yeah, I agree, as long as he doesn't do a lot more probing into why I have such a great sense of smell. I just didn't want you to let on—in front of him—that you do too, in case he's listening in on our conversation and you happened to mention it."

"Thanks for letting me know. And by the way, you are going to be in trouble if you took the case tonight just because you couldn't say no." She raised her brows at him and folded her arms across her waist.

"No worries there. He only called me because I'd worked that case and he thought it might have something to do with the people who stole your car. When I'm on call, that's one thing. When I'm off duty and I have the chance to slip into bed with you? That's a whole other story. I'm not at the bureau twenty-four seven to get a promotion or catch bad guys. I like taking breaks, and on my time off, I aim to play."

She smiled. "Good. I did worry about that."

"That's what I figured." He really didn't want Sierra to be concerned about him being a workaholic.

When they arrived at the hotel, the officer met them, eager to take them to the room that had been broken into. Though Adam was always thorough with an investigation, he really wanted to get it over with and retire to bed with Sierra.

"So what do we have exactly?" Adam asked Roland.

"Same MO as the earlier cases. I read up all about how Ms. Redding helped to break the case wide open. She was in her hotel room showering, and Dover Manning had a key card to get in, courtesy of a clerk he'd made out with the night before. She gave him a master key. And he swore he was aiming his gun at a dog in the room. A big guard dog."

"Okay, but what about *this* case?" Adam didn't want to be reminded about the old case, and he didn't want Sierra feeling like she was on the spot about what she'd claimed had happened either.

"The guy we're after tonight specifically asked the clerk if they allowed dogs in the rooms. And she told him no, that they didn't allow pets. Well, he tells the clerk that his friend went into a room that the clerk had accidentally given him a key for that was already occupied, and there was a big, damn, growly dog in the room. She reassured him no pets were allowed."

"That sure sounds like he was talking about Dover," Sierra said.

Adam agreed.

They reached the room and went inside.

Normally, Sierra would have done a sketch of the would-be burglar, but Adam knew she wanted to go to the room to smell for the man's scent. As soon as they walked into it, she caught Adam's gaze and nodded. It was the same scent as Melissa's kidnapper. "I'll go get the clerk's sketch of the man."

"How did he get into the room?" Adam asked Roland as Sierra left the room.

"Key to the room, just like Dover's method of entry."

Roland was still watching the door where Sierra had left and then turned his attention to Adam.

"Where's the person who was staying in this room?"

"She was moved to another room."

"Single female?" Adam asked.

"Yes, sir."

"Did she see anything?"

"No. She had been taking a shower. Then she heard a noise in the room, and she hurried to lock the bathroom door. She had her clothes and her cell phone in the bathroom, so she called the police and I responded with backup."

"Did he steal anything from her?"

"She said she had one hundred and fifty in cash. She was going to give it to her mother so she could buy some groceries. Ms. Corning got in so late from Medford, she didn't have time to see her mother. Her mother goes to bed at eight."

"Did the guy steal anything else?"

"A credit card and her driver's license. She had taken off her gold ring, watch, and bracelet in the bathroom to shower."

"Okay. But she didn't see him."

"No, sir. She was too busy locking the bathroom door and calling the police."

"Did you have everything in her room dusted for prints?"

"Yes, sir. First thing."

"Okay, I need to speak with the woman who was staying in this room."

"Yes, sir."

They headed up two flights to another wing of the hotel, and when they reached the door the officer motioned to, Adam knocked. He was hoping Sierra was fine on her own for a while and wasn't getting bored waiting for him.

The woman finally answered the door. She was about fifty and scowled at them.

"Sorry, ma'am, for disturbing you. I'm Detective Holmes, and I need to hear what happened to you when the man broke into your room."

"He said you were coming, but I already told him everything." She motioned to Roland.

"Yes, ma'am. He said you were in the bathroom—"

"Showering. And I climbed out and heard someone rummaging through my drawers. I didn't unpack. I was only staying here the night, then spending a few days with my mother, then leaving. Like I told the officer, I got in too late to see her. My mother goes to bed early and there's no waking her once she goes to sleep. Anyway, ever since that case where the man broke into the woman's room while she was in the shower, when I go to shower, I always close the bathroom door, meant to lock it too, and I keep my jewelry and phone in there. *Just in case.* I should have brought my purse into the bathroom too. I had ordered a meal and forgot to bar the door afterward."

"So he didn't take anything else but the money and your driver's license?"

"No. All I had was a few articles of clothing. Nothing in that."

"And you didn't see him. You didn't get a glimpse of him in the mirror..."

"No. My bathroom door was closed. There was no way I was going to open it to get a glimpse of him."

"Okay, thanks. We've got your contact information, and we'll let you know what happens."

"It's bad enough he took my cash and credit card. I've already canceled it. But it really pisses me off that he took my driver's license."

"What about your car keys?"

Her jaw dropped. "Aw, just great." She searched through her purse. "Nope, they're gone."

"You live four hours from here?"

"Yeah, I'm a librarian. I had to work the rest of the day before I could travel, and I didn't get off until six."

"What's the make and model of your car?" Adam asked.

"A 2018 Ford Capri. Red." She gave him her license plate number.

"Where did you park, ma'am?" Adam asked.

"Out front." She went to the back patio, unlocked it, and peered over the balcony.

They followed her onto the balcony and looked at the parking lot.

"It was right there"—she pointed to an empty parking spot—"in between that white van and that blue pickup truck."

Roland had an APB put out on it.

The woman returned to the room and sat down hard on the bed.

"I'm sorry, ma'am. We'll do everything we can to get your things back."

"The money's gone. I won't get that back."

"We'll get him." Adam gave her his card and he and Roland left.

Roland said, "Hell, I didn't think about her car keys. I should have thought of that."

"You called me right away. Maybe we'll get lucky. But that makes me wonder if he had an accomplice with him. Or if he had been dropped off. Or—"

"If his vehicle is still in the parking lot!"

"Exactly."

"I checked the video security to see what he looked like, but he was wearing a baseball cap and was keeping his face hidden from the cameras when he was getting his key."

"And when he left the hotel?" Adam asked.

"I didn't see the same guy leave."

"So he was wearing something different." Adam would check the video to see for himself what the guy looked like. At least now that they knew he'd stolen the woman's car and where it had been, maybe Adam could see him taking it.

They arrived downstairs to see Sierra talking to the desk clerk. He had figured she would be done by now.

She turned to see Adam and Roland. "The lady says that one of their staff was seen flirting with this guy earlier today."

"Just like what happened before. These men have a way with women," Adam said.

"Not *all* women," Sierra said.

Adam agreed and reviewed the security videos. "Yeah, here he is running out of the hotel."

"Light brown hair," Sierra said. "Tall, gangly, not muscular. And you know what? He looks like the man who kidnapped Melissa and brought her to my house, based on Melissa's description of him."

"From the video, you can see he took the guest's car here." Adam pointed to the video. "He was wearing a hoodie then. We need to see what he was driving before that or who had driven him here."

"There. An older car parked and he got out…right there," Sierra said.

Roland and another patrolman immediately headed out the door.

"You ought to be a detective. Let me see the sketch you did," Adam said.

She smiled and showed him the sketch. "He is the same man who was at my house."

"I agree. And he's back to their old tricks."

"It was easy money. I guess they felt they could get away with it again." Sierra sounded disgruntled.

"He got money, the guest's credit card, her driver's license, and her car, so he did, essentially. But these guys won't lie low and we'll catch them before long."

Roland stalked back into the hotel lobby. "We've got the car. A 2010 red Toyota Corolla."

"Have it impounded and check for prints. We might just get a hit on the car, if nothing else."

"I ran it through the system. It belongs to a Lonnie Hicks. He's the guy we have in jail for stealing the boat and selling it to Rivers."

"Home address?" Adam asked.

"Yes, sir."

Adam glanced down at Sierra. She looked tired. "I can have an officer take you back to my place."

"No, we'll do this together."

"All right. Let's go."

Roland and another officer drove to the address where the car was registered, Adam and Sierra following behind them.

"I'll need you to stay in the vehicle, Sierra."

She sighed. "Of course. Just be careful. If you get shot before we go to bed tonight, I'll be more than upset."

He smiled at her. "Believe me, I will too."

CHAPTER 19

Sierra hoped they would learn who the man was who had tried to rob the woman at her hotel, so eerily like what had happened to her. She couldn't believe he was the same man who had tried to set her up for a kidnapping.

"I should have brought a pillow with me."

Adam smiled at her. "This shouldn't take too long."

"It better not. I'm hoping we both have some strength remaining when we finally go home tonight."

"Oh?"

"Yes. So don't take too long."

"I will do everything in my power to capture the culprit and send him to jail at once then."

"Good."

They finally reached the house, and Adam leaned over and kissed Sierra before he left the Hummer. "Don't leave the vehicle. And keep the doors locked."

She saluted him.

Adam left the vehicle and went to the front door of the house, one of the officers going around back to make sure no one escaped that way while the other officer staying with Adam as she watched. Then a woman answered the door. Adam and Roland went inside, and Sierra closed her eyes to rest them.

She was half-asleep when she heard someone trying to open the driver's door. Her eyes popped open and she realized it wasn't Adam but the man from her sketch. The streetlights made it easy to see him and he stared in at her, finally realizing that she was sitting in the front seat.

Then he raced off. She wanted to chase him down in the worst way—as a wolf. It would be the only way to have the advantage, unless he had a gun. She immediately got on her phone and called Adam. "He's headed down the street, south."

"On our way." Adam and one police officer bolted out of the house, the other coming around through the backyard gate to join them.

She opened the vehicle's door. "Down that way." She motioned to the man running down the sidewalk as fast as he could. He was wearing a gray hoodie, blue jeans, and a pair of black sneakers.

Adam was catching up to him while Roland and the other police officer jumped into their patrol car and tore off after them.

Sierra reminded herself she was just a civilian and needed to stay right where she was, even though she really wanted to help track the guy and take him down. Her wolf instincts were definitely coming into play. Instead, to get her mind off the chase and hopeful capture of the guy, she brought out her sketch pad and drew his sketch from when she had seen him peering in through the window at her. She had the drawing she'd done based on the hotel clerk's description of the suspect and could compare the two. But at the same time, she couldn't help wanting to know what was going on with Adam and the other police officers.

Then movement across the front lawn of the house caught her eye, and she saw the man running for the house. She quickly got on her phone and called Adam. "Hey, if you've lost the guy, he just went into Lonnie's house."

"Shit, stay down. He's armed and dangerous."

Great, because *she* wasn't armed if the guy should come back outside and decide to shoot her through the Hummer's window.

The garage door began to open, and she said, "The garage door is opening. Inside is a silver Ford pickup with big-ass grills and tires, and the license plate is… Hell, he's getting ready to ram your Hummer." She quickly finished writing the tag number on her sketch pad and fastened her seat belt, bracing for impact, then told Adam the tag number in case the driver hightailed it out of there before anyone could stop him. Now she wished Adam had left the vehicle's keys with her so she could have at least driven his Hummer out of the maniac's way.

Sirens headed in her direction, and she hoped Adam wasn't running back to the house on foot. But no matter what, she prayed the police would stop this guy before it was too late. Then the truck rammed Adam's vehicle and pushed it all the way into the street, giving her a jolt and scaring the crap out of her. She realized Adam had put the Hummer in park but hadn't used the emergency brake on the level driveway.

The driver pulled away from the Hummer and took off. Man, did she wish she could have plowed into him with Adam's vehicle to stop him, but the Hummer had sustained enough damage, and she didn't think she would make a dent in the pickup anyway. The truck didn't get far down the street before police blocked him and others came up to meet him from behind, further blocking him in. He tried to get around the vehicles but ran into an electric pole, and that finally stopped him for good.

Another police car pulled up to Adam's vehicle, and Adam jumped out to check on her. Good. She was glad he hadn't just gone after the bad guy.

When he came to the passenger door, she got out and he gave her a heartwarming hug, not releasing her even after he was reassured she was okay. "Are you all right?"

"Yeah, thanks, Adam. What a night. Are we going home soon?" She wasn't letting go of him either. She was so glad he was okay too.

"Yeah, let me find out who this guy is and—"

She sighed and handed Adam the two sketches she'd done of him. "See if he really looks like the sketches I did of him while you're at it, just to humor me."

He kissed her mouth generously and sighed. "I will make this up to you."

"What's to make up? If we catch this band of thugs, that's all good."

"Okay, keep your door locked, and I'll be back in a little bit."

"Go. Learn who all is involved in this."

Adam kissed her again, then he said, "I'll be back."

She didn't believe he would be back soon. She figured the next stop was the police station where Adam would interrogate the bastard.

"Burt Barnes," Adam said, looking at the man's ID. Adam couldn't have been any angrier that the man had staged a kidnapping, intending for Sierra to take the fall, no matter how inept he and his cohort had been at the attempt, as well as wrecking Adam's Hummer and putting Sierra's life in danger. He was glad to arrest the guy's ass. "You've been read your rights. Do you have anything to say for yourself?"

The guy just smiled at him, his hands cuffed behind his back. "Your girlfriend buried herself on this one."

That made Adam even madder. "Buried herself on this?" Adam had to act like he didn't know what Burt was talking about so he would incriminate himself further.

"Don't play dumb. You know just what I mean."

"That you're acting on Dover Manning's behalf and want to kill Ms. Redding's dog."

The man stiffened.

"Hey, we found a gun on him with the serial number that matches Ms. Redding's 9mm that had been stolen," Roland said.

"All right, and we have a stolen gun and an eyewitness account of your breaking and entering into a hotel room, evading arrest..." Adam glanced at the other items Roland had collected in evidence bags from Burt's truck.

"The lady's ID from the hotel room, her credit cards, and a hundred and fifty in cash in a bank envelope," Roland said.

Adam smiled. "Good. Book him. I'll question him in the morning."

"I want a lawyer," Burt said.

"Sure. I'll speak with you in the presence of your lawyer." Adam patted Roland on the shoulder. "Good work."

The officer beamed at Adam, and then Adam took off down the street to look over his Hummer. He wasn't even sure it would be drivable. Sierra had her head propped against her window on his jacket—that he'd tossed into the back seat of the Hummer for whenever he needed it—and looked like she was sleeping.

He opened the driver's door and her head popped up.

"Where to now?" she asked.

"Home. Bed." He tried to start his Hummer. It didn't start. "After I get a tow service."

She groaned. It didn't take long for a tow truck to come for the Hummer, and then Roland was right there giving them a lift home.

Adam shook his head. "I can't believe you're taking me home again."

"All in a day's work." Roland dropped them off at Adam's house. "'Night, Detective, Ms. Redding. Have a good night. I'll try not to call you about anything else."

Adam smiled at him. "You did good and we caught the guy. That's all that matters."

Then Roland left, and Adam escorted a tired-looking she-wolf into the house.

"Take a shower and I'll see you in bed since I already took one and I didn't have to chase after a bad guy like you did," Sierra said, heading for the bedroom.

"I will." He followed her into the bedroom, where she'd already turned on the overhead light, and began stripping out of his clothes as he went into the master bathroom.

Then Adam was showering, and he hoped he wouldn't disturb her when he climbed into bed. He didn't figure anything would go on between them except for sleeping. Maybe in the morning before he had to run in and interrogate his suspect, after they got a good night's sleep, they would be in the mood for some snuggling. Or more—if they had time. He sure hoped so.

He finished showering, dried off, and put on a pair of boxer briefs, then turned out the light and joined Sierra in bed.

He had expected she would be sleeping already, but as soon as he pulled the covers over himself, not sure if he should try cuddling with her or just let her get her sleep, she was moving toward him in bed. That certainly worked for him.

Then she was running her hand over his abs and reached down to the waistband of his boxer briefs. "Hmm, you don't ever sleep in the raw?"

"Yeah, I do, but—"

"Don't change your usual routine just for me."

That was when he realized she was naked in bed. He was more than surprised, not to mention thrilled. He quickly shoved his boxer briefs down his legs and kicked them out from under the covers and onto the floor. Then he moved against Sierra, feeling her soft, naked curves and hot body next to his, and he cupped her face and began kissing her.

This felt so right with her like this. She was kissing him back just as eagerly, her body pressing against his, pushing for contact, and he was just as eager to touch her all over. His hand cupped a breast and he massaged it as he continued to kiss her, her lips parting and inviting him to take his fill.

She began stroking his tongue with hers, her body moving against his. He could smell their pheromones heating up, their heartbeats ramping up already. The musky smell of their sex encouraged them to keep going. All the tiredness they both felt melted away in the passion of the moment.

She ran her hand over his hip and his buttock and she squeezed, making his cock even harder. It didn't take much for that to happen with the way he was touching her, and she was touching him right back. He pressed a leg between hers and lifted slightly, connecting with her mound. She moaned softly. The sound undid him, and he swept his hand downward, traversing her short, curly hairs and finding her swollen nubbin between her legs. She jerked a little when he began to rub it, and he kissed her again, wanting to taste her, feel her, listen to her soft sighs and moans, see the way she was drawn under his spell and how she drew him under hers.

She slid her hand down his side and his arm, back to his buttock while he continued to stroke her, his cock ready to plunge inside her, if they had been going for a mating. Once she was free to date, he'd imagined what it would be like to enjoy her like this again and again. He'd tried to keep his mind off it when they were together at work, but the interest and the need couldn't be quashed, no matter how much he'd tried. But now it wasn't just envisioning what it would be like again, recalling all the sensual details, all his senses on high alert whenever he smelled her close by.

He savored every whispered breath, the way she touched him with such abandon stirring in his loins, making him want to skip the dating business and get on with the mating business. Not that he didn't want to take her on fun dates—he would always want to do that—but he realized he *really* wanted her for keeps. Making love to her after hours, working with her on the job, playing with her when they were free. Sure, he'd dated other she-wolves, but he'd never felt this way about another woman.

He continued to stroke her swollen nub and kiss her luscious mouth at the same time, slipping his tongue between her lips and caressing her tongue with his. Her fingers combed through his hair in a sensuous way, but then she seemed to be holding her breath, her whole body taut. She suddenly gripped his shoulders and cried out, her body shuddering with release.

Then he kissed her long and hard, wanting to go all the way.

She reached down and touched his hip. "Do you want to finish up here or in the shower?" Before he responded, she was getting out of bed and pulling at his hand to get a move on. "Come on. We need to get some sleep. Or at least I do."

They soon were in the shower under the pulsating spray of the hot water, and Sierra wasn't in any rush to bring Adam to orgasm. She'd only wanted to get them out of bed in a hurry and make love to him some more. She wanted to take her time just like he had done with her.

She rubbed her body against his first, pressing against his heavy cock, her hands sliding down his body as he cupped her face and kissed her.

When she moved in a sensuous way against him, he groaned. She loved how she could make him malleable like clay in her hands as she slipped her hands to his ass and squeezed. He slid his leg between hers and lifted and she gasped, getting just as hot and bothered as when he was pleasuring her in bed. Man, she loved how he moved against her, stirring all those wild cravings again, to mate, to be one, to be whole.

She was wet from the shower, but she was wet for him again too. She fought giving in to the need to mate. Worried she had latched on to Adam because she was needy for a wolf's affections and attentions after ending her relationship with the ex and concerned he still might be like the ex and have a difficult time giving up his job to spend time with her, she had to hold off on making a decision of that magnitude. To mate or not to mate. That was the question.

For now? She was making the most of this moment, rubbing against his thigh, rubbing against his cock, kissing him to kingdom come. And he was returning the favor, his hands roaming down her back, cupping her buttocks, and pulling her harder against him.

She took a breath from the kiss and looked up at his dark eyes filled with lust. She thought he was feeling like she was, that they should just agree to a mating and get it over with. But she didn't want to ever regret a mating with a wolf. Not when they mated for life.

Sierra smiled up at him, and he shifted his hands to her breasts and massaged them. She slid her hands down his waist and took hold of his cock jutting out and pressed against her. Then she was stroking him, and he leaned down to kiss her lips again, cupping her face and sliding his tongue into her mouth.

She was supposed to make *him* come this time, but she swore if he kept kissing her, kept rubbing against her, and she kept breathing in their musky, sexy scents, she was going to come too. Despite how tired she had been and ready to go to sleep initially, he had totally revived her and changed her mind. Not that if he'd had any intention of sleeping when he joined her in bed, she wouldn't have changed *his* mind. Which was why she'd gone to bed naked.

He moved his hand down and began to stroke her between her legs again. As if she was just as important to pleasure.

Sierra was all for doing this in bed sometime later in the night or early the next morning if they both woke and couldn't get to sleep. He had woken the passionate side of her, and she never wanted to let it sleep again.

She was stroking his cock harder, faster. He was stroking her nub in the same manner, matching her moves as if they were synchronized. He kissed her wet hair, and then he threw his head back and she knew he was about to burst. Even then, he didn't stop stroking her, except to press a finger deep inside her...and she broke! Her second orgasm hit, and she gasped, just as he exploded while she continued to stroke him.

And when she had wrung him out as he had wrung her out,

they clung to each other, her cheek against his chest, her arms around his back. He held on to her in the same way, though his cheek rested on the top of her head. They stood there for a moment, catching their breath and relishing the warm embrace, until she felt the water turning lukewarm and quickly turned it off.

He left the shower and handed her a towel so she could dry off. He began drying off, his gaze holding hers, his mouth curved up.

"What?" she asked.

"You are amazing."

She smiled. "You are incredible. But don't let it go to your head. I might want a repeat performance later, and we'll see if the next time is as good as the others."

He laughed. "I accept your challenge." Then he hung his towel up on the long, brass towel bar, grabbed hers, and hung it next to his, which made her feel extra special. He scooped her up and carried her to bed.

Once they were under the covers, she snuggled in his arms. She couldn't quit thinking of all his hot moves in bed and in the shower and how beautiful he'd made her feel. She could really get used to a life with him if she wasn't thinking too far ahead of herself about being with him forever. But that was what she always did when she was getting to know a wolf better. The possibility of a mating. How they would cope long-term. Would the newness wear off?

She thought that was why she hadn't been able to let go of her relationship with Richard. She knew what to expect from him, even if it wasn't what she *wanted* to expect. There was something to say about the familiarity that lessened the stress of a new relationship. Yet she realized she had long since given up any fanciful notion that she would actually mate Richard.

Now she was at it again—this time with Adam. Okay, so she wasn't going to do that again. She closed her eyes, her head snuggled against his chest, and took a deep breath of him, considering the possibility of them being together for life. So much for *not* thinking about it.

Then she was thinking about how she needed to get some sleep so that if he decided he was ready to make love to her again, she could wake enough to enjoy it.

And then she was mulling over the idea of boating with him, having picnic lunches on the boat—hmm, making love on the boat. Now wouldn't that be a unique experience?

"Does your boat have a cabin?" she asked sleepily.

"Hmm, a cabin, eh?"

"Yeah, a dinghy is out."

"Gotcha. No dinghy. A big bed in a cabin."

She kissed his chest. "Or a small bed." She had no plan to sleep on it. And she knew, unless he had a huge yacht, the bed probably wouldn't be all that big. It would still be perfect.

CHAPTER 20

The next morning, Adam and Sierra had breakfast of eggs, sausage, and toast. He needed to talk to the suspect they'd caught last night, but Sierra didn't need to go in yet. "I was thinking, if Tori was okay with it, you could stay with her and begin helping her unpack so—"

"I would be safe."

"Yeah, she's taking the next couple of days off to get a little more organized before we all land on her on Saturday. And then I'll meet up with you both after I finish interrogating the suspect, if that works for you two. If you don't mind, I need to borrow your car too."

"Sure, no problem. I'll call Tori and see if she is okay with me coming over earlier." Sierra called Tori while Adam began to clean the breakfast dishes and put them in the dishwasher. "Hey, would it be all right if I come over and help you out a bit? You know Adam. He's going in to question a suspect." She put the call on speaker.

"Who is he questioning?"

"The man who helped steal my car, kidnap the girl, and drop her off at my house," Sierra said.

"Ohmigod, you caught him?"

Sierra glanced at Adam. "It appears Tori wants to go in with you to assist you with questioning the suspect."

"No, come over to my place and we can visit while Adam works. Another detective will join him. I'll fix us some tea, if you would like, and we can talk and start to unpack more boxes, but we'll be sure to save some for everyone else who's coming over on Saturday," Tori said. "You don't know how much I appreciate your offer of help. Some days I get home and I'm so tired that the idea of sorting through all this stuff makes me want to just give it all away and start over."

Sierra smiled. "I don't blame you at all. After my last move, I don't want to move again for years." Then she saw Adam watching her and she figured if she ended up mating him, one of them would have to move, unless they got a new place of their own and both moved. "While we're unpacking your boxes, I'll tell you all about what happened last night." Well, not *all* that happened.

Adam winked at her as if he knew what she was suddenly thinking of. "I'll drop Sierra off at your house in just a few minutes, Tori."

"Okay, see you then."

Adam had hoped he could talk to the suspect without his lawyer being present, so when he arrived at the interrogation room, he was surprised to learn Burt had actually waived his right to legal representation. Adam was glad though, because without a lawyer, they might be able to get somewhere with this. Detective Jerome Plumber was there as Adam's backup.

"Okay, let's start with the business with the break-in at the hotel." Adam wanted to jump right in about the kidnapping, but he hoped talking about a lesser crime might get Burt to talk.

"I wasn't at the hotel." Burt made the comment casually, as if he wasn't worried they could prove he had stolen from one of the hotel guests, despite having been caught with the goods.

Adam passed the two sketches of Burt to him. "These were sketches done of you. One was based on a witness's description of you at the hotel, and one was drawn based on an eyewitness account at your aunt's house."

Burt studied the photos and smiled, as if he were pleased that Sierra had caught his likeness. And she had. In both sketches.

He leaned back in his chair, folded his arms, and shook his head. "Nah, not me. Looks similar, but they're not of me. There must be a million guys who look just like that."

"We have video of you coming and going from the hotel. You were found with the stolen goods on you from the hotel room." Adam showed the evidence to Burt in plastic bags.

Burt shook his head again. "Nah. I wasn't in any hotel room. I was nearby though, sure, and I saw this guy—who looked similar to me—run out of the hotel like he was on fire. Then I guess he got spooked and he dropped everything and ran. I figured finders, keepers, you know." He shrugged. "So I grabbed the stuff and took off in my car."

"*Stolen* car. You left your aunt's car in the parking lot after driving it there and tore off in the stolen car. You were videotaped clicking the key fob until you found the car the key belonged to. We have it all on a video recording. You parking in the parking lot in your aunt's car, walking into the hotel, and some minutes later, running out of the hotel, stolen goods in hand. You trying the key fob until you found which car taillights lit up, you speeding off in the stolen car out of the parking lot. There wasn't anyone else in the vicinity. No one who ran out of the hotel like you did. No one was carrying a bunch of stolen goods, then dropping them in the parking lot for you to pick up."

Burt frowned. "Okay, so—if I pled guilty, how much would that get me?"

"Well, we still have the situation with a stolen gun being in your possession. The same gun taken from a house where a kidnapped victim had been tied up and left behind."

"I had nothing to do with any kidnapping."

"Your fingerprints were in the woman's car you stole to carry out the kidnapping," Jerome said, finally speaking up. He smiled at Adam, who hadn't gotten the news yet that they'd actually gotten some prints from Sierra's car. "We have your prints on file for a former burglary—you're a convicted felon."

"The woman gave me a ride one day when my car broke down."

"Really," Adam said. "How do you explain how a witness gave this sketch of you in the kidnapping of a minor? Did you plan the kidnapping? Or did the woman who was your accomplice plan the whole operation? Or was someone else in charge?"

Burt ran his hands through his hair. "Okay, what can I do to make this all go away?" He held his hands up in a placating way.

"We can't make it all go away," Adam said. "Kidnapping is a felony offense. You used a weapon during the kidnapping. You threatened the victim. You're a convicted felon for armed robbery and currently on parole. Tell us who planned the kidnapping and let him…or her…take the rap for that."

"I'm going to prison anyway. That's what you're saying, right? And if I told you who was in charge of it, he would kill me when I got to prison."

"Dover Manning would get out in a few years. But you? You could go away for much longer after all you've pulled. And for what? Doing his dirty work for him? How much did you get out of it? More time in the slammer." Adam assumed between Burt and Dover's girlfriend, Burt was the weak link.

Burt stiffened.

"It's up to you. With everything we have on you, you're going away for a long time, and that's the end of the story. At least for you. Dover's girlfriend is still at large. She could possibly get away without serving any jail time. The next thing you know, Dover's sentence is shortened and he's free as a bird while you're left to rot in prison." Adam paused, letting his words sink in. "Okay, look, Dover's girlfriend, Phyllis Kenton, doesn't think much of you, does she? She thinks you're an idiot. That Dover should dump your ass because you're not good enough for the team. But Dover keeps you on because he needs someone to do his bidding without question and who would serve as the fall guy when you get caught."

Burt slid his hands over his lap.

"You might feel you owe something to Dover, even if he's just using you, because you've been with him for a long time. But Phyllis? She has only been with him for two years, right? And you're no longer in so thick with Dover now, are you? She has come between the two of you, and now you're going to take the fall for something she and Dover wanted you to do. You're the one holding the gun, threatening the girl, forcing her into the car, bullying her at the house. Correct me if I'm wrong, but you're the only one who's going to take the rap for this, and the woman who calls you an idiot is going to get away with it and find another pawn to do Dover's and her bidding."

Burt was glowering at Adam but didn't say a word.

"Did Dover tell you to assist Phyllis in kidnapping the girl, or was it Phyllis who told you that you were needed for the job?"

Burt ground his teeth and folded his arms. "I don't take orders from her."

"Okay, but when you're on the job, who calls all the shots?" Adam could see from Burt's mutinous expression that Phyllis did, but Burt didn't want to admit it.

"She thinks she does."

"She thinks she does, or she does?" Adam needed Burt to confirm she was in charge.

"She tells me what to do, but I've got a mind of my own."

"Did she tell you to do the job at the hotel?"

"No. She's not in charge of me."

"Did Dover tell you to do the job at the hotel?"

"No. He doesn't tell me what to do all the time either."

At least they'd gotten a confirmation from Burt that he'd done the hotel theft. "So where is Phyllis? She thinks she's getting away with this." Adam hoped Burt knew where she was, and they could arrest her.

"Hell if I know. She said we needed to each go our own way, and that was that. I haven't seen her since."

"Why did Dover want you to kidnap the girl and try to frame Ms. Redding for the job?"

"Are you kidding? Sierra Redding lied about her dog being in her hotel room and lied about Dover threatening her in the room. He threatened a growly dog, not the woman! He'd never even seen her before. By supposedly threatening the woman, he got a lot more time than he would have otherwise."

They had Dover jailed, but Adam worried about Sierra's safety when the man got out of jail. Hell, he worried about her safety with Dover still in jail as long as his henchmen threatened her. But Dover was a ticking time bomb. He had been in several armed robberies that they hadn't had enough evidence against him to actually convict him of. Adam had needed Sierra to help them convict him this time. Had he done Sierra a disservice? He was afraid he had.

It still gave him chills to think of what could have happened if Sierra had come out of the shower and found an armed man in her hotel room, if she hadn't changed into her wolf. Would Dover have just left and not threatened her with bodily harm? After she'd seen him and testified against him? She was his first victim who had actually seen him in the act of attempting to burglarize her and had effectively testified against him with such detail that there was no doubt in anyone's mind that she'd seen him do just what she said she had.

Burt was staring at the table and running his hands through his hair, looking distraught.

"Write everything down that happened—the robbery at the hotel, the kidnapping of the minor—in your own words." Adam gave Burt a pen and paper and sat back against his chair. "Did you want anything to drink?"

"A beer."

"Water? Soda?"

Burt shook his head and stared at the paper. "If I confess, you'll state that for the record so I'll get less jail time?"

"We'll let the DA know you were cooperating with us."

Burt glanced at the evidence of the robberies and the sketches of him. "She drew them, didn't she? Sierra Redding? I know that's what she does for the cops. Yeah, she did them."

Then he began to write on the paper.

Jerome folded his arms as he stood near Adam, watching Burt struggle for the words to put on the paper.

When Burt had finally finished writing his confession, he pushed the papers at Adam.

"You need to sign and date them," Adam said, giving him today's date and passing them back to him.

Burt signed and dated them. Adam took the papers and read through them. "Okay, good." He handed them to Jerome to read.

He nodded. "This looks good."

"Are you sure you don't have any idea where Phyllis went?" Adam asked.

Burt shrugged. "Maybe she's with the guy she has been seeing."

"A new guy?" Adam asked, hoping this could be an important new lead.

"No, one of the original crew. If Dover finds out, he'll kill 'em both. The guy goes by Vlad the Impaler, Victor Freemont. He likes to bite the women he's seeing. I've seen the bite marks on Phyllis's neck. And hell, it didn't take her long to jump into bed with him as soon as Dover went to jail."

"Where is Victor?"

"I have no idea. I've just seen them together whenever she was supposed to meet up with me over stuff. That's all I have."

"All right, if that's it, we'll be seeing you."

Once they learned they couldn't get anything more out of Burt, he was carted off to jail and Jerome said to Adam, "Man, how do you and Josh do it? My partner and I were talking about how the two of you could convince more suspects to confess than any other detectives on the force could without even threatening them with mayhem or bargaining with them to reduce their sentences."

"It's all in the sweat, reading their body language, knowing when they're going to fold." Their scent too. And how beta they were. Burt was definitely a beta, and Adam was the alpha. So was Jerome, but he didn't realize he was intimidating the hell out of Burt by just standing there. Burt might be afraid to go against Dover, or he might even feel some friendship and loyalty to him, but when his "alpha leader" wasn't there to protect him, Adam and Jerome had become his alpha leaders.

"You sure have them pegged. I could learn a thing or two from you in the art of interrogation. And here I thought I knew it all." Jerome grabbed all the evidence to put back in the evidence room.

Adam slapped him on the back and headed for the door. "Anytime you want a tip, I can give it to you."

"Thanks. Oh, and thanks for coming in last night. My partner wanted me to tell you that since he was the one on call."

"No problem. I know if either of you were working on a case, you would want to go in about it."

Jerome chuckled. "Hell, on my night off? My wife would give me the boot."

Adam knew him better than that. He and his partner would have gone in about their own cases if it meant they might get a break in them.

Adam headed outside to Sierra's car and got a call from the auto-body repair shop. It would cost him a couple of thousand dollars to repair the Hummer. *Hell.* Well, that was another charge that Burt would have to face. Adam pulled off his suitcoat and laid it neatly in the back seat of the car, then drove off.

When Adam called ahead to tell Sierra he was on his way to pick her up for work, she said, "Well, it's about time. Though I already did two eyewitness accounts. Tori took me."

"Ah, hell, honey."

Sierra chuckled. "She was happy to do it. We were having a blast unpacking boxes, and I just had to run out to a couple of crime scenes to do witness sketches. We're getting lunch delivered. What kind of sandwich do you want?"

"Okay, good. Do they have hot corned-beef sandwiches?"

"Yes. We'll get that for you."

After lunch, he and Sierra left Tori's place to return to work. Sierra was busy on other cases that detectives needed her to do sketches for, and he was still trying to run down other leads he had to finish up. Then it was time to return home. "Dancing tonight at the wolf restaurant and club?"

Sierra yawned and smiled at him. "How about tomorrow night? TGIF. No work the next day, just helping Tori unpack her boxes. I barely helped her at all before I had to start sketching perps per witness accounts."

He smiled back at Sierra. "I think we need to go to bed early tonight."

"No wolf run?"

"No. Let's do that Friday night too. We'll be at the wolf club, and it's near the pack leader's ranch. We can just run afterward. Like you said, we don't have to go to work the next day."

"Okay, so what do we do tonight?"

"I can grill chicken for dinner. We have avocados, spinach, tomatoes for a salad, with roasted potatoes. And we can just watch something on TV and go to bed. We've been burning the candle at both ends, so we'll need to get some sleep."

She smiled as he parked her car in the garage. "I imagine we'll get to a bit more than that."

"Exactly. That's why we need to retire early…so afterward we can still get some sleep."

She chuckled as they went into the house.

"Oh, and about my car… It's going to cost a couple thousand dollars." He pulled chicken out of the fridge.

"Oh, no. Can you afford it? I can help out if you can't." She got the potatoes out of his pantry.

He smiled. "Yeah, Burt Barnes's car insurance is covering it."

"Oh, good. So when will your Hummer be repaired?" She began peeling the potatoes, then wrapped them in foil for the grill.

"Monday morning. That means, if you don't mind, I'll just be driving your car for a while longer. Or I can rent a car. The insurance will pay for it."

"No, that's okay. As long as we're going to work together and I just need to ride with whoever needs a witness sketch, or I'll be at the office. And that way I'll be protected."

"That's true."

They had dinner while watching a movie, just chilling and enjoying themselves. Once the movie was done, they went to bed. It was only nine, but they weren't going to sleep just yet!

Friday was a hectic day, and after doing sketches of four bodies in the morgue they needed to identify, Sierra was so ready to call it a day and just dance the night away at the wolf club. Adam was careful not to show her a lot of affection at the police bureau or it wouldn't be professional, but when she had viewed the last body of the day and returned to the bureau, he gave her a hug and a kiss.

She really didn't think she'd ever get used to doing morgue sketches. But she was so glad Adam was there to give her a hug afterward and make her feel so much better.

"Do you still want to go dancing tonight?" he asked as they got into her car and headed home.

"Oh, yeah. Unless you don't feel up to it." Even though she wanted to go, she had to make sure he was feeling just as eager to go out. She could just envision dragging him onto the dance floor and him being tired and worn out and wishing they'd just stayed home. They were going to be busy all weekend too.

"Yep, I've thought of nothing else all day."

She laughed. "Yeah, I bet." She figured he would have been busy thinking about all the cases he had to work on, not about dancing with her tonight.

"Truly. What better way to show the whole pack we're together than to go to the restaurant and dance with you, have dinner with you, and show off we're a couple."

She smiled. "Okay, gotcha." She should have known that was why he wanted to go with her there. "Uh, you do know how to dance, right?"

CHAPTER 21

As soon as Adam and Sierra arrived at the Forest Club, she was surprised to see how busy it was. Of course that meant that the food was great, the music was riveting, and the patrons were a lot of fun. But they probably should have made a reservation first.

"It's packed," she said, worried. They could probably dance a few dances, but getting a table wasn't happening. Not tonight anyway.

"I've got reservations."

She threw her arms around Adam and hugged and kissed him. "You are so my hero."

He laughed and kissed her, waving at another couple who had just arrived. "I learned my lesson when I came here on a Friday night a year ago with a date and there were no seats to be had. She was an out-of-state wolf, just passing through, and she was so disappointed. I took her to a steak restaurant instead, but I never saw her again after that. No great loss, but I never did that again."

Sierra hurried him inside. "I'm glad we weren't the ones who were out of luck. I've never been here to dance. My brother kept raving about their steaks, so he bought his mate and me lunch there. I always wanted to go dancing here, but I had to call it quits with Richard first."

"I learned from a girl I dated when I was younger. She loved to dance. She was more like a sister to me than anything, but I was always glad I had learned."

"My brother and dad taught me."

They were shown to their seats and given menus and glasses of water. The place was full of wolves, some eating and drinking, others already dancing.

As soon as Sierra and Adam had ordered their meals, she was

taking him to the dance floor to prove to her that he liked to dance, just like she did.

This was so nice, the decor woodsy as if they were in a forest, lights flashing over the dance floor, and a great band. And Adam was a dream to dance with.

They moved across the floor in slow motion, glued to each other during the slow dances and shimmying to the fast ones.

"This could be a mistake, you know," Sierra said as she waltzed with him again, their bodies pressed intimately against each other's.

He glanced over at their table. "You mean because our meals were just delivered to our table?"

She nipped at his chin. "No, because we'll want to take this to somewhere a lot more secluded."

He smiled down at her and kissed her nose. "Now you're talking."

They finished the dance and then headed to their table to eat. Though they saw their pack leader and his mate and several others they knew, everyone was just waving at them, smiling but not intruding. She was impressed. She wasn't used to that because when she and Richard went somewhere to eat, there were no other wolves about, no pack, so she hadn't realized how the pack would react to her dating Adam.

Then she saw Ethan with Brad's sister-in-law, Dorinda, waltzing on the dance floor.

"Ethan's here," Sierra said, cutting into her New York strip steak.

"Yeah. He's gone out a couple of times with Dorinda. I don't know if it means anything, or they're just single and enjoying each other's company." Adam took a bite of his T-bone steak.

"Not like us."

Adam took a deep breath and let it out. "I'm glad for that. I didn't realize how stressful it was dating other women until I began dating you, and it's been like night and day for me. We enjoy most of the same things, we work well together—"

"Oh, I love how you are always telling me I can do something, like drawing sketches of deceased people. You're always so positive with me when I don't have a lot of confidence in something."

"You are for me too."

She raised a brow. "I've seen you work your cases. You always have everything completely under control."

"When I stepped out and did something not in my comfort zone—like taking your art class—you encouraged me the whole time."

She laughed. "That's my job as an art teacher. There's nothing worse than someone telling you that you can't do something and you should just give it up. Try something else. That's what's so fun about art. If one kind isn't your thing, some other kind could be. And like anything, practice makes it better. One of these days, you can even enter something you've created in a contest. Some art really stands out."

"Oh, mine stands out all right."

She chuckled. "You are one of my cutest students. Why do you think I started dating you?"

"Damn, I knew signing up for your art classes was the thing to do."

"And when we're not busy doing other stuff on the weekends, I can give you some private lessons."

"Oh, hell, yeah. Now I'm all for that."

After dinner, they danced until late, then drove over to the pack leaders' ranch to run as wolves. They'd almost skipped it and gone home, they were so ready to just make love and call it a night. But they were so close by the ranch and running as wolves was a great way to finish a beautiful evening before they made love.

As soon as they dropped their clothes at Brad's house, Brad and Janice, Ethan and Dorinda all came to run with Sierra and Adam. Even though running as a couple was fun, so was playing with packmates. Then they went home to make love and Sierra was wishing they had the whole weekend off just to do this before the workweek started again and she began teaching art to the kids again too.

On Saturday, Adam and Sierra showed up a little later than they had planned to at Tori's place. Josh and Brooke were already there. Tori was making mimosas for everyone. The coroner was there and so was their DEA agent, Ethan, and Josh's brother, Maverick, all bachelor males hoping to court Tori.

Adam had to laugh. He hadn't expected a party.

Maverick was busy flattening boxes when they walked inside. In that moment, it seemed like all time stood still. And then Adam realized why. Everyone had stopped talking and laughing and turned to see his and Sierra's arrival. There wasn't any denying how he felt about being with her and vice versa.

They'd made a dent in unpacking boxes, but many were still stacked everywhere several high and several deep. By the time lunch rolled around, at least there was room to sit on the couch and the chairs and eat at the coffee table or dining table if anyone wanted to. Boxes were stacked next to the kitchen island too, and there were pots and pans and cutlery sitting all over the counter.

The lunch boxes arrived and Adam realized Tori had gotten him his favorite—corned beef on rye. Once he and Sierra finished their sandwiches at the kitchen table, they began working on one of the boxes together.

Tori opened boxes with them so she could hear what all had happened during the interrogation, since she'd been off work for the last two days. Even Josh had to hear the story. He might have retired from the police bureau, but he was still a detective at heart.

Adam took a couple of swigs of his margarita—*that* was good—and cut open another box. "So what do I do with all this stuff?" He didn't figure Tori would want him to take everything out of the box and pile it all up on the floor.

Sierra was right beside him, pulling out towels and bathroom items. "In the linen closet." She handed him the stack of towels and led him to the linen closet. The she carried the toilet paper and cleaning supplies into the bathroom. Once they were done, she said, "Okay, next box?"

They worked on the boxes until they were all gone and most everything had been put away. Ethan and Maverick helped Tori hang pictures while everyone else was telling them which way to move the one, first over an inch, up two inches, over another inch.

Everyone was laughing and having a good time. Then Adam realized how late it was getting—nearly dinnertime, and he had wanted to do something special for a date with Sierra. They hadn't even discussed what they wanted to do yet.

"Dinner's on me," Tori said. "Thanks for all the help you gave me. My house is livable now, and I can't thank all of you enough. It would have taken me months to get all this done, what with my work commitments."

"We totally understand," Brooke said, "and we were glad to help. And it was fun while we were doing it too."

Everyone agreed with her.

Adam wrapped his arm around Sierra and looked down at her, silently asking her what she wanted to do about dinner. "Dessert is on you," she said softly for Adam's ears only.

He raised a brow and smiled.

She punched him lightly on the arm. "I meant at an ice cream parlor I love to go to. They have the best hot fudge sundaes."

He chuckled.

"Yeah, I know what you were thinking."

"You can't blame me for that."

She laughed. "I don't. I want the same thing, but after my dessert—the ice cream sundae kind."

CHAPTER 22

After having barbecued ribs delivered to Tori's house and enjoying the camaraderie of the wolves that were there, they finished dinner and Adam and Sierra gave Tori a hug and thanked her for the meals.

"I got a lot of work out of both of you, so I'm the one who needs to be thanking you," Tori said.

"No problem at all," Adam said.

Sierra smiled at Tori, glad to be her friend. "It was lots of fun. And we made fast work of it with everyone being here."

Before they left, Josh and Brooke were saying their goodbyes, while the bachelor males appeared to be staying a while longer.

"I wonder if any of them will outlast the others," Sierra said to Adam as she drove them to her favorite ice cream parlor.

"None of them will leave until she kicks them all out," Adam said. "You know, I had planned to take you out to dinner tonight and tomorrow night. We won't get to do either now."

"I know, but we had fun anyway. Getting to know each other isn't all about just being together at a restaurant but how we interact with others and each other at work and play. I love seeing the way you joke back and forth with the guys. I didn't think we would ever get that last picture hung because you and the others were making Josh and Ethan move it so many times."

"They're good sports. I'll be on the hot seat next time. We take turns."

"I haven't checked the weather for boating tomorrow. What does it say?"

Adam looked up the ten-day forecast on his phone. "Sunshine, only ten percent chance of rain that day."

"Okay, good, then it will be a beautiful day. What about Josh? Did you check with him to see if they were coming?" She pulled into the parking lot of her favorite ice cream store.

Adam was texting on his phone when she left the car, and he hurried to join her. "They said they would definitely come with us on the boat trip."

"Oh, great." Then she got a call from Brad and put it on speakerphone. "Hi, Brad. Adam and I are going into the ice cream shop for dessert. What's up?"

"Mom and Dad wanted to do something with us tomorrow morning, but we are already going boating with you. Would it be all right if they come with us on the boat?"

Adam said, "Yeah, sure. Josh and Brooke are coming too, and we have plenty of room."

It looked like this was going to be a family excursion, plus Josh and Brooke who were like family. She hoped Adam didn't feel obligated to take her parents with them too.

"We'll see you all tomorrow then," she said, and they ended the call. "Since my parents are coming, did you want to ask your parents to come along for the ride?"

"Yeah, they love to boat."

"Okay, invite them then."

"You know what this is going to sound like," Adam warned.

"A welcoming committee for my parents. They're the same age as your parents, so hopefully they'll become fast friends."

"All right. I'll ask them." Adam called his parents and said, "Yeah, Dad, we're boating tomorrow, and Sierra's parents are coming. Would you and Mom like to join us so they'll feel welcomed to the pack?" Adam smiled. "Yeah, of course Sierra's coming. All right. See you in the morning."

Sierra and Adam walked inside the ice cream shop and were greeted with a fifties-era nostalgic look: a black-and-white-checkered floor, red-vinyl-topped chrome stools at the counter, red booths, little café tables and chairs, and fifties music playing overhead. Pictures of fifties stars hung on the wall behind the aqua counter, and vintage-style Coca-Cola lamps hung over the booths. A red replica vintage gas pump was filled with cold sodas. She loved the atmosphere here, but she especially loved their sundaes. She couldn't think of a better place to have dessert on a date.

She and Adam were soon ordering their sundae treats to die for. Hers: brownie waffle sundae topped with chocolate-chip mint ice cream, hot fudge sauce, whipped cream, colorful sprinkles, and two cherries on top. And his: a Black Forest sundae with Oreo cookies, vanilla ice cream, and cherry pie filling, topped with whipped cream, walnuts, and a couple of cherries.

With sundaes in hand, they took their seats in a booth.

Adam asked her, "So what do you think about kids?"

She had just taken a spoonful of ice cream, and she swallowed it before she answered the question. She was surprised he would ask that of her so out of the blue. It sounded to her like he was getting really serious. "I like kids." Most wolves did. It was something innate to their wolf halves—the love of all little wolves and taking care of them in a pack. "I love to teach art to the ones at the ranch."

"I mean, about having your own."

She smiled. She figured that was what he was getting at, but he hadn't wanted to just come out and say it. "You mean about…?" Her job? Raising kids? Mated wolves wanted to have offspring, if they could, to continue their species. It didn't mean they could always have kids. But sure, she wanted some. She continued, "Working while raising them?"

"Uh, yeah."

"You mean having kids with you."

He smiled, his ears tingeing red.

"You have been at your job as long as Josh has, and he retired." She didn't want to assume Adam wouldn't want the role of stay-at-home daddy. Maybe he did. Maybe he was tired of all the running around, trying to catch the bad guys, especially since Josh had retired.

"Uh, yeah."

"Or I have my retirement income from the military, and I could take care of the kids while you continue to be a detective."

He let out his breath and looked relieved. "Yeah."

She laughed. She wasn't really surprised. With Josh, it was different. He wanted to help Brooke with her business. "Don't worry. If we mate and have kids, I want to stay home with them. I can still teach art to the kids at the ranch. Someone will surely look after the little ones when I teach the others. As to being a sketch artist? That's a toss-up."

"You could do it on the days I'm off and I could watch the kids."

She smiled. She wanted to laugh, but he was being so serious, as if they had already agreed to a mating, that she didn't want to make light of the situation.

"What about money?" she asked. If they were going to talk about being a couple and the issues that came with that, money was often a top concern.

"I save a good portion of my income every month, spend what I need, splurge when I feel the urge, and I shop around for the best deal I can get on major purchases. What about you?"

"That sounds like me." She ate some more of her ice cream. "What about the house situation?"

He smiled, looking pleased they were having this discussion. "We can sell one or rent it, or sell or rent both and buy a new one. If you were to stay home with the kids, then you should have the biggest say in that since you'll be living there more than I would be."

"Until you retire."

"Yeah, someday. I like what I do for now, though I won't be able to do it forever."

That was one problem with their longevity. The humans aged faster than the wolves.

"Okay. And"—she reached over and stroked his hand—"we can't drift apart in the intimacy arena."

He chuckled wolfishly. "You can count on *that* not happening."

She laughed, already feeling all tingly with need. "Communication. We have to tell each other what's going on if something's bothering us. That means not telling Tori that we're upset over something to do with the other but instead you and I talk it out with each other."

"I agree with you there. My parents are great with talking to each other about issues. Most of the time, one of them didn't realize how the other felt about something, and once they cleared the air, everything was fine."

"Okay, good. My parents are good about talking to each other too."

"That's good." He finished his ice cream. "That hit the spot."

"Lots of energy for what comes next, right?"

"You better believe it."

CHAPTER 23

ADAM WAS THINKING ABOUT A MILLION THINGS, TRYING TO stay focused on the pretty little she-wolf sitting across from him, licking every bit of hot fudge syrup off her spoon, instead of the things he was mentally noting he needed to take care of. He needed to meet with Sierra's parents and have a heart-to-heart talk to let them know he would do everything in his power to make Sierra happy if he mated her.

"Hey," Sierra said, reaching over to grab Adam's hand. "Ready to return to the house?"

"Yeah, I sure am." Forget about anything else; it was time to go home.

"What were you thinking about when you were zoned out back there?" Sierra asked, driving them home.

He chuckled. "What did I miss?"

"Me confirming our dinner date with my family tomorrow. Brad is asking your parents to come over too, since we're going to all be on the boat the rest of the day. You're invited, of course."

He laughed. "Yes. That sounds good."

"What were you thinking about? Dover? The case?"

"No. I was thinking of your family, mine, us."

"Oh, good," she said. "I mean, if you were thinking about how you were going to take down these guys who have been causing us trouble, that would have been good too. But I like knowing you were thinking along the same lines as me."

"For sure," Adam said.

She glanced at him. "You're good for it, right? We're not jumping the gun on us getting together with them, are we?"

Smiling, he shook his head. "I absolutely want to do this, and if you must know, I wanted to talk to your parents about my interest in you."

"Really? You're so sweet."

But what came next was hot and sexy, nothing sweet about it.

After making love again Sunday morning, Sierra and Adam hurried to dress and headed out to the marina to meet with her brother and sister-in-law and their parents and Adam's. Brooke and Josh were hurrying to catch up to them. The morning was cool, the sun rising, reflecting off the rippling water in the fussy breeze. Seagulls were flying overhead, fish splashing in the water, ducks floating on the surface. They used a cart to wheel their bags of sunscreen and beach towels and other essential items for a day out boating and ice chests full of beverages and containers of potato salad, coleslaw, and fixings for sandwiches.

Sierra was excited about seeing Adam's boat and hoped it wouldn't be too crowded. She hoped his boat was at least as nice as some of the ones her father had owned, just because she wanted him to impress her father, even though she shouldn't have been worried about that. She should just be glad Adam had a boat, period, to enjoy when they could. Otherwise, trying to rent one at this late date for the summer probably would have been impossible. They would all be booked up.

She kept thinking about Adam and how good he was to her and how much she enjoyed his company when her mom met up with her. Sierra knew she would want to talk to her about Adam.

The guys were hauling most of the stuff, passing covered boat slip after slip as Janice, Brooke, and Adam's mom, Beverly Holmes, were talking about something on the walkway way ahead of them.

Sierra's mom said to Sierra, "It was all your dad's idea to come along. We both wanted to do this, but I thought you two might have needed the time alone together. Your dad has dreamed of getting another boat since we sold ours when Brad and you moved away."

"We're glad you could join us. If things go well with Adam and me, we'll take you out again when you move here."

"Yeah, but that's why you need the time to be alone together. Not with all the parents being here. You need the time to get to know each other."

Smiling, Sierra hugged her mom. "We've known each other since I moved here."

"As in dating?"

"Well, no, but Adam has always brought me my favorite coffee when I'm at work."

"The hazelnut and chocolate caramel?"

"Yep. He's always been a bright spot in my day, and he seems to feel that way about me too. Adam wants more from life like I do. Anyway, this doesn't mean we're mating, but we are definitely dating. And now—so that he keeps me safe from Dover's minions—we're spending the evenings together. And we're quite alone."

Her mother's expression brightened. "Oh. Oh, that's good."

Sierra chuckled. "Yeah, it is."

Then her mother frowned. "You don't think it's too soon after breaking up with Richard, do you?"

"You broke up with a wolf you were dating, and how long did you wait to date Dad?"

"Two days."

Sierra smiled. "Well, I've known Adam for longer than that. We always chatted during pack social events. I didn't go with him to them, but I always met up with him there because of our connection on the job."

"And he got you that job. I like him."

Sierra was glad. She loved her parents, and if she did mate

Adam, she wanted them to welcome him like a son. Adam's parents had been reservedly friendly, and she suspected that was because they knew Adam had cared for her all along, but she hadn't been available and maybe they were afraid she would break his heart. She was glad they had come too, but she didn't want everyone to believe this was a done deal between her and Adam in case it wasn't and then they'd be disappointed.

"Well, you take your time, dear. You have all the time in the world to decide on a mating."

"Like you and Dad did?"

Her mom smiled. "When the love bug bit, we couldn't keep our hands off each other."

That was how Sierra was feeling about Adam. She kept telling herself she should wait and date him longer, but she realized she couldn't.

She watched as her dad talked animatedly to Adam and his dad and Brad as if they were one big happy family already.

"Everything will work out the way it's supposed to," Sierra said to her mother, and then she and her mom caught up with the other ladies.

"We were talking about gardening," Janice said.

"I can't wait to build our home on the ranch so I can begin to grow flowers again," Sierra's mom said.

Sierra saw the yacht the guys were loading the stuff into. It was beautiful.

"It's a West Bay Sonship West," her dad said with pride, as if it was *his* boat. "Three state rooms, two heads, washer and dryer even, kitchen, dinette table with booth, tons of seating on the covered deck and lots more inside. It's just beautiful."

Sierra gave her dad a hug. "Remember you're with Mom."

Her mom laughed. "Kirk's first love has always been a boat."

"Aww, but he always named them after you," Sierra said, loving her dad for that.

The guys had already carried all the supplies onto the boat, and Adam had given her dad the grand tour. Everyone else had been on the boat before, so once Sierra and her mom climbed aboard, her dad gave them a tour of the boat.

She loved the boat, from the spacious kitchen to the equally spacious living area. This was big enough to be a real party boat. Everything was decorated in blues and greens, her favorite colors—the upholstered seating for the dinette in the salon and the same kind of upholstered covering on the seating in the living area. She eyed the queen-size berth covered in a blue bedspread in the captain's stateroom and had the sudden urge to pull the captain away from his duties and make wild and passionate love as the boat began to move out of its mooring. If they did that, their activity would be the talk of the pack for sure!

Now she wished she'd come boating with Adam before this. She had been so protective of her relationship with Richard when she could have just started over and enjoyed herself to the fullest. Like now.

The other staterooms were nice, the one with a double-size berth, covered in a green and blue floral bedspread, and the smallest stateroom with a double-decker twin-bed set. Six people could sleep comfortably in the staterooms, and actually, more could sleep on the bench-style seating in the living area.

She loved the seating at the stern of the boat too.

Sierra joined the rest of the "crew" up on deck. She saw cedar waxwings flying back and forth across the river catching flying insects, a bright-yellow band around their tails helping her to identify them. And closer to the water, a variety of swallows were zooming in to catch their own prey.

As they continued along the river while Adam captained the vessel, Sierra saw ducks and geese, seagulls, and then a hawk flying off in the distance. She was having so much fun watching fish jumping out of the water and the birds overhead and the wake the boat churned up and seeing other boaters at the early morning hour. She envisioned coming out here and watching the sunrise or the sunset someday.

Her dad joined her on the foredeck. "This is nice, isn't it?"

"Yeah, Dad. I understood why you got rid of the boat. It was too much upkeep and trouble for just the two of you after we left home, but don't you love it? Getting out on the water again?" She breathed in the fresh air.

"Yeah. You can't let this one get away, honey."

She laughed. "The boat or the wolf?"

He smiled down at her. "Both."

"Can you pilot the boat without a boater education card?"

"Yeah. Adam has one, and so do both his parents and Josh. As long as one of them supervises us, we're good."

The air was cooler on the river, and some of them were wearing windbreakers as they motored toward the falls.

Brooke called out that she was serving pastries, coffee, tea, and hot chocolate in the galley. Sierra gave her dad a hug and then they made their way to the companionway to join the others in having a fun breakfast.

Josh had taken over piloting the boat, and Adam joined Sierra to grab some coffee and a chocolate-covered doughnut. Sierra smiled when she saw that Adam had gotten her favorite special coffee: hazelnut and chocolate caramel. He smiled and kissed her.

"I can't believe I said no to going with you on a boat ride before."

"I know. I can't believe it either."

She laughed. "This has been so much fun." And they'd just started the day.

Adam set his coffee and doughnut down on the table and wrapped his arms around her waist while everyone else grabbed their treats and drinks and headed to the stern cockpit to lounge and enjoy their breakfast. She noticed her dad was going to the helm to talk to Josh instead, taking a coffee for both Josh and himself and a couple of doughnuts each. She knew before long, her father would be piloting the boat.

She would have loved to be with Adam and no one else, but it was special to be with her whole family too, bringing back all the happy memories of boating of her youth.

Sierra's mom was talking to Adam's mom about moving to the ranch and the location they had picked out. But then Josh handed over the helm to Janice and began talking to Adam about the case involving Sierra, and the conversation quickly switched to that. Adam's parents were both retired civilian police officers; Sierra's mother, a retired air police officer; and Sierra's dad, an army military police officer before moving up in rank. With them, plus Josh, a retired police detective, and Adam currently working as a police detective, Sierra felt they had their own private investigative force onboard.

"Okay, so what is going on with this investigation?" Josh asked.

"We're still trying to track down the rest of the people involved in this business with Sierra. At least we have enough evidence that we have a good chance of convicting them of several crimes. We just have to arrest them," Adam said.

Sierra wanted to be part of the conversation, but she didn't want Brooke and Janice to feel left out, and she was enjoying the day too much to want to talk about the ongoing police cases. But she was glad the others were trying to come up with solutions to take care of them.

She and Brooke joined Janice at the helm.

Brooke waved her cup of peppermint mocha at Sierra. "I hear the chocolate hazelnut coffee is your favorite, and Adam is always getting it for you."

"Yeah, he's the sweetest."

Janice smiled at Brooke. "I need to train Brad to get my favorite coffee for me."

"Josh ended up loving my peppermint mocha so much, I have

to make *him* some whenever I get myself some," Brooke said. "Josh was a real keeper. Just like your brother was for Janice. Adam's a keeper too."

"Yeah, I hear you." Sierra took another sip of her coffee.

"So?" Janice asked, raising a brow at Sierra.

Sierra chuckled. But what could she say? She and Adam would mate if or when they mated. For now, she was just having fun.

High overhead, a chirping sound caught their attention and everyone looked up to see an osprey calling out as it spied a fish in the river, dove headfirst for its prey, and skimmed the water with its talons, catching the fish near the surface and shooting back up into the sky.

Sierra had never seen anything like that before, and she was thrilled.

"We'll have to go fishing," Sierra's father said to Adam as if the osprey fishing suddenly made him think of that. Her father loved to fish.

"Yeah, we will have the best time. The ladies are welcome," Adam's dad said.

"Or shopping, movies, happy hour," Adam's mother said.

Sierra raised her hand. "I'm with you..."

The ladies all laughed. "That sounds like fun," Brooke said.

Everyone took turns at the helm, and while Sierra was captaining the ship, Adam was with her, the first real time they had been alone together while on the yacht since breakfast.

He rested his arm over her shoulder and leaned down and kissed her cheek. "You know, I could really get used to you being the captain of the ship and I'll be your first mate."

"Hmm, I could take you up on it."

"Good. That's exactly what I wanted to hear."

"This is a beautiful yacht, Adam. We will have to take it out every weekend we're off now."

He laughed. "First, I couldn't get you to take me up on it, and now?"

"Yeah, it's all your fault, you know."

"Oh, how's that?"

"When we went to see the River Patrol Unit about the stolen boat, just breathing in the air, listening to the sound of the water lapping at the boats, the seagulls crying overhead..." She sighed. "It just brought back so many good memories with my family. Of course there have been disasters too."

"Oh?"

"Yeah. I got seasick when we ran into a storm on one trip on our sailboat. Man, was I miserable. And another time a drunk driver hit our boat, put a hole in it, and was thrown from his boat."

"And?"

"Amazingly, he survived, but my dad wanted to rescue him in the worst way."

"Not your mom?"

"Um, no. She was staying with me and Brad, ready to rescue my dad if he needed to be after going after the guy. But the boat patrol told Dad they couldn't do anything until the boat ran out of gas. It was going in circles around the guy, hitting its own wake and changing course. The guy was lucky the water was warm—Texas, you know, not like this water—and that the boat didn't hit him, or he didn't just plain drown from being drunk."

"And?"

"When the boat ran out of gas, the boat patrol pulled the guy out of the water, charged him with driving a boat while intoxicated and the damage to our boat, towed his boat, and pulled his license. It could have been a lot worse for all of us. We were able to reach the boat ramp under our own power, but Dad had to put the boat in the shop for repairs and there was no boating for weeks. He was not a happy camper. Well, none of us were."

"I don't blame him. I'm just glad none of your family was injured. You're not afraid to boat then?"

"No. I love it out here. This is just wonderful. I have to ask… Just how soft is the captain's bed?"

Adam chuckled darkly. "Perfect while sharing it with the first mate."

She lifted her head to kiss him. "One of these days, we will have to try it out."

To their surprise, Josh was steaming up lobsters in the galley for lunch as a special treat, something they'd brought to celebrate Sierra's parents joining the pack and just the get-together, so the sandwich fixings were for anyone who didn't like lobster. Everyone opted for the lobster.

"They're fresh from this morning," Josh was explaining to the rest of the guys. "I bought the live lobsters, blanched them in salted, boiling water for two minutes, put them in an ice bath for twenty minutes, placed them in freezer bags and squeezed the air out of them, then put them in the ice chest. You can double-bag them and freeze them for up to a year. After that, it's time to boil them and eat them with a little lemon and butter."

"I was afraid we were going to be late getting here," Brooke said, rubbing Josh's back. "We were still putting them in the ice chest when we noticed the time."

"I'd say it was perfect timing," Sierra's dad said.

This was a slice of heaven, Sierra thought as she gave up the helm to her mom and Dad joined her mom up there. Sierra sat with Adam and the rest of the crew on the deck seating in the stern to have lunch, and she was thinking about her dad's comment about not letting Adam get away. She had no intention of it.

CHAPTER 24

While Sierra had been talking to Brooke and Janice at the helm, Brad had told Adam how glad he was that he finally got Sierra to go for a boat ride.

"You knew how much she would love it," Adam said to Brad.

"Yeah. She has always loved being near water. And boating... She was the first one to pack everything to go on a trip. If anyone was waffling about it—sometimes my mother, who wanted to garden or do something else—Sierra was always there to encourage her to go with us. She would tell Mom that it wouldn't be the same without her. If you're looking for a mate who loves boating like you do, Sierra's the one for you."

She had so much more to offer Adam as a mate, beyond that she loved boating. He was thinking they could run after dinner tonight at Brad's home since it was on the pack leaders' ranch. He really enjoyed running and playing with her. And she already had him hooked on ice cream dates. He would offer to take her to her favorite ice cream parlor after they ran as wolves tonight.

They finally reached the Willamette Falls in the Willamette River, a horseshoe-shaped, block waterfall, forty-two feet high and fifteen hundred feet wide. They felt the spray on their faces as some of them stood on the bow deck.

"Oh, this is beautiful," Sierra said, her parents agreeing.

Everyone else had seen the falls before, but Brooke said, "I always love seeing them."

"Me too," Josh said.

They were all taking cell phone pictures of the falls.

Then they headed back to the marina again, everyone vying for a time to captain the boat. Everyone got a couple of turns on the five-hour trip.

When they finally reached the marina, it was time to unload the boat. Brooke and Josh went home after that, everyone thanking them for the lobster lunch. The rest of them were driving in their separate vehicles to the pack's ranch.

Adam drove Sierra's car, hoping his Hummer would be repaired by Monday like the body shop had promised. "So what did you think about the boat ride and the family get-together?"

"It was wonderful. My folks and yours really hit it off. And everyone had a great time boating down the river. Did you and your new crime team solve any of the crimes you've been working on while I was talking to Brooke and Janice?"

He chuckled. "No. Though your dad believes the coroner is correct that the drowned men died accidentally, since he's a wolf like us. Your dad gave some scenarios he knew of where boats were found, and the boat captain or others had drowned. Of course then my dad was looking up cases for the local area, and our moms were trying to outdo them. Josh and I were getting the biggest kick out of them. They might all be retired from their original jobs, but they're all great detectives. How are you feeling about going for a wolf run and returning to Portland for our favorite ice cream spot after dinner with our families?"

"Boy, are you saying all the right things."

"Good, we have a date."

Adam got a call on Bluetooth from Tori and hoped he didn't need to go in about anything. She was on call today, and if she needed his backup, he would go in. "Yeah, Tori, what's up?"

"I was looking into Mr. Kinney's background after going over the statement he gave concerning the carjacker, and something didn't add up."

"We wondered about that too," Adam said. "So what did you learn?"

"Mr. Kinney has a record. He has spent time in jail for theft."

That didn't sound good. "And...?"

"Guess who he served time with."

"The carjacker," Adam guessed. "The description he gave didn't match the carjacker in the least, and then when we told him he was dead, Kinney was highly irritated we hadn't told him already. If he hadn't been so angry with us over it, I would have just figured he hadn't remembered the carjacker's description because of the head injury."

"Yep. And he'd been in jail with the guy we just picked up for taking part in the kidnapping of Melissa, Burt Barnes."

"Aww, hell, they're all in this together?" Adam couldn't be any more furious about it than he was. Here he was feeling sorry about Kinney being injured and that he could have been fatally killed, and all along he was one of the gang?

"It sounds like they could be."

"So that means they had a falling-out?" Why else would the carjacker have hit Kinney so hard as if he intended to kill him and then stolen his car?

"I figure that's what it is all about. The carjacker was trying to kill him, steal the car, and get rid of it."

"Are you arresting Kinney?" Adam wasn't planning on going in, despite how much he wanted to deal with this personally. He glanced over at Sierra and smiled.

"I want to gather more evidence against him, but I'm going home for now. I'll run in again if we have any more developments."

"Okay, sounds good. Keep me posted."

"I will. I didn't want to disrupt anything. You two have a fun day."

"We're going to have dinner with both of our families. We're almost there."

"Oooh, sounds serious. Enjoy your dinner!"

"We will, thanks," Adam said.

Then they said goodbye and Sierra said to Adam, "You could have gone in if you needed to."

"No way. Unless Tori needs emergency backup, I'm here to do this with you."

"I just wanted you to know that it's okay with me if you have to go in, even if we have plans," Sierra said.

"Only if it's a matter of life or death." Adam reached out and took Sierra's hand and kissed it. "Otherwise, this is more important."

She sighed. "Good. Though I'm serious about if you need to go in about work when we have something planned. I don't want you to think I'm clingy or anything."

"I would never think that, honey. I'm just glad we're together. And the same thing goes for you. If you get called up for anything, don't worry about any plans we might have. We'll make up for it."

"Okay."

They finally arrived at Brad's home on the ranch, and he and Sierra's and Adam's parents greeted them. Janice was in the kitchen pouring glasses of wine for the ladies. The guys were having beers.

The dads and Brad went out to grill the steaks, while the ladies talked about Sierra's parents relocating.

"When are you going to propose a mating to Sierra?" Kirk asked, getting right to the point as he was drinking a beer with Brad and Adam on the back patio.

Adam smiled at his dad while Brad put the steaks on the grill.

Sierra's dad frowned. "We tried to stay out of Sierra's love life, but both of us agreed that we didn't think Richard was right for her. His work always came before her, even when there wasn't a good reason for it. We all know how important promotions are in the military, but the family is important too. She deserves more. Better."

"I agree, sir. I definitely thought the same when she was going out to see him. And then he had the gall of coming out to see her here without telling her he was going to," Adam said.

"I heard about that." Kirk chuckled. "And there you were. That must have killed him, but it served him right. I'm glad you were there for her."

"I was glad to be there for her. Though neither of us could have anticipated his showing up like he did," Adam said.

"Once she called it quits with him, we knew she would eventually find a mate and settle down. When all the grandkids start showing up, we want to be here for them," Kirk said.

Adam laughed.

Kirk slapped Adam on the back. "Boating as a family again would be great too."

"I agree," Adam said.

"And anytime Adam's tied up at work, he's fine with me taking the boat out. We can all go out together," Adam's dad said.

Adam was glad his dad was making Sierra's parents feel welcome.

Sierra suddenly joined them on the back porch and slipped her arm around Adam's waist. He immediately settled his arm around her shoulders, leaned down, and kissed her uplifted lips. She was smiling at him, and he thought she had come out to rescue him.

"We're just talking about boating as a family again," Kirk said as Brad served up the steaks and they headed inside to eat.

"Oh, really," Sierra said to her dad.

Adam laughed.

She kissed him again. "We sure had a great time."

"We did," Adam said, remembering a day long ago when his father would take his family boating on the Willamette River. "We'll do it again when you all get settled in."

"Sounds good to me. We're all running as wolves on the ranch after dinner, right?" Kirk asked as they joined the others inside the house.

"Yeah," Brad said. "We'll probably have some other wolves join us too. But we'll go as a family."

"That's what we've missed while living in San Antonio." Rhonda, Sierra's mom, set out the plates and silverware. "A safe place like this to run wild. We've been running every night with Adam's parents since we arrived here, and we're thoroughly enjoying it. Leidolf showed us the stream and the waterfall, the forested land, all of it."

"Well, I couldn't be any gladder," Sierra said.

"Me either," Brad said, Janice agreeing.

"Where will you be living?" Sierra asked.

Adam was wondering that too.

"We're going to build a home on the ranch. Leidolf hired us to provide security for around the property. Adam's parents are already providing some of the security, so we'll swap off days. We'll be chasing down hunters, watching the security videos. With our military police backgrounds, they were eager to hire us," Kirk said.

Adam was glad they would be working with his parents in security.

"The best thing about it is that we can run as wolves sometimes while we're doing it." Rhonda took Kirk's hand and squeezed, looking up at him, and he smiled back at her. "We've missed running as wolves so this will be an enjoyable change of pace for us. We'll also be able to monitor things from the house, once it's built. We'll be watching things from Leidolf and Cassie's house until then. We have to return to put the house up for sale and move our household goods here. The whole pack has offered to help us get things sorted out once the house is built. Because of military personnel coming and going all the time in San Antonio, the market is good, and we should be able to sell the house quickly."

"We already picked a location and have agreed on the house plans. The building will begin soon," Kirk said.

Adam thought Sierra's parents really looked happy about the prospect. He was glad they would be living here soon.

When they finished up their dinner, Janice and Sierra hurried to clear away dishes, but Brad and Adam began helping too.

"Just set everything on the counter. We'll clean up later," Janice said. "We're going to run now so the two of you can return home and have the rest of the night to yourselves."

Brad chuckled.

Sierra blushed and Adam smiled. He was all for it.

Then they were going to different rooms and stripping out of their clothes. This time, Adam and Sierra were together. She didn't seem to want him to give her space this time, despite her parents being in the house. He was glad their relationship had truly changed. As soon as they were naked, he pulled her into his arms and kissed her. He couldn't help himself. He wanted to make love to her and spend the rest of the night with her in bed.

But running with the family as wolves was important too, and he loved to run with her as a wolf. This time, Brad and Janice and her sister would run with them, not on guard duty, and her mom and dad and his parents would be with them too.

Sierra smiled up at him and whispered, "Thanks for making my parents love you."

"They do?" He was glad to hear it.

She smiled again. "Yeah. And of course Dad loves your boat." Then she kissed Adam back and sighed, releasing him. "Let's race off to the falls."

They both shifted and licked each other's faces as if they had to kiss in a wolf's way too before they headed out. Then she led the way and they found everyone sitting in their wolf forms waiting on them.

Rhonda led the way, Kirk following his mate out the door, then Adam's parents, Sierra, Adam, Janice, and Brad next. When everyone was outside, Brad and Janice were in the lead.

Adam wasn't sure how to behave with Sierra now that her parents and his were here. It was funny how a change in a group would make such a difference in the dynamics. He would have bitten her and played with her, but he didn't want to look foolish. He and

Sierra were following behind the crowd, and he was watching where they were going when Sierra bumped into him.

At first, he thought she wasn't watching where she was going, and she had bumped him by accident. But then she nipped his ear, her eyes bright with excitement, and he was ready to play with her and forget his and her parents, her brother and sister-in-law. He was ready to enjoy this. That was part of what being a wolf meant to them. Being protective, sure. Loyal, yes. But playful too? Definitely.

He chased after her and she raced off, away from the rest of the family. He was bound and determined to catch her, and she was just as determined to keep out of his reach. This was so great, and they were working off their dinner at the same time so they could have dessert. He loved her, he realized. Unconditionally. He couldn't have found a better mate in Sierra, but he still wanted to give her time to feel the same way about him.

He finally reached her tail and nipped at the tip, and she wheeled around and tackled him with a woof and a growl.

Sierra loved Adam. She knew he was hesitant to play with her in front of the rest of her family and maybe his, but she wanted him to know that no matter who they were with, he could be himself—either as a human or in wolf form. Still, she moved him away from her family, just so he would feel comfortable playing with her.

She loved being aggressive with him, like she'd been with her brother growing up.

Adam tackled her right back, gentler than he would with his male wolf friends because she was smaller. Her brother had been really rambunctious with her, but her parents had made him settle down if he got too wild.

She was having a ball play-fighting Adam, breaking off from the fight and then running off again. He was on her tail in a flash. She was trying her darnedest to keep out of his path. She was a fast runner, but so was he. And she loved it. How fun would that be if he could never catch up to her? No fun at all!

He tackled her again. Okay, she *really* needed a head start!

Then she heard her mom woof, wondering where they'd gotten off to. Sierra woofed back to let her know they were fine as Adam was chewing on Sierra's neck in a play bite. She retaliated with a bite to his muzzle, and he mouthed hers back. God, she loved him. She had so been missing this in her life.

Adam gentled his play-bites and nuzzled her muzzle. She figured he wanted them to rejoin her family. Which was fine by her. She had just wanted to get some of her wolf aggression out in playtime with him first. Every chance she got.

She waited for Adam to run off so she could nip at his tail for a while, but he was panting, smiling at her, giving her the evil wolf eye. He wasn't going for it. Fine. Next time, she was chasing him!

She raced off and he tore off after her. *Give me a head start the next time!*

He nipped at her tail and she rounded on him. They weren't going to get very far like this. But what did they care? They were having a blast.

After finally visiting with her family for a while as wolves, they all headed back to the ranch house. Sierra would have raced off to play some more with Adam after their hour or so restful walk through the land, but she was enjoying the walk with the family. She hadn't done this with the whole family together in a long time. She'd run with Brad and Janice since she had arrived in Oregon though. It could be a while before she would have time to run with her parents after they moved here.

They finally reached the house and shifted and dressed. Janice had shifted and dressed and was already in the kitchen getting glasses of water for everyone, though they had all been drinking down at the stream as wolves before they returned to the ranch house.

Then they all said their goodbyes.

On their way home, Sierra said to Adam, "Did Dad lecture you about anything while Brad was grilling the steaks?"

"No. He thought I was the right mate for you."

She smiled. "Ice cream still next on the agenda?"

"You bet."

CHAPTER 25

When they finally arrived home, Sierra pulled into his garage and parked the car. She closed the garage door, and she and Adam got out of the car. "I had fun, but I'm glad to be home," he said. *With* Sierra.

He wanted in the worst way to tell her he had to have her for his mate for all time.

"That was a great weekend. Busy, but great," Sierra said.

He felt the same, but he hadn't had this much fun in a long time. Though he wished he had more time to spend alone with her.

"I mean, as far as helping Tori with her unpacking and the next day seeing my family and yours, the boat excursion, dinner, and the running as wolves. And ice cream both nights. Everything was fun." She looked like she'd had a great time, and he was glad about that.

"I agree. Weekends can be boring for me, just chilling out, while Josh is having fun with his mate." He was about to pop the mating question.

Sierra smiled at Adam. "Yeah, it sucks when your best friend gets hitched and leaves you all alone."

He sighed. "Sometimes I would go out with Ethan or Josh's brother, Maverick. But they can be busy on the weekends too."

"You'll still get to plan outings with them. Or we can do, um, couple stuff with Josh and Brooke too," she said.

That was just the prompt he needed to lead him into the mating question. "About the couple stuff, I don't know how you feel, but—"

"About us?" She went into the kitchen and poured a glass of burgundy for both of them and drank some of hers.

"Yeah." He drank some of his wine.

She sighed and set her glass down on the kitchen counter. "I've waited forever for the right wolf to sweep me off my feet, and now that I've finally realized what I've got, I'm not letting you go. I just wouldn't allow myself to see what I knew was right before my eyes all these months."

Hell yeah! "So you're saying—"

"I love you? Yes! With all my heart."

"All right! I love you too." He wasn't waiting any longer to mate his wolf.

She smiled and wrapped her arms around his neck. "No matter how many times I try to consider the cons of mating you, all I can think of are all the pros."

He encircled his arms around her waist and kissed her forehead.

"When it comes right down to it, I know just what I want. You." She kissed his mouth, tongued his tongue with rapture, then pulled away before he could get more into the kiss. She grabbed his hand to haul him toward the bedroom and get down to business.

But he swept her up in his arms and carried her into the bedroom, then set her down on her feet. She began unbuttoning Adam's shirt, and he leaned down to kiss her willing mouth as she lifted her head and offered her sweet lips to him. She kissed him back, nibbling on his lower lip. Then her hands tugged at his shirt as if she were eager to undress him. She kicked off her sandals and made him sit down on the bed. Then she began to remove his shoes and socks.

Adam was over the moon about it as he rose to his feet and unfastened his belt.

He began kissing Sierra's soft lips again, their bodies pressed together with interest and intrigue. He kissed the tender skin below her ear, and she sighed. He had wanted this between them for so long.

Already his cock was hard and ready, her seductive body

pressing against him, making his blood burn white-hot. His fingers itched to yank off every article of clothing she was wearing, but he fought the inclination. He wanted to savor this moment for all time.

She ran her hand over the front of his Bermuda shorts. It made him think of wearing his suit for work now and coming home to peel out of it and make love to Sierra every night. After a day on the boat, she was wearing a thin-strapped tank top and jean shorts.

She ran her hands up his abs in a sensual caress and then thumbed his nipples, sending a streak of need shooting straight to his groin. Slow and steady wasn't going to do it.

He began pulling off her tank top, and she lifted her arms for him. Then he pulled her top off and tossed it aside and stared at the sexy bra she was wearing. He was so busy getting dressed this morning for the boat trip that he hadn't noticed what she was dressing in, only what her street clothes looked like. He ran his hands over her formfitting bra and felt her nipples pressed against the intimate see-through fabric trimmed in lace.

"Hmm."

"Do you like?" she whispered against his cheek.

"Oh yeah," he said, kissing her head, his hands still snugly wrapped around her breasts. He swept his thumbs over her rigid nipples and she moaned softly.

She slid her hands down his pants and squeezed his buttocks, rubbing her mound against him.

She smelled of coconut butter, the wind and the sea and the woods, and now she would be all his.

His heart sped up and he skimmed his hands down her sides until he could reach her shorts. He unfastened them and slid them down her hips. She immediately reached for his shorts and unzipped them, and they slipped off his hips.

He kicked them off. Then he moved his mouth over her breasts and licked her nipple through the fabric. She hummed with pleasure and slid her hands down his boxer briefs and cupped his ass again, which made his cock twitch with need.

"You are sooo hot," she said, kissing his shoulder.

Her mouth was warm and inviting. "So are you." He kissed her mouth and unfastened her bra, then slid the straps off her shoulders, letting her bra fall to the carpeted floor. He massaged her breasts, loving the feel of them and the fragrance that was all Sierra, sweet and sexy. His mouth caught hers again, their tongues teasing and tasting—all sweetness.

She moved her hands up to run them over his back, her fingernails skimming his skin lightly, tickling—not meaning to—and he fought chuckling.

Then he slid his hands down her sides and pulled her scrap of silk panties down. She immediately seized his boxer briefs and removed them, his cock springing free. He grabbed her up, her legs wrapped around his, and carried her to the bed. He was past ready to ravish the seductive she-wolf and make her his.

She kissed his chest as he moved against her body, kissing her mouth that softened against his. He rubbed his body against her, inciting their pheromones to take off in a mating frenzy.

Their tongues clashed in a fevered dance and his blood felt on fire. His hand grazed the curve of her breast, but it wasn't enough to satisfy him, and he covered her breast with his hand and rubbed the palm over her rigid nipple. She sucked on his tongue and he was about undone. He immediately reciprocated and she moaned, then swept her hand down his back and cupped a buttock and squeezed.

"Perfect," she said, pressing a kiss against his lips and nuzzling his mouth before nipping on his lower lip in a gentle, sexy way.

His cock was raring to go. He slid his hand down to her dewy, curly hairs and found her nub and began to stroke her.

"Oh, yes," she whispered, breathless, their hearts hammering out of sync, their pulses rapid.

Her hands were exploring everywhere she could touch, and his skin tingled with her caresses. Her body arched to the feel of his touching her nub, stroking, plying his skills to arouse her. And she *was* aroused, just like he was, her feminine sexual scent an aphrodisiac to him.

He kissed her belly and worked his way to a breast, his finger still stroking her nub. And then he was taking her rigid nipple in his mouth as she ran her fingers through his hair and lightly massaged his scalp, making him feel like he was in heaven. She practically stopped breathing, grew very still, and then bucked against him.

He hurried his strokes, kissing and licking her nipple right before she cried out, "Oh, A...dam," in a husky breath.

He smiled and kissed her mouth long and hard and deep. When he pulled his mouth away from hers to catch his breath and ask her if she was truly ready, she held her finger to his lips and said, "Yes!"

Then he nudged her legs further apart and slid his cock between her legs and embedded himself as far as he could go. He began to thrust, long, slow, deep thrusts, filling her completely. He couldn't believe the fun-loving she-wolf he had known for several months was now his to mate.

He was one lucky wolf as he continued to thrust, breathing in their sexy, wolfish scents, burning up with white-hot friction and hot-blooded desire. He hadn't thought he would ever be this lucky or feel the kind of bliss he felt with her.

And then he exploded deep inside her and she cried out again as the climax consumed them both. He collapsed on top of her, inside her, having claimed her for his very own wolf. "I so love you."

She wrapped her arms around him and kissed his mouth with enthusiasm. "Hmm, I love you right back."

Adam snuggled with Sierra, thinking how she had been the one who had captured his imagination as a possible mate. He was glad she had chosen him as a mate.

"We need to tell everyone we're mated," Adam said, caressing her arm, wanting to get this out in the open to let all the other bachelors out there know she wasn't available any longer.

"Hmm," she said and kissed his chest.

He continued to run his fingers lightly over her soft skin. "A wedding date?"

She sighed.

"A honeymoon?"

Her breathing grew light.

He closed his eyes. "All right. We'll decide it all tomorrow."

She chuckled under her breath and he smiled.

They woke early the next day after making love a couple more times during the night and showering afterward. Sierra glanced at the clock this morning as she snuggled with Adam and groaned. "I sure wish we had the whole day to ourselves instead of having to go into work."

And she was thinking she could get more done at home if she was working part-time again. Now that she was with Adam, she wanted to spend every spare moment she had off with him. At least for now as newly mated wolves. Would that change? Probably. But she knew, no matter how much work they were both doing, she would want to spend time with him and enjoy every minute when they did.

Sierra rested her chin and arm over Adam's chest, looking at his smiling eyes and lips. "We have to go to work."

He combed his fingers through her hair. "Hmm."

She was ready to make love to him all over again. She licked his rigid nipple. "I think we're a bad influence on each other."

Smiling, Adam stroked her arms, sending heat streaking across her air-chilled skin.

She sighed. "I just needed to take a chance on a new relationship, and I soon knew you were the one for me."

"No regrets?"

"Are you kidding?" Her chin resting on his chest again, she shook her head. "You're the best mate I could have ever asked for." She kissed his chest. "I think I was ready the day I left Texas to live in Oregon."

"Hell, if I'd known that, I would have made it known I wanted to date you from the beginning."

"You did, in your way." She patted Adam's chest but before she left the bed, he pulled her into his arms and rolled her onto her back so he could kiss her, one leg between hers, telling her they were together.

No more guessing how either would react.

"I guess I'm lucky you weren't relying on weeks of dates to help you make your decision," he said.

She laughed, wrapped her arms around his neck, and kissed him back. "I didn't need to date you to know I loved you." She reached down and patted his bare butt. "We have to leave if we're going to get to work on time."

He groaned, then let her up, and they both hurried to dress. He pulled on a pair of boxer briefs. "I can't believe I don't want to go to work."

She laughed. "You always know the right things to say."

He grabbed his trousers and pulled them on.

She was dressing in a pantsuit but paused to pull him into her arms and kiss him. "I love you."

He kissed her like he wanted to take her right back to bed. "I love you too. Today will be entirely too long a workday."

She smiled up at him. "I agree. More later." Then she released him and brushed out her hair.

He pulled on his socks and shoes, then finished buttoning his shirt.

"Don't do any foot races with bad guys today. You're going to need your strength for more bed play tonight."

He smiled at her, looking ready to take on the challenge. "I'll be ready. Oh, and do you want to call the pack leaders about us mating, or should I?"

She grabbed her phone, smiled at Adam, and pressed a contact's name. "Hello, Cassie? Adam and I are officially mated."

CHAPTER 26

As soon as they were in Sierra's car on the way to work, Adam got a call and said, "Okay, thanks." He put his phone away. "Good news. My Hummer has been repaired. We could drop by there on the way to work and pick it up."

"Oh, that's wonderful. Yeah, sure, that would be great. One less thing on our to-do list and then you can run in to work anytime you need to, and I can too, without having to ask others to drive us."

"I still want someone to watch over you, just in case."

She let out her breath in exasperation. Not because Adam was being protective of her but because he needed to be.

They changed direction and drove to the auto body shop.

They finally arrived at the car dealership, and he leaned over and kissed her. She kissed him right back, glad she'd finally made her desires known.

He smiled at her. "I'm ready to call in sick. Just say the word."

She laughed. "Then we would put Tori in a lurch. Though the anticipation of being alone with you tonight after work will make the day seem even longer."

"I agree." Adam gave her a hug. "I'll be right back." Then he left her car to go inside and pay for his vehicle.

She texted Tori to tell her they were on their way into work, but Adam had to stop at the dealership to pick up his Hummer.

Sierra looked up to watch for Adam coming out of the building and saw the woman who had kidnapped Melissa, just as she had described her, minus the wig, walking toward the customer service building. Sierra's jaw dropped. Was it Dover's girlfriend? Her heart racing, Sierra hurried to text Adam: Dover's girlfriend,

Phyllis Kenton, is headed into customer service! I'm pretty sure that was her.

Adam didn't respond to Sierra's text, and she frowned and texted him again. Suddenly, Phyllis ran out of the building and headed straight for a red Fiat parked in the lot. Sierra hurried to back her vehicle out of the parking space and drove it behind the Fiat before Phyllis could start the engine and back out of her space. Sierra sufficiently blocked her in, and Phyllis couldn't make a move. Sierra just hoped Phyllis wouldn't ram her car into Sierra's. But the Fiat was smaller than Sierra's car so she thought Phyllis wouldn't.

The woman honked her horn at Sierra, angry that Sierra had blocked her vehicle.

Adam came running out of the building, and Sierra honked at him to let him know where Phyllis was.

The woman got out of her car, ran at Sierra's car with a gun in hand, and pointed it at Sierra's window.

Her heart practically seizing and not wanting to get shot, Sierra drove the car out of the way. Immediately, the woman rushed back to the Fiat to jump into the driver's seat, but Adam intercepted her and grabbed her arm, wresting the gun away from her, and cuffed her.

"Yes!" Elated Adam had shown up in time and caught the woman, Sierra parked her car again. She didn't know whether to leave her car and see if she could do anything for Adam or not, since it was police business and he didn't appear to need her help. He was on his phone, probably calling in the arrest.

Then Sierra opened her window and heard Adam reading the woman her rights. A couple of sirens sounded in the distance, and the police vehicles were headed in their direction.

Good. Hopefully, they were coming to back up Adam. She knew the bureau had a warrant out for Phyllis's arrest, so Sierra suspected the police would put her in the back of a squad car, take her in, and process her in at the jail. Sierra assumed Adam would question Phyllis after he picked up his Hummer and drove in to work.

As soon as two patrol cars arrived, Adam handed Phyllis off to one of the officers and walked over to Sierra's vehicle.

"Good catch," she said, getting out of her car and hugging Adam. "Where were you when I texted you?"

"Disputing the charges for my vehicle when I got your text. They had the wrong account. Before I answered the text, I looked up and saw Phyllis entering the customer service lobby. I thought it was Dover's girlfriend. She saw me and bolted, and then I knew it was her. I raced after her, and when I saw your car blocking her in, I was reminded what a great mate you are." He kissed Sierra.

"Until she pulled a gun on me."

"That's where I came in."

"Good thing!"

"Yeah, well, I'm glad she didn't shoot you."

Adam didn't tell Sierra that she shouldn't have done even that much. It wouldn't have done him any good if he had. They needed to get all the gang and put them in jail, and if it meant taking a chance to help catch them, Sierra was doing it.

"Are you going to be all right?" Adam asked.

"Yeah, I'm just glad we got another one of them. Now you and Tori can question her."

"We'll sure do that. I'm going back inside to finish paying for my vehicle, and then I'll be right out."

"Okay. I'll watch for any more bad guys."

Adam smiled at her. "You do that." He hugged her and kissed her again, then headed back inside the building.

She was serious.

Adam hadn't wanted Sierra to get involved in apprehending the bad guys. That was *his* job. Though he was glad she'd stopped Phyllis, he certainly hadn't wanted Sierra to risk getting injured, but he figured no amount of saying so would change Sierra's mind about helping him solve a case if she thought she could. And he was glad he didn't have to be involved in a car chase with the woman, risking lives.

As soon as he was in his Hummer, he drove out of the parking lot and Sierra followed him into work.

She called him on Bluetooth. "You didn't like that I stopped Phyllis from backing out of her parking space."

He sighed. "I just don't want these people hurting you."

"I have to admit I was afraid she would run into my car and then I would end up having my car in the shop for repairs."

"I was more afraid she would shoot you."

"Which is why I moved my car."

"I'm just grateful you weren't injured. I'm going to call it in to Tori and let her know we got Dover's girlfriend."

"Tori will be thrilled."

"She will be."

He ended the call with Sierra and called Tori next. "Hey, we caught Phyllis at the dealership where I was picking up my Hummer."

"Oh, wow, great going!"

"Yeah, she's in custody now. We'll see you in a few minutes." He was glad Tori had made arrangements to speak with Kinney this morning first thing. He glanced in his rearview mirror and saw Sierra right behind him. He smiled. He couldn't wait to get off work tonight to be with her and enjoy mated life with her. She was a real trouper.

Sierra and Adam had barely walked in the door at the bureau when the chief called Sierra into the office.

Now what?

"Yes, sir." Sierra was afraid she'd really screwed up on one of the sketches.

Tori glanced up from her work at her desk and raised a brow.

Adam was frowning at Sierra, looking worried for her. She patted his shoulder with reassurance. "Everything's fine, no matter what it's all about." She didn't want him worrying about her when she knew he had to question Kinney and Phyllis this morning and needed to remain focused. Then she walked into the chief's office.

"Shut the door and take a seat."

She did, figuring the chief was going to complain about something she had done. Or maybe say something about her dating Adam. She wasn't sure how her boss felt about people working in the same office and dating each other.

"The woman that the hiker found in the woods and you sketched for us? Her daughter recognized the sketch and confirmed her mother had been hiking alone and hadn't told anyone where she was going. The autopsy revealed she'd broken her ankle, and the area where she was found was so remote that no one located her for weeks. There wasn't any evidence of foul play. It was just an accident. But the daughter was glad to get closure. You do excellent work."

"But?" She knew there was a "but," as serious as her boss sounded.

"I posted the full-time position and interviewed someone who can fill the job. He was a friend of Willy's so he knew all about his retiring and you taking over Willy's position. I needed to make sure you really want to go back to working just part-time and doing witness sketches."

She wanted to say yes, so she could do all the things she liked to do, and she did have her army retirement check. "Did this other person agree to me doing just witness sketches if he took my full-time job?"

"Absolutely. He was doing all the sketches in Medford, but his girlfriend got a better paying job in Portland and he wants to move here with her. Now, I didn't confirm he had the full-time job because it's yours and you're great at it. I just wanted to learn your thoughts on this. It's strictly up to you. But if you would like to go back to working part-time, we can do that."

"You're sure he wouldn't decide he would rather do the witness sketches instead?"

Her boss gave her one of his rare smiles, then grew serious again. "Listen, no matter what, he'll have to do the forensic sketches. I told him my full-time artist does both right now. He doesn't mind doing either. He just wants to have a job here. He's a former police officer who is an artist on the side."

"Okay."

"I know you had the arrangement with Willy that you would do just witness statements, but if you go back to working part-time and the new guy takes the full-time position and is swamped and needs a forensic sketch done—"

"Right. I would do it. Can I think about this overnight?" Normally, she would have just decided it right then and there. She loved doing this part-time. But there were the perks of getting more paid vacation time and health insurance coverage that she didn't have as a part-time employee. And she wanted to talk to Adam about it now that he was her mate.

"Of course. Let me know as soon as you decide so I can get back with him and tell him if he's got the full-time job or not."

"Okay, I'll give you my decision tomorrow."

"All right, that's it. And you're doing great."

"Thanks. I'm glad we got the identification on the woman." Really glad. She had needed the validation of her work. Then she left the chief's office, and both Tori and Adam were waiting to hear what the chief had to say.

"What did the chief want?" Adam asked, not waiting for her to clue them in.

Sierra thought Adam and Tori would have left already to question Kinney.

"Well, he has an applicant who is qualified as a sketch artist to fill the full-time position."

"But you're doing fantastic work," Tori said, frowning, as if she thought Sierra wouldn't want to give up her job.

"Thanks. It's only if I want to give up the full-time job. The chief isn't making me."

"So what are you going to do?" Adam asked.

"Take the part-time job," Tori said, patting her shoulder. "Only witness sketches, right?"

"Unless the new guy needed me to do one of his jobs if he got swamped."

"But you enjoy doing the witness sketches. I haven't known you for long, but being what we are, I could sense it. You stress out every time you have to see a dead body. And you're having to come in all the time now. You have an army retirement, so you're not hurting for money," Tori said.

"And I could go back to teaching art when I'm not required to be here to do the sketches all the time. I can garden and do some other things I enjoy doing. I feel like I'm kind of back in the rat race again. I really liked working part-time. I thought I would get used to working with dead bodies, but it's not happening right away. And it's not as fun for me now."

"Then I think you have your answer," Adam said. "When did the chief need an answer?"

"I told him I would tell him tomorrow."

"Sure, you could sleep on it," Tori said.

Tori was right about the way Sierra stressed every time she had to see a dead body. "Actually, you're right, Tori. I've been hoping the chief would find someone else for the job and I would go back to what I was doing. I just needed to bounce it off you guys. So I'm ready to just give the chief my decision, and the other guy won't have to wait to learn that he has got the job."

Adam pulled Sierra into his arms and kissed her. "I just want you to be happy, no matter what you decide."

"Doing part-time work." She kissed him, glad he was leaving the decision-making up to her. "Thanks, guys. Uh"—Sierra glanced at Tori—"did he tell you?"

"You're mated?" Tori asked, whispering.

"Yeah." Sierra smiled brightly and Tori gave her a hug.

"I'm so thrilled for the two of you." Tori gave Adam a hug too. "Finally, you did it. And no, he didn't tell me."

"Yeah, we finally did it. We told Cassie this morning, but I'm sure the word will soon spread. Be back in a sec, but don't wait on me. I know you're busy." Then Sierra returned to the office and knocked.

The chief was on the phone, but he motioned for her to come in.

"Same arrangement as before. Part-time. Witness sketches only, except for when the new guy gets swamped and needs me to help," Sierra said to her boss.

"Are you sure?" the chief asked.

Sierra nodded. "I'll be glad he has the full-time job, but I really enjoy doing this part-time. So we're good."

"All right then. You'll keep this job until he can move up here and you can switch with each other."

She thanked the chief and felt so lighthearted and happy. She knew this was the right decision to make. To Sierra's surprise, Tori and Adam were still waiting for her to tell them what the final decision was. They were so sweet.

"I did it," Sierra said, smiling. "I feel great. I'll work full-time until he gets to Portland and can take over. I really am relieved."

"I'm so glad," Adam said and gave her another hug and kiss.

Tori gave her a hug too. "I knew it. Okay, we've got to go do some interrogations. We'll see you in a little bit."

Sierra smiled, but then she got a call to do another dead-body sketch. Man, was she hoping the new guy would get here soon. She grabbed her camera and was about to head out when her boss called out to her. "He'll be here Wednesday."

"Okay, great." Yes! Only two more days of doing dead-body sketches. She took off to get this one done.

CHAPTER 27

After Adam called Josh to let him know he was mated to Sierra, he and Tori headed into the interrogation room to speak to Kinney first in the small room featuring a table, three chairs, and a one-way mirror.

"Okay," Adam said to Kinney, taking a seat in front of him while Tori stood nearby, "we know you were in jail with Burt Barnes and Ollie Thomas, the carjacker, who tried to kill you."

Kinney stiffened.

"Do you want to tell us about it?" Adam asked.

"I did my time," Kinney said.

"Right, for the burglaries you were convicted of. But the rest?"

Kinney smiled. "You don't have anything else on me."

"Okay, so don't you want to get these guys after they nearly killed you?"

"Only Ollie did that. And he's dead."

"Good thing for you. What if Dover tells the rest of the guys loyal to him to finish the job? That's who gave the orders, right?"

Kinney cleared his throat.

"Do you need some coffee? Water?" Tori asked.

"Uh, coffee, thanks."

An officer soon brought him a cup of coffee, and when he left, Adam said to Kinney, "Dover ordered your death, right?"

"I can't say for sure. You would have to ask Ollie, and he's dead."

"Who were the others in the car with him? The driver? The other passenger?"

"I don't know. It was like I said. I couldn't see the one in the passenger seat." Kinney took a long, deep breath. "Ah hell, the driver was"—he let out his breath—"Victor Freemont."

"The guy that's having a fling with Phyllis." Adam let out an exasperated sigh. "Why didn't you tell us that before?"

"Victor would want me dead. And yeah. Dover would be pretty sore at both Victor and Phyllis if he learned they're together."

"So why was Ollie trying to kill you?"

"I was trying to go clean."

Adam wasn't sure what to believe.

"I know you don't believe it, but I promised my wife and my daughters I was going straight. I'm on parole, I have a job, I'm working hard, and I don't want to lose my family. My wife will leave me if I go back in."

"Dover wanted you on a new job?"

"Yeah. To steal the car of the woman who testified against him for breaking into her hotel room. I was supposed to help kidnap some random kid off the street and dump the hostage at the woman's house, then call the police to say the kid was tied up there and frame Sierra Redding. I wasn't going to do it. Like I said, I've done my time. I don't want to get involved in any of Dover's revenge plots. But once you work for Dover, he thinks he owns you. For life. No one says no to doing a job for him."

"But you did." Adam admired Kinney for finally trying to do what was right. He just wished he'd informed the police that Dover was planning to send his henchmen to do the job for him before it happened.

"And look where that got me. Nearly dead."

"Do you know of any others who refused to work for him that he had killed?"

Kinney ran his hands through his hair. "No. Look. He's angry that the woman who did my witness sketch put him away. No one's done that to him before. He blames her. He wants revenge. Until he can force her to recant what happened—say that she did have a dog, the one in the hotel room—so he can get his sentence reduced, maybe even commuted, he'll continue to cause trouble for her."

"Will you testify to this? To Ollie trying to kill you under Dover's orders?"

"I don't have any proof."

"All right, how about this. You work for us. You wear a wire. You tell Dover you'll do what he wants as long as you have his word he doesn't try to have you killed again."

"What about the others?"

"His girlfriend and Burt Barnes are in jail. They're not getting out anytime soon. Lonnie Hicks is in jail too."

"Okay, I'll do it."

"Good." Then they wouldn't have to threaten Kinney with giving false information concerning the appearances of the carjacker and others who were involved in the carjacking.

"It was Victor's car, a red 1997 Ford Expedition," Kinney said. "Listen, after Dover went to jail, the regular crew began doing jobs for him on the outside, but they were also doing their own thing."

"Such as?" Adam asked, glad Kinney was still talking.

"Hell, Burt Barnes was bragging about a captain of a boat hitting his boat's wake really hard, and the two men sitting on the transom fell off. From the distance, Burt and his crew, Victor Freemont, Phyllis Kenton, and Lonnie Hicks, couldn't see the men in the water. All they could see was the captain driving back around to pick them up. Then the captain left the controls and dove in to get them. When Burt drove up to help, there was no sign of the men anywhere."

Adam's heart rate sped up. "On the Willamette River?"

"Yeah, the men must have drowned. And there was a boat just sitting there, ripe for the picking. Someone else would have taken it if they hadn't. That's what Burt said. Phyllis drove their old boat to the boat ramp, and Burt and the other guys drove the other boat there. They ran into the River Patrol Unit, though, and had to pretend they didn't have any ID on them, just because they didn't appear to have life jackets onboard. Burt had no idea if there were or weren't. They cited him for not having a permit to pilot the boat. He has one, but he didn't want the officers to know his real name. He said he and the other men were sweating bullets, afraid the officers knew who the boat really belonged to. Burt showed me pictures of the boat. I thought it would be some old clunker, but it was a beautiful boat."

"Like this?" Adam showed him a picture of the boat.

Kinney frowned as he eyed the picture. "Uh, yeah, that's it. You found it already?"

"Do you think they were telling the truth about the men drowning accidentally?" Adam asked.

"Yeah, they just got lucky." Kinney shrugged. "It was a fluke. Easily lifted. I mean, I know they'd done it with a couple of other boats they found in slips and sold them, but nothing that grand."

"The three men who were on that boat were found dead in the Willamette. They didn't report that the men had gone overboard, that they could have drowned. And you didn't report it either," Adam said.

Sweat beaded up on Kinney's forehead. "Hell, no. I mean, I wasn't doing any more jobs for them. Burt called me up out of the blue and was bragging about it, like he was telling me what I was missing. But I'd never helped them to steal boats. Truthfully, Dover didn't approve of it. Burt said they were making way more money selling stolen boats than we were when we were stealing from hotel rooms. By then, I was clean and staying that way. I wasn't there. I only know what Burt told me. And he's been known to exaggerate or lie.

"If anyone would have had it in him to kill anyone though, it's Victor Freemont. Or Dover's girlfriend, Phyllis. She thinks she's in charge most of the time, but so does Victor, now that Dover's out of the picture."

"What makes you think Victor and Phyllis might be capable of murder?" Adam asked.

Kinney scoffed. "The two of them are like Bonnie and Clyde

when they get together, waving guns around, acting big, shooting off their mouths. Victor has got his grandmother's farm way out where they go for shooting practice. I've been there once. I don't know the address. I rode with Burt that time."

An investigative officer knocked on the door, and Adam paused the interrogation. "Yeah, Roland?"

"You had me looking into Victor Freemont's properties, and we found he had inherited this property from his grandmother."

Adam smiled. "Good going."

"No GPS directions out there though."

"Okay, thanks." Adam returned to the room and said to Kinney, "We have the address to Victor's place. Do you think you could give us directions?" Adam asked.

"Uh, I could tell you where to start, but I would have to go with you to tell you where to turn off."

"I'll take you," Adam said, eager to get further on the case. What if they found shell casings and bullets on the property that were connected to any shootings they might be looking into, like when Adam and Sierra were running as wolves in Forest Park?

"Do you know of any other robberies they've committed recently?" Adam asked.

"No. Once I said I wasn't going to work with them any longer—and to tell the truth, not only do I not want to mess up my parole or lose my family, I can't stand Victor or Phyllis—none of them have had any contact with me. Until they tried to kill me. Except for Burt bragging to me about the boat on the phone the one day. I really don't have anything else I can add. I need to be getting to work in a couple of hours."

"All right, thanks, Kinney, for all your help. The DA is dropping any charges against you. We'll get with you on speaking to Dover so you can try to pin him down on the attempt to kill you. But we'll take you out to Victor's place in the meantime." Then Adam called the judge to get a search warrant.

"Thanks." Kinney got up from the table and shook Adam's hand, then Tori's. He looked relieved he wasn't involved with the others in criminal activities, particularly if they had resorted to murder.

On the way out of the interrogation room, Adam said to Sierra, "We'll be back in a little while."

"Okay, I'll be here, unless I'm out on another job."

He thought she looked happy, like she was glad she would soon only be working part-time again. He was happy for her. Adam arranged for some of the officers to help collect evidence at Victor's place. Then he, Tori, and Kinney went out to the parking area. Kinney wanted to drive himself so he could leave after they found the house.

In his Hummer, Adam and Tori followed Kinney, while the other officers were behind them. Tori was on her cell phone, checking her emails.

"Sierra seems really happy. I'm sure it has a lot to do with being with you, but I think going back to part-time work agrees with her." Tori texted someone.

"It does. I'm really glad she decided to go back to part-time. Especially since we will have to decide where we'll be living. Not to mention the wedding business when we get around to it. So it's going to be a lot of work and stressful. At least she can take some time off and chill. I think that has been bothering her."

"You mean because now you're taking up all her spare time."

He laughed. "Yeah, kind of. It's good, but I'm sure she needs some time to herself too."

They drove for what seemed like forever through the countryside, past farms, ranches, acreage lush and green from recent rains, took two false turns, and backtracked both times.

"Do you think Kinney really remembers where it is?" Tori asked, sighing.

"I sure hope he does." Then they turned off on another road, and this time Kinney wasn't driving as slowly and Adam thought he might finally know where he was going.

About a quarter of a mile after that, Kinney slowed down and pulled onto a rutted private dirt drive.

Kinney turned his truck around and called out to them, "It's down that road."

"Are you sure?" Adam asked.

"Yeah. They have a gate up, but I don't want to get that close to it. No security, but I don't want to run into anyone if someone's out here right now."

"Okay, thanks, Kinney. We'll set you up for talking with Dover as soon as we can." Adam really appreciated his helping them.

"Thanks," Kinney said and drove off. Now that he wasn't trying to find the place, he headed out in a hurry.

Adam drove up to the gate and saw the overgrown vegetation covering the farmhouse from years of neglect.

"That's what happens when nature takes its course," Tori said.

"Doesn't it look like a great place to run as a wolf?" Adam asked.

"I'll say."

They cut the lock to the gate and drove onto the property.

Adam was hopeful they would find enough evidence to put all of them away for a good long while.

Once Adam and Tori were inside the farmhouse, he smelled Phyllis's scent right away.

"Yeah, I smell her too."

"And I smell the men who had been on the stolen boat that we picked up," Adam said.

"Which includes Burt Barnes, the other kidnapper in Melissa's case."

"Kinney's been here, but his scent isn't recent." Adam was glad for that. "The carjacker's scent is here too."

A couple of policemen came in to check for the list of items they were looking for. "We found tons of spent casings and bullets out there," one of them said. "They've been doing tons of target practice. And we've got some men searching an old barn now too."

"Okay, good," Adam said, wearing gloves and peering into drawers in one of the bedrooms.

Tori was checking out a closet. "Boy, they have lots of great vintage clothing in here."

Adam chuckled. "You would love Brooke's antique shop. She has some vintage clothes. In fact, we're doing a 1920s-themed celebration in the winter."

"Oh, wow, that would be fun."

"Where?" an officer asked, coming into the room.

"Oh, just a few friends getting together." Adam hadn't meant for anyone else to hear.

Tori smiled at Adam.

"Sounds like fun." The officer left the room in search of anything else related to the burglaries.

"Look what I found." Tori brought a red wig out of the closet.

"Great. That's just what we needed. As long as it's the same one used in the kidnapping of Melissa."

"It has Phyllis's scent on it. And there are hairs inside that might be from her own hair. Long, dark-brown strands."

"Good." Adam got a text and pulled out his cell phone. Sierra had texted and he instantly worried about her. "Hey, honey, what's up?"

"My car tires were all punctured."

"When you were getting a witness sketch at a crime scene?"

"No. At the police bureau. I had to have an officer take me to speak to the witness."

"Did you have someone check the security videos at the bureau?" Adam was furious someone would do that to her car. And at the bureau in broad daylight? He couldn't believe it.

"Yes. They said a teen did it."

"Your car only or others too?"

"My car only. The police are out looking for him and two

buddies of his. Hopefully, they'll catch them. I've got a tire company serviceman taking care of the tires."

At least Sierra was safe and not in harm's way. That was the only consolation Adam had.

"How are you doing out there? I don't have any sketches to do at the moment."

"Good. Take a break. We're getting some evidence here. We just found some stuff that had been stolen from various hotels that tie Victor in with the thefts. They were in a locked closet. And in the bathroom were sample bottles of shampoos and conditioners from the various hotels they stole from."

"Oh, that's great."

"And we found the wig Phyllis probably wore when she kidnapped Melisa. We'll have to look for a DNA match, but—"

"You smelled she had worn it."

"Yes. And we found a stash of passports and driver's licenses that match the names of some of the victims we had reports on. Credit cards and debit cards too. We're verifying the rest of them now based on victim reports."

"You really hit the jackpot."

"We did. Phyllis has been in jail before, so we have her DNA on file. We should be able to match her with the wig. We found a stash of guns, including a couple of rifles, and the picture of your brother in his wolf form."

"Oh, wonderful on all those things. I'm so glad you got the photo of my brother back. I only had the one copy. Kinney told you all about this place?"

"Yeah."

"Are you going to put him in witness protection?"

"We may have to. If Victor learns Kinney ratted him out, he and his family could be in danger. I'll check with Kinney and see what he wants to do. I'm not sure if he knew all this stuff was here, but now that we've found it, he could be in worse danger. I have to look for some more evidence, and we've issued a warrant for Victor's arrest."

"Okay, good. Hopefully, he's the last of the gang."

"We can only hope so."

"I'll let you return to work. I'll talk to you in a little bit."

"For a lunch date. Decide on where you want to go," Adam said. "Ask Tori to come with us if she would like."

"I'll do that." Then he ended the call and Tori came out of the kitchen carrying some lockpicks and a master key card for one of the hotels. She was smiling, probably feeling like he was, elated they'd found so much evidence to put these guys away.

"Do you want to have lunch with Sierra and me when we're done here?" he asked Tori.

"Yeah, sure, that would be fun."

Once they were done there, Adam called Sierra and told her they were on their way back to the bureau to pick her up.

"What were you talking to Sierra about concerning seeing the bureau's security videos?"

"Some teen flattened all four of her tires."

Tori's jaw dropped. "At the police bureau?"

"Yeah, and Sierra's car was the only one targeted."

"Do you think it had to do with Dover?"

"Could be. Unless she did a sketch of someone and the person is paying her back by hiring a teen."

"Wow. I hope they catch the delinquent and learn what the deal was then."

When they reached the bureau, Sierra hurried to greet them. She gave Adam a hug and kiss. "All of you did great on that haul. I'm starving. Where do you want to go?"

"A hamburger place?" Adam asked.

"Yeah, sure, that would be great," Sierra said.

"Hmm, mushrooms and blue cheese on mine. And french fries… Sounds so good," Tori said.

"Too bad we don't have time to stop by the ice cream shop too," Sierra said.

Adam laughed. "It's becoming our standard after-meals treat."

"Good thing we like to run." Tori climbed into the back seat of the Hummer, and Sierra sat up front while Adam drove to the hamburger shop.

"When do I get my picture back?"

"It'll be used in evidence at a trial for the kidnapping charges so it will be a while."

They finally reached the restaurant and ordered their meals. Ethan walked in, and they all smiled at him and waved him to their table.

Adam handed him a menu. "Imagine you coming here today."

Ethan chuckled. "I was going to the fast-food chicken place when I saw your Hummer here and thought I would join you." He caught the waitress and placed an order. "So what's going on with you all?"

"Tori and Adam made a huge haul based on an informant's statement." Sierra sounded proud of them. "Maybe we'll catch the rest of the people involved in the hotel robberies and boat theft."

Adam sipped from his water glass. "And those who are causing trouble for Sierra."

"Now *that's* good news," Ethan said.

"Yeah, it is. What about you? Got any good cases?" Adam asked.

"Sierra's sketches of the men nailed them. We picked a couple of them up based on some good tips this morning." Ethan smiled at her and raised his water glass in a salute.

"Oh, great. That's wonderful. I'll be working part-time again, starting Wednesday, so I won't always be there if you need me."

"Is that what you wanted?" Ethan was frowning like he planned to speak to the chief himself about it and make him change his mind.

She smiled. "Oh, yes. That's all I've wanted."

Ethan relaxed. "Okay, that's great then."

"Oh, and we're mated."

Ethan laughed. "I'm not surprised and congratulations."

Their hamburgers arrived and they began to chow down. Adam and Tori had a lot of work ahead of them this afternoon, first of all, questioning Phyllis. But he was anxious to spend the evening with Sierra and enjoy their time together.

Later, they would set Kinney up to speak to Dover at the jail.

"By the way, Kinney wants to cooperate this time, afraid they're going to come after him again," Adam said.

Tori said, "How are things going for you so far, Sierra?"

"Oh, good. With working part-time starting Wednesday, I'm back to teaching art classes on Thursday and I'm moving my things to Adam's home until we decide what we want to do."

Tori smiled. "Moving? Now that's when the real fun begins."

"Yeah, what a job."

After lunch, they said goodbye to Ethan, and Sierra returned to the office. Tori and Adam went into the interrogation room to question Phyllis. She sat stiffly in a chair behind the table, and this time, Tori took over. They had to feel out who would be the best at getting the truth out of their suspects—and if it didn't work with Tori, Adam would take her place. He realized that having a female partner in this business could be a real boon. Some might be more comfortable talking to a woman, others, the opposite.

"Tell us who planned the kidnapping of the young girl." Tori placed the sketch drawn of Phyllis based on the girl's description on the table.

"I have an alibi for that day," Phyllis said. "You have the wrong person."

"An alibi? Okay, so where were you and who witnessed you weren't anywhere in the vicinity of the Chinese restaurant where you allegedly stole the car and at the strip mall where you grabbed the girl, then tied her up at Ms. Redding's home?"

"At home with a male friend."

"He's in jail. I mean, you have matching tattoos, so I was thinking you meant Dover." Tori frowned at her. "Oh, sorry, you mean the new guy you're with."

Phyllis's eyes narrowed. "I'm not *with* him. We're just friends."

"Name?" Tori had her pen poised to write the name down in her notebook. When Phyllis didn't answer her, Tori said, "No name, no alibi. That's how this works."

"Victor Freemont. He's a bartender and he's home during the day."

"So he's up late at night."

"Right."

"And sleeping during the day, like around the time you allegedly were stealing a car and kidnapping a girl."

"No, he was awake then. I was with him. We were having lunch."

"What did you have for lunch?"

"How do I know. Tuna fish sandwiches, I guess."

"Can anyone else verify you were with him then? Dover, maybe?"

Phyllis's eyes widened, then she frowned at Tori. "He's in jail. What a stupid thing to say."

"Right. He's in jail, but wouldn't he know you're with this Victor character now? Maybe you mentioned it to Dover?"

Phyllis chewed on her bottom lip. "He wouldn't know what I'm doing on a daily basis unless I told him. And why would I tell him I made tuna fish sandwiches for Victor and me?"

"Would he care?"

Phyllis glowered at her, her arms folded across her waist, her chin tilted up, her look superior.

Adam took that as a yes. But he knew she wasn't having lunch with Victor when Sierra's car was stolen and the girl kidnapped. Now they knew she was seeing Victor for sure and Dover didn't know about it. Adam was thinking Kinney might drop that little bombshell on Dover when he went to speak to him and hopefully get him to confess on tape to some of the crimes he had done.

Tori brought out some photos of video surveillance in the area. "You were seen driving here and then here. Then you drove out into the country to get rid of the stolen car. But there's a car following you too. That car is registered to...Victor Freemont. Your new boyfriend. I wonder what Dover will think of you stealing boats and selling them and having a new boyfriend."

Phyllis looked panicked, her arms tightening against her waist, her hands clenched into fists.

Then Tori pulled out a plastic bagged wig from an evidence box. "From Victor's grandmother's house."

Phyllis's eyes widened. Adam figured she was immediately thinking about all the stuff they had at the house that could be used as evidence. If it had been him, he would have certainly been considering that.

"This is the wig you wore to Ms. Redding's house, and hair fibers in her car and in her house place you in both the vehicle and her house. Your hair fibers were also inside the wig. Even the kidnapped victim had a couple of the wig's hairs on her," Tori said.

Phyllis chewed on her lip. "Kinney told you about Victor's grandmother's house, didn't he?"

Adam shook his head. "It's a matter of public record."

Phyllis let out her breath and pulled her hair back off her shoulders, then released it, narrowing her eyes at Adam. "Dover will kill me if he knows I've been with Victor since he was incarcerated."

"You don't think he already knows?" Adam asked.

Her eyes grew big again.

"Maybe that's why Dover sent you on the mission to steal Ms. Redding's car, kidnap a girl, and break into Ms. Redding's house. You've never done anything like that before, right? And he knew you would get caught. And when you didn't get caught soon enough, he had Victor pay some teens to slash Ms. Redding's tires.

Who would get hurt by this if you got caught? Whose idea was it to kill Ms. Redding's dog for revenge when she doesn't even own one?" Adam asked.

Phyllis started to say, "She has one and she lied—"

"It's Dover's payback for a perceived wrong. I get it. But who is going to pay the price? Dover? You? For his vendetta? And you're with Victor now, so why should you care about some revenge issues Dover has? Ms. Redding did you a favor when she helped put Dover away so you could be with Victor, right? And this is a great way for Dover to kill two birds with one stone. He told you that you and Victor had to do the job and make sure Burt had the gun and threatened the kidnapped victim with it, correct? That way, it sounded like he was setting up Burt.

"But in truth, he was setting up the lot of you. How hard do you think it would be for Dover to figure out that you and Victor have been together since the time Dover was incarcerated?" Wise up, Adam wanted to say to her.

Phyllis shifted in her chair.

"Not once have you visited Dover in prison. No visits to the jail before he was tried. No letters or postcards, care packages sent to him, nothing. You don't think he would get suspicious? Especially since Burt Barnes is the only one bothering to visit him. You don't think Dover would ask him what was up with you? Do you think Burt would be loyal to you or to Dover?" Adam asked.

Her eyes narrowed.

He raised his brows. "Then we have the sale of the stolen boat to a Mr. Rivers."

"I don't know anything about that."

He folded his arms. "You were driving the other boat while your cohorts took possession of the boat you tried to sell. Then we have the case of you and your cohorts trying to kill Kinney, one of your fellow associates in crime, since he was trying to go legit."

Her jaw dropped, then she gathered her composure. "There is no way I can be implicated in that."

Adam just smiled at her.

"I didn't have anything to do with Ollie trying to kill Kinney," Phyllis added.

"You were in the car following Kinney. Victor was driving," Adam said.

She didn't say anything to that. Then she let out her breath. "I want a lawyer."

"Sure thing," Adam said. "You're going to need one." He wondered then if she had been the other passenger in the car that Kinney didn't identify.

Adam and Tori left the interrogation room, and one of the officers took Phyllis to jail.

"How did it go?" Sierra asked.

"Great. But let me tell you, once Adam is on a roll, there's no stopping him," Tori said.

Adam felt his face warm a bit. "Sorry, Tori. I meant to let you deal with her the whole time."

Tori laughed. "I don't have an ego. Any way we can get anything out of them works for me. She knows we have her over a barrel. You were brilliant in coming up with the idea that Dover already knew about her affair with Victor. I didn't even consider that she hadn't been visiting him in jail. She'll be thinking it over as far as the business with Dover setting her and the others up. Hmm, he might even be pissed he was in jail and they all got off without spending any time there."

"That's certainly a possibility. Here he's the one who's in charge and he got caught."

Sierra smiled. "All because of me."

CHAPTER 28

After they were finished with work, Adam and Sierra said good night to Tori and then headed out to their own vehicles.

"You know, when I mated you, I never dreamed how much better *everything* would be. Not just with being mated to you but enjoying my time off. It didn't bother me about having to go into work before. Now I want to spend the time with you instead. You make it really worthwhile."

"Same here with me. I hope I don't keep you from solving your cases though."

"We can still discuss them and try to come up with solutions when we're having fun." He walked her to her car. "I'm glad you had your tires fixed." He checked her car over to make sure it looked all right.

"When you were in with Phyllis interrogating her, the police caught the three teens involved in slashing my tires."

"That's good news."

"They said some guy by the name of DM paid them, but the description I got from them matched Victor Freemont as the one who handed them the money."

"Good. I hope they learned their lesson."

"They've done some minor thefts prior to this, one of the officers said, so I don't know if this will help deter them or not. What do you want to do about dinner tonight?" Sierra was thinking in terms of something quick and easy to make.

"I'm taking you out on a date."

She was surprised that Adam wanted to take her out for dinner. She thought they would end up in bed first before they even came up with an idea for the meal.

She smiled. "Sure, I would love to." She really would. Though it was a toss-up. Dinner at home and making love for dessert or having dinner out and ice cream to follow, *then* making love at home? "Where did you want to go?"

"Your choice. Somewhere special," he said.

She had to remind herself she had all the time in the world to enjoy being alone with Adam and this was something he really wanted to do with her. And she wanted it too.

She pulled out her phone and looked for restaurants. "Okay, how about a Spanish restaurant? Greek? Or German, for something different?"

"Let's go to the Spanish restaurant and we can save the other restaurants for another night."

"That sounds good. We can get some ice cream afterward."

Adam smiled. "Sure, at your favorite ice cream place?"

"Absolutely."

Adam made reservations at the Spanish restaurant and then they drove to his house and dropped off her car. Then in his Hummer, they took a drive through the housing development where Carver's place was, looking for a home that they might want to check into further.

"Oh, this is fun." She began taking house numbers down for homes for sale and the name of the Realtor who had listed them.

Then when it was time, he drove them to the restaurant for an early dinner. Once they arrived, they were seated right away. Spanish songs played overhead, and pictures of the coastal regions of Spain were hanging on the plastered walls that revealed old brick for an old-world appearance. Because of the early dinner hour, the restaurant wasn't busy yet, which was nice.

Sierra ordered seafood paella, while Adam got the steak paella. It wasn't long before their server brought them bread, water, and salads. They were just finishing their salads when the dinners arrived. Hers was shrimp, clams, mussels, and sausage on Spanish rice. She loved eating here because she could take home half her meal, normally, and eat it for lunch the next day. Adam's main course consisted of steak and shrimp and peas on a bed of rice.

"Remember to save room for dessert," she said.

He gave her an interested smile.

She smiled back. "I mean ice cream."

Adam smiled at her before he buttered his bread.

Sierra took a sip of her white wine. She truly thought the world of him. "This is a lovely date."

"I love you, you know?" Adam took a bite of his steak.

"I love you right back." Sierra ate some of her shrimp on top of some rice. "How's your steak paella?"

"Divine, but so is the company."

They finished their meals, paid for dinner, and headed to the ice cream shop, ditching their suit jackets in the Hummer.

"Are you getting the same thing as you got before?" he asked her.

She shook her head. "This time, it's coffee ice cream and hot fudge topping. I like to do something different every once in a while. What about you?"

"I think I'll have chocolate with butterscotch on top. Try some variety."

"That sounds good. I'll have to try that the next time," Sierra said.

At the ice cream shop, they ordered their sundaes, then took them to a booth and sat down. Adam said, "I thought we could call a Realtor to have him or her show us some homes this weekend."

"Oh, yeah, I would love to do that. I loved some of the ones they have up for sale next to Forest Park, if we can find one we both love that is for sale and affordable."

"All right, that's what we'll aim for. Something close to Carver's place, if we can get one, and we'll help watch over his place and vice versa."

"When we sell both of our homes, we should be able to afford it," Sierra said.

"That's what I figured. We could put them both on the market at the same time, and if we sold one, we would be able to purchase the new house with the proceeds. My house is free and clear. What about yours?"

"Yeah, mine too. With as many years as we live, I save lots and have investments, and I sold my home in Killeen to purchase this one. So we should be good." She took a scoop of her ice cream.

"Better than good. I've always liked the idea of living next to the park. It makes you feel as though you have a lot of acreage, even if it's not yours. And we could run anytime we wanted to after the park closed for the night."

"I would have dumped Richard sooner if you had lived in a house backed up to Forest Park and if I'd known you had such a gorgeous boat."

Adam laughed.

It wasn't long before they were heading home for a second course of dessert—even better than the first.

At home, Adam and Sierra headed for the bedroom, pulling off their shoes as they hurried, and once there, they tackled each other to the bed, falling onto it and laughing. But then they were kissing and sitting up. He pulled her onto his lap so she was facing him. They were tugging at their clothes—him trying to unbutton his shirt, her unfastening her pants—and then she tackled his belt and zipper.

Once he had unbuttoned his shirt, she moved her mouth from his and kissed his chest, then licked his nipples and nibbled. "You are so hot and sexy," she whispered against his chest before she kissed his mouth again.

"Like you are." He kissed her lips and speared her mouth, their tongues dancing in heated passion.

"Hmm," she murmured, skimming her thumbs over his nipples, and he was quickly unbuttoning her blouse, then pulling it off her shoulders. He tackled her bra next, trying to unhook it.

He struggled with it and she thought of reaching behind her and unfastening it, but she was too busy running her hands over his hard chest, loving the feel of his exquisite muscles. Then the bra came undone and he was pulling it down her arms and tossing it aside. She felt so naked, her breasts free until he cupped them and massaged, then kissed her mouth again, but he wasn't letting go of her breasts. She loved the way he eagerly touched her and made her want for more.

Their hearts were beating wildly and their kisses building up steam. Her blood was on fire as he massaged her breasts. He uplifted her, made her feel glorious and wet and needy. She rubbed her mons against his cock, wanting him seated inside her now.

He released her breasts and was struggling to get his shirt off the rest of the way. She began to pull his shirt off while pressing sweet kisses all over his warm, broad shoulders. His fingers curled through her hair, and she felt all tingly between her legs. She looked into his green eyes filled with love and lust and was sure hers looked the same.

She tugged his shirt off the rest of the way and tossed it aside and sighed deeply.

His hands on her arms, he pulled her to the side, unseating her from his lap. Once she was on her back, he kissed each budded nipple, licked them, then blew on the wetness, making them tingle, and she arched against him, wanting more.

He cupped her mound covered by her slacks and then drew his finger through the crease between her feminine lips. Desperately, she wanted him inside her, and she yanked at his pants to jerk them down his hips. Smiling wolfishly, he moved his hands down her back, slipping them beneath her slacks and panties, and gently squeezed her buttocks.

She couldn't get his pants any lower with the way he was lying half on her so she grabbed her own pants and began to slide them over her hips. He quickly pulled his hands out of her panties to help her and drew her pants down her legs. Then he hurried to yank off his own pants the rest of the way.

He inserted himself between her legs, pressing his heavy cock against her mound, and moved, rubbing her, getting her all hot and bothered. They were both still wearing their underwear, and she was eager to rectify that. She grabbed his waistband and slowly peeled it down his toned butt while he was kissing her mouth. But she couldn't get his boxer briefs any lower than just below his buttocks. He smiled and hurried to pull them off and toss them.

Then he was sliding his finger between her feminine lips again, her silk panties not much of a barrier, and he stroked her like that for a few seconds. He slid the fabric aside and began to stroke her nub in earnest.

There was something erotic about being partially clothed while making love. She slid her sock-covered foot up the back of his leg. Their pheromones were driving them insane, inciting them to finish this now!

He pulled her panties down only low enough so that he could stroke her good. She was already feeling the rising climax calling to her, and she was anticipating the cataclysmic conclusion. Then he finally pulled her panties off the rest of the way. He continued to ply his wonderfully skillful strokes to her clit, bringing her to a crescendo of pleasure, and she was in heaven.

Before he entered her, he kissed her mouth hard and long, his cock pressed against her entrance, wet with readiness. He pressed his cock into her, deep, deeper still, and then he pulled very nearly out. She wanted to grab him and hold him in place, needing him inside her. But then he pushed into her again and began to thrust.

His biceps bunched as he held himself above her, driving deeper before he consumed her mouth with his. Delicious butterscotch and chocolate kisses. She was still in a state of bliss when she felt a second climax building. She put her hand in between them and began to stroke herself while he thrust into her. He quickly took over the role and stroked her nub again until he groaned out loud at the end and she cried out in sheer pleasure.

For a long moment, he remained inside her, just breathing her in, and she was doing the same with him. Then Adam pulled out of her and she settled against his chest.

She ran her fingers over his shoulder. "I can't believe I waited so long to see the light and didn't jump at the chance to be with you like this much sooner after I arrived." She sighed, still reveling in the ripples of orgasm flowing through her. "What about you?"

"Oh, hell, I was ready from the first time I saw you. To date, anyway. I had to get to know you first. But I knew I really liked you, even from the beginning. We complement each other. Brad kept telling me you needed me to change your mind about going back to Texas. But that had to be something that you were ready for."

"Well, I was definitely ready." She sighed and nestled her head against Adam's chest. "I don't want to go to work tomorrow."

He chuckled and kissed her head. "Usually, I'm ready to go back in and catch the next bad guy on the list. I'm usually thinking about the cases I need to solve. This time? I would much rather take a couple of weeks off and enjoy being a newly mated couple."

"A honeymoon. We definitely need it."

CHAPTER 29

A WEEK LATER, ADAM GOT A CALL FROM TORI EARLY IN THE morning, and he groaned and hurried to answer it. Mornings and work always came too early now that he was mated to Sierra.

Sierra yawned and waited to hear what it was all about.

"Yeah, Tori? What's up?"

"Phyllis wants to make a deal. She insists she wasn't involved in trying to sell the boat illegally and she didn't have anything to do with carjacking Kinney's car or Ollie trying to kill him. She said the other person in Victor's car was Lonnie. And she said she'll give up Victor's hiding place for a deal. And when I questioned her about the postcard sent to Sierra, she said that none of them did it. But we found Phyllis's fingerprint on the front of the card."

"Hot damn! Great. I'm coming in." Adam kissed Sierra's smiling mouth, her beautiful blue eyes half-lidded. "Sleep. Chet Crawford said he would handle everything and not to worry until you're ready to come in." Adam really liked the new full-time sketch artist. He was always there to cover for Sierra when she had art classes to teach or was trying to handle the sale of both houses because Adam was working full-time.

Though no matter what, getting up in the morning had become a chore for both of them, their fault, of course. Either one or the other was always waking up in the middle of the night and wanting to make love.

As to the sketch-artist job, Sierra always made up the time at work later, but he was glad Chet was accommodating. Chet was so grateful to Sierra for giving up the job to him so he could relocate to join his girlfriend. Not once had he given her a dead-body sketch to do.

"I have to get up anyway," Sierra groaned, running her hands through her red curls. "I have an appointment with the Realtor in an hour. I think my house might have sold. And you know what that means."

"We have to find a new house to move into so we can move both our households at the same time."

"Exactly."

"Good luck on the house deal."

"Thanks and hopefully we'll sell yours soon too."

Then they were both hurrying to dress and grabbed a quick breakfast of eggs and toast. They kissed and hugged, and she was off to see the Realtor and he was off to speak with Phyllis and her lawyer.

"Okay," Tori said in the interrogation room at the bureau, Adam giving her the floor again with Phyllis and planning to stay out of it unless she needed him to back her up on something. "The prosecution has agreed to the plea bargaining, if Victor is where you say he is and you testify against him and against Dover about ordering the kidnapping of the girl."

"Unless Victor believes I'll turn on him and he's taken off, he should be in either one of two different locations. He's stayed at Lonnie Hicks's place. I know Lonnie is in jail, but Victor's got a key to the house. The other location is a room above the Fast Time Bar and Grill. He rents it under the name of Vlad Romansky."

"Okay, let's go." Adam called it in to the judge, and they got search warrants for both places.

Tori smiled at Adam as they headed out in his vehicle.

"What? You did all the talking, and when we wrapped it up, it was time to go."

She laughed. "I love working with you. When I worked with the FBI, I didn't have a wolf partner, and this is so much better."

"I'm glad you're my partner too."

"So which place do we go to?" she asked.

"We'll send a unit to Lonnie's house, and you and I will go to the bar and grill. We don't want to spook him if he has an informant tell him we're searching one of his places and he runs from the other."

"Good idea."

When they reached the bar and grill, they found stairs to an upper apartment, and with backup, they headed up the stairs. One of the police officers knocked on the door, but no one answered. Then they heard someone inside and the officer kicked the door in.

"This is the police!"

They heard a window opening in a back room, and Adam and an officer raced to intercept the person. As soon as they reached the window, they found Victor on the fire escape. Adam radioed to the other police that Victor was on his fire escape out back while he headed down after him.

Suddenly, Victor turned and looked up at Adam, drawing a gun at the same time. Adam knew that look. Victor wasn't going to give up without a shoot-out.

"Drop the weapon!" Adam yelled, his heart pounding.

Victor fired at him, but the round ricocheted off the metal ladder as Adam ducked. Adam fired his gun and the round hit Victor in the hand, and he dropped his gun.

Adam continued to race down the steps while Victor reached the bottom of the ladder and landed in the alley. Adam caught up to him as other police officers surrounded them with guns drawn. Adam took Victor down to the pavement, and one of the officers called for an ambulance.

Tori retrieved Victor's gun and made sure Adam wasn't the one injured, then returned to the apartment. Once they had read Victor his rights and treated him for the gunshot wound, he was taken to the hospital. Adam knew he would have to do a bunch of paperwork and wished he hadn't needed to shoot Victor, but he hadn't had any choice.

Adam soon returned to the apartment to help with the investigation to find any other criminal evidence against Victor, while Tori called the other officers who were checking out Lonnie's place to let them know Victor was in custody.

"It's a good thing you didn't get shot," Tori said to Adam.

"I know. Sierra probably would have been upset with me." He opened a drawer and smiled. "More guns, more stolen credit cards."

Tori waved a piece of paper at Adam. "A rental receipt for a boat storage unit fourteen by forty-four feet and the key to it." She held up the key with a tag on it.

"Since they were involved in the theft of boats, I think we should check it out," Adam said and gave a call to the judge, who okayed the order for a search warrant. "Let's go."

They had two officers come with them, and when they arrived at the boat storage unit, they unlocked and opened the door and found a 2019 SeaArk EasyCat. Adam checked the list price. "Going rate on one of these is around $54,000. I suspect this wasn't the boat they were in when they stole the other."

"Nope, unless it was stolen too. This for sure is," Tori said, checking the serial number on the engine with a list of stolen boats she had on her phone.

When they finally finished processing both crime scenes and the boat was hauled off as evidence, they returned to the office and found Sierra at the bureau, sketching a witness's account of a man who had stolen the witness's purse at the grocery store. Unfortunately, the place where he stole it wasn't in view of a camera.

Sierra smiled at Adam, and he hoped she had good news about her house. As soon as she was done with the lady, she came over and gave Adam a hug. "I sold my house, and your house has an offer."

"All right. We've got good news too. We caught Victor."

"Yes! That's the last of them, isn't it?" She frowned as she saw a small amount of blood on Adam's sleeve.

"It's not my blood. It's Victor's. I had to shoot him in the hand so he wouldn't shoot at me again." Adam let out his breath in exasperation. "Which means tons of paperwork. But we need to go out and celebrate the sale of your house tonight."

"And the capture of Victor without you getting shot."

"Absolutely." He began to do the paperwork and Tori was checking into a couple of cases at the same time.

Roland came to him with a bit of good news. "Ballistics came back on those shell casings and bullets found at Victor's old farmhouse, and we had a match on a couple of the rifles used in the shooting incident in Forest Park."

Adam smiled. "That's great news!"

"Yeah, I thought you would want to know right away." Roland left to do some other work.

A police officer motioned two men to speak with Adam and Tori, and they learned the men had witnessed the boat accident where the three men had drowned on the Willamette River.

Adam and Tori sure hoped they could have confirmation one way or another about what Kinney's former cohorts had witnessed concerning the men's drownings.

"We saw the driver of the boat make a turn and cross its own wake," the older gray-haired man said, his face weathered and tan. "During the maneuver, the two men seated near the transom of the boat fell overboard. The captain of the boat turned it around and motored over to the men, then he dove into the water."

The other man said, "Yeah and by the time we reached the location, the boat was gone, and so were the men. We figured the men who had left the boat returned to it and were fine. Later, we saw three men on the boat and figured our assumption was true. The men were okay. We've been out of the country and didn't see the description of the boat or about the three drowned men until this morning and realized their boat had been stolen. We immediately canceled our fishing plans and came into the bureau to see you."

"Okay, thanks for the information. We're grateful you came in and told us what happened." Adam was glad that the men they had up on charges of theft of the boat hadn't murdered the three men to steal their boat. It was just accidental, as the coroner had thought.

"The currents are strong and the water was cold. None of the men must have been wearing life jackets or were strong enough to withstand the cold," the one man who had witnessed it said.

Adam shook his head. "They weren't."

When the men left, Tori said, "Hey, Kinney's going in to see Dover at the jail today"—she glanced at the clock—"in half an hour."

"Let's hear what he has to say."

They drove over to the jail in the van they used for surveillance with a couple of officers who did regular surveillance.

They were all talking about summer plans, boating, camping out, when Kinney began to talk to Dover and the officers got quiet to hear what was being said. "Hey, Dover, I guess you know Phyllis got caught."

"Yeah. What are you doing here?"

"You know Ollie tried to kill me, only he ended up killing himself after stealing my car."

"Yeah, so?"

"Ollie didn't do anything without someone ordering him to do it."

"So what are you saying?" Dover asked.

"You wanted me to do the job of kidnapping the girl and frame Ms. Redding for it. I said I couldn't. I have to stay clean. The next thing I know, Ollie is trying to kill me."

Dover didn't say anything. Hell, they weren't going to get anything out of him, Adam was afraid.

"Things really fell apart once you were no longer in charge," Kinney said, changing tactics.

"I'm still in charge."

"That's not what Phyllis and Victor say. First, they hooked up as soon as you lost your case and you weren't getting out of jail. Then they started stealing and selling boats because they said they can make more money at it than from stealing from hotel rooms. When I told them that you didn't want them doing that, Victor said you weren't in charge any longer. Then Burt tried to do what you taught him to do, but he got caught at the hotel room. And Lonnie got caught trying to sell the stolen boat. Of course, Victor and Burt were there also. Phyllis was driving the other boat, so she was involved too. That was some of the reason I quit. Victor had taken charge and I can't stand him. He's all in it for himself."

"Is Victor still on the loose?"

"I heard on the news he got caught. A police officer shot him, and Victor is at the hospital now."

As soon as Victor was out of surgery, Adam and Sierra would have to question him.

"Nothing fatal, I hope." Dover sounded sarcastic when he said it.

"No. He was shot in the hand."

"So why are you here?" Dover asked again.

"I wanted you to know that if you told the others to kill me, I wasn't the one who was being disloyal to you. Victor and Phyllis have been."

"I wouldn't have ordered anyone to kill you, Kinney. I like you too much." Again, the sarcasm in Dover's tone of voice was evident.

Adam figured Dover knew Kinney was wired, and that was why he wasn't incriminating himself.

"You want to know if I ordered the hit on you? I didn't," Dover finally said. "I didn't tell Phyllis to kidnap the kid either. You either. That's all on her and Burt. I'm sure Victor had a hand in it. Yeah, I knew she was screwing around with Victor. I suspected it when she wouldn't visit or call me or take my calls. If she had gotten in touch with me, I could have seen right through her."

"Burt said the kidnapping of the girl was your idea," Kinney said.

"Burt said that? He's a fool."

"He said Phyllis said so too."

"Why didn't you tell me in the beginning what was going on between Phyllis and Victor?"

"I wasn't sure about it right away. I just figured they were getting together to make plans. But Burt knew right away. I figured he would have told you. I never heard what other plans anyone had because I'd said no to doing the kidnapping job, except that Burt told me about the theft of the boat. I don't blame you if you had hoped Victor and Phyllis would blow the kidnapping case and get caught. But why involve me?"

"I didn't involve you. I told you already. That had to have been Victor or Phyllis's idea. And when you said no, they did the job with Burt."

Kinney laughed out loud and nearly broke Adam's eardrums. Tori immediately glanced at him and he knew it had hurt her ears too. "So you told Phyllis to do it and she tried to make me do it with Burt, betcha. But I wouldn't, so she had to do it."

"If you see her before she gets out of the slammer, tell her I'll be seeing her. *And* Victor. Gotta go."

Kinney let out his breath and must have turned the mike off after that.

As soon as he left the building, Adam called him. "This is Detective Holmes. Meet us at the bureau."

"He didn't say anything," Kinney said.

"I know. But we'll talk."

When they all arrived at the bureau, Adam and Tori waved at Sierra and then headed into the interrogation room to speak with Kinney.

And then they listened to the recording. "So what do you think about Dover ordering the hit on you?" Adam asked.

"I'm not sure. I'm thinking it might have been Victor and Phyllis because they had to do the kidnapping bit with Burt instead of me. That made them more of a target for the police."

"What about Dover ordering the kidnapping of the girl?"

"Oh, hell, yeah. No way would Victor and Phyllis have tried to incriminate Ms. Redding for the kidnapping if Dover hadn't told them to do it. Dover wanted revenge. Pure and simple. Victor and Phyllis had no reason to do it otherwise. And they figured he would learn about it if they didn't do it, so they tried to con me into doing it."

Adam sat back in his chair. "But they needed a third person driving the getaway car."

"Yeah, that would have been Lonnie, but Burt said they couldn't get ahold of him. I think Dover assumed I was wired at the jail, and that's why he asked me twice why I was there. It would have been better to have sent Burt to see him. He has been visiting him since Dover went to jail."

"Well, thanks, Kinney. You gave it your best shot."

"I feel better knowing Dover didn't try to kill me, if I'm right in my assumption. I just hope you found enough evidence to put Victor and Phyllis away for a long time."

"We hope so too. Thanks again, Kinney."

Kinney left and Adam went to talk to Sierra. He'd barely had a chance all day.

She smiled at him and kissed him. "So what's next on the agenda?"

"Tori and I have to speak to Victor in the hospital as soon as—"

"He's out of surgery and now is awake. The bullet went through his hand," Tori said, hurrying to join them with her phone in hand.

"Okay, good luck, you two. If I don't see you before I leave, I'll be going to my house to begin packing up all the rest of my clothes and food to take to your house, Adam."

"Our house. They both are now."

"And remember, I'm helping you both after all the help you were with me," Tori said.

Actually, everyone who had helped Tori had offered to help Adam and Sierra move too.

"As soon as I'm done with the interrogation of Victor at the hospital, I'll meet you at your house," Adam said.

"Okay, see you there." She gave him a hug and kiss, some other officers smiling and shaking their heads.

Then Adam and Tori took off for the hospital.

"So who gets to question him?" Tori asked.

"You can, if you want. Or we can feel him out and see which of us he might be more willing to talk to. That's how Josh and I did it. Sometimes someone was more hostile toward him and other times toward me, so we just feel the situation out and then go with whoever we believe can get the most out of the perp."

"Okay, sounds good to me."

They finally parked at the hospital and went up to the room where Victor was recuperating before they took him to jail.

Adam and Tori spoke to the guard, then went inside the room where Victor was lying in a bed, his head partly elevated while he watched TV.

Tori turned off the TV, and though Victor had been read his rights, she gave them to him again. She glanced at Adam, but he motioned with his head to let her question Victor first.

She began going through the list of charges against him and ended with the boat they had found in the storage unit. "Dover's not happy that you and Phyllis hooked up. He wants a word with you when you join him."

"Who told him that?" Victor asked.

"She wasn't seeing him or taking his calls. Then Dover learned for sure that you and Phyllis have been an item. He says it was your idea to do the kidnapping of the girl and frame Ms. Redding."

"Like hell it was. Dover tasked us to do it. He gave the order. He wanted revenge. We had no reason to do it otherwise."

"So why do it?" Tori asked.

"Phyllis was feeling guilty about not seeing him. And she worried he would do something about it if she didn't do the one thing he wanted her to do."

"Why did you order the hit on Kinney?"

Victor ran his good hand over his arm.

"Phyllis is testifying against you."

Victor's eyes widened. "I don't believe you."

Adam brought out the recorder and played the part where Phyllis had given up Victor's location and promised to testify against him.

"Hell. She's the one who ordered the hit on Kinney. She was so angry he wouldn't do the kidnapping so she wouldn't have to be involved and risk her pretty neck, and we couldn't find Lonnie, so she had to do it."

Adam just sat back while Tori questioned him and he gave all the same answers that the others had given, except that Phyllis had ordered the hit on Kinney. They'd have to verify that with the others to see if it was true, if the others knew the truth.

Once they had gotten as much out of Victor as they could, Adam said to Tori on the way to the vehicle, "I'd say the den of thieves are all turning on each other."

"Just the way we like it." Tori smiled at him.

He got a call from Sierra and answered it on Bluetooth. "Hey, what's up, honey?"

"You know the hotel where Dover broke into my room? They have a seafood restaurant that has the best shrimp scampi. Only this time, I'm eating with you in the restaurant. Ask Tori to join us too."

He smiled at Tori and she was smiling and nodding. "We'll meet you there." But he dropped by the bureau so that Tori could follow him in her own car.

He hoped that all the perps would be tried and convicted. And that would be the end of the harassment Sierra had been getting.

Before long, he was sitting down to eat with Sierra and Tori, and they all had shrimp scampi, since Sierra so highly recommended it.

With glasses of champagne, they toasted each other. "To crime solving and selling my house," Sierra said.

"Hear, hear!" Tori and Adam said.

Then they discussed what had happened today, from witness sketches to interrogation and searches they'd conducted.

They were halfway through their meal when Sierra got a text. She answered it, then gave her phone to Adam. "What about this place bordering Forest Park? One of the bedrooms could even be my art studio."

He looked at all the pictures of the spacious living area, island counter and seating, the large deck out back, huge kitchen for large parties, a large den, fenced-in yard, five bedrooms, and three baths, and he smiled. "Is this the one you want?"

"Yeah. I saw it with the Realtor this morning after I sold my house. I just walked in and it felt like home."

They clinked champagne glasses again.

"To your first home together," Tori said.

"Yes!" Sierra said.

But Adam was already on the phone, making an offer. A home for the two of them. He couldn't be more thrilled than to make his mate happy. And tonight, after they finished dinner, he was all for making her happy all over again.

Sierra adored Adam. She had thought he would want to see the house first before committing to it, but she was thrilled when he went ahead and made an offer. This summer had been the best—what with working at the bureau and mating Adam. Just the best.

Her parents had even sold their home this morning and were getting ready to move to the ranch. Two of her art students had won contests. Not once had she had to do dead-body sketches since the new sketch artist had come on the scene. Nothing could be better.

Then a hotel clerk ran into the restaurant, having recognized Adam from investigating the hotel theft before, and hurriedly said, "We've had a robbery in one of the guests' rooms and the man just left the elevator."

"Go," Sierra said to Adam when he glanced her direction as if making sure it was all right with her.

Tori and Adam raced off, but Sierra paid for the meal and hurried after them and the clerk with sketch pad in hand, just in case the detectives didn't catch the thief and the security video hadn't either. "So what did he look like?" she asked the clerk.

Life would never be the same. But it still was all good.

EPILOGUE

Four months later

After having dinner and fancy ice cream sundaes, then leaving through the back-gate wolf door of their new home in Forest Park as wolves, Sierra and Adam were having a ball running with Josh, Brooke, Brad, Janice, Tori, and Ethan. But things had changed. Sierra, Janice, and Brooke were all pregnant with twins, and the guys were still fussing about them running as wolves. Which sure didn't stop the ladies.

Sierra was still giving art classes a couple of days a week at the ranch, and Janice and her parents couldn't wait for her and Brooke to give birth. Sierra was also still doing the part-time police sketches, mostly witness sketches, and the new guy was still totally grateful she gave up the full-time job to him. She'd even planted her Pacific Northwest wildflower seeds at their new home as soon as they'd moved.

And Sierra loved her art studio. She took all the pictures Phyllis had torn up and redid them for her clients. Sierra had even painted Mount Hood in the distance, including her whole family in the woods—all in wolf form—to hang over the fireplace mantel.

Tori, Cassie, and the moms helped Brooke, Sierra, and Janice decorate the twins' rooms for their arrivals while the guys barbecued steaks and ribs and helped out with whatever the ladies needed.

Tomorrow, they were all going for a ride on the boat, just like Sierra and Adam had talked about before they were mated. Her parents and Adam's and Brad and his mate enjoyed the boat when Sierra and Adam had to work, and she was glad the boat wasn't sitting idle. They had even managed a couple of love fests on the water, and the captain's bed was indeed soft and just perfect for what they had in mind.

They finally ran home, and once inside, Brooke and Josh shifted and dressed in one of the guest rooms, Brad and Janice in one, Tori in another, Ethan in the den, and Adam and Sierra in the master bedroom. Since it was eleven that night, everyone gave a round of hugs and told them they'd see them at the marina tomorrow. Maybe Tori wouldn't get seasick this time.

"'Night all," Adam and Sierra said, remembering the time four months ago when she and Adam were running as wolves and Dover's men were shooting at them. With all the bad guys incarcerated, they had no more trouble and wolf runs were a joyous nightly occurrence. Though Sierra was really glad she could sleep in most mornings now.

"Are you too tired for what comes next?" Adam asked, lifting Sierra into his arms and hauling her to bed.

She laughed. "No. Never. We shouldn't have put on so many clothes."

"That's the fun part, stripping them off each other again." Then he howled in the bedroom and she howled back.

Best of all, they were finally taking their honeymoon—leaving in two days for South Padre Island, Texas, for two whole weeks—and this time, she knew she wouldn't get bored!

She loved her adoring wolf.

Life couldn't be any richer than with Sierra as his mate. Adam couldn't believe that he was going to be a daddy at the same time as his best friend, Josh, and his brother-in-law too. He had a lot of learning to do, and Cassie had been giving the guys lessons on diapering and feeding infants. He was ready as he began stripping

Sierra out of her clothes and leaned down to kiss her belly. Then they were making love, and he was so thankful that she had come into his life, decided to settle down, and took him as her mate.

"Love you, my beautiful she-wolf."

"You were always the only one for me, wolf paws down."

Read on for a sneak peek of Terry Spear's
exciting return to Arctic wolves in

While the Wolf's Away

Coming soon from Sourcebooks Casablanca.

CHAPTER 1

Eager to get their clandestine meeting started, David Davis got ready for his weekly Skype session with Elizabeth Alpine. It was their only opportunity to visit face-to-face since she lived in Yellowknife, Northwest Territories, Canada, and he was located near Ely, Minnesota, the gateway to the Boundary Waters Canoe Area Wilderness.

They had to do this in secret because her Arctic wolf-pack leader, Kintail, would have done something drastic had he known they were still in touch. To say Kintail had issues with his pack members trying to break free was an understatement.

Not that David would ever consider himself one of their pack, even if they did, technically, save his life. It was either be turned or die of a heart attack during a bear hunt gone terribly wrong in Maine. And he was glad he wasn't dead, no complaints there. But once he was turned, Kintail and his pack thought they owned him.

David had other ideas. And so did Elizabeth, which was why she'd helped him to escape.

She'd meant to escape with him so they could make a home together in Seattle, Washington where he was a PI and be free of Kintail and the pack, but Elizabeth's grandmother, Ada, had gotten sick. Elizabeth couldn't abandon her only family; she would forever have regretted it. Ada had often told David that Elizabeth just needed to leave to be with him and get on with her life, and the pack would take care of Ada just fine.

But Elizabeth wouldn't have been just fine if she had left her grandmother in other wolves' care. Especially with the way Kintail treated his pack. The other wolves might really want to help Ada but be prevented from doing so by Kintail.

David drummed his fingers on the table as he placed the Skype call and waited for Ada to pick up. She was always trying to sneak in some "before time" with him. And sure enough:

"Oh, David, you're looking more handsome every time I see you." Ada smiled. "I want you to come and take Elizabeth away from here *before* I'm gone. Kintail and his men are bound to be watching her to ensure she doesn't leave as soon as I've passed on to join my dearly beloved mate."

They'd been over this a dozen times before. David smiled gently. "Elizabeth needs to be there for you for her own peace of mind and for yours. But as soon as—"

"No. Now. I feel it in my bones that I could go any minute now. Oh, scratch that. You smile at me and look at me with those big, adoring brown eyes, and I almost forget I'm as old as an ancient oak tree. If Elizabeth and I could trade places, I would be racing out of here to be with you. She's a silly goose to waste her life away here without you."

Sometimes, Ada's curly white hair was piled high on top of her head in a chic coiffure, as if she were getting ready to go to a dance. Other times, like today, her hair was long and silky and down around her shoulders as she lay in her big bed. She did seem more tired than usual, but she still had good days too. Besides, David was used to this line of conversation. Ada had been saying she could go any minute now ever since Elizabeth had returned home to take care of her. He smiled wider and gave her a wink for good measure. "You're not going anywhere and good thing too. Who would sing my praises if you weren't around?"

"Are you on Skype already?" Elizabeth asked, hurrying into her grandmother's room with a couple bottles of water. She sounded mildly accusative, but David knew it was a game the two women played, Elizabeth pretending to be late to the session, David and her grandmother getting on just a little early so she could chat privately with him.

"Grandma, you know you're not supposed to be on Skype without me. I never know what the two of you are plotting." Elizabeth's beautiful brown curls were partly up and partly down. She looked like she'd been working in her grandmother's garden again.

He hoped Elizabeth would love gardening in the plot at his cabin. He hadn't planted anything there yet. He wanted it to be her garden. Every summer he kept it weeded, just in case he had to go rescue her and bring her home. In the winter, it lay dormant waiting for the spring. Waiting for her.

"What am I plotting?" Ada said. "Running away with this handsome wolf since you won't? We would make a lovely pair, wouldn't we?" She sighed dramatically. "But alas, he only has eyes for you. You need to go to him."

"I can wait," David said, like he'd said so many times before, because there had never been anyone like Elizabeth and he knew there never would be. "I'll wait forever for you, Elizabeth, honey." And he would. He would wait as long as he had to. But being together like this wasn't the same as *being* together. The last time they'd actually been together, they'd been on the run from her pack leader. But staying in hotels and having unconsummated relations because wolves mated for life hadn't really counted.

Yet, they'd known then and they knew now they only wanted each other.

Still, he couldn't help the doubts that crept in. When they were finally able to physically be together, safe from danger, would they still feel the same way about each other? When they finally lived in his cabin on the lake, and he was off working as a PI and she was... She was what? He didn't even know what she would do when he was away on missions. Would the magic still be there?

"She's treated like an omega wolf here," Ada was saying. "I'm not just crying wolf. She needs you and your pack's protection. And she needs it now."

"Grandma, shush. I'm fine. I'm happy to be here with you, and I won't leave until it's..." Elizabeth took a deep breath, but the tears in her eyes said it all.

David hated that Kintail was such an ass. He wanted nothing more than to swoop in and take Elizabeth away from her pack, get her out from under his control. David had been glad Elizabeth had more time with her grandmother before the end came, but he hated that Kintail and the other pack members were still giving Elizabeth grief for having freed David and his friend Owen. It'd been years since then, but Kintail knew how to hold a grudge; losing new wolves wasn't something he would ever get over.

Losing yet another wolf wasn't something Kintail would stand for either. And Elizabeth *would* leave, the first moment she could. It might have been a different story with a different leader. If Elizabeth had been met with kindness, with understanding, maybe she would have stayed. But Kintail was who he was: Controlling. Demanding. Greedy for power. Kindness was weakness, and weakness was death.

That's why Elizabeth needed to be free.

"Okay, so let's go over the new plan of rescue and evasion, shall we?" That was Ada's favorite topic of discussion when they had their weekly Skype sessions.

"If I drove long days and didn't stop for much, I could make it in three days going up and we could make it in three days coming back," David said.

"Right," Ada said, as if she were making the trip herself.

Elizabeth let her grandmother dominate the calls with David because her grandmother loved them, and it always gave her something to look forward to for the next week. David enjoyed talking with her too. He'd loved his own grandparents, but they were gone now, and Elizabeth's grandmother had adopted him, whether he ended up mated to Elizabeth or not. He loved Ada just as much as Elizabeth did.

David continued going over their plans. "And flights are around twenty-two hours, depending on layovers. Some are longer. Layovers are two hours in Calgary and seven hours in Edmonton."

"I don't like that plan. While I want the two of you out of Canada as soon as possible, Kintail and his men will be watching Elizabeth after I'm gone, and they'll be watching the airport to see if you turn up."

Elizabeth's grandmother had never liked the idea of them escaping by plane, but David didn't want to discount it either. Driving would mean a delay in reaching Yellowknife to pull Elizabeth out after Ada's funeral. It was risky to wait.

"True. But I was thinking I could solicit Amelia—Gavin Summerfield's mate—to help us," David said. "He's another PI partner and long-time friend, and she's a pilot. Then we wouldn't have long layovers because we can take a more direct flight instead of having to fly their scheduled routes."

"Oh, yes, that sounds much better. Also, I don't want a funeral," Ada said. "I'm being cremated, and Elizabeth has instructions to scatter my ashes over the roses in the backyard. Well, if the yard isn't covered in snow. I'll try not to leave when it's snowing out." She always said "leave," like she was just planning on taking a trip—which, in a way, was exactly how she thought of it. "Oh, and I'll try to leave when it isn't the full-moon phase."

The phase of the full moon could be an issue for David. Not for Elizabeth. She and her family were royals, having very few purely human roots in their genetic makeup. But David had been turned by one of her pack members, so he'd been born as a human and dealing with a full moon was harder for him. It tugged on his need to shift, though now he was better at controlling it than he used to be. He still couldn't entertain the thought of flying during that phase, though, unless either Amelia or her brother, Slade, piloted him. Their father, Henry, flew planes too, but David figured, as a royal like Elizabeth, Henry would be holding down the fort while either Amelia or Slade helped David and Elizabeth get out.

"If it's winter, you could sneak in at a rendezvous point and snowmobile out of here," Ada mused.

That was the thing of it. They had so many things to take into consideration—time of year, the moon phases, getting to and out of Yellowknife in the Northwest Territories, whether extra help was needed or not.

His three partners wanted to help him, not to mention their mates too. They all knew Elizabeth from Maine, whether personally or through stories of her bravery, and were ready to jump in whenever David needed them.

"You can't get your partners and their mates involved in all this," Ada said, seemingly reading his mind. "We don't want a pack war up here. You'll never beat them, and they'll bury the lot of you. So don't even think of it. Come alone... Well, except for Amelia or her brother, if they can fly you here all right. When Elizabeth is finally safe back home with you, your pack members can help, if Kintail and his men are foolish enough to follow you."

"I like that idea," Elizabeth said. "If Amelia or Slade fly in, it won't matter if the full moon is an issue for you. And if I could reach the airport without Kintail being aware of it, we would fly off into the sunset and be gone before they could do anything about it. Hopefully we wouldn't have to involve your pack at all."

David didn't want a pack war either. The thought of putting his packmates at risk ate at him. But he would—for her.

He couldn't understand why Kintail was so adamant about not losing a pack member. If a wolf was unhappy with the pack, let him go. Once her grandmother was gone, Elizabeth had no kin left there, and most of Elizabeth's friends had turned their backs on her.

But letting Elizabeth go wasn't in Kintail's plans. He couldn't have anyone "mutinying" and that's exactly what he would consider it. Mutiny. What if more of his pack members saw that as a sign to leave too?

Kintail would do anything in his power to stop Elizabeth from leaving. *Anything.*

Just as David would do anything to help her break free.

Ada sighed. "I know she will be in good hands with you and your packmates. I'm going to rest my eyes a bit and let you talk in private with my Elizabeth, but no talking over trip plans without me."

He smiled. "I love you, Grandma." And he meant it.

"Oh, how I wish I was younger." Grandma smiled in return and blew him a kiss.

Elizabeth kissed her grandmother's cheek. "I'll come check on you in a little bit." Then she took her laptop out of the bedroom, closed the door, and went into the living room, settling into her recliner. "She loves making plans to get us together. She says when these calls end, she thinks for hours about how to help us. About the life we could have. She remembers the time when she was a young woman and went with her mate, my grandfather, to see the States. If her memories of my grandfather weren't so tied to this pack, she would leave with me to join you."

"I would welcome her into my home gladly," David said.

"I know. And she does too. You've done her a world of good. Thanks for including her in our chats."

"I wouldn't have it any other way. I miss you though. I can't say that enough." He longed to be with Elizabeth, sharing kisses with her, and more. There was so much he wanted to experience with her. She was truly the light of his life.

"I miss you too," Elizabeth said.

Despite the closeness he felt with his own pack, it wasn't the same as being with a mate. He thought about her constantly. About running with her as wolves and playing chase and tag. About making love with her and having little wolf pups of their own. About being a family, when he'd never thought he would be interested in such a thing. Not until he'd met Elizabeth—and lost her.

They just had to get her out of Yellowknife and out of her pack's reach. Until then, nothing else mattered.

CHAPTER 2

Elizabeth loved her grandmother and was grateful she'd had her in her life for so long. She hated her pack leader for vowing to kill David, and any of his pack members, if they dared set foot in their territory.

Her bond with David went deeper than any bond with her pack, with the exception of her grandmother. Her feelings for him transcended place and time. In the beginning, she'd worried about their relationship. What if he had only really needed her for the comfort he'd craved when he was turned, going from an ordinary human to an extraordinary *lupus garou*? What if he wasn't as into her as it seemed? That the newness of being together, or the fact she'd helped him and Owen escape, was the reason he'd been attracted to her?

If it hadn't been for Kintail, David could have made the trip to see Elizabeth and her grandmother from time to time. But she knew spies in the pack were always watching, waiting, making sure David didn't show up. And she was certain they would ensure Elizabeth didn't slip away from the pack once her grandmother died.

Only two places offered funeral services in Yellowknife, so it would be hard to keep her grandmother's death quiet when the time came. The pack would eventually find out; they always did. But Elizabeth promised her grandma she would keep it a secret as long as she could. The longer the pack was in the dark, the better chance Elizabeth had of escaping.

Her best friend, Sheri Whitmore, had said she would take care of the cremation when the time came and would spread Ada's ashes in her rose garden, just as she wanted. Elizabeth hadn't wanted to tell either David or her grandmother of Sheri's offer because no one in the pack was supposed to be in on their plans. But Elizabeth loved Sheri like a sister, and she was her best shot at buying some time.

Still. Involving Sheri came with risks, not in the least to Sheri herself. If the pack ever found out Sheri had helped her, she would end up in the same position Elizabeth was in now. Friendless. Her family under suspicion. *Watched.*

Elizabeth shook off her dark thoughts and refocused on her call with David. She couldn't believe he had waited for her all this time, though she'd been doing the same for him. If he'd had a chance to find a mate, she had wanted him to take it. To find love.

And at the same time, she hated the very thought of that.

"Still no she-wolves on the horizon?" she asked David. She always asked.

"You're the only one for me. To think I've waited this long and then I would just give you up? No way. You need me and I need you."

She smiled. He had never wavered once about waiting for her. Even when his other PI partners had all found mates, he continued to wait for her. She couldn't help but appreciate him for it. She so longed to be with him.

"How is it out there today?" She pictured all the forested land they had around his pack members' homes. He'd taken her and her grandmother on a video tour of the house and shown them the views of the lake and forest, just so Elizabeth could see the area, could envision herself there when she moved to the Minnesota pack to be with him. And Elizabeth loved every bit of it. Her grandmother had been glad to know how beautiful everything was in the area too. She told them she saw it when she worked on their plans after their calls, adding it to the details in her mind, imagining Elizabeth there with him, happy in the woods and by the lake and in the home he'd built.

"Sunny and warm, perfect for us to go swimming," David said. "We will take the canoe out, paddle to the island. We can shift and have a nice run through the woods."

"Hmm, it sounds delightful. And I'd make brownies for dessert."

"Yes, I love your brownies and the way you always made extras for me."

"You were always so grateful for them."

"And for you for freeing Owen and me and for coming with us."

"I miss that. I wish I was with you now."

"I don't miss the danger, but I sure miss you."

"Yeah. Hopefully, we can do it this time without the chase scenes and all. Okay, I need to speak with you about something else. I know we talked about not getting anyone else involved—especially from my pack. But my childhood friend has offered to help me with Grandmother when she passes. I didn't talk to her about it, I swear. She just knows me too well."

He didn't say anything for a moment, and Elizabeth continued. "It might give me a chance to slip away. It might give me a little bit of a head start."

"Would she say anything to anyone about it?"

"No."

"But they would learn soon enough that she had helped you with your grandmother."

"Yeah. They would."

"Can you get someone else to do it? Someone you trust? Someone human, instead of a pack member?"

"It would be hard to explain why I had to ask someone else to do it. And even if I said something about having an emergency I had to attend to, I wouldn't want to leave Grandmother's ashes to a total stranger to take care of."

"I understand."

"You know they're going to be watching me all the time anyway. As soon as I start leaving the house for more than a trip to the grocery store, they're going to know something's up." Then Elizabeth had another idea. "Wait, maybe we've been thinking about this all wrong. What if we let it be known that you have a mate already and there's no way you're ever coming for me, or that I'm ever going to join you either?"

A long silence followed her suggestion. His face went still, but his eyes spoke volumes. Finally, he said, "It's a good idea. That could be our answer. I'll start working on it."

She was so relieved they might have finally figured out a way for her to leave without anyone being the wiser. "I'll call Sheri with a sob story, make it sound as realistic as I can."

"But we keep on with our weekly chats." He sounded like he couldn't do without them, just as much as she couldn't.

"Oh, absolutely. I'll let my grandmother know what's going on." This would work. It had to. "I can't wait to be with you, David."

"I can't wait to be with you either. I love you."

"I love you too." They ended the call, but Elizabeth didn't feel the same sense of letdown she usually did when they hung up. They had a plan! She checked David's Facebook page and saw right away that he had posted a picture of a woman who didn't look anything like Elizabeth. Fast worker! She hoped that would be the first step in getting everyone in her pack to believe he had wanted someone new in his life. Someone *not* Elizabeth.

Another update popped up. "Candy" was listed as his wife. *Candy?*

Half an hour later, she checked his Facebook page again and found all kinds of pictures featuring David and the blond—Candy—hugging and being together at the lake, swimming, eating a meal together. It wasn't real. But it would be someday, with her.

Then she smiled, realizing who the woman was. She'd only seen her once; she'd dropped by while David was sitting on his deck at the lake doing a Skype session with Elizabeth, and the woman had to come over to say hi. She was Owen's mate, Candice-now-Candy, a romance author.

David must have contacted her the moment they hung up to come and help him with the deception. Elizabeth was so thankful for David's pack; she couldn't wait to be part of it. She loved all of them. She just wished her grandmother had wanted to go with her and be with them. She would have loved them too.

Speaking of, she heard a bell ring, and she went to see what her grandma needed and to tell her the good news.

"My hot tea?" Grandma asked. "You finished your talk with David, I hear." She still had the best hearing.

"Oh right." Elizabeth turned on her heel and headed to the kitchen. She heated the water in the teapot, then brought in a cup of hot Earl Grey, her aunt's favorite. "Okay, I have to tell you the great news. David found a mate."

Grandma looked puzzled, but she was a crafty old wolf, and it didn't take her long to smile. "Aww, I'm so angry with him."

"Yeah, so am I." Elizabeth left again, then returned with her laptop. She popped open the lid and showed her the pictures of David's mate.

Her grandmother frowned. "Photoshopped?"

"No. That's Owen Nottingham's mate, Candice, wearing a wig. She's the romance writer. She makes a great actress, doesn't she?"

"I'll say. I would have believed it."

"In his posts, David doesn't call her by her real name, though, just Candy, so no one will really know who she is. And the wig looks real. I saw her once on a Skype call, and she doesn't look at all the same."

"Does she have her photo anywhere else? A Facebook page that shows her and her real mate or something?"

Elizabeth checked Candice's account. "She shows Owen is her mate, but see? She doesn't look anything like the pictures David uploaded."

"You're right. Between the makeup and hair, she really doesn't. And she doesn't look anything like you either."

"Exactly, like he was going for someone completely different."

"When are you going to tell Sheri?"

"After I cry a bit."

Her grandmother laughed. "Make me some roast-beef hash from last night's leftovers, and then you can cry over cutting up the onions."

Elizabeth laughed too. "It's a deal." She went into the kitchen and started making the hash. While it was cooking, she FaceTimed Sheri, tears in her eyes from all the onion chopping. "David found a mate."

"Oh, no, Elizabeth, I'm so sorry. I'll be right over."

Elizabeth hated lying to her best friend. "No, it's"—sniffle, sniffle—"time for Grandma and me to eat dinner. She's upset about it too. I just had to tell you."

"I'm so sorry. You let me know when you want me to come over, then."

"I will."

"How's Grandma doing?"

"Raging at David on my behalf but fine otherwise."

"Well, as much as I hate to hear it, I'm not surprised. If he finally found someone, it's understandable." There was a pause, then: "He's not a royal anyway. Maybe you'll be better off with someone who's ..." Another pause, like she wasn't sure what kind of reception this line of discussion would get. She plowed ahead though. "Who's like you."

Elizabeth wasn't bothered by the whole royal thing, not that anyone from the territory who was a royal was interested in her. And she wasn't interested in anyone like that either. But it did worry her that Sheri said "if" he finally found someone. Did Sheri have doubts about Elizabeth's story?

"Right," she said, playing along, hoping that Sheri bought it. "I don't know what I saw in a newly turned wolf anyway. He would have been nothing but heartache, and having kids by him would mean our offspring wouldn't be royals. Why would I do that to my own children?"

"Exactly. I'll let you get to your meal and I'll talk to you later. Feel better."

"Thanks, Sheri." Elizabeth was already feeling much better. She served up the hash on a platter and took it in to her grandma. She was still eating well and had an iron stomach, Elizabeth thought, which she was thankful for.

"Did Sheri take it hook, line, and sinker?" Grandma asked.

"I think so. And because she thinks that will somehow make everything all right with the pack concerning me, she'll spread the word. Not because she's a gossip or anything."

"Hopefully it will throw Kintail and the pack off the track. They'll figure you'll have nowhere else to go. You won't want to join Cameron's pack now since you'd have to see David with his new wolf mate all the time." She held a fork full of hash suspended in front of her mouth. "Whose idea was it?"

"Mine. I suddenly figured out what might work. I don't know why I didn't think of it earlier."

"Well, it's an excellent plan," Grandma said.

They finished eating and watched a wild thriller—her grandma's favorite kind of movie. When it was done, Elizabeth kissed her good night. "Love you, Grandma. Call me if you need anything."

"I will, dear. Love you too."

Three days later, in the middle of the night, Elizabeth heard a noise coming from her grandmother's room and went to check on her to see if she needed anything. She pushed open the door, listening to the quiet darkness within. Her grandmother had died peacefully in her sleep.

Tears ran in tracks down Elizabeth's face as the reality of her grandma's death pierced her heart. But like Grandma had told her, when the time came, she had to bury her sorrow for the moment and put a plan of action in place right away.

Elizabeth dried her eyes and called David, waking him from sleep. "David, Grandma's gone." Her voice cracked with emotion.

"Oh God, Elizabeth, I'm so sorry. How are you doing?"

"I don't know. I mean, I have expected this forever, and yet, it's never seemed real to me. Even now, I can't believe it. But"—the tears flowed again, unchecked—"Grandma died peacefully in her sleep, at home, just like she wanted, and she would tell me to get my butt in gear and get going. So that's what I'm going to do."

"I'll get ahold of Amelia right away and get a flight out as soon as I can. If she can't do it, maybe her brother can. I already have a bag packed. Did you tell everyone in your pack that I had mated Candy?"

"I told Sheri. She would have told the rest of the pack."

"Okay, good."

"I'll call to have my grandmother's body picked up. I don't know for sure, but I don't think they'll do anything...with her..." Her voice went soft, nearly a whisper, as she struggled to say the words. "With her body until morning at least."

"Elizabeth, honey, it'll be okay. I promise." His heartbreak for her came through in every word. "Don't think about that right now. I'll call you back as soon as I know what time we are leaving and when we'll get in, and we'll go from there."

"Okay." She sniffed. "At least the waxing gibbous moon phase is here, so you won't have a problem with shifting for a while. And it's summer." She sighed through her tears. "No moon *and* no snow. I swear my grandmother planned it that way. I love you so much."

"I love you too. Your grandma was a great woman. For the time I got to know her—even though it was just on Skype—I loved her and miss her too. It's time for us to be together now though."

"I know she wanted this for me, for us. I know she did. She

knew how much I wanted to be with you. I love you. I'll talk to you soon."

Then Elizabeth ended the call so she could take care of her grandmother, one last time.

CHAPTER 3

Hating to hear her feeling so destitute after her grandmother died and unable to hug Elizabeth like he wanted to, David was immediately on the phone to Amelia, waking her. He didn't waste time with niceties. "Hey, it's on."

Amelia responded like he hadn't just awoken her from a dead sleep. "Elizabeth's grandmother died."

"Yes."

"Okay, I'm calling my mom to have her get ahold of a couple of standby pilots to take Slade's and my flights for the next couple of days. I've already talked to Slade about going with us so we can switch off on flying. We always have a bag packed for emergency flights so we're ready to leave at a moment's notice. This is definitely an emergency rescue mission. I'll take care of the flight plan. We'll be going to Winnipeg, refuel, and then to Calgary, which is two hours from there. And another three hours from Calgary to Yellowknife. Are you sure that the business with being mated to 'Candy' was enough to have Kintail call off his watchdogs?"

"We won't know for sure until we get there. I'll rent a car and pick her up at some place we can agree on, someplace not anywhere near the airport so they won't think she's taking off. We'll meet you back at the airport after that."

"Okay."

Then he called Elizabeth back. "How are you doing?"

"I wish you were here already. What's the plan?"

"I'm flying out with Amelia and Slade. You need to pick a place where I can come and get you. If you have any indication that they'll be on the lookout for us at the airport, let us know and we'll change our plans in a hurry."

"What if Amelia comes to meet me at a restaurant instead? There's a place called the Wildcat Café. Hopefully, if anyone's following me, they won't think twice about me having dinner with a friend."

"Okay, though it's going to kill me to be so close to you and not be able to see you. I'll stay with Slade." And pray this worked out all right. "What about your car?"

"I could have Sheri drop me off at the restaurant and tell her I was going with Amelia to do something after dinner. I'll call Amelia by some other name though. I hate lying to Sheri about any of this, but I can't tell her what's really going on. I'm afraid Kintail would force it out of her if he suspected anything."

"What if Sheri wants to join you for the meal?" David asked.

"Actually, she could. It might even seem more natural if we all went out to eat together and then I left to do something with Amelia, telling Sheri that Amelia will drop me off at home afterward."

"Sounds good." He told her the flight times to the various airports, then they said another rushed goodbye. But this time the goodbye was tinged with hope because their next hello wouldn't be over the phone.

It would be in each other's arms.

"I'm so sorry about her grandmother, but I'm damn glad Elizabeth is coming back with us. And if she decides she can't live with you, there's always me," Slade said to David, smiling.

Amelia shook her head. "You'd better not even think of it, Slade. I don't want to be on the outs with the whole pack because of you stealing the woman away."

Slade laughed. "As if that would ever happen. I'm just glad David and Elizabeth can finally work something out between the two of them if it's meant to be."

That was the thing. No matter how much David was sure it was, they wouldn't really know for certain it was meant to be until they'd had the chance to be together in a normal setting. At least they'd have a playground—so to speak—in their backyard where they could run to their hearts' content when he wasn't working. And a home they could make their own. And a pack where she knew most of the members already, members who loved her. Maybe he had nothing to worry about. Maybe her transition to his pack, his life, would be easy for her.

Maybe everything would be just fine.

They loaded up the plane, and it wasn't long before they were heading to Winnipeg. Slade took the first shift, being more of a night owl. Amelia and David would get some sleep, but not until after he explained Elizabeth's plan and Amelia's role in it.

"Oh, I bet they'll have bison burgers. I haven't had any of those since we left Alaska," Amelia said.

"Bring us some back, will you?" Slade asked. "I haven't had one since then either."

"Anyone watching might wonder why Amelia is taking a sack of burgers to go," David said.

Slade sighed. "All right. But don't you get yourself kidnapped by Kintail's pack, Amelia, or Mom and Dad will have my head. And David's too."

Six hours later, they landed in Winnipeg, grabbed a quick bite, then refueled. Slade turned the pilot's seat over to Amelia, his eyes already closing as he slumped next to David.

David called Elizabeth to see how she was doing. "Hey, how are you?"

"Nervous. And I can't stop crying. I start to think I'm doing okay, then all of sudden I'm crying again." She stopped and blew her nose, the sound loud and clear through the phone. "She's already been cremated, so at least that's done. I waited until morning, then told Sheri that my grandmother had died. She had practically adopted her. She's upset because she loved her too. I didn't tell anyone else, but you know how fast word spreads. I know Kintail will hear soon."

"Okay, that's to be expected, even though we hoped he wouldn't learn about it until *after* you were well on your way out of there. What about a bag of your things? Your personal belongings?" David hadn't even thought about that before now. He'd always thought someday they'd be together, and she could bring whatever she needed. Whatever she didn't have, they'd just get in Ely.

"I'm going to need a whole new me. It's not like I can pack a bag and bring it to dinner. Kintail would know for sure something was up. I did mail some documents and things to you just yesterday, thinking it was past time to do it. And I can fit some things into my purse, but when we get to your place, I'm going to have to go shopping."

He smiled. "I'll take you shopping for whatever you want or need." He thought of texting Candice and seeing if she could run to the store for Elizabeth so she would have what she needed as soon as they got in, but decided against it. Elizabeth would probably want to pick out her own things. "This is really happening, Elizabeth. We're on the next leg of our journey." It was his turn for emotions to clog his voice.

"I know," she said softly. "All right, I'm going to spread my grandmother's ashes in her rose garden, though I'm going to bring some of her ashes with me to put in a memorial garden for her. Then Sheri's coming over to have lunch and be with me for a while."

"Don't let on about anything. I know she's your friend, but we have to be careful."

"I won't say a word, but she's going to know something's wrong if I don't have her over. I won't mention going to dinner with a friend until later, in case you don't get in on time. It might seem odd if I kept delaying the time for dinner."

"We need to come up with a story about who Amelia is and why she's meeting with you—" David said.

"I was living in Alaska and met Elizabeth in Yellowknife once," Amelia said.

David put the call on speakerphone. "Did you get that?"

"Yeah."

"And I was going to be in the area again and wanted to see her."

"That should work," Elizabeth said. "We just need to come up with a reason you were in Yellowknife and how we met."

"I'll think about it while I'm flying."

"All right." Elizabeth sighed, more a sound of relief than anything else. "Thanks, Amelia. Love you, David."

"I love you right back."

"Guess that leaves me out of the running," another male said.

Elizabeth guessed it was Slade and was so appreciative he'd come too. "Slade?"

"Yeah, sometimes it seems I'm just invisible when it comes to women," Slade said.

Elizabeth laughed.

Amelia said, "Don't believe him. He's charming and irresistible, but he just hasn't found the woman for him yet."

Well, Elizabeth wouldn't be the one as she had her heart set on David.

ACKNOWLEDGMENTS

During this COVID-19 threat and trying times, I want to thank Donna Fournier and Darla Taylor for reading over the book to help make it better. And thanks to Deb Werksman, who is always there for me. And to the cover book artists who always do such glorious work. Thanks!

ABOUT THE AUTHOR

USA Today bestselling author Terry Spear has written over sixty paranormal and medieval Highland romances. In 2008, *Heart of the Wolf* was named a *Publishers Weekly* Best Book of the Year. She has received a PNR Top Pick, a Best Book of the Month nomination by *Long and Short Reviews*, numerous *Night Owl Romance* Top Picks, and two Paranormal Excellence Awards for Romantic Literature (Finalist and Honorable Mention). In 2016, *Billionaire in Wolf's Clothing* was an *RT Book Reviews* top pick. A retired officer of the U.S. Army Reserves, Terry also creates award-winning teddy bears that have found homes all over the world, helps out with her granddaughter and grandson, and is raising two Havanese puppies. She lives in Spring, Texas.